A Life of
Her Own

Marc Brandel

A Life of
Her Own

Houghton Mifflin Company
Boston   1985

Library of Congress Cataloging in Publication Data

Brandel, Marc, date
A life of her own.

I. Title.
PS3503.R25784L5   1985   813'.54   84–22472
ISBN 0–395–37724–2

Printed in the United States of America

S 10 9 8 7 6 5 4 3 2 1

For my daughters, Antonia, Tara, and Shaena.
And for Edith

A Life of
Her Own

One

It was only the third day of waiting and already the repeated ordeal of hope and despair had created its own routine.

Max Ludlow's lawyer in Los Angeles had told her to be at the port, waiting under the Fisherman's Monument, from ten to noon each day. A man driving a white camper would meet her there. A man named Lindsay, the lawyer added, as one might say, Let's call him that. Max Ludlow's lawyer could not tell her how long it would be before Lindsay kept the appointment. It depended on a number of things, he said. It depended mainly, of course, on Max Ludlow.

Although it was less than ten minutes' drive to the port, Carol left the hotel every morning before nine. With an hour to spare, she could not force herself to sit around the lobby or the pool. From the moment she had finished breakfast and persuaded the elusive Mexican waiter to bring her the check, she was goaded by a sense of urgency.

She hurried straight from the restaurant to her rented VW. Each morning there was the second of panic when the car failed to start up at once. The panic persisted like a bruise as she drove out of the parking lot, along the flat, straight road, already fluid with mirages, to the intersection of Highway 15.

At nine o'clock in the morning the highway was clogged with trucks and buses. Impatiently she followed their stertorous progress into Guaymas. Pursued by horns, she drove down the main street, through the town, and out into the open stillness of the Plaza of the Three Presidents.

She parked her car on the far side of the square and walked on toward the jetty. She was still in a hurry; she might still fail Vanessa. Only when she had reached the end of the jetty and was sitting on the low stone wall under the Fisherman's Monument did she feel safe. She had made it. She could do nothing then except wait.

It was 9:06 by her watch. Not time yet to begin expecting Lindsay. She would have to idle through another fifty minutes before she could start watching the traffic around the port for the sight of a white camper. Her anxiety was like the awareness of a nodule in her breast: it might or might not be malignant; Vanessa might or might not be unharmed. She tried to find ways to distract her mind from it.

All her life she had found pleasure in watching other people. From sidewalk cafés in Rome and Paris, at Irish horse fairs, years ago waiting for the streetcar on Santa Monica Boulevard. She was alone on the jetty except for occasional children. They tried to sell her Chiclets. She gave them coins, not to drive them away, but hoping that the outright gift of a peso would give them a moment's pleasure. To her the children seemed beautiful, with their dark umber eyes. Up close their feathery hair was not as black as it seemed at a distance but had a coppery sheen. They did not at first remind her of Vanessa. Then she noticed how rarely they smiled, these Mexican children. Their gravity was as thoughtful and private as Vanessa's had been at their age. After that she avoided looking at them as she handed them the inadequate coins. She could not remember Vanessa in the past — the happy secure years in the Chelsea house, then later in Ireland — without instantly being reminded, in contrast, of the horror of the present.

The first morning on the jetty she had found all the interest she ever would in the statue of the fisherman. A man in a broad-brimmed hat, gripping a moribund fish by its tail while he trod on its head with his bare foot. There was no purpose in his face, no conviction in his grip on the fish. He was posing with it for a statue. The first morning Carol had read both inscriptions on the monument, over and over, until she knew them by heart. One of them was a poem, "La Barca de Guaymas," the other its moral, "Raise in your soul — like a pilot bird — sweet hope."

Sweet hope. For a time she had tried to see an augury in that, but the word "soul" contradicted any promise it had for her. She did not think she believed in the soul. Max Ludlow did. The last time she had seen him, sixteen years ago in Rome, he had used the word when they parted. "You've tried to destroy my soul, Carol," he had said at the airport. "I'll make you pay for that if it takes me the rest of my life."

She wished she had killed him that winter, pushed him out of the window of that sixth-floor tenement room in Trastevere. No one would have taken it for anything but suicide. Instead she had, in a way, saved his life.

She would not think about Max Ludlow. In the end he had done what he had said he would. He had made her pay. He had her daughter, Vanessa. Somewhere over the gulf, in that desert called Baja, Max was holding Vanessa "against her will," as she had told the American police.

She looked at the high-prowed fishing boats, the statues of the three presidents on the other side of the square. They stood twelve feet high in gilded bronze — Huerta, Calles, and Rodríguez — wearing square-cut proletarian suits, the kind Molotov used to wear. Rodríguez, incongruously, had a bow tie. Behind each of them was a concrete pillar. The presidents stood against them as though facing a firing squad. The second day, Carol had managed to pass some time fantasizing about that, their last thoughts before they were shot, the brave underdog causes for which they had lost their lives. That night at the hotel she had asked the manager about them. Huerta had died in bed, an old man, over seventy; the manager wasn't sure about the other two. They had all been *cabrones,* "pricks." Their statues had been put up in the square only out of provincial patriotism, because they had all been born here in the state of Sonora.

Looking at their statues from the end of the jetty, Carol tried to think about them now with less illusion. She tried to imagine they were men who had sold promises the way others sold wine;

they had been greedy and ruthless, coldly indifferent to any consideration except their own advancement, their own enrichment.

She didn't believe it. People were more complicated than that. They were often cruel only out of resentment or fear; or, like Chris Deniken, out of carelessness.

That rotten shit, Chris. It was his part in Vanessa's kidnapping for which she blamed herself most bitterly. She should have run when Chris left Ireland, taken Vanessa to France or Spain and hidden her again. She simply hadn't believed Chris would take the trouble to betray her to Max Ludlow.

"Isn't life horrible?" It was Sylvia who had said that.

"Sometimes," she had replied. Even then, after Timmy was shot, she wouldn't admit Sylvia was right. All her life she had been like that stupid monkey, she thought — "See no evil." She had always known it was there, that whole area of the day-to-day world in which people tortured and killed each other, in which the only motives were money and power and hatred. She had always stepped away from it: from that aspect of the war, with its murderous area bombing, the blind careerism of the generals, the sordid opportunism of men like Vince Campion; she had withdrawn from it in Rome and Madrid, from those studio pricks and their crass values, finding with Jason some corner for herself where people were kind and trustworthy; she had tried to do it with Timmy and the IRA.

Again and again she had been faced with the ugliness of life and each time she had smugly and selfishly avoided it. Well, it had all overwhelmed her now. Served her right.

She still couldn't believe Max would harm Vanessa. How could anyone harm a child of fifteen? But of course, they did. Every second that passed, somewhere, someone . . .

She looked at her watch again: 9:23. At least another half-hour before she could hope for the sight of a white camper, a man named Lindsay to bring her instructions from Max Ludlow.

She sat there under the Fisherman's Monument, a woman in her early fifties, still lithe and attractive, still, in her own individual way, beautiful.

Still hopeful.

More than any other emotion, hope had influenced the actions of her life. It had all begun so hopefully, so lightheartedly.

Two

Carol Clavering?"

"Yes."

"That's you?"

"Yes."

"This your passport?"

"Yes." I could see he didn't believe me. "Don't you think I look like my photograph?"

"How old are you?"

"Eighteen." I felt I was expected to give more exact information. "I was born on the twenty-eighth of March in 1921."

"Where?"

"At St. Louis, in Missouri."

The immigration officer took the cigar out of his mouth and rested it against the ashtray on the table between us. It was the first time I had seen anyone smoke a cigar in a holder. He looked at me. I was wearing a double-breasted gray flannel suit, the jacket of the suit buttoned on the left to show I was a girl. My hair was cut straight across just below the level of my ears, parted, and held in place by a tortoiseshell comb. I couldn't have looked more like my mother's idea of a well-brought-up English girl if I'd been carrying a prayer book.

The immigration officer frowned and picked up his cigar. "Next." He handed back my American passport.

I found I had to deal with this situation again and again during the next few years. No one could believe I was American.

It was chance — sheer luck as I saw it — that had made me one. In the fall of 1920 my father had been offered what seemed to him more money than he could sensibly refuse to come to the United States as a visiting poetry lecturer at Washington University in St. Louis. There had, I learned from my mother later, been a protracted discussion about whether he should take his two small daughters and his pregnant wife with him. He was fervently hoping his third child would be a boy. It was important to him that his son be born in England. In the end, predictably, his needs were stronger than his chauvinism. He was to lecture at Washington University for eight months. He needed his socks mended, regular meals, to be protected against doorbells. And who would bring him his morning tea in America? He took his whole family circle, including an English nanny, to St. Louis with him.

I was born there six months later.

I slipped the blessed evidence of this — my American passport — back into my bag. I had already tipped the cabin steward. My luggage — two large suitcases filled with the kind of clothes I was wearing — was waiting for me in the customs shed. I felt a startled excitement that reminded me of going swimming in the nude — a thing I'd only done twice in my life — as I walked down the gangplank into America.

I knew very little about the United States. I had read very little American history. In my English boarding school, the colonies had no history once they ceased being colonies. The Americanization of Europe had scarcely begun in the thirties. I had never eaten a hot-dog or tasted Coca-Cola. But the hundreds of Hollywood movies I had seen had left me with a vivid impression of Americans. They were an enterprising, reckless people. They were impulsive; they made cynical wisecracks. They were not, like the English, dull and conventional. They were unpredictable, eccentric. They were wildly exciting.

My mother had arranged for me to stay with the Harts, friends from the twenties and the south of France. They lived in Washington

Heights. I had a letter from Mrs. Hart telling me how to get there: I was to take the Eighth Avenue subway to 183rd Street. As soon as I had been cleared through customs, I started out with my two suitcases to find the subway station. Before I'd gone twenty yards, the suitcases were almost too heavy to carry. I was grateful when a stout man in a plaid jacket offered to help me.

"Where you going?" He took one of the suitcases from me and headed out of the customs shed.

"The Eighth Avenue subway."

"You're English, huh?"

"No."

He nodded, chewing his cigar. Did everyone in America smoke cigars? In Europe they were a symbol of wealth.

"You'll have to change your English money. I'll do it for you, save you going to a bank."

"No, thank you." I had changed all my pounds in the purser's office the evening before.

"I'll give a good rate. Four-twenty."

"No, thank you." The purser had given me four-ninety-five.

"What you want the subway for?" The man in the plaid jacket no longer sounded helpful. "Where you going?"

"Washington Heights."

"You don't want to take the subway up there. I'll give you a ride." He was out of the customs shed ahead of me. I caught up with him on a broad street filled with careening traffic. I had a quick, sunbright impression of garish haste. I had never realized New York taxis were yellow; in the movies America was black and white. The man in the plaid jacket put my suitcase down beside a battered plum-colored car. He opened the front door.

"Get in. I'll put your bags in back."

"No, thank you." I stepped away from him.

I didn't imagine the man intended to beat and rob me if I got in the car. In broad daylight? He wouldn't dare. The possibility of sexual assault never crossed my mind. At eighteen I didn't regard myself as desirable. I was too skinny looking. My shoulder blades stuck out. They embarrassed me on the beach or when I was wearing an evening dress. I knew he only wanted to drive me to Washington Heights, wherever that was, and then demand an exorbitant fare.

I shook my head politely. "I'm going to take the Eighth Avenue subway." I might have been telling him I had promised the subway I would and I didn't want to disappoint it.

"You don't even know where the subway is. Go on, get in, I'll drive you." He raised his hand as though to push me into the car.

"No, thank you." I hadn't spent five years at an English boarding school for nothing. A teacher had once written on my report card, "Obedience: very poor." What she meant was that I wasn't easy to bully. "I can find the subway, all right. Don't you worry." I was no longer altogether there on a New York street; I was facing two older girls in a dormitory. "And you'd better leave me alone or it will be worse for you."

He closed the door of his car. Something of my determination must have reached him, or perhaps he just thought I was a hysterical nut case. He didn't want any trouble with me anyway; there were police on the pier. He showed me how to find the subway.

The Harts' apartment house, Hudson View Gardens, was a long red-brick building with a profusion of entrances. It took me some time to find the right one. Virgil Hart. The name under the bell in the downstairs hallway seemed to me to have an aura around it.

Virgil Hart was a writer, a sort of writer, in my father's words. Back in the twenties he had written a popular success, the story of an Arkansas mule. He had come to the south of France to celebrate it, bringing a letter of introduction to my father from a New York publisher. Mrs. Hart and my mother had taken to each other at once and had corresponded fitfully ever since. My father had not taken to Virgil — there were few writers he did like — but at the age of seven I adored him. Virgil Hart became one of my childhood heroes.

He was the first American I remembered knowing. An avid reader of French children's magazines about *les Indiens Peaux-Rouges* and *le Wild Ouest,* I saw in him everything I expected an American to be. He had none of my parents' polite restraint. In a restaurant he would send dishes back to the kitchen as though holding the waiter at gun point. Once when my parents were making one of their endless moves from one rented house to another and the landlady was raising a fine, hysterical French row about the inventory, Virgil suggested tying her to a tree. After eleven years he still remained a hero to me for this. As I took the elevator to the third floor, the thought of seeing him again was as tinted with wonder as the expectation of finding Buffalo Bill in buckskin and boots waiting there.

A stout, corseted woman met me in the doorway of the apartment. I had no recollection of Mrs. Hart at all. She had a broad, powdered face and untidy white hair that seemed, like wisps of smoke, to be trying to escape from her head. In an accent which I found hard to understand at first — she was from Virginia — she greeted me with effusive surprise at how grown-up I was.

I hefted the two suitcases into the apartment. There was no sign of Virgil.

"How's Mr. Hart?" I meant *where* is he?

"Virgil's working for a man who writes a column. He'll tell you all about himself just as soon as he gets home. Put your things in here, Carol."

That was the last time she mentioned him. Showing me my room, offering me a shower, giving me a cup of tea, Mrs. Hart welcomed me to the New World. This was not my excitedly anticipated New World of America; it was her world of white, middle-class Washington Heights. While I waited for Virgil to come home, I heard a great deal about the Jews, the persistent idleness of the unemployed, the criminal selfishness of the labor unions.

I was relieved when I finally heard the front door open. Mrs. Hart talked on, paying no attention to the footsteps approaching across the hallway. I stood up expectantly.

"Well. Say. N. E. Clavering's daughter." Virgil was filling the doorway. Physically he was much as I remembered him: a very tall, bald man in a loud checked suit and a polka dot bow tie.

But as he lumbered forward and shook my hand and, folding himself into the nearest chair, began to talk about my father, it occurred to me that I did not really remember him at all. A child of seven had invented a fantasy hero. This tired, middle-aged man was a total stranger to me.

He rambled on about my father for several minutes, his reputation as an editor and critic, how thrilled he had been all those years ago to meet the celebrated N. E. Clavering. He didn't sound thrilled now. I heard an envy in his voice that was almost hostile.

"Of course your father never had to make a living with his writing," he said at one point. "He could afford to look down on poor boys like me who had to write for money."

At six-thirty, after listening to Lowell Thomas's news broadcast, the Harts took me down to the apartment-house restaurant. It reminded me a little of school. The waitress placed a glass of ice water in front of me with brisk authority. "Drink that," she might have been saying as she stood there waiting to take my order. I sipped it cautiously. My father had once told me the reason "all" Americans suffered from dyspepsia was because they drank ice water.

I looked at the menu. Virgil recommended the fifty-five-cent special.

While I ate it, he talked about Lowell Thomas. Not about his broadcast — the ominous news from Europe didn't seem to concern either of the Harts — he talked about Lowell Thomas's success, his fame, his friendship with ex-presidents. He went on to praise other famous men. He stressed their modest beginnings. "Why, Henry Ford was just a country farm boy like me," he told me over his apple pie. "Why, Rockefeller . . . Why, Carnegie . . . Why, Jerome Kern . . ." He spoke of them all with the same enthusiasm. It didn't matter how they had achieved fame and wealth — the cornering of the wheat market, a popular song — it was all one to Virgil.

Mrs. Hart had been listening restively to her husband. "It's all Roosevelt's doing," she interrupted briskly. "That cripple. He's never made a success of anything in his whole life. That man's done nothing but try to pull this country down. He's got the unemployed believing it's not their fault they're out of work. They don't even want to believe in opportunity anymore."

So far neither of them had shown much interest in me except as an audience. When we were back in the apartment and Mrs. Hart was making coffee, Virgil abruptly asked me what my plans were.

It was hard to answer that. I didn't have any plans, only impulses and desires. The strongest of them had already been realized: to get out of England, away from my mother, my two elder sisters, all those people who felt they owned me because they knew my family. What did I want next? I wanted to try myself out, not as the Claverings' daughter, but as me, Carol. I was happily convinced I was absolutely special, singled out, and I wanted to meet people on my own terms at last.

Once at school Beatrice Lillie had come down to present the end-of-year prizes. She was Lady Peel at the time; that was why she was invited. I had won a prize for drawing. I waited my turn to go up and shake Beatrice Lillie's hand and be awarded a leather-bound classic stamped with the school crest. I was terrified. I was afraid Beatrice Lillie would "recognize" me. She had never seen me before, but she would look at me and say, "What are *you* doing here?" meaning, What's someone like you doing among all these ordinary people?

Beatrice Lillie didn't say anything. She handed me my book and waited with cheerful indifference for the next girl's name to be called. I didn't hold it against her. Beatrice Lillie, special and unique though she was herself, had simply failed to pierce my disguise, the drab school uniform, my enforced similarity to the other girls. No more of that for me. From now on people were going to be able to look at me and see me.

It didn't occur to me to try to explain all this to Virgil; I couldn't have explained it to anybody.

"I thought I'd look around for a few days and then try to get a job."

"What kind of job?" Mrs. Hart had reappeared with the coffee tray.

"Can you take shorthand?" Virgil asked.

I couldn't; I had no skills or training. I had spent a year since leaving school, at seventeen, studying commercial art. I could draw quite well, but I had no talent.

"I thought of trying to find a job in a publishing house," I said. "My father gave me some introductions to people. Sinclair Lewis and Curtis Brown, the agents."

"Well, say, you're lucky," Virgil told me.

The Harts went to bed early. Alone in my small room, I sat on the bed and thought back over my first day in America. I was off to a bad start. I was never going to be able to be myself so long as I stayed with the Harts. They were my mother's friends, not mine. I could never be anything to them except the Claverings' daughter. I decided not to unpack my suitcases. As soon as possible I would leave, find a furnished room somewhere.

Mrs. Hart was in the kitchen, drinking coffee, when I got up the next morning.

"Sit down, dear."

I sat down. "I hope I didn't disturb Mr. Hart by having a bath."

"Virgil's gone to the office."

"Oh." I realized I must have overslept. "Have you already had breakfast?"

"He stops by at the drugstore on his way to the subway." Mrs. Hart poured me some coffee. "Virgil and I were talking about you just now."

I reached for the sugar on the tray.

"Your mother must be worried to death about you."

"She was glad to get me out of England before the war starts. So was my father. It isn't as though I'd be any use —"

"She wouldn't worry so much if she knew you were with friends."

"She knows I'm here."

"That's what I mean. You'd better stay on here, Carol." A wisp of white hair had drifted down over her eyes. She pushed it out of the way. "I'd be happy to have you, dear."

"No, really, I couldn't. It's terribly kind of you —"

"Virgil and I thought you should pay us eight dollars a week."

I didn't say anything. I was determined not to stay there, but I couldn't think of any way of getting out of it when she put it like that. I had already stayed one night and let Virgil pay for my dinner.

Mrs. Hart asked me if I could let her have a week's rent in advance. I gave it to her. "Your dinner last night will be our treat," she told me.

I had no idea where to look for a furnished room in New York. I took the subway to Forty-second Street.

There were several hotels on the side streets around Times Square, advertising rooms for rent, a dollar a night, weekly rates. I went into one of them. The small lobby was full of people and suitcases. I had to pick my way to the elderly man behind the desk.

"Where you want to go?" he asked me.

I told him I was looking for a room. I asked about the weekly rates.

"It's five dollars a week, nice room, or seven with a toilet." It struck me how American his accent was; I still wasn't used to the idea that everyone around me was American.

"Could I look at one?"

He glanced around the crowded lobby. "Why don't you sit down over there? I'll be with you in a minute, soon as I get rid of the Cleveland bunch. The guy's loading his car now."

I hadn't the least idea what he was talking about. I found an empty chair at the back of the lobby. Three young men were sitting on the tubular steel sofa next to me. They were all three dressed in brown slacks, fawn jackets with leather buttons, and two-tone shoes. Even their shirts and ties were identical. The man at my end of the sofa gave me a quick, wary look without moving his head. He leaned over and whispered something to the other two.

"Ask her," I heard them say. "Hell, they promised us only three passengers." "Go ahead, ask the kid."

"You going to Chicago?"

"No." I shook my head.

They all three smiled, obviously relieved.

"Where are you going?" one of them asked.

"Nowhere."

That seemed to puzzle them all. They were silent for a moment, then the one farthest from me put his suitcase on the floor so that he could take a good look at me.

"You're English, huh?"

"No."

He nodded. All three suddenly became friendly. They introduced themselves as the Blanco Brothers. Breaking in on each other, finishing each other's sentences, they told me they were jugglers.

"We're on our way to Chicago." "A nightclub date." "In the Loop." "Two weeks, minimum." "Just waiting for the guy to finish loading his car."

The hotel, they explained, was an agency for people who were driving cross-country and wanted to take paying passengers with them. All the people in the lobby were on their way somewhere. "It's a better deal than the bus." "Of course sometimes you have to wait around for a day or two." "If you're going to Los Angeles or someplace like that."

I was beginning to like the Blanco Brothers. I had never met any jugglers before. They weren't depressing, like the Harts; they were all excited about their date in Chicago, and they treated me as an equal. They asked me again where I was going. I told them I was looking for a room.

"You don't want to live in a dump like this." "Not in this neighborhood." "It's full of floozies." "You want to go over to Third Avenue." "Get a nice room over there for four dollars a week." "If you don't mind the El."

The elderly man was still behind the desk, still apparently trying to get rid of the Cleveland bunch. I thanked the Blanco Brothers and walked back to Times Square. Where was Third Avenue? I bought a map of New York and studied it at a drugstore counter while I ate a chicken sandwich. The layout of the city delighted me with its simplicity. Madison Avenue, where the Curtis Brown office was, was on the way to Third Avenue. I had the letter of introduction in my bag.

I had been to the office in London and met Curtis Brown himself. We sat in leather club chairs in front of the fire and he gave me a cup of tea and talked about my father. "Such a pity he never tried his hand at fiction. I used to tell him, even Chesterton, even Belloc. Still, he did very well out of that book of verse." When he had finished his tea, he sat down at his desk and wrote a letter of introduction on a sheet of vellum. As I left he was jabbing at the coals in the fireplace with a cast iron poker.

The atmosphere of the New York office was different. The reception room reminded me of a boudoir. My letter was addressed to Miss Mavis Beeton. I gave it to the beautiful young woman behind the white lacquered desk. She thanked me. I waited.

"Do you require a receipt?"

"I'd like to see Miss Mavis Beeton, please."

That seemed to surprise her. She looked at the letter and then back at me, standing there in my gray flannel suit and lisle stockings, with a tortoiseshell comb in my hair.

"May I inquire the nature of your business?"

"It's in that letter." There was no return address on the envelope. "It's from Mr. Curtis Brown in London."

"I see." She might have been saying, "What *is* this?" "Miss Beeton doesn't see anyone without an appointment. Did you wish her secretary to call you and make an appointment?"

A year or two later I would have agreed to this at once; not that I was all that brash at eighteen, I was just more English. The woman behind the desk, for all her chill beauty, was a functionary to me, like a stationmaster or a clerk in a post office. I had been brought up to believe that the way to deal with functionaries was to be very polite and tell them exactly what you wanted them to do.

"Would you please give that letter to Miss Mavis Beeton and say I'd like to see her."

Perhaps it was my clothes, my English accent, the fact that she couldn't fit me into any known category of nuisance; she took the letter and disappeared through a doorway. I wasn't in the least surprised when she returned almost at once, without the letter, and said Miss Beeton would see me.

Mavis Beeton was in her thirties, small and dainty as a porcelain doll. She didn't offer me a cup of tea, but she was friendly and charming and invited me to sit down.

"So your father's a friend of Mr. Curtis Brown's?"

"Mr. Brown used to be his agent."

"Your father's a writer?" She glanced at the letter that was lying on her desk.

"He's N. E. Clavering."

I said it with the confidence acquired from years of hearing people say, "Oh, yes, that anthology of British and American verse." I could see at once that Mavis Beeton had never heard of him. She asked me how long I had been in New York.

"Just a few days." I didn't want her to think I had come here straight from the ship.

"What can I do to help you?"

I told her I was looking for a job in publishing. She asked me if I had any experience. Any qualifications, then? I had to admit I didn't have any *particular* qualifications. I mentioned my father's one-time position as chief editorial adviser to Collins, the largest publishing house in England. I tried to explain that I had been exposed to books and writers all my life.

She was kind enough not to laugh at me. She lit a cigarette

with a mother-of-pearl lighter. "Publishers are going through a very difficult time," she told me. "Of course, everything's slow." She went on for a few minutes to explain the Depression; she didn't blame Roosevelt. "But publishers have been particularly hard hit for years because it's a luxury trade." She didn't try to let me down lightly: as an inexperienced, untrained young girl, I had absolutely no chance in the world of finding a job in publishing at that time.

I was fascinated by the way she smoked her cigarette, as daintily as a Chinese princess sipping tea.

"Is there anything else I could do to help you?"

"My father said I ought to see Sinclair Lewis."

"I'm afraid Red's in California."

My father had never called him Red. I asked when Mr. Lewis was expected back in New York. She thought he would be in Hollywood for at least another two months. "He's at the Beverly Hills Hotel, if you'd like to write to him." She gave me the address on a sheet of blue paper. I stood up and thanked her.

"I'm afraid I haven't been very encouraging."

It was true, she hadn't. But as I walked out onto Madison Avenue, I didn't feel discouraged. Mavis Beeton had given me an idea, a way of getting away from the Harts without hurting their feelings. I walked back to Times Square and went to a double feature.

Mrs. Hart had given me a key. She was in the living room when I let myself in around nine. She seemed to rouse herself to notice my presence. There was a pot of coffee on the table. She offered me a cup.

I thanked her and said I was going to bed.

"Sit down, Carol." She was always telling me to sit down.

I perched on the sofa. She stirred sugar into her coffee, twirling the spoon in a thoughtful way.

"What are you going to do, dear, if you don't find a job. How are you going to manage to live?"

"My father's going to send me three pounds a week."

"That's all right, then." She took the spoon out of the cup. "I'm so glad you're going to live with us."

I braced myself. Here I go. No sense putting it off. "I'm afraid I won't be able to stay here, Mrs. Hart."

"Why not?" She dropped the spoon on the table.

"I went to the Curtis Brown office this afternoon. I talked to a woman named Mavis Beeton. She didn't think I had a chance here. She told me Sinclair Lewis was in Hollywood. She thinks I ought to go out there and see him. She thinks Sinclair Lewis might be able to get me a job."

"What kind of job?"

"Well, in the script department at one of the studios. After all, Sinclair Lewis is pretty well known. He ought to be able to help me."

She couldn't argue with that. The idea that the rich and famous ran everything, were entitled to run everything, was almost a religion to her. She asked me when I thought of leaving. I told her in a day or two. Now that I'd made my break, I was no longer in any great hurry. I had hardly seen anything of New York.

I stayed on at the Harts' for a week, keeping out of the apartment except to sleep. That was one thing about the Harts: their way of life gave me a refreshing amount of freedom. For the first time in my life, I was free of the inflexible timetable of regular meals. The Harts did not have regular meals. Mrs. Hart picked at things in the kitchen; Virgil stopped by at the drugstore.

I walked for miles around New York. Everything was new and exciting to me. I would never have believed a city could be so lively. It was so different from London. The people were different too. They were astonishingly direct, especially the women. They weren't patronizing and interfering with small advice the way English women were when talking to a girl of my age. "Don't lose your bus ticket." "You've got dandruff on your collar." Perhaps intrigued by my English accent, American women asked me startlingly personal questions about myself and then responded by confiding intimate details of their own lives. I had never felt treated so completely as a grown-up. It gave me a new, excited confidence in myself.

Toward the end of the week I went back to the hotel where I had met the Blanco Brothers. The elderly man behind the desk surprised me by remembering me at once.

"That's right, you want a room, don't you?"

I told him I wanted to go to California.

"I got a car leaving for L.A. tomorrow. You going to L.A.?"

"Hollywood."

"That's right. I got a nice ride for you, a couple, going all the way, thirty-three Pontiac, cost you twenty-five bucks." He told me to check in with him the next morning at ten o'clock.

I felt I owed it to the Harts to spend my last evening with them. We ate at the same restaurant. I insisted on paying for myself this time. The waitress no longer reminded me of school; I felt if we were alone together she would soon be telling me about her boyfriend. Virgil no longer puzzled me with his indiscriminate admiration for the rich and famous. He had once touched success with the story of an Arkansas mule; he had to believe it was still possible to do it again. I felt embarrassed for him when he slipped a dime under his plate for the waitress.

The next morning the clerk at the hotel told me the couple who were driving to Los Angeles hadn't arrived yet. I sat in the lobby, waiting, watching other travelers.

A young man caught my attention. He was standing by the desk, talking to the clerk. His jacket didn't match his trousers. They weren't sports clothes, they were parts of different suits. It gave him a careless, eccentric look. I liked his face — his slightly arched nose, his wide mouth, his strong cheekbones, his no-nonsense chin. He reminded me of something; it took me a moment to remember what: the illustrations in those *Wild Ouest* magazines I had read as a child. It was easy to imagine him squinting into the desert sun, scouting *Indiens Peaux-Rouges*. His hair was reddish brown and needed cutting; he didn't use hair oil.

He nodded to the clerk and walked toward me. He had an easy, rangy gait.

"You mind?"

Without waiting for an answer, he sat down in the chair next to me. He had no luggage except a canvas bag. I glanced sideways at him: his eyes were dark blue and had a thoughtful, confident look.

"You're going to Los Angeles?"

I told him I was.

"So am I. I hope we're alone in the back seat."

That startled me a little. Did he mean he hoped he'd have me to himself? The idea pleased and flustered me. I had had very little experience of being alone with young men.

"Why?" Might as well see what he did mean.

"It's a long trip. If there are only two of us in back, we take it in turns to put our feet up. Your feet get swollen if they're lower than your head for too long."

"Oh." That was what he had meant.

I asked him how long he thought the trip would take.

"Five or six days. Depends if they want to stop anywhere."

"We'll stop to sleep, won't we?" I had packed my favorite dress in the top of one of my suitcases, imagining myself changing into it every evening after·the long day's drive.

"I hope not." He smiled; he had very white, even teeth. "I haven't got much money for hotels."

He talked on like that in a friendly, confiding way. About himself. About California. He had been born out there, had lived there most of his life. I had never met anyone like him before. He was so *American*. The eagerness, the quality of enthusiasm in him, caught me up, inciting me to believe in him as I had believed in those *Wild Ouest* heroes as a little girl. After a while he told me his name.

It was Max Ludlow.

T*h*ree

T*h*e couple arrived to pick us up at noon.

Their name was Erikson, Don and Wilma. They were both in their thirties. Don's face has left no impression on my memory at all. I remember only his determination. He did everything — shaking hands with me and then Max, complaining about the size of my suitcases, taking a drink from the water fountain, loading the car — with the same wooden, let's-get-on-with-it intensity. Wilma was dark, with a long, pinched face, her hair wound into coils over her ears. She was outwardly less purposeful than Don, but I soon learned she was the one who made the decisions.

"Take the bridge," she said as we crossed Eighth Avenue.

Don argued that the bridge was out of the way.

"It's free," Wilma told him.

We passed the piers where the liners docked, their prows sharp crags above the elevated highway. The *Queen Mary,* the *Normandie,* and the *Bremen* were all there. I saw an officer in a belted uniform on the *Bremen;* with a chill I realized he was German, a Nazi.

Max and I had become friends in the two hours we'd been waiting. He was a film cutter, irregularly employed, "way down on the list," as he put it. He shared a house in the hills with a group of other people who were often out of work too. He made it sound fun. When I told him I was hoping to get a job in the script department at one of the studios, he didn't try to discourage me. He was silent now in the car; he didn't seem to want to talk in front of the Eriksons.

We crossed New Jersey: marshes and factories and dark, abandoned-looking towns, then miles of open land on which nothing was growing except weeds; an occasional farmhouse, great wooden barns with advertisements plastered on them; yards full of junked cars and tractors at the approach to another town; streets of frame houses that looked parched for paint. It all made me remember how tidy England was.

My awareness of the outside world waned as we entered Pennsylvania. The Eriksons had stowed several small, heavy canvas sacks in the back of the car. Every time I wanted to shift my feet I had to lift them over a sack and find a space on the other side. After a few hours, the effort of trying to get comfortable absorbed all my attention.

We stopped at a gas station at about five o'clock. I went to the rest room. Wilma came in as I was washing my hands.

"Is that man a friend of yours?"

I explained that Max and I had met while waiting at the hotel.

"What do you know about him?"

The suspicious way she asked made me feel an instant loyalty to Max. I shook my head. "Nothing."

"I do. I know his kind. I can spot them at once. He's one of those troublemakers."

As we walked outside I wondered what she meant. What kind of trouble? I didn't ask her; I had a more pressing question. "When are we going to stop for dinner?"

"We brought sandwiches." She sounded accusing. "Didn't they tell you to bring sandwiches?"

"Nobody told me anything. I thought we'd be stopping for meals."

"You can get a Coke and a candy bar here if you're hungry."

There was a tank full of watery ice in the office. I fished out a Coke and bought a chocolate bar. Max walked in as I was paying for them.

"We're going to drive straight through the night," I told him.

"I'm sorry."

"Couldn't we insist on stopping somewhere to eat?"

"Okay, if you want to."

"Oh, well." I remembered what he'd said about not having much money. "It doesn't matter. It wouldn't be so bad if we didn't have all those bloody sacks."

"You know what's in them?"

"No."

"Bibles." He accepted a bite of my chocolate bar. "They're all full of Bibles."

Somewhere in Ohio the next morning I tried to persuade the Eriksons to stop for breakfast. They didn't want to waste the time. That was all right for them; they still had sandwiches left and a Thermos of fresh coffee. Max supported me. Wilma glared at him, confirmed in her judgment: he was making trouble. Don finally pulled up in front of a diner. I got out thankfully. The ground felt wonderfully still. It was like being back on the dock after a night in a rowboat. Wilma told me to hurry up. I walked around the car and stood waiting for Max. He stepped out of his door, still holding onto the handle.

"Bring me a couple of doughnuts and a container of coffee." He slipped some change into my hand.

"Aren't you coming in?"

"Better not."

While I ate I could see him by the open door of the car. His body had a natural grace, even when he was still. When I went back outside with his doughnuts and coffee, he drew me aside.

"It's okay now." He smiled. "Wilma's taking a pee."

I didn't understand; he had to explain it to me. If we both left the car at the same time, there was nothing to stop the Eriksons from driving off without us.

"They can't do that. We paid them to go to Los Angeles."

"They could pick up another couple of passengers in St. Louis."

He was still smiling. There was no complaint in his voice, he was simply speaking from experience, like a guide saying he knew the trail.

"I know these Bible thumpers," he told me. "They think it's their God-given right to rob you."

So we kept it up, all across Indiana and Illinois, each time we stopped for gas or food. It was like a game of Prisoner's Base. Max and I were safe so long as either Don or Wilma was out of the car; otherwise, one of us had to stay with them.

They drove on and on in three-hour shifts, taking turns dozing in the passenger's seat. Max scrunched down on the floor for a few hours to give me a chance to stretch out. I was scarcely aware of the country we were traveling through; the interior of the car, the smell of gasoline, my own sticky body became the only facts of my existence. It was dark when we went through St. Louis. I remember only a wide square, bland public buildings. I couldn't pretend to have any strong emotions about my birthplace — I was only three months old when my parents took me back to Europe — but if I hadn't been so exhausted, I might have felt curiosity.

Early the next morning we were in Joplin, Missouri. There, everything changed. The Eriksons lost their momentum. We all went into a diner for breakfast. I took my toilet things out of my suitcase, brushed my teeth and washed my face. After we'd eaten, Max and I headed back to the car while the Eriksons were paying their check. We reached the car before they did. Max was opening the back door, when Wilma caught his arm.

"We've got some stops to make in this town," she said. "Why don't you two walk around and we'll pick you up here at noon."

"We'll go with you." Max got in the car.

Don and Wilma walked away, whispering together.

"We're in the Bible belt," Max told me. "They're going to try to sell those goddamn Bibles. We'll be here all day."

All at once I had had enough of that Prisoner's Base game.

"Why don't we do what they say?" My voice was a bit shrill. "Let them pick us up here later. They won't run off." I didn't care if they did; at that moment I would have been willing to spend the rest of my life in Joplin, Missouri, so long as Max and I could spend it walking around in the fresh air. It looked like a pretty little town.

"Sure they will. We'll never see them again. Or your suitcases either. Come on, get in."

I got in. It was like climbing into my own coffin.

We drove around until late afternoon, stopping at frame houses, churches on the side streets. At each stop Don and Wilma disappeared with one of the canvas sacks. Sometimes when they came back the sack looked lighter, sometimes the Eriksons were sullen, muttering. "Call themselves Christians," I heard Wilma complain.

At least it was a respite from the road. While they were gone, Max and I could sprawl under the trees that shaded the sidewalks. For the first time since we had left New York, we could talk freely.

We talked about the Eriksons, their Bibles, religion. Max asked me if I'd been brought up in any church. I hadn't. Although he had lately developed an interest in spiritualism, my father had been a lifelong agnostic. For the first years of their marriage, while my mother was still in love with my father, she had also been an agnostic. After we returned to England from Switzerland, when I was twelve, she started to go to church again. But I was too old by then to be persuaded to go with her.

"So you're still an agnostic," Max said approvingly.

"No, not really." I wanted to be honest with him. "I wish I could be. But whenever I get in a panic about anything, I can't help saying, 'Oh, please help me, please,' to myself. Sort of praying. And I can't stop believing that if I do something awful I'll be punished for it. There'll be a day of judgment for me some day." I felt I was being too serious; I tried to make a joke of it. "I'm a God-fearing agnostic, really." I asked him what he was.

"I was brought up a Catholic." Max was chewing on a stalk of grass; I noticed again how beautiful his teeth were. "Both my parents were very strict about it. Then after they died and I was living with an aunt, I began to see it was all a racket. Pie in the sky. A way to keep the masses down. You know?"

I nodded. Even when he was criticizing, denouncing something, his voice had that quality of eagerness and enthusiasm.

"Take the Bible," he went on. "The Old and the New Testament. One preaches vengeance and the other forgiveness. Take your pick. If you want to justify oppression, slavery, exploitation of women, child labor, just turn to the Old Testament and you'll find they're all okay with God. If you want your slaves, your colonial peoples, your tenant farmers, your labor force, to lie down and let you walk all over them, you can go to the New Testament. Give them Jesus meek and mild. In the last analysis" — he was watching the church as the Eriksons came out — "the Bible's probably the most harmful book ever published."

He jumped up. We hurried to the car and stood guarding it. The Eriksons stopped a few feet away, confronting us. I noticed Don's canvas sack was empty.

"We're going to stay here the night." It was Wilma, as usual, who took the lead.

"What about us?" Max leaned back against the car door. "What do you expect us to do?"

"Go to a hotel." Wilma ignored him; she was talking to me. "You've been wanting to stop for the night ever since we started."

"Not on your life." Max answered for me. "If we went to a hotel, if we let you out of our sight, we'd never see you again."

"Wilma's too tired to drive anymore and the Reverend here invited us —"

"If that's the way you feel" — Wilma interrupted Don with a smile; it was the first time I had seen her smile — "you can have ten dollars of your money back."

"Ten dollars!"

"I never wanted to take you anyway. The moment I saw you —"

"Ten dollars," Max repeated. "We paid twenty-five."

"We had to pay the tolls on the Cut-out."

They argued about it, more and more fiercely.

"Give him twelve dollars, Don," Wilma finally conceded.

Don fingered through his wallet and gave Max the money. I hadn't said a word so far.

"I don't mind taking *you* on to L.A." Wilma was looking at me again. "There's a nice cheap hotel here. We'll drive you to it. You get a good night's sleep and we'll pick you up there in the morning."

I often wondered later what would have happened if I'd done what Wilma suggested. Would she have picked me up at the hotel the next morning? Would I ever have seen Max Ludlow again? At the time I didn't hesitate. I was on Max's side. With all my heart.

"Please give me back my twelve dollars, too."

Less than a minute later, Max and I were alone on the sidewalk with my suitcases and his small canvas bag.

"Okay, let's try and find that nice cheap hotel." Max picked up my suitcases and then put them down again. "Do you have any gloves?"

"Gloves? Why?"

"So they won't see you're not wearing a wedding ring."

I was astounded, flabbergasted. Here was this young man whom I'd only just met, taking it for granted I was going to spend the night in a hotel room with him. Go to bed with him? Fornicate?

Up to that time I had been kissed by three young men, two at Christmas parties and one suddenly and rather roughly at the tennis club. I hadn't particularly either liked or disliked it. The intimacy of their mouths had dismayed me a little, the close, tobacco odor of their breath. Altogether it had been little more than a new experience, part of growing up, like wearing lipstick for the first time. Eventually, of course, there would be someone, probably a husband, who would do much more than kiss me. I knew what he would do, I wasn't sexually ignorant. The teachers had been very sensible about that at school in Switzerland. I was even quite prepared to enjoy it all when the time came. My married sister, Sylvia, had told me it was "rather lovely," once you got used to it, "like reading poetry together."

But *now?* With this man I had never even kissed? Go to a room together? Take our clothes off? Go through that whole elaborate, naked process with each other's bodies?

"Certainly not," I told him. I wasn't shocked; the idea was too absurd to be shocking. It was out of the question.

"Certainly not what?"

"I'm not going to bed with you."

Considering the bleakness of my refusal, he took it very well. "Okay," he said gently. "I guess you're a virgin, huh?"

"Of course I am." I was *eighteen years old.* Every girl that age I knew was a virgin. Every girl I knew to speak to, anyway.

"Okay." Max picked up my suitcases.

We found a hotel off the square, single rooms $1.50. What I could see of the lobby had a bare, pinewood look, like a hotel in a Western movie. I started in, expecting Max to follow me. He put down my suitcases.

"Aren't you coming in? Aren't you going to take a room too?"

"I'd better get out on the highway and start to hitch."

I walked back to him. It made me wince to think of him out on the highway. He hadn't had any more sleep in the last few days than I had. It would be dark in a couple of hours. I felt a quick sympathy and affection for him. I wanted to explain that I really liked him. It wasn't the idea of going to bed with *him* that bothered me. It was just the idea.

"I'm sorry." I couldn't think of any way of saying it all.

"It's okay. I don't mind." He was feeling through his pockets. "I enjoyed meeting you, Carol." It was the first time he had used my name. "I like talking to you." He had found a pencil and a piece of paper. He leaned against the glass door of the hotel and began to write while he went on talking. "You'd better take the bus tomorrow. I mean, don't try to hitchhike alone. The All American is cheaper than Greyhound. You'll probably get to L.A. before I do. Go to this address. See Mrs. Hainert. She's an old friend of mine, and a very nice woman, and she can rent you a room. It's just off Sunset Boulevard, right in Hollywood."

He gave me the piece of paper. I thanked him. We shook hands. I watched him walk away down the block with his little canvas bag. Then I picked up my suitcases and went into the hotel. I felt terrible.

The bus took three days and two nights to reach Los Angeles. It wasn't any more comfortable than the Ericksons' car. The center armrest was immovable, so that even when no one was sitting beside me I couldn't stretch out. Max was right, my feet did swell up.

I remember the vagrants. They were everywhere, men in dirty ragged clothes, in the bus stations, squatting by the side of the road, clinging to the freight trains.

I remember Oklahoma City, flat and still and dusty in the hot sun. The man behind the counter in the lunchroom was wearing cowboy boots. And then, vividly, I remember the desert. I felt instantly at home there: the vast emptiness, the purple silhouette of the distant mountains, was like the landscape of some secret reverie. Much later, I remember Barstow. The desert ended there as abruptly as the coming of a spring shower. California: the land was suddenly green and fresh; white Spanish houses and orange trees. The clarity of the sunlight gave everything a bright, birthday promise.

We backed and ground into the Los Angeles bus station in the late afternoon. A porter helped me onto a Hollywood streetcar. The address Max had given me was on Las Palmas. I got off there and, with frequent stops to set down my suitcases, found the house just south of Sunset. It was a wooden bungalow with a patch of grass in front of it and a screened-in porch running the width of the house.

A woman appeared out of the dusk when I touched the bell beside the porch door. She was in her early fifties, trimly dressed in a dark suit with a white ruffled blouse. What impressed me about her at once was her air of distinction: she had that rare quality of personal dignity.

"Mrs. Hainert?" I asked.

"Yes, I'm Mrs. Hainert." I was getting used to American voices; she didn't sound exactly American.

"I was told you might have a room for rent."

"Who told you?"

"Max Ludlow."

Her cool reserve vanished at once. "You're a friend of Max's?" She switched on a light and opened the screen door for me. "Come in."

I struggled up onto the porch with my suitcases.

"You must be one of the East Coast —" She hesitated, studying me in my rumpled linen dress, my lace-up shoes. "Where do you know Max from?"

"I met him in New York."

"Through the —" She hesitated again. "Where in New York?"

I told her. She listened with amused interest to my story about the Eriksons.

"You'd better come and see the room. You must be half-dead." She led me through a living room filled with books, down a short passage to a large, pleasant room with a small porch of its own overlooking the backyard.

"It's lovely."

I would have taken it at once if it had been a dungeon, rather than walk another step on my swollen feet, but I was delighted with it. The furniture was ordinary enough — a sturdy table, a basket chair, pine bookcases. What pleased me was that there was not a single ugly or tasteless object in sight. I had a sudden panic; it must be more than I could afford, with a porch of my own, certainly more than the eight dollars the Harts had demanded. I asked Mrs. Hainert how much the rent would be.

"Four dollars a week?" She made a question of it.

I was still carrying the piece of paper Max had given me with her address on it. I put it down on the bureau while I opened my bag and gave her the first week's rent, thanking her, telling her how glad I was to be there.

"I expect you'd like to go to bed. The bathroom's off the corridor to the left." She stayed watching me while I found my toilet things. She was gone by the time I came back. I pulled out my pajamas and unpacked a few things. It was while I was doing this that I noticed Max's piece of paper was no longer on the bureau where I had left it; it was on the table. I was almost asleep when it crossed my mind that Mrs. Hainert had waited until I was out of the room because she wanted to look at it. To make sure Max had really sent me there?

She had left by the time I got up the next morning. I found a note slipped under my door, telling me she would be back from work at six and to use the kitchen whenever I wanted to.

I spent most of the day idling around Hollywood, the Movie Capital of the World. It was a dull, sleepy little town. I looked at the hand- and footprints outside Grauman's Chinese Theater. They gave me absolutely no feeling that Clark Gable or Greta Garbo had pressed their hands and feet into the cement there.

Mrs. Hainert was in the kitchen making soup when I came home. She offered me some. I didn't want to impose on her, so I told her I'd already eaten. I accepted a glass of milk and sat talking to her while she ate. Max was right: she was a very nice woman, intelligent, kind. She had traveled a lot, and she was interesting about it, comparing customs and cultures. She was a listener, too, asking me about myself. She had heard of my father; some of his books were in the library where she worked. She had only read one of them, his endorsement of Fabian socialism. She didn't comment on it. She had a gift for swerving away, like a bird in flight, from any subject she wanted to avoid. I asked her about Max. She didn't refuse to answer my questions; she gracefully evaded them. "That reminds me," she would say, or pick out one part of them, perhaps his work as a film cutter, and talk about that.

I soon stopped mentioning Max's name altogether. But I couldn't forget him. I thought about him constantly during the next few days. He was like an unseen presence beside me as I explored Los Angeles, took the streetcar out to Santa Monica and walked on the pier, wrote to Sinclair Lewis at the Beverly Hills Hotel, joined the public library where Mrs. Hainert worked. Many of my thoughts were addressed to him.

I had been at Mrs. Hainert's almost a week, when one night the doorbell rang. She went out onto the porch. I heard her voice, soft and cautious. I had been reading a book about the abolitionist movement, and something in Mrs. Hainert's tone made me think of those New England women welcoming runaway slaves: "Did anyone see you? Were you followed?"

I knew I was being absurd, fantasizing melodrama out of nothing. It was probably some salesman she was talking to; people were always coming to the house selling things. I left my room and walked a little way down the passage so I could see the front door.

Max was standing out there on the porch.

I couldn't help myself; I ran out to him. I was smiling, laughing, like a rewarded child.

I was so glad to see him again.

Four

"I'll drop you off here." Max stopped the car he had borrowed just short of the Beverly Hills Hotel driveway. "How long do you think you'll be?"

"You don't have to wait for me."

"I'll pick you up later. What time will you be through?"

Max's voice had the gentle persuasiveness I had learned to recognize in the past two weeks. It meant he had something he wanted me to do for him, but didn't wish to explain. A few days ago he had offered, in that same persuasive way, to drive me to Santa Monica. When we got there, he had taken a package out of the trunk and asked me to deliver it for him, making me memorize the address. I hadn't minded walking the few blocks to the house on Montana Avenue, handing the package to the woman who answered the door. It had hurt me a little that he wouldn't tell me why he couldn't deliver it himself, wouldn't answer any questions about it.

"I don't know how long I'll be. He might invite me to stay to lunch or something."

"I'll come back at noon." Max leaned over and opened the car door for me. "If you're not here, I'll wait."

I didn't argue with him; my mind was too busy with my own

immediate purpose. I was all dressed up, hat and gloves and my best afternoon dress. "You must have something in case you're invited to a garden party," my mother had said when she bought it for me. I had carefully ironed it the evening before.

God knows what I must have looked like, walking up the drive to the Beverly Hills Hotel that day. The dress was a flowered print with a sash and a full skirt that came down to my ankles. The hat was the kind ladies used to wear to Ascot, wide-brimmed straw with a ribbon tied in a bow at the front. At least no one stared at me in the lobby. The desk clerk was noticeably polite. After a brief phone call, he invited me to go straight up to the suite.

"Come in." The door was flung open before I could knock. The impatience in the voice suggested I was late. "Come in," it repeated in the same rasping tone.

I went in. The door was slammed behind me. I did my best to smile at my host.

It wasn't easy to hold the smile. My first thought was that he was the ugliest man I had ever seen. His scanty, sand-colored hair strayed moistly over his forehead. His pockmarked cheeks tapered to an insignificant, pitted apple of a chin. His mouth was never still, constantly twisting into a series of grimaces. His nose looked peeled at the tip and was wrinkled at the sides. But it was his eyes that shocked me most: yellowed, bloodshot orbs with pale blue irises, they were so protuberant they seemed in danger of falling out of their sockets. The lower lids peeled down, revealing their raw inner membrane.

"Mr. Lewis?" I asked timidly.

"Sit down. Sit down." Everything he said seemed to be followed by an unspoken "for Christ's sake." I sat down on the sofa under the window. A woman in tailored slacks was standing in the doorway to the next room.

"This is Carol Clavering," Sinclair Lewis told her curtly. "N. E. Clavering's daughter. You know N. E. Clavering, the god-damn British critic."

The woman murmured something that might have been her own name; I didn't catch it. Sinclair Lewis had collapsed into a chair, his thin legs twisted around each other, his chin resting on his tie. "For Christ's sake take that hat off," he told me. I took it off. The woman in the slacks disappeared through the doorway. A moment later I heard her talking on the phone.

Sinclair Lewis sat glaring at me in silence. Every part of him was motionless except his grimacing mouth, but his stillness held no suggestion of repose; he was as taut as a cricket.

"What are you doing out here? What made you come to this loathsome place?"

I said something about the war, being an American citizen, wanting to get out of Europe. He didn't interrupt, but it was difficult to tell if he was listening. His jaundiced eyes had an absent expression of thoughtful intelligence.

"I mean *this* place," he rasped at me when I had finished. "Hollywood." It was astonishing how much disgust he managed to get into the single word.

When I told him I was looking for a job, his eyes lost their thoughtfulness and became wary. "You want to be an actress, a movie star?"

"No. Of course not."

"A lot of goddamn girls do." For the first time he showed a personal interest in me. "Why don't you want to be a movie star?" He spread his hand in front of his mouth, clawing at his pockmarked cheeks with his fingers.

"The whole idea's ridiculous."

"Why?"

"Being held up in public, so that people can gawk at you like a freak."

"You think actors are freaks?" He didn't wait for me to answer that. He was on his feet, stalking about the room. He walked like a man on stilts. "You're right. Maybe that's why I've turned into an actor. I'm a freak, all right. Look at me. Did you ever see such a goddamn freak? So I might as well get up on a stage where the bastards can gawk at me every night."

He collapsed into another chair, into the same deceptive stillness as before. He asked me what kind of a job I was looking for. I mentioned manuscript reading.

"Call Jed Walker." He turned in his chair. The woman in the tailored slacks was standing in the doorway again. "Tell him to get Carol a job as a reader."

"It's very kind of you." I meant it. Why should he bother with me? Just because he had known my father?

"You'll never get anywhere in this godawful place unless someone helps you." His smile briefly relieved his ugliness. "And nobody ever will. They're too busy in their own troughs."

I thanked him again, wondering if I ought to leave. I stayed on, hoping he would talk about himself. He didn't. He continued on about Hollywood for a while, the brutal, cattle market aspect of the studios, then suddenly seemed to lose interest in the subject and switched to the coming war in Europe. He stalked up and down. He was the most restive human being I had ever met; it was as though he were driven by some maddening physical irritation. The constant grimacing movement of his lips reminded me of the flick of a horse's skin when a fly settles on it. After ten minutes I put on my hat and stood up to go. He didn't try to detain me. As I was leaving, the woman in slacks handed me Jed Walker's office address. "Go and see him tomorrow at ten o'clock," she told me. I thanked her, too. Closing the door, I had a last glimpse of Sinclair Lewis, cricketlike in a chair, his dreadful eyes staring at his own knees. It shocked me how unhappy he looked.

I had to wait half an hour for Max on Sunset Boulevard. I sat on the bench at the bus stop, thinking about Sinclair Lewis. He was a Nobel Prize winner. He had written *Main Street* and *Babbitt* and *Dodsworth,* but he hadn't talked about that. Except for the single sardonic reference to his recent acting career, he hadn't talked about himself at all. He had made no attempt to impress me, to play the great man. He had no pretense in him, it seemed to me, no vanity. I decided it wasn't only because he had been kind to me that I liked him.

Max was in a hurry when he finally arrived. He stopped the car across the street and waved to me to join him. He didn't ask me about Sinclair Lewis; I didn't try to tell him. We drove along the Strip, past the big agents' offices, Utter McKinley's funeral parlor, the Garden of Allah. A cluster of women waited outside the Trocadero, hoping some movie star would show up for lunch there.

"Where are we going?"

"My house."

I had seen Max almost every day for the past two weeks. He would stop by Mrs. Hainert's in the late afternoon. We would walk through the Crossroads of the World to Hollywood Boulevard and have a hamburger in a drugstore. Sometimes he and I and Mrs. Hainert would eat together in her kitchen, then later, after I had gone to bed, he would stay on for hours talking to her. We never made dates. I could never be sure whether he had come to see me or Mrs. Hainert. He had never taken me to his house before.

We turned up Laurel Canyon and then off into the hills, twisting up steeper and steeper and less and less well-paved roads.

"Put your head down."

"What?"

"Get down in the seat, out of sight."

We were on a dirt road now. On one side was a high overgrown bank, on the other, a sheer drop. Out of sight of what?

"Go on." Max used his persuasive voice again. I slid down in the seat until my face was below the window.

Max drove on for another few minutes. When he stopped I could see sloping beams through the window; we were in a garage. He wouldn't let me sit up until he had closed the garage doors.

He led me through a side door, past a small, smelly kitchen, into a large, dark-curtained room. A half-dozen people were sitting around on the scanty furniture, mostly on cots pushed against the walls. It was hard to make out their faces at first, but I could see they were all fairly young, the men in slacks and open shirts, the women in plain cotton prints.

"Christ," someone said.

I had forgotten I was still wearing my Ascot hat, my long afternoon dress.

"This is Carol. Sit here, Carol." Max pushed an orange crate forward for me. I took off my hat and sat down. Nobody said anything. It was like some party game, Guess Who She's Meant to Be. I could feel them all studying me. I half expected someone to guess "Eliza Doolittle," and Max would say, "Right first time," and they would draw open the curtains and the game would be over.

"I'm Leda." A woman moved forward and peered down into

my face. She had short hair and pursed lips and horn-rimmed glasses.
"How old are you, Carol?"

"Eighteen."

"Christ," someone said again.

They all started questioning me after that. They didn't do it in
the casual way Sinclair Lewis had, this was an exam; I was being
tested. They asked me in detail about my background, my education,
my reasons for coming to California.

Why did I answer them? Perhaps it was partly vanity, the pleasure
of being the center of attention, but mostly, I think, because of
Max. If I'd refused to answer, I would have been letting Max down.
He was standing beside me and touched my shoulder now and
then in an encouraging way.

It went on for about half an hour. I was beginning to distinguish
individuals among the group. Apart from Leda, there was one very
thin young man in a ragged sweater, who put his questions to me
in a scornful, bullying voice as though he expected me to lie. I
heard someone call him Mannie. I didn't find out until years later,
when he went to jail for contempt of Congress during the McCarthy
era and his picture was in *Time* magazine, that his name was Emanuel Orville Lind.

Gradually the questions became less personal. They asked me
what I thought of Roosevelt, Hitler, Stalin. "I like him." "I hate
him." "I don't trust him." I would have found it hard to explain
why I didn't trust Stalin; it was something about his eyes. Many
of the questions I couldn't answer at all. I had never heard of the
Wagner Act, or Norman Thomas, or Lovestone. I was a little better
informed when they moved to English politics. I was vaguely in
favor of the Labour party but despised Ramsay MacDonald. My
particular hero was James Maxton of the ILP. "Why?" Because I
felt he was the only honest socialist in parliament. Although I didn't
say so, I had acquired that opinion from my sister, Sylvia.

I felt a stir of approval when I praised James Maxton. After
that, inevitably, I started telling them what I thought they wanted
to hear. When they questioned me about my socialist beliefs, I
moved to the left of my father's Fabians, whom I was afraid they
would think old-fashioned and stuffy, and closer to Lenin.

There was a long, fidgety silence when the questioning ended,
an occasional whisper from one of the cots.

"Would you mind going into the garage for a few minutes?" Max touched my arm, guiding me out past the smelly kitchen.

I didn't mind; I was glad to get out of that darkened room. I spent ten minutes poking around in the garage, among the coils of frayed hoses, the broken garden tools. The only thing of any interest I found was a crumpled sheet of wrapping paper. I was pretty sure it was the paper that parcel had been wrapped in, the one I had delivered to the house on Montana Avenue.

When Max called me back into the living room, I was glad to find the curtains had been drawn open. I sat on the same orange crate and examined the room with interest. The walls were unpaneled, of roughhewn logs. Apart from the orange crates and cots, the only piece of furniture was a wooden table that looked as though it had been nailed together out of firewood. This was Max's home. How many people shared it with him? Were they all men, or did some of these women live here too?

"How would you like to go to Mexico?" Leda was leaning forward on the nearest cot.

"Mexico?"

"We'll pay your fare, don't worry." The young man they'd called Mannie still sounded bullying and scornful.

"What for? What am I supposed to do there?" I was looking at Leda; she seemed friendlier to me than the others.

"We want you to go to a hotel called the Monte Carlo —" She stopped; I must have reacted to the name of the hotel. "What's the matter? Do you know it?"

"It's where D. H. Lawrence used to stay." I remembered that from my father's book about him.

"Oh." Either she had never heard of D. H. Lawrence or she thought the information was irrelevant. "Register in your own name. A woman will get in touch with you there. She'll ask you a few questions, and if she thinks everything is okay, she'll give you an envelope. You leave the next day and bring the envelope back here."

I didn't say anything.

"You don't have to make up your mind right away." Max put his arm around my shoulders.

"It'll be an interesting trip for you," Leda urged me. "You like traveling, don't you? And if they decide they can trust you in Mexico City . . ." She hesitated, glancing at the others. One of the young men nodded. "If they decide you're okay, you might even get to meet the old man."

"Wouldn't you like that?" Mannie taunted me. "Wouldn't you like to meet Trotsky?"

Five

I don't know."

I was slumped down in my seat, keeping my face out of sight, as Max drove me back along the dirt road.

"You don't have to make up your mind right away, Carol."

"Why me? Why doesn't one of you —?"

"It's not safe for any of us to go. We might be stopped and searched at the American border coming back."

I've wondered since if Max was right. Were the FBI already keeping a surveillance on left-wing groups way back then in 1939?

They probably were, but I found it hard to believe at the time. Perhaps it was my secure, smug English background. Max's conspiratorial behavior, the furtive way he had smuggled me into his house, seemed absurd to me. It didn't make any sense. It wasn't as though he and his friends were Nazi spies or something. Trotsky was a famous man; he wrote books about himself; my sister Sylvia admired him. And here were these people behaving as though they belonged to some dangerous secret society being watched every minute by the American government.

It was an indication of my respect and affection for Max that I didn't say any of this aloud.

"If it's not safe for you, why is it safe for me?"

"There's nothing to connect you to us. And besides, you know, the whole way you look. You can sit up now."

"How? How do I look?" I sat up with my hat on my knees.

"You're so obviously, well, middle class."

"Why don't you say bourgeois?" I was annoyed. I didn't like to think of myself as belonging to any class; that was one of the reasons I'd wanted to come to America.

"You don't have to make up your mind right away."

He dropped me off at Mrs. Hainert's. I went in and sat on my porch. It's ridiculous, I kept thinking. Mexico City, a secret contact with a woman at a hotel, smuggling an envelope back across the border. What was in it, anyway? What *could* be in it that was so special and dangerous? It was ridiculous.

Soon after six o'clock I heard Mrs. Hainert come back from work. She knocked on my door. I was glad to see her; maybe I could talk to her about it. She was so sensible, so down-to-earth.

"Why, Carol, you look lovely."

I was still wearing that bloody dress.

I felt so silly in it I had to explain it to her. I told her all about Sinclair Lewis. She was interested. We were still talking about him when the doorbell rang. Max had come for my answer.

I changed into the simplest, drabbest clothes I could find before I went out to him. We walked down to Santa Monica Boulevard and sat on a bench.

"I don't know, Max." I still hadn't made up my mind. "For one thing, I don't want to leave here now. Sinclair Lewis made an appointment for me to see an agent tomorrow. He's going to try to find me a job."

Max didn't say anything for at least two minutes, leaning back on the bench. The orange glow of the street lamp made his face look tanned, even more Western. I thought how natural he would look in cowboy jeans on horseback. He was still wearing the same unmatched jacket and trousers. He didn't seem to have any physical vanity at all.

"You think that's more important?"

"More important than what?"

"That getting a job is more important than what we're trying to do? We're trying to change things, Carol . . ." I didn't interrupt him as he went on to explain. He was persuasive and convincing without ever making me feel he was lecturing me or that what he was saying was something he had learned from other people or from books. It all seemed to be coming from Max and he seemed to be saying it all for the first time. He started with the migrant lettuce pickers in the Salinas Valley, their wages, the hours they worked, the way they lived. He made it sound ghastly without sounding exaggerated. Silently, while I listened, I began to try to excuse myself. It wasn't my fault I'd been born one of the lucky ones, well fed, educated, white, privileged, and protected by the way I looked and talked. It wasn't my fault I didn't have hookworm, wasn't working in the sun twelve hours a day for just enough to keep myself from starving. I didn't even like lettuce; I never ate it. I still felt guilty.

Max went on from the lettuce pickers to a more general criticism of the capitalist system. Ten years after the Wall Street crash, over ten million people were still unemployed in the United States, four million Americans were still without homes, vagrants. But economic depression was nothing new: there had been regular, predictable panics and crashes for the last hundred years. Max knew their dates. He explained them in terms of Marxist theory: surplus value, overproduction, glut.

"You think you're going to change all that?" I asked him.

"Sure." He stretched his arm along the back of the bench behind me. "It's just a question of educating people, organizing them. Don't you want to help us?"

He sounded so sure of himself. I wished I could feel as confident as he did. I had begun to understand there was a quality in Americans that made them different from Europeans. I had glimpsed it in the Harts' indiscriminate admiration for success. I had heard it in dozens of boastful voices across drugstore counters in Hollywood. It wasn't a particularly engaging quality; it was what made Americans so truculent about being equal to *anyone,* while hating the idea that anyone was equal to them. It was a stubborn belief that their dreams were true. Demonstrably true. "Why, Edison . . . Why, Carnegie . . . Why, Ford . . ."

I would have found it hard, then, to put all this into words, but sitting on that bench on Santa Monica Boulevard I knew that Americans, 95 percent of them, anyway, would never accept Max's ideas; he would never be anything but a "troublemaker" to them. Because they would put up with anything rather than give up their belief that every success was due to their own individual efforts, even if it meant admitting that every failure was their own fault.

"Max." Something had been puzzling me all evening. "You could find someone else to go to Mexico, couldn't you? I'm not the only person —"

"Sure. Sure, I guess we could if we had to."

"Then why me? Why do you want me to do it so much?"

"Because I like you." He dropped his arm from the back of the bench and put it around my shoulders. "I want you to be in this with me. It's my whole life and I want you . . . I want you to be a part of it. You will go, won't you, Carol?" Our faces were very close together. In the way you do at eighteen, because it's all new to you and your senses are so responsive, I could feel the emanation of his physical vitality brush my lips like the touch of a feather. It was exciting; it made me smile.

"Okay. I'll go if it really means so much to you, Max."

Max was smiling too. He kissed me. It was the first time I had enjoyed being kissed. It made me breathless and eager, and then confused about what I was eager for.

I stood up. Max walked me back to Mrs. Hainert's. I could hear him talking to her until I fell asleep.

Jed Walker handled writers for one of the big agencies, Dove and Roberts, with offices on Wilshire Boulevard in Beverly Hills. He was young and smart and not bad-looking, and I felt at once there was no substance to him. He was one of those people whose whole personality seems to be an imitation of what they think its supposed to be. One of the things Jed Walker thought a Hollywood agent was supposed to be was hot cheese with women. All women. He never made any advances to me, never so much as patted my shoulder, but he spent a lot of time telling me what hot cheese he was. I never liked him and I owe him a great deal: he didn't find me a job; he gave me one.

"I haven't time to read," he told me. "A client gives me an

original he's written. It's a hundred and twenty pages. The New York office sends me a property they're handling." He picked up a book and glanced at the last page. "It's three hundred and seventeen pages. Who's got time to read three hundred and seventeen pages?"

I did. That was my job, to reduce all those words to something Jed Walker did have time to read, a twenty-page outline of what he called the subject. "Don't tell me what you think of it," he warned me. "That's my job, whether the studios'll buy it. I just want to know the subject so I can talk to them about it."

He wanted six copies of the outline, presumably so that five other people in the agency could talk about the book without having to read it, either. He would pay me five dollars a property.

"Say hello to Red," he told me as I was leaving with the book. "Red's a sweetheart."

I bought a portable typewriter on time from a store on Hollywood Boulevard, and got some paper and carbon and erasers. Back home, I wrote Sinclair Lewis a letter thanking him. I had to retype it three times before it was neat enough to mail. Then I sat on my porch and started to read the property. It was about a woman who was in love with a married doctor. His wife was an invalid. I was very conscientious and made notes on the subject as I went along, although the more cynical side of my mind kept telling me I could write the whole outline without reading the rest of the book.

The wife had just gone over the cliff in her wheelchair when I heard Mrs. Hainert come home. She tapped on my door; I put the book aside and invited her to sit on my porch with me. She noticed my new typewriter; I told her about my job.

"I'm sure you'll be very good at it, Carol." She smiled. "I think you're the kind of person who'll be good at anything you set your mind to."

Compliments always embarrassed me a little, but it meant a lot to me, coming from her. I respected her so much. She lit a cigarette and offered me the pack. I shook my head; I didn't smoke. "You're very sensible." She was still smiling. "It's a ridiculous habit."

I didn't agree with her; I wanted to smoke. Everybody I knew smoked; it was a symbol of being grown-up and it added a whole facet to your personality. The way you held your cigarette, tilted it in your mouth, was as much an individual characteristic as your hair or your clothes. The way John Garfield smoked showed he was tough and disillusioned. Ronald Colman's pipe was an emblem of jaunty sophistication. By not smoking I was losing an important chance to express myself. The trouble was I didn't like smoking. It made me feel sick.

When Mrs. Hainert smoked, she concentrated on it, thoughtfully, like someone tasting wine.

"This new job, Carol . . ." She was no longer smiling. "I hope it doesn't mean you won't go to Mexico City."

"Who —" I couldn't hide how startled I was. "Who told you about that? I suppose Max —"

"Of course not. Max is only —" She shook her head impatiently. "*I* suggested you, Carol."

God, how I wished I smoked. I had to sit there with nothing to do with my hands or my mouth while I absorbed that.

"I thought you would be a good person for us." She put out her cigarette. Was she going to tell me I was bourgeois looking, too? "And I thought it would be good for you."

"Why?"

"You're an intelligent girl, too intelligent to waste your life on yourself. There's a terrible emptiness in that, in personal ambition, in having a good job, getting ahead, making money, and you're too good for it." Her usual gentle distinction had vanished. The ardor in her eyes reminded me, inappropriately, of Mrs. Hart denouncing the unions. "The world's in such an appalling mess — Russia, Germany. There's so much to be done. You've got to help us do it, Carol, for your own sake as much as ours." Mrs. Hainert stood up. I realized the doorbell was ringing.

I sat there in the twilight as she went to the front door. I felt suddenly wary, trapped. It wasn't that I minded going to Mexico City; I had promised Max I would, and it might even be rather exciting. It was the way Mrs. Hainert had talked that made me uneasy, the tone of her voice as much as her words. She had made me understand that in carrying out this errand I would be committing myself. I would be entering a new separate world, a world of causes and faith. It would be like joining the church, I thought, devoting myself to Christ. Promising to believe all kinds of things. Without questioning them. And I didn't think I could do it. It was against my whole nature.

I heard footsteps approaching. Mrs. Hainert came back onto the porch with Max.

"I think we've made a convert, Max," she said. "I know Carol's going to be a valuable new member in our group."

I turned my head from side to side, looking at her and then at Max. "You mustn't," I said loudly. "I mean, just because I agreed to do this for you, you mustn't think I'm going to give up my life to the socialist cause or anything. I'm afraid —" I broke off. Mrs. Hainert was staring at me, her usual kindness and charm frozen into severity. "I'm afraid" — I went on, still too loudly; I was determined to get it said — "I'm just not the right kind of person for you. I'm too selfish and sort of independent and rebellious" — Obedience: very poor, I remembered — "and I'm just no bloody good at taking orders from anybody."

"That's only because you're young, Carol." Mrs. Hainert was smiling again.

"No, it isn't." I looked at Max. He still hadn't said anything.

And then he did something I never forgot. He did it against his own interests, his own side, out of kindness and understanding and affection. He came over and put his arms around me, and shook his head, almost imperceptibly, telling me not to worry.

He turned back to Mrs. Hainert. "I came to tell you," he said cheerfully. "They don't want Carol to go after all. They're sending someone down from New York."

"Won't it get you into trouble, Max?" We had escaped from Mrs. Hainert's and were sitting on the same bench on Santa Monica Boulevard.

"I don't want to get you into trouble with them."

"Don't worry." He took my hand. "I can fix it. Easy. I've got a friend in New York who has more authority than Mrs. Hainert, even. All I have to do is call him and he'll send someone down from there. I can fix it."

"You're sure. Because I still don't mind going."

"No. I'm quite sure."

"Why —?" I could feel his hand tight in mine; I could feel it all the way up my arm and across my breasts and down to my knees. "Why did you change your mind? Why did you suddenly decide you didn't want me to go?"

"I don't know." The street light was making him look tanned again. God, he had such a wonderful face, the quiet, easy confidence in it. "I just got to thinking about it, that's all. About you. And it didn't seem fair. You never really wanted to go. You were just being sweet about it. And besides" — he smiled — "you'd have been gone at least a week. You might have lost your job. And I'd have had to spend a whole week worrying about you, in case anything went wrong at the border."

"Thank you. Thank you, Max."

I hoped he was going to kiss me again. He didn't. He held my hand for a little while longer, then he had to go call New York.

I started my first outline the next day. I had no difficulty writing it; writing précis had been one of the few useful things we had been taught at school. Typing it was another matter. I had never learned touch typing. I used two fingers of my right hand and one of my left. I had to hit each key hard to carry through all those carbons. If I hit the wrong one, I had to make six separate erasures. It took me half an hour to type the first page and it still looked terrible. I did it over again. As I went along I did several of the other pages over again too. I got stuck on page six. I couldn't get it right. It reminded me of those awful hours of childhood, being sent to my room to do something — mend a dress I had torn, "and do it properly, Carol" — and my fingers couldn't do it at all. I remembered the lonely taste of tears, the relief of rage. I wasn't a child, I told myself. I was doing a responsible, grown-up job. This was no time for tantrums. I worked until midnight and finished at noon the next day.

I took the streetcar to Beverly Hills and delivered the six copies to Jed Walker. Why are we told in childhood that everything will be counted? Effort will be rewarded. It leaves us with doomed expectations. Jed Walker didn't even take my outlines out of the envelope. "Tell my secretary to file them," he said. "She'll give you a petty-cash slip to take up to the eighth floor." I thanked him and started out. He handed me a script off his desk.

"Say hello to Red," he reminded me. "Red Lewis is a sweetheart."

Red Lewis was such a sweetheart, I averaged three properties and earned fifteen dollars a week. I never managed to get complete control of that portable typewriter, but I learned to hit the wrong keys less and less often. After a while I quite enjoyed the work. I read an extraordinary manuscript by a writer named Dalton Trumbo. As far as I know, nothing I read was ever made into a movie.

Unless he was working late in the cutting room at one of the studios, I saw Max every day. We went for long walks together and we kissed a lot, but we never went any further than that. In those days it was difficult to go very far on public benches or on Santa Monica pier. But even when Max managed to borrow a car and we parked up in the hills, he never tried to feel my breasts or put his hand up under my skirt. And when we were alone together in my room at Mrs. Hainert's, he never touched me at all. It was as though we had reached some understanding in Joplin and we were waiting for something, some circumstance in our lives, to break that barrier between us.

I never knew exactly what Max had told his friends in the group about me, how he had explained the sudden change in the plan to send me to Mexico City, but they obviously decided I was okay. Leda, the woman in the horn-rimmed glasses, and several of the others adopted me like a little sister. Even Mannie, who despised and distrusted everyone, took the trouble to instruct me sometimes. I never committed myself to their beliefs, and so long as I felt I could retain my independence of mind I was glad to learn from them. They gave me some understanding of American history. As Marxists they believed in economic determinism, but as young Americans they filled me with their own idealistic enthusiasm about the best of America. I shall never be able to read the Gettysburg Address without having to clear my throat.

At the same time, Leda, in particular, had a healthy skepticism. She soon talked me out of my belief in the American myth of a classless society. "Jefferson meant all *white men* are created equal," she explained to me one afternoon while we were picketing a department store in Hollywood. "He didn't mean women or Negroes."

The Trotskyists weren't much concerned with the Negroes in

those days, either. Perhaps the whole problem of educating the masses about race was too much for them. They would have liked, like Max, to be concerned with the migrant workers, but the Stalinists had gotten there first in the lettuce fields. "Those crypto-fascist bastards would kill us if we tried to go down there and organize the pickers," Mannie said. He was probably right. The two Communist parties reserved their deepest hatred for each other.

The Stalinists had gotten there first in the industrial unions, too. We were forced to concentrate mostly on white-collar workers. We kept after that department store on Hollywood Boulevard for weeks until we organized enough of a union to threaten a strike. The management refused to recognize it. We might finally have managed to force recognition through the NLRB, but we lost control of the employees. Mannie said we'd been betrayed by the Stalinists again, but I never believed that. I thought we lost control because the salesgirls, who made eighteen dollars a week, wouldn't be able to keep up the payments on the clothes they were wearing if they struck, and they were scared helpless by the thought of what the roughnecks from the collection agencies would do to them.

We held meetings and study groups. Mannie bawled us out for any deviationist tendencies he suspected in us. We received regular policy directives from Mexico City. Some evenings we sat around on the cots in the house above Laurel Canyon and sang protest songs, "I'm Sticking with the Union" and "The Ballad of Joe Hill." I began to avoid those evenings; they embarrassed me. It wasn't that I minded communal singing, I just couldn't believe in the songs. I'm sure Joe Hill was a wonderful man, but I thought that ballad was a piece of sentimental rubbish. On an emotional level, it was as trite as "God Save the King." There was no difference.

And then late in August everything changed.

"There's only us now," Max told me excitedly when he brought me the news.

I read the headlines. I was so shocked I felt physically cold. I kept staring at the picture on the front page. Ribbentrop. A weak, vain, empty face. Molotov. His expression so noncommittal he might have been stuffed. Nazi Germany and the Soviet Union had signed a nonaggression pact.

"It's the end of the American Communist party," Max was saying.

"Do you think there'll be a war now?"

"I don't know." He didn't seem to think that was very important. What mattered was that the Stalinists had revealed themselves to the whole world as the fascists they were. "Even the Russian people will turn against them now. And they'll . . ."

I stopped listening to him. I had only been asking him for reassurance anyway; I was quite sure there was going to be a war now. The Hitler-Stalin agreement had finally made it inevitable. Superciliously, ineffectually, Chamberlain had been trying for months to turn Hitler against Russia. He had failed. Now, peevishly, superciliously, he would declare war. I didn't see how England and France could ever win that war. I couldn't see how it could ever end; it would go on forever. My mother and father listening to the BBC news six thousand miles away were suddenly more immediate than Max sitting next to me on the porch. The backyard, the palm trees above the neighboring houses, were as irrelevant as snapshots in someone else's album. I could only see my sister Sylvia in her apartment in St. John's Wood, my other sister, Daphne, waiting for a bus outside her training school. I was frightened for them. My fear made me sick with anger against Chamberlain, Halifax, Henderson, that whole pathetic bunch of self-righteous frauds.

"The stupid idiots," I said aloud. "Look what they've done. Look at what their smug, stupid lies have got us into."

"Don't worry, the American Communist party won't be able to lie —"

"Oh, shut up about the Communist party, Max. This is *real.*" The word just slipped out. Had I been suppressing it for weeks? "I'm talking about the bloody British government. How can they defend Poland? They lost the last chance of ever stopping Hitler at Munich." I thought of the refugees I had met on the ship coming over, the thousands and thousands still trapped in Europe. They would all be murdered now. "It's going to be horrible, Max. Can't you see that? Absolutely horrible."

He should have corrected me, pointed out my error, criticized my thinking. He didn't. That was one of the things that made me love him; he could be so sensitive when I least expected it.

"I guess your whole family's over there, aren't they?" He touched my cheek.

I avoided the group for the next few days. I didn't go to any of the emergency meetings they called to discuss the Trotskyist line in case of war. I spent a lot of time walking up and down Las Palmas Avenue. At the top of it, on the corner of Hollywood Boulevard, was a newsstand that sold papers from all over the world. I walked up there two, three, sometimes four times a day to see if the latest *News Chronicle* or *Manchester Guardian* had come in from England. They were days behind the local papers in telling me what was going on in Europe, but they seemed to bring me closer to it. The American papers had suddenly become foreign to me.

I walked up to the newsstand around noon that Sunday when Chamberlain read his plaintive announcement that a state of war existed between Britain and Germany. I bought a *Los Angeles Times* to find out exactly what he had said, then started looking for the latest papers from England. A woman was riffling through the German papers beside me. There was nothing about her to attract attention: she was in her forties, with a homely face, rimless glasses. She twisted her head to try to read the headlines on my *Los Angeles Times.*

"*Bitte,*" she said, "*ist England macht,* make —"

"*Krieg?*" I helped her. "*Ya. Heute.*" I remembered enough German from school in Switzerland to be able to translate the first paragraph of the story for her. She thanked me. I picked out the *London Times* from the rack. She looked at it suspiciously.

"*Sie sind Engländerin?*"

For once I didn't deny it. I felt English that day. I asked her if she was Austrian? Czech?

"*Deutsch.*"

So there we were on Hollywood Boulevard, and six thousand miles away our two countries were at war. It seemed to create a bond of misfortune between us. I asked her if she would like to come and have a cup of coffee with me.

It was like touching the wrong lever on a machine; instantly she was all sound and motion. She didn't actually strike me, but I thought she was going to. Her fists kept hammering at the space between us.

"We will win," she shrieked at me in German. "We will win.

We have leaders. You have no leaders in England. We will beat you. We have leaders. We will win."

She was right, of course, in her crazy way. We didn't have any leaders. We had an old man who looked like a turkey. We had a cabinet that didn't believe in the war. I still thought it would be interesting to talk to her. I told her so in my schoolgirl German.

It was as though I had attacked her. She backed away. "Leave me alone," she yelled. It sounded musical and rather sad in German. *"Lass mich allein."* She was edging across the street. "We will win," she shrieked at me over her shoulder.

The absurd encounter reassured me. It made the war less of an abstract horror. The bombs I pictured killing my father and mother, destroying Sylvia's apartment, no longer had any evil magic. They were made by people like that woman, and if they were all as crazy as she was, perhaps they wouldn't win after all. I went home; I had an outline to finish typing.

My job became more important to me after the war started. The English papers said there would be strict currency restrictions. My father wasn't going to be allowed to send me three pounds a week any longer. I wrote and told him not to worry about me. It was amazingly cheap living in Hollywood. I could manage on what I earned from Jed Walker and I'd saved almost two hundred dollars over the summer.

Max was busier than ever with emergency meetings. The Wehrmacht defeated the Polish army in a few days; Russia grabbed the other half of Poland; the French Communist party was outlawed; Stalin took over the Baltic States and threatened Finland. Each of these events had to be interpreted and explained from the particular point of view of the American Socialist Workers' party. Trotsky himself was often no help. He publicly predicted the United States would be in the war within six months. Max came to see me after the emergency meeting about that, looking as though he'd been through the October Revolution.

I was collating an outline and the pages were spread all over the furniture. I cleared a space for him and gave him an ashtray; he sat there smoking while I went on putting the pages together.

"Why don't you come to New York with me, Carol?"

"What for?"

"I don't want to go without you."

I was so busy looking for the sixth copy of page eight that I hadn't understood what he was saying until then.

"You're going to New York, Max?" I put the outline down.

"I think I ought to."

"How long for?"

"I don't know. Why? What's the matter?"

He was going away. Oh, no, please, no.

If we had been out on the street I would have hugged and kissed him, urging him not to go. I couldn't kiss him in my own room with the door closed, it would have had too much significance. It would have been like suggesting I wanted to go to bed with him. Did I? Well, yes. Sometime. Soon? Yes.

I finished collating my outline. Max put out his cigarette. We parted with nothing settled between us.

Jed Walker was in a meeting when I went to his office that afternoon. It was always a relief when this happened: his secretary gave me my petty-cash slip and the new property, and I didn't have to listen to the latest installment of Jed Walker's sex life. This time he had left word that he wanted me to wait. I sat in the outer office, looking through a newspaper I had already read. Each time I glanced up, I found his secretary watching me. She was a plain woman in her thirties, who had never given the least hint of having any existence of her own. She was "Jed Walker's secretary"; that seemed to be all she wanted anyone to know about her.

I was surprised when she gave me a timid smile. "I expect you'll be going back to England now," she said.

"No. Why?"

She moved her hand as though shooing away a fly.

"The war."

"Oh. No." I explained I was American. She went back to her typing. That was the end of the only personal contact I ever had with her. I wonder what her name was.

Jed Walker sent for me a few minutes later. He was on the phone when I went in, trying to get one of his clients a job at a studio. "He'll work for less," I heard him say. "He needs the money." I tried not to listen.

"I guess you'll be going back to England now, huh?" He had finished his phone call.

"No." Did I have to explain about being American again?

"Now that Red's all tied up."

I shook my head vaguely; I didn't understand what he was talking about.

"Didn't you see this?" He handed me a press clipping. It was from a New York paper, a gossip column. Halfway down I saw Sinclair Lewis's name. "The Nobel Prize winner has a new interest in life, and it isn't literature. A little bird told me her name is Marcella and Red is really KO'd by her. Is that ringing in his ears wedding bells?" It meant nothing to me.

"You think he's going to marry her?" Jed Walker asked.

"Who?"

"That little actress."

"How would I know?" I was going to say it was none of my business anyway. He interrupted me.

"Too bad. It's a tough break for you, kid, I guess. But that's the way things go."

He picked up the phone, waving me away. It was the first time he had dismissed me without saying Red Lewis was a sweetheart. I got my pay slip from his secretary. She didn't have a property for me. I asked her if she would call when Mr. Walker had something he wanted me to read. She seemed surprised.

"Mr. Walker's taken on a new reader," she said. "I guess he thought you'd be going back to England."

I got my five dollars from the eighth floor and walked out onto Wilshire Boulevard. The windows of the hotel across the street threw sunlight back at me with that brittle clarity that was so startling in California in those days, as though the air itself were a focusing lens. I had always known, obviously, that Jed Walker had only hired me because Sinclair Lewis had sent me to him. What I couldn't understand was what he imagined my relationship with "Red" was. Did he think I was his mistress? I'd only seen Sinclair Lewis once in my life. As I waited for the streetcar, it occurred to me that, having invented himself, Jed Walker couldn't help seeing everyone else as an extension of his fantasies. That was as close as I could get to understanding it all.

By the time I reached home, one thing, at least, was clear: I had to find another job. Mrs. Hainert was in the kitchen. I told her what had happened.

"Don't worry about the rent," she said briskly. "It doesn't matter if you can't pay me for a few weeks."

That almost made me cry. I tried to thank her and explained I had enough money to live on for months. She asked if I thought I could get another job as a reader.

I suddenly realized I didn't want to. I was tired of struggling with that typewriter; it was such a waste of time. The only reason I took so long hammering out those six copies was because I was so inept. I would never be able to do it neatly and quickly unless I got some professional training as a typist.

"Do you want to be a secretary?" As usual her agile, swooping mind was way ahead of mine. "Because don't think it's going to lead to anything, Carol. Not the way things are for women in this country. If you become a secretary, that's what you'll remain, just a secretary."

I thought she was probably right, but what she was saying didn't seem to have anything to do with me. If I learned to type and take shorthand, it wouldn't make me a different person; I wouldn't have to surrender that private sense of my own uniqueness; I wouldn't have to become like that woman in Jed Walker's office. Mrs. Hainert herself seemed to prove that.

"Do you think of yourself as just a librarian?" I asked her.

She shook her head; I caught a glimpse of that ardor in her eyes again. "That's not the important part of my life. It's just a way to support myself. The movement is my life, I've been in it since I was your age. My husband and I were —" She broke off. Max was at the door.

I brought him into the kitchen. Mrs. Hainert told him about my lost job. Max lit a cigarette. Like most of his friends in the group, he smoked a brand called Wings because they were union made. They always seemed to shed scraps of tobacco in his mouth. He frowned now as he picked some flakes off his tongue; it made him look thoughtful.

"Why don't you come to New York with me, Carol?" He explained his plans. Mannie and Leda were driving cross-country in a borrowed car. They had the loan of an apartment on the West Side. Because of the war in Europe, New York had become the center of Trotskyist activity; we were all needed there.

"Come on. Come with us. Come and help us."

I looked at Mrs. Hainert. She was waiting for my answer. I could feel her urging me to agree, to go on, give myself to the movement as she had; I would never regret it if I did; it would give my whole life meaning.

I knew I wasn't going to do what she hoped of me. I had no intention of giving myself to the movement. I had wanted to help those salesgirls in the department store because I could put myself in their place. I couldn't put myself in the place of people like Trotsky. I didn't understand them and I didn't trust them.

I wanted to go to New York, though. Because of Max. The thought of staying in California without him was unbearable. I wanted to tell him that, to shout, "Yes, of course. Of course, I'll go with you." Mrs. Hainert was still watching me. I was afraid she would misunderstand if I said that. I liked her so much; I didn't want to deceive her.

"If I go to New York with you, Max," I told him, "I'm not going to spend all my time working with your group. I'm going to secretarial school and then I'm going to try to find a job."

"Sure. Sure. But you can still help us, Carol. It's so important. We've got to force the United States into the war before Hitler turns against Stalin. We've got —"

"Perhaps it's not your fault, Carol." Mrs. Hainert interrupted him with gentle severity. "There are just some people who are so involved in themselves, they can't see beyond that. They shouldn't even try."

I couldn't defend myself against that. She was right in a way; I couldn't help it. I was the kind of person who had to keep on making up my own selfish mind about one thing at a time.

"I've got an appointment." Mrs. Hainert stood up and walked out, leaving us in the kitchen. I heard the front door close softly behind her.

Max wanted to go on explaining about Hitler and Stalin. He was all steamed up with that buoyant enthusiasm I found so attractive in him. But for once I didn't want to listen to him. Hitler and Stalin had nothing to do with it, as far as I was concerned. I felt it was time I admitted that to him.

"I want to go to New York with you, Max," I said. "Because

I can't stand the thought of your going away. I'd miss you too much. But I do want you to understand — I don't want to pretend — if I come with you, I'm going to get on with my own life, too."

"Okay." Max agreed to that at once. He would work for the group and I would go to secretarial school. There was nothing wrong with that. "I'm glad you're coming, Carol. I'd miss you, too," he said eagerly. "I don't know. I've never felt like this about anyone before. I don't want to be anywhere without you."

We were shy with each other after that. We had made an unspoken commitment, an indefinite tryst. I would go to bed with him. Somewhere. Sometime. Probably quite soon. If he'd said, "Let's go to your room," right there and then, I would have gone in with him and taken my clothes off. Right there and then. He didn't say anything. We left it all in the future.

Except for parting with Mrs. Hainert, I wasn't sorry to leave Hollywood. It was such an ordinary little town, and yet there was something specifically sad about it — the reactionary loyalty of the dress extras, the grips, and the carpenters who made up most of its population; those middle-aged women constantly scanning the traffic, hoping for a glimpse of some movie star; saddest of all, the young men and women standing in their best clothes for hours every day on Hollywood Boulevard, hoping some producer or director would come by and "discover" them.

I cried when I said good-bye to Mrs. Hainert.

"We'll see each other again," she said crisply. "And I'm not going to tell you to take care of yourself, Carol, because I know you will."

I was still thinking about that as I climbed into the car. I knew I could never be unselfish in the way that she was, but at least I could try to be more like her. I made up my mind to be kinder, more thoughtful, more understanding from now on.

It wasn't easy on that journey. Because of the insurance, Mannie and Leda had to do all the driving. Max and I were helpless passengers again. Like the Eriksons, our drivers made all the decisions.

In some ways they were worse than the Eriksons. They quarreled incessantly — not about the war or the materialistic interpretation of history or anything else you'd expect a couple of devoted Trotskyists to quarrel about; they quarreled about where to stop for a hamburger or which windows to have open or whose turn it was to drive. They quarreled before they made any of these decisions and they quarreled even more bitterly afterward. Max and I sat in the back, trying to get comfortable, and occasionally, tensely, holding hands and doing our best to ignore their nagging, accusing voices.

After two days and nights of straight driving, it was impossible to ignore them. We began to join in. Sometimes we took Mannie's side and sometimes Leda's; sometimes we screamed at them both to shut up. Mannie had a boil on the back of his neck. When he was driving I was directly behind him. The car was smaller than the Eriksons'; no matter how far back I crouched in my seat, Mannie's boil was always, hour after hour, within my reach. I couldn't look at anything else. I became obsessed with it. People have told me it's the same with vertigo: what you're really afraid of is that you'll let go, you'll jump. The last thing in the world I wanted to do was to touch that boil, but hour after hour I had to keep active control of myself for fear I'd grab Mannie's neck and squeeze my nails into it.

Sometime in the evening of the third day, I half woke from a half sleep. We were entering a town; Leda was driving.

"Where are we?" I asked unsteadily.

No one knew. Somewhere in Ohio, Max thought. City streets were coming into focus, the lights of stores, restaurants, a movie house. They had no air of inviting gaiety, but in my trancelike state I saw hope in them, the blessed relief of stillness. In a few minutes they would be gone; we would be back in the speeding darkness of the countryside, out of reach of those safe, motionless buildings.

"We're going to stop here." I grabbed Max's arm. "We're going to find a hotel and spend the night here."

It was one of those times when he responded at once with his unpredictable sensitivity. He was my instant ally against the others. He shouted at Leda to stop. For once she and Mannie were allies too. There was no sense in stopping. We'd be in New York in twenty-four hours.

"If you don't stop I'm going to jump out of the car." I yanked at the door handle.

"Me too." Max already had his door open.

Leda pulled to the curb. "How are we going to find a hotel?" she asked plaintively. "We don't even know where we are."

"There," I yelled. "There's a hotel across the street." It was a tall, sheer building with a neon sign: Sheraton.

Leda craned to look at it. "We can't go there." She was horrified. "It'd cost a fortune."

"I don't care." I was already out of the car. Hurrying around to the back, I waited impatiently for Leda to open the trunk for me. She was arguing with Max, insisting it was insane to go to a Sheraton hotel. By the time they joined me, they had reached a belligerent agreement. She and Mannie would go somewhere else, "somewhere sensible." They would pick us up the next morning at eight. "We'll be in the coffee shop," I told her.

Max took one of my suitcases as we started across the street. He stopped under the marquee. "It's going to cost at least five dollars," he warned me. "Maybe ten."

"I'll pay." I fished in my bag and gave him a ten-dollar bill. A man in a long overcoat with silver buttons carried my suitcases into the hotel. I felt no shyness as we registered as Mr. and Mrs. Max Ludlow, Hollywood, California. Max paid for the room in advance; it cost $7.75. He gave the man in the overcoat a quarter.

Another quarter for the bellhop, and Max and I were alone in a musty room with twin beds and long brown-velvet curtains. I still hadn't lost my wild momentum.

"I'm going to have a hot bath," I told Max, "and change my clothes, and then we're going to go out and have dinner and we're going to have wine with it."

That made Max laugh. "Okay," he agreed. "It's crazy, but why not?"

We found an Italian restaurant down the street and had lasagna and half a bottle of Chianti.

When we got back to the hotel room, I felt sleepy and cheerful and no longer in the least crazy. Max locked the door and I took off my shoes and then suddenly there we were. What was I supposed to do next?

I had no experience to guide me. I had no experience. The one thing I was sure of was that I didn't want to undress in front of Max. I took my pajamas into the bathroom, and when I'd brushed my teeth I changed into them there. Max was sitting on one of the beds when I came out. He stood up. He was wearing brief, tight shorts and nothing else. I had never seen his bare chest before. I thought it was beautiful, spare and supple. I was so glad he didn't have hair all over it.

"I'm afraid I left my pajamas in my other bag."

"It doesn't matter. I mean, I like you like that."

I found out later it wasn't true anyway; Max didn't own any pajamas. I pulled the cover off the other bed and turned down the sheet and blankets. I sat down on it; Max stood over me. There was a lumpy looking bulge in his shorts only a few inches from my face. It disconcerted me. I lifted my legs and slipped into bed.

Max sat beside me. He took me by the shoulders and kissed my cheek. The physical feel of him was reassuring; it was like dipping my foot into a bath and finding it was all right to get into it. I held onto him; he stroked my hair.

"We don't have to do anything if you don't want to, Carol."

I sat up. "Oh, come on, Max." I meant, For God's sake do it and get it over with. "Come into bed with me," I told him.

"I've got to get the what's-its-name."

I didn't know what he was talking about. He walked over to the bureau and rummaged in his canvas bag. When he came back to the bed, he was holding something in his clenched hand.

For a wild moment I thought it might be an aphrodisiac. "What is it?"

He unclenched his hand and showed it to me. I knew what it was. Just. I'd found one in Sylvia's bathroom cabinet once when I was staying with her, and she had told me what it was for.

Max put it on the night table, turned off the light, and got into bed with me.

I hadn't the least idea what to do next. I thought it might help if I undid the cord of my pajamas. Max was trying to get his arm under me; I raised myself slightly to make it easier for him and slipped my pajama trousers down to my knees. He had both arms around me now. We were lying pressed flat against each other. He kissed me. I wanted to be transported, swept off into a blissful trance, a state of swooning sensuality. All I felt was what I always did, kissing Max, breathless and eager and a little confused about what it was I was eager for.

He had his hand up under my pajamas and was stroking my

back. I liked that, it was reassuring. But when he brought his hand down to my bare behind, it startled me.

It startled me even more when he squeezed his other hand between my legs. I had never been touched there by anyone except a doctor, not since I was a baby, anyway. I had a shocked impulse to jump out of bed, pull up my pants, and stop the whole thing right there. I resisted the impulse. I loved Max, didn't I? I knew I did. And I had made up my mind days ago to go to bed with him. It seemed childish and cowardly to back out now just because his hand felt so foreign when he touched me there. I would have to go through with it sooner or later, anyway. I wasn't going to remain a virgin for the rest of my life, was I?

He was still kissing me. At least the taste of his mouth was familiar to me. I began to feel happy and playful. I hoped he would just go on kissing me for a while.

He was pulling away from me, reaching around behind him. The bedside light went on.

Taking the rubber out of its wrapping, he tugged down his shorts. I had never really seen a man's penis before. I say "really" because sometimes on the beach in England when a man was changing out of his swimsuit, trying to wriggle his trousers on under his towel, he would expose it for a second. Part of it. Max sitting up with his shorts down, trying to roll on the transparent elastic, showed me the whole thing for quite a long time.

It startled me how ugly it was. It didn't look in the least like the penises on sculptures in museums. It was veined and the tip was pink and raw looking; the sack hanging below it was as wrinkled as a wattle. The whole thing reminded me of some internal organ, something that wasn't generally visible, like an intestine.

Max got the rubber on at last and turned off the light. His hand was between my legs again. He was gently urging me onto my back.

The room was pitch dark but I closed my eyes tight while he rolled on top of me and fiddled around trying to open me up and get that elastic-covered, by now completely impersonal, instrument into me. It was like being operated on. I thought with a flash of black humor that I should have insisted on having an anesthetic. A moment later I had to clench my teeth not to cry out. The pain, though sharp, was mercifully brief. After that there was only a feeling of intrusion, of having something done to me, not exactly against my will, but without my having any part in it.

At least it didn't last very long. Quite suddenly the body on top of me stopped threshing around and became rigid. With a sense of relief, I felt something plop out of me. Just being rid of it made me feel like myself again, all recovered.

Max rolled his hips off me. His cheek was still pressed against mine, his chest across my breasts. I couldn't see him, but I could feel his exhaustion. His stillness had a sweet, spent quality.

"Carol." He was clinging to my shoulders. "Carol. Carol. Carol."

The gratitude in his voice touched me. I was moved, too, by the way he kept repeating my name. For the past few minutes I had forgotten who he was. He hadn't been anybody, only an activity. I was grateful to him that he had remembered who *I* was. All his striving had been directed at me, Carol.

I stroked his hair and his back. I felt like saying, "There, there." Before I could say anything, I realized he was asleep. I managed after a while to ease myself out from under him without waking him up. I turned on my side in the darkness and pulled up my pajama trousers. Suddenly it all seemed so silly I couldn't help giggling.

Well, anyway, thank God, I've done it, I decided as I fell asleep. Thank God it's over.

Everything was wonderful in the morning. We both woke early. I remembered immediately, without any regret, what had happened, and I wasn't for an instant surprised to find Max in bed with me. We were warm and friendly and loving together in the way I'd always hoped I would be with a man after he'd made love to me. When I got out of bed my pajamas fell down around my ankles. I kicked them off; I didn't feel shy about being undressed in front of Max any longer.

I had changed. However lacking in ecstasy my experience in bed with Max had been, I had made an irreversible commitment. I had joined the family of man. As I soaped my body under the shower, I realized it was no longer so privately my own. I had shared it with Max. It had changed me.

Other things had changed that morning, too. When Mannie

picked us up at the coffee shop, he had a Band-Aid on the back of his neck. Leda agreed to drive without quarreling about it. Max and I sprawled comfortably across each other's laps or huddled in each other's arms all the way to New York.

The apartment was a cold-water flat on the Upper West Side. The front door opened into the kitchen, and beyond it five other rooms led into each other with curtained doorways between them. The toilet was outside on the landing; the bath was in the kitchen. It had a white enameled-metal cover, and no matter how often you washed the tub or poured in Clorox, the moisture in it became stagnant after a few hours and smelled like a drain when you took the top off. The furniture consisted mostly of mattresses.

The two weeks Max and I spent there were the happiest time of my life up to then. We had a room with a double mattress to ourselves, though we had no privacy in it. I never knew how many other people were staying in the apartment at any given time, and since "our" room was next to the kitchen, half-naked strangers were constantly stumbling over us in the night on their way to the outside toilet. That sometimes interrupted my sleep but it never disturbed the contentment I found in the warm, blanket-covered sanctuary Max and I made of that mattress.

I began to love sleeping with him. My sister Sylvia had misled me; it wasn't in the least like reading poetry together. It was much more personal and intimate than that. I loved Max's body. I loved being *fondled.* For years one of my senses, touch, had grown numb from disuse. I hadn't been handled affectionately since I was a baby. I had tried to compensate for this deprivation with daydreams of running naked through fields, being stroked by the wind. I didn't need to daydream anymore. After that first night, Max's hands never felt foreign or intrusive. I welcomed them eagerly, as I would have welcomed sounds if I'd been half-deaf for years. When we nestled under those blankets together, the warmth of his body, the friction of his skin against mine, pleased me so much I often found myself trembling with laughter.

In a more subdued way I was happy all day, too. In spite of my determination to get on with my own life, I didn't even get around to copying a list of secretarial schools out of the phone book. I was too busy. Mannie had a girl somewhere, "One of those

Junior League liberals," Leda told me. He spent most of his time with her. Free of his goading presence, Leda and I became close friends. People were always dropping in, arguing, writing directives, mimeographing handouts on the machine in the front room. They always seemed to be hungry. Leda and I fed them soup and sandwiches and coffee. We mended and washed their clothes for them. When we had time, we handed out leaflets and went to meetings with them. Most of them — I never knew their names and I've forgotten their faces. Only one of them remains clearly in my memory.

Max brought him home one evening, a big man with wild hair and a loud voice. His shirt was unbuttoned, his tie pulled halfway down his chest, and his suit looked as though he had lived through a war in it. In spite of his slovenly appearance, he established himself at once as a man of authority, a world figure. I'm not sure how he managed this; many of the Trotskyists who came to the apartment were as overbearing as he was. Perhaps it was the sheer energy of his arrogance. A young poet I knew at that time described him as a manic-impressive.

Max was excited about having him there. "Do you know who he is?" he whispered to me as I was making coffee in the kitchen. "That's Philip Rahv."

I had never heard of Philip Rahv. That was obviously my fault, my political ignorance. Max explained that he was a famous critic and journalist, an editor of the *Partisan Review,* one of America's leading left-wing intellectuals. I was impressed. When I took in the coffee, I sat on a mattress and listened to him.

He had only one subject of conversation: himself. But that included a great deal. To Philip Rahv, Philip Rahv was mankind. His experience was universal.

He was lecturing Max about the intellectual disadvantages of being an American Jew. "To understand the anti-Semitism of the Nazis, you have to have been born in Europe, preferably in Russia." I found out later that Rahv had been born in the Ukraine. "You have to have gone through the emigrant experience yourself. You have to have lived through a pogrom. You can't see these things through your parents' eyes. You'll never understand them if you've spent your whole childhood in Brooklyn." Every time he bellowed out the word "you," he banished Max to some intellectual Siberia. "*You* probably think . . ." "The way *you* look at things . . ."

I was indignant for Max, but he took it very well. He sat listening, smiling in his quiet, Western way, while Philip Rahv stormed on. When he finally managed to interrupt long enough to explain he had been born on a ranch near Fresno, he had never spent any part of his childhood in Brooklyn, the great man threw out his arms as though he were being crucified. Here he was, wasting his time on a peasant, a goddamn goyisher American hayseed. How could they do this to him?

"What are *you* doing in the Trotskyist movement?" he demanded. "What do *you* know about social injustice?"

A few minutes later he left. His exit seemed accompanied by thunder and lightning. He never came back to the apartment; I never saw him again, but Max was spending a lot of time with him at meetings and discussion groups. And Philip Rahv was slowly beginning to drive him crazy. Max was still good-humored and patient about Rahv's personal attacks on him; what upset him were Rahv's political opinions, his eccentric shifts in attitude about America and the war. Max was determined to impress his own views on Rahv, to make him see he was pursuing the wrong line. In other words, he was trying to convince him that a native-born American might know more about American public opinion than a Ukrainian Jew.

I knew it was hopeless. I was sure no one could ever persuade Philip Rahv that anybody could possibly know more about anything than he did. But Max wouldn't give up. The more he saw of Rahv, the more frustrated he became. After we'd been in New York for about two weeks, he came home one night in despair. I was already in bed, reading.

"When I try to explain the Middle West to him, he keeps telling me I'm as bad as Mary McCarthy," he reported bitterly. "What does Mary McCarthy have to do with getting America into the war?"

I didn't know. I closed my book; I wanted Max to come to bed. He sat on the orange crate I'd moved into the room as a table, smoking one of his union-made cigarettes.

"It's hopeless," he went on. "He doesn't understand. None of them understand. That whole *Partisan Review* crowd. They're too involved in their own intellectual conceit. The way they talk, you'd think Stalin was a character in Dostoevski. All we've got to do is prove our own moral superiority and history will do the rest. Can't they see we've got to fight Stalin now while he's still on Hitler's side? We've got to fight both those criminals at once. Rahv's just *helping* the Stalinists."

I'd been shopping and making sandwiches and ladling out soup and listening to raised voices denouncing the Stalinists all day. I didn't want to hear any more about it. I wanted Max to come to bed. He said he was too restless. He sat smoking and frowning and picking shreds of tobacco off his tongue.

"We're leaving," he said suddenly. "We'll never get anything done here."

I had been lying back on our only pillow. I sat up when he said that. If Max wanted to move into an apartment of our own, I was all for it. It was time I got something done myself, time I found a secretarial school and a part-time job.

"How much money have you got left, Carol?"

I wasn't sure. I had been dipping into my savings since we'd been in New York, for coffee, for food, doling it out to people for cigarettes and subway fares, trying not to worry about it. I reached for my bag and looked.

"A hundred and twenty-eight dollars." I was slightly shocked it was so little.

"It's more than enough. We can go to that hotel again."

I didn't understand. It irritated him that he had to explain.

"We'll go to that hotel where we met and get a ride to Laredo and take the bus from there." He was waving his arms like Philip Rahv. "We're going to Mexico City. I'm going to talk to the old man. He'll listen to me. He thinks America should be in the war now. He'll make Rahv get into line."

"You want me to go to Mexico City?" I shouldn't have laughed. I couldn't help it; we were back where we'd been all those months ago, off to see Trotsky.

"What are you laughing at?"

"Oh, come to bed, Max. We'll talk about it in the morning. I've had enough of this Trotskyist nonsense for one day."

I had never seen Max lose his temper before. It was a totally unexpected side of his character. That quiet confidence of his was suddenly transformed into cold rage. "You don't care about anything, do you? You have no sense of responsibility." He was no longer waving his arms; he was dangerously still, his voice low and even. "You don't care about anyone except yourself. They don't even exist for you. No one exists for you except you. You. You. You. Carol Clavering. And your trivial little life. You're so selfish, so shallow, so hopelessly frivolous. Like some vapid character in a Noel Coward play. Mrs. Hainert always said you were. She said you'd never be able to be serious about anything. You haven't got it in you to see what's really important. You . . ." On and on it went, that low-pitched monotone like the sound of a dentist's drill. When you grow up with two sisters, outbursts of temper are a commonplace rite. You've been accused of every character fault you can think of by the time you're twelve. Particularly selfishness. Daphne had often grown tearful over my selfishness.

It all sounded different coming from Max. It hurt. It hurt so much that all at once I couldn't stand it any longer. I jumped out of bed.

"Shut up," I screamed at him. "Shut your stupid mouth. Can't you see how ridiculous you are? I'm sick of you and your childish games. Pretending anyone cares what your bloody Trotskyist party does. Thinking you'll ever change anything. It's all a lot of silly, stupid make-believe. And I'm sick of it."

I snatched the pillow off the bed. I pushed my way through the curtain into the next room. A young man was lying on the mattress there with an older woman. They were both wearing glasses. They stared at me, pained, dismayed. I felt like throwing the pillow at them. I pushed my way into the next room, and the next, all the way to the end of the apartment. There was an empty mattress beside the mimeograph machine. There were no blankets. I found some heavy wrapping paper and made a nest and crawled into it.

When I woke up the next morning, I knew at once that something terrible had happened. I lay under the stiff, coarse paper, hugging the pillow and thinking about our quarrel. I shouldn't have said those things to Max. I shouldn't have attacked his beliefs. They were so important to him, his whole life. And I had thrown them in his face, ridiculed them, shouted at him that it was all a childish make-believe game he was playing.

Well, he had certainly provoked me to it, hadn't he? Yes, he had. Still, I shouldn't have done it. It was all right to lose my temper, but I should have just told him to shut up. I shouldn't have said that about the bloody Trotskyist party. Everyone in the apartment must have heard me. Well, I didn't care about them . . .

I did care about Max. More than I'd ever cared about anyone. Anything. I would go and tell him I was sorry.

He wasn't in our room. He wasn't in the kitchen. Leda was making coffee. I asked her where Max was.

"He left." She sounded distant and resentful.

"Left? Where?"

She didn't know. He had packed his bag the night before and walked out.

"But he must have said where he was going. He must have said something, Leda."

"He said good-bye. He said he wasn't coming back."

Oh, no, please, no, please don't, please don't let him be gone.

But it was no use praying to myself in that atavistic way of mine.

Max *was* gone.

And so, too, I discovered when I looked in my bag for a comb, was a hundred dollars of my savings.

Six

My lunch hour wasn't an hour; it was forty-five minutes.

I had to get my hat and coat from the locker room, which was on the fifth floor, then I had to punch my timecard in the employment office, which was on the second. By the time I was out on Seventh Avenue, I usually had only thirty-five minutes before I had to clock in again.

It was cold by the end of November. I had never lived anywhere as cold as New York. If it had ever been that cold in Switzerland when I was at school there, I didn't remember it. Every cross street was an ordeal. I approached each one with tight apprehension, waiting for the pain of the wind off the river. Each time it came I was unprepared for it. It hurt my eyes most, seemed to get in behind them and find some nerve there that responded to chill the way a cavity responds to a dentist's probe. I ran the gauntlet of the eight blocks to Forty-second Street with tears dribbling down my cheeks.

I didn't do it every day, only the last two or three days before payday. It was my own fault. I was earning $18.24 a week, net. Four evenings a week at the secretarial school cost eight dollars. Four dollars for the little slip of a room on Perry Street. Subway fares to work and back, fifty cents a week. That should have left me eighty-two cents a day for food and stockings and toothpaste and soap and whatever. I was lucky about clothes; I still had the things I'd brought from England. So eighty-two cents a day should have allowed me to spend twenty-five cents for lunch, a hamburger and coffee and a piece of pie.

What kept me broke were the weekends. I got my pay on Friday afternoon. I didn't go to secretarial school on Fridays, and when I left the store at six o'clock, there they were, all those hours until Monday morning. I did read a lot, getting books from the public library on Tenth Street and lying on my bed with my head at the foot of it and the window behind me. I practiced on the portable typewriter I had bought in Hollywood. I washed my stockings and my underwear. I borrowed an iron from my landlady and pressed my dresses for the next week. All that kept me busy for several hours on Saturday. But I couldn't cook in my room. Around two o'clock I would go out to the White Tower on Greenwich Avenue for a hamburger. And then I didn't want to go back, back to the silence and the feeling of being closed in. I would buy myself little presents, candy and magazines and fruit, sometimes flowers, anything festive that would give me a moment of expectation and pleasure.

Or I would go to the movies. I went to Loew's Sheridan or the Waverly or the Academy of Music on Fourteenth Street. The Academy of Music was my favorite. I found out from a book that when Edward VII came to New York as Prince of Wales, a ball was given for him at the Academy of Music. Four thousand people came and the floor collapsed but nobody was hurt. It was still possible to feel some of the rakish splendor of that age — Lillie Langtry and the Boyos and Lillian Russell — all that lovely, boisterous, conspicuous consumption. Besides, the Academy of Music had Screeno on Friday nights. One Friday, only once, I won five dollars. Nothing that ever happened to me afterward in my life — no raise, no trip to Rome when the studio was paying for it — made me feel as rich as that five dollars. When the double feature was over, I walked up and down Fourteenth Street, feeling I could have anything I wanted.

Most Sundays I went to the movies, too, and then, oh, God,

because it was Sunday evening and that's the saddest, loneliest time in the world, I would have spaghetti and a glass of wine afterward.

So on Monday morning I would have two dollars left, and by Wednesday or Thursday I would be walking up Seventh Avenue to Times Square on my lunch hour.

There was a stand-up counter on Forty-second Street where you could get either a hot-dog or a potato knish for a nickel with a root beer thrown in. The root beer was served in a mug with a trick bottom: it looked like a lot, but it was only a couple of swallows. I never liked root beer much anyway. I usually had the potato knish; it was more filling than a hot-dog.

As soon as I'd finished, I had to hurry back to the store. My haste had a frantic edge to it now, because I didn't know what the time was. There was a clock above a jewelry store on Forty-first Street, but it wasn't reliable, and I'd hocked my watch after I'd moved down to Perry Street to keep going until I found the job at the store.

If I checked back in a minute late, the store would fine me half an hour's pay, twenty-five cents. The whole place was organized like that. It prided itself on being a New York institution, like Carnegie Hall or the Met, and it was an institution in the other sense, too. There were niggling prison rules about everything. The real bosses, the wardens, were the buyers, but discipline was enforced by the department seniors, "trusties."

I sold towels. The trusty in towels was Miss Horn. Miss Horn had been "with" the store since 1926. She had survived the Wall Street crash, the Hoover winters, and the Great Depression. All those precarious years, clinging to her job, had left her with a fervent loyalty to the store. She identified with it. She wanted me to identify with it, too.

In particular she wanted me to wear black shoes, "like everyone else." I pretended I didn't have any. Standing and walking around on a carpeted floor all day made my feet feel like live coals and the only shoes I could bear it in were my brown English oxfords. I could have had them dyed black but it would have cost $1.20, two movies and a *New Yorker*. Day after day I showed up in my brown shoes. Day after day Miss Horn told me off about them.

The way she did it, the way she gave me any order or reproof, was based on the assumption that I was lucky to have the job.

There were thousands of other girls who'd give anything, and so on. At least once a day I wanted to kill Miss Horn. I could feel myself doing it, squeezing her throat until her eyes popped out and her head swung back and forth like a balloon on a string.

Half my time in towels was spent folding them. It was a labor of Sisyphus. A minute after I had them all neatly stacked on the display counters, some woman, some woman who had no intention of buying anything, would drift by, pulling out the bottom towels. Down would come all the top ones, tumbling onto the floor. A minute later Miss Horn would be standing behind me.

"Just look at those display counters, Miss Clavering." There were no first names in towels. "I tell you, if Mr. Griffin sees them like that" — Mr. Griffin was the buyer. All the buyers seemed to be men — "I tell you, you'll be lucky if Mr. Griffin doesn't let you go." Miss Horn never said "fired." After all those desperate years, the word was too frightening to be spoken aloud.

I would start refolding the towels. Miss Horn would supervise me. That was usually when she told me about my brown shoes, all those thousands of other girls. That was usually when I wanted to kill her.

The thing that restrained me and saved Miss Horn's life was the spiteful sense of superiority I felt toward her. I knew she was an anachronism, a relic of a doomed regime. I knew it was no longer true about all those thousands of other girls. Miss Horn, the store itself, were on shifting, perilous ground. I could see the evidence of this in all the departments on my floor. The conscientious, soft-spoken young women who came to work in gloves and hats were disappearing one by one. They were being replaced by a rowdier element, young women who said "them towels" and surreptitiously chewed gum. The store could no longer insist on a college education as an essential qualification for selling diapers. The war in Europe was slowly bringing about what no act of Roosevelt's had quite succeeded in doing. The Depression was dragging to an end at last. Mr. Griffin would not "let me go," not unless I set fire to the cash register, anyway.

I think Miss Horn knew it. It embittered her loyalty to the store. She was like someone who has clambered hand over hand up a mountain to find a busload of tourists having a picnic on top.

The one part of the job I didn't mind was the work I'd been

hired to do. I rather enjoyed selling towels. My customers interested me. They represented an attitude, a whole side of America that was new to me. They hated the store. No matter what the store's advertising said about quality and low markup and providing a service to the community, they were convinced the store was there for one purpose only: to cheat them. They entered it like hostile Indians lured into a stockade, suspicious, aggressive, and ready for instant flight. "No, no," they would mutter edging away from the counter as I spread out my towels for them. "No, no, that's not the right ones. That's not what you said in your ad in the *News*. No, no." Shaking their heads, tightening their grasp on their handbags, they would be halfway to the elevator before I could show them anything else.

There was a sadness in their suspicion because it was partly their own fault: they misrepresented themselves. God knows, like me, they had to make every cent count, but they were ashamed of it. They were ashamed to ask for the cheapest towels; they pretended they wanted something better.

I learned to appease them after a while. I showed them the cheapest towels first. I confided that these were the best we had, all the others were overpriced. I wasn't trying to con them; I got no commission on what I sold. I did it because I was lonely. These wary, hostile women were the only people I had to talk to.

Leda and the other Troskyists wouldn't have anything to do with me after my quarrel with Max. I might have made friends with some of the women at the secretarial school, but I messed that up right at the beginning. Two of them asked me if I'd like to come and have coffee with them after class. It was a Wednesday night, and I had twenty-five cents to last until Friday. I handled it badly, brusquely, because I was embarrassed. Like my customers in towels, I was ashamed of my poverty. None of them ever asked me again. They stopped talking when I went near them: they had decided I was a stuck-up little bitch with my silly clothes and my English accent.

I wasn't able to make friends with anyone in towels. It was difficult to talk on the floor: if Miss Horn saw two of us chatting for a moment, she would find something for one of us to do. Four evenings a week I had to hurry off at six to get to my secretarial class on time. Some Fridays I would hang around the locker room hoping someone would speak to me, but everyone was in a hurry on Friday nights; they had their pay, dates, plans.

Men, even young men, accosted me occasionally on the street. Most of them did it for their own amusement, commenting on my legs or my behind. But some of them genuinely seemed to want to get to know me. They asked me to go to a bar or to the movies with them. I could never quite manage to make myself do it. There was always one instant when I was going to respond, to smile, and then I would be running away. I didn't think they were going to try to rape me; I didn't know what they were going to do. I was too scared to want to find out.

My landlady on Perry Street was not unfriendly; she was always generous about lending me her iron. The trouble with talking to her was that she hated to listen. Or perhaps it was just me: she wouldn't listen to me for an instant. If I tried to say anything about myself, she would start to fidget, turn her back on me, walk out of the kitchen.

Then I would finish my ironing and go back to my own room.

But after an hour or two I couldn't stay there. My loneliness would become as positive as hunger.

Most of all I craved Max. I longed for his companionship, his understanding, his physical affection. I longed for him in bed at night. I missed him the moment I woke up every morning. I didn't care about my hundred dollars anymore. I had been hurt and angry about it for a while. I hadn't exactly blamed Max; I could see that from his point of view he had taken the money for the cause, to go and see Trotsky in Mexico. I just wished he hadn't done it to *me.*

The loss of the money no longer seemed to have anything to do with my present poverty. Miss Horn, potato knishes, had become an accepted, temporary condition of learning to be a secretary. Missing Max, wanting him, was impossible to accept. I wrote him a cheerful letter, making fun of my life at the store so he wouldn't feel guilty about me. I told him I'd love to hear from him.

I didn't know where he was. Back in California? I mailed the letter to Mrs. Hainert.

Every evening when I came home I went through a whole crazy

ritual. I closed my eyes, clasped my hands. Please, please let there be a letter from Max on the hall table, please. There never was.

I wrote to Mrs. Hainert. I tried to sound cheerful and casual to her, too. I asked how Max was. Did she know where he was living? I never heard from her, either.

Decorations went up in the store, colored lights and tinsel and sprigs of holly. "Aren't they cheery?" one of the rowdier element exclaimed several times. "Don't you just love Christmas?"

I didn't. I dreaded it more acutely each day. The tinsel did not look cheery to me; it was as ominous as a dead albatross. Never mind all the nostalgic associations of home and family and presents and lovely hot food and paper hats and charades and real candles on the tree. What was I going to do? Christmas was on a Thursday that year. Four whole days. What was I going to do?

I thought of buying a gallon of wine and drinking it in my room. In the end I couldn't do it. I had always had a strong sense of the pathos of inanimate objects — a pair of shoes, a broken watch, almost anything, under certain circumstances. I couldn't stand the thought of that damn bottle of wine, sitting on the window sill, waiting to be opened.

Christmas came. It was all right. I discovered something. A lot of the doom I'd been feeling had nothing to do with me; I'd been seeing myself through other people's eyes, a girl alone in a furnished room, a brave pathetic character out of O. Henry. So long as I didn't think of it that way, it was just like any other four days. Better. The people on the streets were friendlier.

After Christmas came the sales. My customers were less wary; they grabbed my towels so fast I couldn't keep up with the sales slips. The last of the soft-spoken young women disappeared. Except for Miss Horn and one older woman, I was the senior salesperson in the department. In February I passed my shorthand and typing tests. I bought the *New York Times* every Sunday; I marked the want ads and wrote neatly spaced letters to employment agencies. I invented an impacted wisdom tooth, repeated dental appointments, so I could go out for interviews. I turned down several jobs. This time I wasn't just looking for a wage, I was determined to do something that interested me.

One Friday morning in March, Miss Horn told me I was wanted

in personnel. Waiting in the outer office on the second floor, I figured I had been having too much trouble with my teeth; Mr. Griffin had finally decided to let me go. I was all primed with lies about them being all right now, when I was told Miss Waring, the assistant personnel manager herself, would see me.

Miss Waring had short hair and pockmarked cheeks. She politely invited me to sit down.

"Do you smoke, Miss Clavering?"

That disconcerted me. Several of the rowdier element on my floor smoked. They slipped out onto the fire stairs for a few hasty puffs. I couldn't understand what that had to do with me.

I said I didn't smoke. Miss Waring lit a cigarette; she had been offering me one. The whole interview was getting stranger and stranger.

"I've been watching your work — do you mind if I call you Carol?" I nodded. "You have a fine record, Carol."

I did?

"Mr. Griffin says your sales have been excellent."

I didn't think Mr. Griffin even knew my name.

"Now that I've met you myself, I can see you're exactly the type person we want here."

Hadn't she noticed my brown shoes?

"You're what I'd call first-team material, Carol." She enlarged on that. She told me there were great opportunities at the store for persons like me. In a few years, why, she could hardly imagine what I might become.

I could.

Miss Waring was explaining the "first-team training course" she wanted to put me through, when a small explosion took place inside me. The ingredients of it — the niggling tyranny of the store's rules, the constantly suppressed impulse to throttle Miss Horn — had been accumulating for months. The detonator was Miss Waring's sad, pockmarked face.

I'm not sure exactly what I said when I exploded. I sputtered a lot. I know I said some gratifyingly candid things about team spirit.

"It's a swindle, can't you see that?" I asked Miss Waring. "They try to do it to you all your life. Your school and your country and every place you work. 'Join us. We'll give you a bit of petty power, too.' That's the way they get you. They cheat you out of thinking for yourself. Can't you see that?"

Miss Waring, understandably, didn't seem to be able to see it. She kept saying, "What?" She sat staring at me, smoking her cigarette with quick nervous movements of her fingers.

"I hate the store," I explained to her. "You've been trying to bully me into submission for months. Nagging me about my shoes and my hair, fining me every time I'm a minute late. Telling me when I can go to the *toilet*. Okay. But there's one thing you're damn well not going to do to me. You're not going to pat me on the back."

Miss Waring was still staring at me, still saying, "What?" I realized I wasn't getting through to her; she was beyond help; I might as well give up on her. I told her to write me a note to the cashier for whatever they owed me, and let me out of there. I was out on the street with a whole week's pay ten minutes before my usual lunch hour.

There was a warmth in the air, soft as a promise. I decided to do something I'd wanted to do for days. I walked over to the Plaza and took one of the double-decker open-topped buses down Fifth Avenue to Washington Square. It cost a dime, twice as much as the Seventh Avenue line. I felt rich sitting up there, high above the crowded sidewalk, as I rolled past Scribner's and the Brevoort Hotel.

It was the twenty-first of March, the vernal equinox. I loved those words, "vernal equinox." They filled my head with images of pagan festivity, the intoxicated relief of youths and maidens leaping and dancing and tumbling together in the fresh grass. Winter was over.

In a week it would be my birthday. I would be nineteen.

I sat for an hour on the stone circle in Washington Square. I decided not to be in any hurry about finding a job. If I ran out of money, I could work for a day or two as a temporary secretary. There would be no more Miss Horns for me; from now on when I woke up in the morning I would look forward to spending the day with intelligent people who were working at something they cared about and who treated me like a friend.

No youths or maidens were dancing in Washington Square today. It was full of pale and exhausted-looking young people, lifting their faces to the sun as though begging it to heal them. I was wearing a wool dress with long sleeves and a skirt that came down to six inches above my ankles. I made up my mind to go home and change into a cotton dress and then spend the whole afternoon in the square doing absolutely nothing.

I saw it the moment I opened the front door, and I knew at once it was for me although I had never received a letter that looked the least like it before. Sitting on the bed in my room, I examined the cheap envelope, the unfamiliar handwriting. There was no name above the return address, only a number, 71823. The address itself consisted partly of numbers, too. The postmark was Toronto, Canada.

Even after I'd opened it and read the first few lines — *Dear Carol, I don't know if Mrs. Hainert told you. When I left New York I hitched up to Montreal and joined the Canadian Air Force* — I still couldn't entirely believe who it was from. *I heard from Leda about your hundred dollars. She said she took it to make you pay for your disloyalty to the Trotskyists. She said it served you right, but I was furious with her . . . It isn't bad here.* He was stationed near Toronto. Bomber Command. He would be getting a week's leave as soon as his training was over. Probably in August. He could come to New York then, if I'd like to see him. *Please write to me Carol. All my love, Max.*

I sat there holding the letter in my hands like a magic charm. I knew I would read it again and again until I knew it by heart. But first I wanted to treasure it, whole and complete, the way it had been when I first saw it on the hall table.

As I picked up the envelope to replace the letter inside it, a money order dropped onto the bed.

It was for a hundred dollars.

Seven

Fitz wants to see you, Carol."

I left my cubicle and walked down the long corridor. As I passed the typists' desks outside the newsroom, I got the usual treatment.

"Mr. Fitzpatrick wants her."

"Mr. Fitzpatrick can have her."

"Mr. Fitzpatrick has had her."

I couldn't blame them. I'd been sitting at one of those desks myself, the most junior typist, three months ago. Now I had my own office and a title: Research Assistant. Mr. Fitzpatrick sent for me three or four times a day, and I had lunch with him at least once a week. The typists didn't know it, but I also spent frequent evenings with him in his apartment in Gramercy Park and called him Fitz.

He was standing by the window in his office at the end of the corridor. Fitz always seemed to be standing by the window when I went in to see him; he said it helped him think. "Someone's got to think around here," he once told me. "Bill can make the decisions. It's my job to think."

"Come in, Carol. There's something I want you to look at. That bullshit on my desk."

There was a lot of bullshit on his desk — memos from the network, pressuring letters from sponsors and advertising agencies, "bumf" from the British Ministry of Information — but I knew the bullshit Fitz meant. I read it. *And now there's a story I'd like to leave you with tonight. It's about a young Spitfire pilot. He's nineteen years old and . . .*

I felt as though someone was drawing his nails across a slate quite close to my ear, but I read it to the end.

"What do you think?" Fitz was watching me; he knew what I thought. "Don wants to use it on his eight o'clock tonight."

"I guess it's what people expect from Don. That's why they listen to him."

"Would he really say that, that pilot? 'A piece of cake'?"

"I'm afraid he probably would."

"But, goddamn it, Carol, he's going to get killed any day. Ed says their casualties are much higher than they admit."

"I don't know. People start imitating themselves, don't they? Particularly English people. The few debutantes I've met sounded like a bad parody of Evelyn Waugh. They . . ." Fitz always listened to me with thoughtful attention when I tried to explain the English to him. He was a naturally skeptical man, but for some reason he trusted me.

That was why I had been promoted out of the typing pool. I'd been working for the network about two months when one of the news writers pushed past my desk one morning and looked into the cable room.

"Anyone here speak French?"

He wasn't asking me, but when no one else answered, I said I did.

"I can."

"Who're *you?*" He had walked past my desk a dozen times a day but he seemed surprised to see me sitting there.

I told him my name.

"You have a French grandmother or something?"

"I went to school in France and Switzerland."

"Come in here."

I followed him into his office. He had a recording of a speech of Reynaud's he wanted translated. I did it on my lunch hour, listening to it again and again through the headphones to make sure I got every word right. By the time the news writer came back from lunch, I had it typed up for him in English.

A few days later Fitz sent for me.

"You went to school in Europe?"

"Yes."

"How long were you there?"

He asked me to sit down. He questioned me about my life, my family. He was the best listener I'd ever met. If I had told anyone else so much about myself, I would have felt embarrassed afterward. When I left Fitz, all I could think about was how much I liked him.

A week later he sent for me again. According to some British source, the Cowes Yacht Club had "played a vital part in the Dunkirk evacuation." Fitz wanted to know if I thought it was true. I said I didn't know, but I didn't see how racing yachts would be much help getting people off a shallow beach and I didn't think there'd be all that much deck space on them for 340,000 soldiers.

Fitz listened to me thoughtfully. "Why do they put out a story like that?"

"Maybe they're afraid Americans have the idea the British upper class are a bunch of silly-ass pro-Germans. They want us to know they're doing their bit."

The next day I was a research assistant.

I was still looking at Don's story about the young Spitfire pilot. "Does he have to say 'wizard show' as well as 'piece of cake'?" I asked Fitz. "Would Don mind if you cut out 'wizard show'?"

"He'd mind like hell. But I'll talk to him anyway. Sit down, Carol." Fitz went back to the window. That meant he wanted to think aloud for a minute. It was my job to listen and not say anything unless he asked me a question. I watched him while he organized his thoughts.

He was a good-looking man, although he wasn't conventionally handsome. His features were rather blunt, like a wood carving, and he must have been about fifty. His hair was gray. He was sturdy, without softness, and over six feet tall. Like Max, he had blue eyes, but a different, lighter blue that reminded me of my father's. Altogether he was just like the man I'd pictured as a child in stories about being rescued, the woodcutter in "Red Riding Hood." He was unremittingly kind and reliable; you could never doubt it.

"What are we getting into?" he asked without looking at me. "Almost every word we broadcast as news is pro-British. Ed often refers to the Germans as the enemy. The America Firsters hate us for that. They hate Ed. They think the FCC ought to cut him off the air. That's Bill's problem, thank God. What concerns me is that we're doing something without taking the responsibility for where it leads us. Where do you think it leads us, Carol?"

"Getting America into the war."

"Is that what we should be doing? Is it any part of our job as a radio news department? It may be what we want to do as individuals, but do we have any right to use commercial broadcasting facilities, licensed by the government —"

The phone was ringing. He picked it up. "Yes, I'll take it." He nodded to me; that meant "later." He was talking to Ed in London as I left.

I went back to my cubicle. There was a note on my desk from the news room: Hastings had been bombed; they wanted to know its distance from London, population, main industries, any features of special interest, and so on. I walked over to the British Library of Information in Rockefeller Center and asked the helpful but distant English secretary there to let me see anything they had on Hastings.

Sitting in the reading room making notes, I kept thinking of what Fitz had said. Should America get into the war? Obviously, personally, I *hated* the idea of England being occupied by the Nazis. My family, all the people I knew there, would be bullied and half starved, the way the French were now since the fall of France. But from an ordinary American's point of view, was England all that worth saving?

"What's the alternative?" Fitz asked me a few evenings later when I was having a drink with him in his apartment. "Say the Germans defeat England? Where does that leave us?"

"People like Lindbergh would say it leaves us three thousand miles away across the Atlantic."

"If England goes down, then so will the Dutch East Indies, Malay, and Burma. And then India and Australia. We'll find ourselves sitting there with the Germans on one side and the Japanese on the other. The Germans will infiltrate Latin America. They've got a lot of friends down there. We'll be completely boxed in. We'll either have to fight them off for the next fifty years or have the kind of government that can get along with the Nazis. I don't know which would be worse."

I knew he was right, but I felt he wanted me to argue with him. "Russia?" I asked in a rather squeaky voice.

"Germany and Japan between them could soon take care of Russia. Kaltenborn thinks Hitler's only waiting to knock England out of the war before he turns against Russia anyway.

"Oh, God, I hope not."

"Why do you say that?" Fitz looked at me, surprised. "What are the Russians to you?"

We were alone in his apartment that evening. Sometimes when he invited me over, he would have two or three other people there. They were never the kind of people I would have expected a man in his position to entertain. I never met any senators or government officials at Fitz's, not even broadcasters or foreign correspondents. There were a few young women who were regulars like me, remarkable chiefly for their respectability. One was the daughter of a department head at Harvard; another, a sweet, shy woman, whom I came to like very much, was the great-granddaughter of General Grant. Occasionally there would be professors from Columbia or Yale, polite young men in their thirties. I could never figure out what Fitz's relationship with any of these people was; he just seemed to like having them around.

He was waiting for me to answer his question about Russia. What did Russia mean to me?

Max.

"It's just that I've got a friend in the Canadian air force. I think the only reason he joined is because he wants to fight the Russians."

I began to explain Max's connection with the Trotskyist party. Fitz soon had the whole story out of me — my aborted mission to Mexico City, the two weeks Max and I had spent together in New York, his differences with Philip Rahv.

"Do you agree with him about the Stalinists?"

"I never really believed in the Trotskyists the way Max does. But I can see what he means. He thinks if this war has anything to do with right and wrong, then Stalin's on the other side."

"Are you in love with this young man?"

Fitz asked the question so casually and unconcernedly that it never occurred to me not to tell him the truth.

"Yes. Yes, I am. I think I fell in love with him at once, when I first met him. But I only realized how much . . . well, about a year ago now." That night in Ohio?

I heard Fitz let out his breath; it was a faint, natural sound, but I understood it at once. He was relieved; I was in love with someone else, thank God.

That made it even easier to talk to him about Max. After that first letter, we had been writing to each other two or three times a week. Max seemed to be enjoying his air force training. He was full of enthusiasm for Britain's "decent stand," bitterly contemptuous of American neutrality.

"He's coming to New York next month," I ended excitedly.

"I'd like to meet him."

The idea pleased me at once. Because I loved him, I was proud of Max; I was proud of the way Fitz had befriended me. I wanted to show them off to each other.

When I left around midnight, Fitz kissed my cheek. "You're swell, Carol," he said. Those women in the typing pool would never believe it, but that was as close as he ever came to making a pass at me.

Max was due the first week in September; he was coming down from Toronto by bus on Friday. He wasn't sure what time he would get in, so I arranged to leave the key for him at the Chinese laundry next door. I had moved out of Perry Street when I became a research assistant and found a studio apartment on East Tenth. It had one large room with a high ceiling and windows overlooking the street, an alcove kitchen and a quaint Victorian bathroom with brass fixtures. The previous tenant had sold me her scanty furniture and told me the place had great possibilities. In the three months I had been there, I had done very little to try to realize them: a huge map of Europe on one wall, a bookcase from a Third Avenue junk shop. I was a sloppy housekeeper, too. Slothful about getting up in the mornings, I often came home to an unmade bed. In the week before Max's arrival, I tried to make up for this. I scrubbed the wooden floor, bought two vases and filled them with flowers, found a green baize cloth to cover the scarred table and several colored cushions to hide the irremediable stains on the bedspread. I had never seen Max show a second's interest in his domestic surroundings; I was doing it for myself. I wanted to present my new life to him as attractively as possible.

I prepared for his arrival in another way, too. Feeling a little brazen, I went to a woman doctor in Washington Square and had myself fitted for a diaphragm. She was a nice woman, with no illusions about human fallibility. "If you want my advice," she told me, "either carry it in your handbag or wear it all the time." After I left her, I went to Lord and Taylor's and bought a sheer, lace-trimmed nightdress, black with a pale blue ribbon.

Friday was a bad day. I didn't want to think about anything but Max. I planned to enjoy the idea of him quietly on my own, the way as a child I had enjoyed the expectation of a birthday. It didn't work out that way. Fitz sent me out to the Brooklyn Navy Yard with a reporter. One of the overage destroyers Roosevelt had traded to Churchill was in dry-dock there. I spent the day making notes about it. It was a grotesque object, a Gothic fortress that didn't look as though it could even float. The reporter was interested in its history as a U.S. naval vessel. It turned out the damn thing had never done anything except be shifted about from one base to another like a useless pawn in a long, dull chess game. When I got back to the office, it took me two hours to type up the list of its uneventful moves.

It was almost seven o'clock by the time I stopped in at the Chinese laundry.

"Your fliend take the key, yes?"

The street door didn't lock; I hurried up the stairs. Outside my apartment, I suddenly lost all momentum. Max was in there. I hadn't seen him for a whole year. I was scared. Would he seem a stranger to me? Max. Max. Max. I stood there saying his name to myself, trying to conjure up the old intimacy between us.

It didn't work. When he let me in, Max looked more of a stranger than I would have believed possible. I had never seen him so tidy.

His hair was trimmed and combed; all his jacket buttons were fastened; his tie was pulled in tight to his collar. So help me, his shoes were shined.

Then I realized he was doing what I had tried to do with my apartment. He was presenting himself to me, the new, spruce, soldierly Max in his blue air force sergeant's uniform. That revived all my old intimate affection for him at once. I hugged him. He felt stiff for a moment, then his hand moved down and fondled my bottom. He had always liked doing that. I liked it too; it was flattering that he could find pleasure in such an everyday part of me. "Your sit-upon," my mother used to call it.

"You're wearing a hat." He stepped back and looked at me.

I took it off.

"Your hair's longer." It was down to my shoulders. "And, Jesus, your — I mean, you've sort of — you've filled out a bit, haven't you?" It was true, I wasn't so skinny looking anymore. "And your face. God, you're beautiful, Carol."

Wait till he saw me in that nightdress.

"Do you have anything to drink?" He lit a cigarette. He no longer smoked the union-made kind.

"I bought some wine." I started to the alcove kitchen for it.

"You don't have any whiskey?"

"I didn't think . . . you never used to drink liquor, Max. I'll go out and buy some."

He said he'd come with me. He put on his cap with its brightly polished badge, adjusting it rakishly on the side of his head. I made him stand still for a moment so that I could see him in it.

"Oh, Max, you look wonderful." He did. "You look like one of those Spitfire pilots, so young and so brave and so few."

"I'm in bombers." But he was obviously pleased.

"Do they say 'piece of cake' in bombers? Do they say 'wizard show'?"

"Not in Canada."

"What do you say?"

"Well, when we go home on leave, we say, 'Get up them stairs.' " He smiled. "Do you know what that means?"

"No."

"I'll show you when we get back from the liquor store."

He did. We were hardly inside the door with a bottle of Canadian Club when he started to undo my dress. By the time I'd made the drinks I was in my slip. We took our glasses to bed with us. By then I had nothing on but my stockings and my garter belt. Max was naked. His body had always been spare. He was as lean and hard as a marathon runner now. I had loved going to bed with him in the Trotskyist apartment because he was so cozy. He wasn't cozy anymore; he was wild and uncontrollable. After we had made love, he couldn't let go of me. His hands kept clutching at my breasts and my behind and burrowing between my legs. If I'd ever imagined myself in bed with a man who wanted me with such hunger, it would have scared me. It didn't with Max; some erotic responsiveness I'd never known I had was delighted. In a little while I was behaving in the same wild, starved way myself. We finally stopped around nine o'clock to go out and eat in a Mexican restaurant. I was in my new nightdress and back in bed ten minutes after we returned to the apartment.

Max didn't want to get up in the morning. He didn't want to get up all weekend. He did get out of bed now and then to lie in a warm bath, but then he wanted me to lie on top of him or sit at the other end within easy reach.

Okay. Why not? I was all for it. He'd been up in Canada all those months being trained to save civilization. Living like a monk, probably. Doing all those Canadian air force exercises. He deserved to have anything he wanted. It was lovely how much he wanted me. "Lift your legs a little." "Lie on your side, Carol." "Let me do it with my tongue, darling."

The one thing Max didn't want to do was talk about the war. I had imagined long conversations about American neutrality, Russia, the Burma Road. He wouldn't let me mention any of them. Lying beside him, between our bouts of coupling, I read *Swann's Way,* which I'd been taking to the office with me for weeks. Max went through back copies of *The New Yorker,* starting an article and then going on to another until he suddenly dropped the magazine on the floor. I would pretend to go on reading as he turned onto his side, started to caress me through my nightdress, slowly drew it up above my hips. Then Proust would go plonk onto the floor, too.

"Ah," Max would say. "Ah, Carol." There was a sweet wonder in the way he said it, the hushed surprise of someone discovering some marvel he had never altogether believed existed. I loved it. I had never altogether believed myself that my own ordinary, familiar body had such power to please.

Sometime during that weekend my attitude as a woman altered. I crossed a border into an area of sexuality where physical passion with a man was no longer a new, rather tentative, experience; it was a natural, accepted part of existence.

Sometime during that weekend, too, Max drank the bottle of Canadian Club. It was empty when I got up to go to work on Monday morning.

I had only just arrived at the office when one of the reporters looked into my cubicle.

"Fitz wants to see you, Carol."

I started down the long corridor.

"Mr. Fitzpatrick wants her."

"Mr. Fitzpatrick can have her."

"Mr. Fitzpatrick has had her."

I stopped and looked at the typists sitting at their desks outside the news room. I couldn't help it; I grinned at them. Had *they* ever done all those marvelous things Max had taught me to do since Friday? Did they carry on like that with *their* boyfriends? I longed to know; I couldn't very well ask them there in the office. Still grinning, I walked on down the corridor. The typists never gave me the treatment again.

For once Fitz was sitting behind his desk. "Did your friend arrive, Carol? Max —"

"Max Ludlow. Yes, he arrived."

"How long is he staying?"

"He has to go back on Friday morning."

"I happened to mention him to Don." I sat down; I had an idea what was coming. "An American who's serving with the Canadian air force. He is a flyer, isn't he?"

"He's a gunner. On a bombing plane."

"Don got all excited. He wants to interview him on his eight o'clock on Thursday."

"I don't know . . ."

Fitz waited.

"Max doesn't seem to want to talk about the war."

Fitz waited again.

"And then — Max — if Don has him on the air — you can't tell what Max might say."

"Don can handle him."

I wasn't so sure. Max had been quiet enough about his politics over the weekend, but I would never forget that night in the Trotsky-ist apartment; Don couldn't handle Max if he slipped into that mood.

"I don't know, Fitz."

"Don only wants him to talk for two minutes, just his reasons as an American for getting into the war."

"He hates Stalin. I told you —"

"He must hate Hitler, too."

We left it at that. I promised to ask Max. If he agreed, I was to bring him to the office on Wednesday so he could meet Don and rehearse what he was going to say.

There was a letter for me in my box when I got home that evening. I opened it in the downstairs hall.

Dear Carol, I'm sorry I have taken so long before writing to you."

It was from my father. I sat down on the stairs and read it through.

You've probably heard by now that your mother and I have parted. Why hadn't Sylvia or Daphne told me? . . . *I and a very dear friend of mine, Joyce Dyson-Smith. Perhaps you remember her. She used to live in Brighton, just around the corner on Chesham Place.* I remembered her name, but not her face; Sylvia used to call her Father's little bit of nonsense. She had done typing for him. *Please, don't think I have abandoned your mother.* There was a lot about that, the money he had settled on her. . . . *very painful decision for me, but I felt I could not continue my work without Joyce's spiritual support and encouragement. She is a very fine woman and has great psychic powers.* Oh, God, she was one of those, in touch with the other world. *I did not want to embarrass your mother.* They had moved to Bath and were living there together. *Carol, my dear, you must not think for one moment that there is anything physical in our relationship. We do kiss sometimes, but we are trying to cut down on that.*

Oh, God, poor Daddy. As though I'd grudge him a bit of fun after all those years with my dutiful, virtuous, churchgoing mother. I put the letter away in my bag. Poor Daddy, I would write and tell him I didn't blame him.

Max was in bed. He hadn't been in bed all day; he had gone out to buy another bottle of Canadian Club. I sat beside him; he wanted me to get undressed. "Up them stairs," he said in his "Ah, Carol" voice.

"I can't, Max." I moved away from him. "Please get up and get dressed. We'll go out and have dinner."

"Don't you want to?"

"Of course I do. You know I do. But not now. I've been working in the office all day and there was a ghastly air raid on London last night, and my sister's in London, and there's another invasion scare, and my mother's living on the south coast." My father's letter had brought it all, my family, close to me in my mind. "I'm sorry, but I can't just switch all that off, Max. Besides, there's something I have to talk to you about."

We had lasagna and Chianti in a restaurant on Sixth Avenue; the same meal as in that nameless town in Ohio before going back to the Sheraton. I remembered my crazy momentum that night. I felt rather sad now; I kept thinking about my father, his pathetic guilt.

We had strega after dinner and I told Max about Fitz's suggestion. "You don't have to do it. As a matter of fact, I don't think you should."

"Prime time. My God, what I'd have given for an audience like that when I was a Trotskyist."

Was a Trotskyist? "You mean you've given all that up, Max?" I couldn't believe it. The Trotskyist party had been his whole life, his family.

"Have you ever read Saint-Exupéry?" Max asked.

"I've read *Wind, Sand, and Stars.* Oh, and *The Little Prince.* Why?"

"The thing he's saying, and T. E. Lawrence, too, is that the significance of all action is subjective. Political dogma, all dogma, is irrelevant. Any cause becomes the people who support it. It's the intensity of our own experience that matters."

He ordered another strega and explained it all to me. He had found a new faith, a semimystic belief in danger and hardship. I decided I liked it better than Trotskyism. The personal element in it was more sympathetic to me, and it seemed to come not from someone else's teachings but from inside Max himself. It had very little to do with Saint-Exupéry, really, I thought. Max had formed his new belief out of his own experience in the air force, from the stoicism he had acquired living in barracks, being forced through basic training, ordered around. Deprived of independence, he had tried to idealize self-discipline as an alternative to dumb obedience and indignity. It pleased and touched me. That Westerner's integrity I had always sensed and admired in him had taken on a new form, a new dimension.

We finally got back to Don's radio news program. "You don't have to do it," I told him again.

"I don't know. I rather like the idea. Prime time. There are things I'd like to say to an audience like that."

"It's up to you, darling." I felt a little uneasy. I didn't think Max and Don were going to see things quite the same way.

I was right.

"Christ, he's a stupid, ignorant bastard," was the first thing Max said about Don when he came into my cubicle after their meeting on Wednesday morning. "How did a clot like that get to have his own news program?"

"We only put him on twice a week. The Western affiliated stations like him. They say Kaltenborn talks down to people. Don talks with them."

"He kept calling me a gallant airman." Max sat in my chair and put his feet on the desk. He was wearing his cap at that rakish angle; he did look like a gallant airman.

"I'm going to give them a mouthful tomorrow night," he went on. "I'm going to let millions of Americans know what at least one person thinks of their smug neutrality."

"Did you tell Don that?"

"More or less." He lit a cigarette. "Who's that other guy, Fitzpatrick?"

"He's my boss. He wants us to have dinner with him after the broadcast tomorrow."

"He's pretty damn stupid, too, isn't he?"

"No, he isn't." I said it too sharply.

Max took his feet off my desk. "He's crazy about you, too. He said you were swell."

"Fitz says that about a lot of people. He's one of the kindest men I've ever known."

"You call him Fitz? Are you having it off with him or something?"

This was getting ridiculous. I told Max I had work to do. "I'll see you this evening." I closed the door so I could kiss him.

After he had left, I sat at my desk for several minutes without moving. It wasn't only that I could still feel myself being kissed; I was like a tuning fork, still vibrating to Max. Oh, God, I loved him. He was the only man I'd ever loved, could ever imagine myself loving. Because he was the only man I'd ever been to bed with? That struck me at once as a damn silly question. I didn't want to go to bed with anyone else. Ever.

I went back to work.

Fitz and I watched the broadcast from the control room. Don started off in his usual Pollyanna way. He had an ancient messenger's attitude toward bad news: let someone else deliver it; his master, the audience, would have his head if he did. That Thursday when German planes were bombing London for the sixth straight night and Allied shipping losses were approaching fifty percent of all convoys, Don's lead story was the settlement of a threatened strike in Chicago. He went on from that to a speech of Wendell Willkie's in which the presidential candidate had said the United States was the strongest industrial nation in the world.

I was watching Max. Don had put him on his left, but not directly next to him, leaving at least six feet between them. Max looked a little lonely sitting in front of his own mike in his smartly pressed uniform. He also looked ominously relaxed. I wondered how much Canadian Club was left in the bottle he had bought that morning.

Don didn't get to him until after the commercial break. He gave him a fulsome introduction. "The other day I happened to meet a young American I thought you'd be interested in meeting, too. He's taken a step that may seem strange to some of us. It may even seem the wrong step for an American to take." Don's audience was heavily Middle Western isolationist. "But one of the fine things about American democracy is that we're free to follow our own conscience. And now I'd like you to meet this young man." He shifted slightly so that he was half facing Max with his own mike still in front of him.

"Will you tell us your name?"

"Max Ludlow. I'm a —"

"Where are you from, Max?" Don could be very fast with an interruption.

"Fresno, California. I'm —"

"Are your parents living in Fresno?"

"No, they're dead. They —"

"I'm sorry to hear that, and I'm sure our audience is, too. Now, you're a sergeant in the Canadian air force."

"Yes, I'm a gunner. I went —"

"You went up to Canada and volunteered, Max?"

"Yes, I felt —"

Don raised his hand in a casual friendly way and turned away from Max. I saw the director in the control room lift his circled finger and thumb: okay. I didn't immediately understand why.

"Max's parents are dead. He has no immediate family." Don's voice was coming over the speaker. "But he did have a young cousin . . ."

Then I saw that Max was paying no attention to Don. He was leaning over his own mike. His lips were moving, but his voice wasn't audible. His mike had been cut off.

"Max Ludlow's cousin lived in the old country, in Norway . . ." Don's voice came through clear and maudlin as he told us his story about Max's cousin. It turned out he had been killed at Narvik. "So you see, no matter how terrible and distant this war may seem to us, it is very close to some of our fellow Americans."

I wanted to throw up.

I had to wait until the second commercial break before I could leave the control booth. As I stood up, I saw two studio attendants lean over Max and say something to him. Politely, with smiles, they escorted him to the door. Don gave him a cordial thank-you nod as he left. I found him in the reception room outside the studio.

"What did you think?" He put his arm around me and kissed my cheek. "What did you think of my little speech?"

Max didn't know he'd been talking into a dead mike. Without even thinking about it, I decided not to tell him. "You were fine." I took his arm. "Let's go."

"Aren't we going to have dinner with your boss?"

"Fitz won't mind. Your last night —"

"No, I'd like to. Let's wait for him."

I was going to insist, drag him out of there if I had to. It was too late; Fitz had slipped out of the control room. "Come on. That's enough of that bullshit." He shepherded us through the swinging doors, down the corridor. If there were other people waiting for the elevator, I might manage to get close enough to Fitz to whisper to him, "He doesn't know. Don't tell him."

No one was waiting for the elevator. It took a long time coming. We stood in that silent, suspended fraternity that overtakes people in dentists' offices. I could see Fitz was organizing his thoughts. Maybe I *should* throw up, I thought crazily. Max would have to take me home.

"I don't know what you wanted to say, Sergeant, but personally I think you should have been allowed to say it."

I listened helplessly while Fitz went on. I couldn't think of anything to say without making it worse. The elevator came. The three of us were alone in it.

"When did he cut me off?" Max sounded mildly curious. I was afraid that was a bad sign; the longer he suppressed his anger, the more violently it might explode.

"After you said your parents were dead," Fitz told him.

"He turned away from me. I thought he was giving me a chance to speak my piece. I guess he went on talking."

"He certainly did."

We were in a taxi by the time Fitz had finished with the Norwegian cousin. It seemed to puzzle Max at first. "My family came from Cornwall," he said. "I don't have any relatives in Norway."

"Don's so full of bullshit."

"Do you often make up stories like that on what you call the news?"

"Don —"

"I guess that's freedom of the press." I was holding Max's hand; it was as cold as his voice. "The First Amendment. The right to tell lies — so long as they sell refrigerators."

"We have to tell the truth about refrigerators. The FCC insists on it."

"I guess it's not your fault. You're only the head of the news department."

Things got worse after we reached the restaurant. It was one of Fitz's regular places, a pleasant, casual grill room near Gramercy Park. O. Henry was supposed to have spent a lot of time getting drunk there. Tear sheets of his stories were framed on the walls. We settled into a booth. Fitz ordered drinks. I watched Max drink half his double Canadian Club the moment it arrived. It was like watching someone loading a gun.

"Don's a mess," I said quickly. "He thinks —"

"But the affiliated stations like him." Max wasn't going to let me take the initiative away from him. He leaned across the table, squeezing me into the corner of the booth.

"Do you know anything about the Greeks?" he asked Fitz.

"The ancient Greeks?"

"Yeah. When the young men went off to fight at Thermopylae, don't you think the old men who stayed home must have had a great time with the chicks. They —"

"It was the Spartans who fought at Thermopylae, Sergeant." Fitz's blue eyes were amused and understanding. "They were a fairly celibate lot, especially —"

"Okay, take Napoleon's Grand Army then." Max finished his drink. "I bet they all got cuckolded, too. It's funny, isn't it? Every army's an army of cuckolds. I guess that's why we have wars. The old men start them so they can get laid. Carol says —"

"What are you going to eat, Max?" I pushed the menu at him; he ignored it.

"Carol says you're all for American intervention, Mr. Fitzpatrick. I should think you would be. Get all the young pricks into the army. Send them overseas. That'll give you a clear field with the gash. You'll have twenty girls in every office who . . ." It went on and on.

Fitz still looked quietly amused. "I think you're a little drunk, Sergeant," he said at one point.

I did my best to stop it. "Shut up, Max," I told him several times. I tried to persuade him to eat something; he wanted another drink. We got into a futile argument with the waiter about it. He was a mild, patient man, obviously used to drunks. Maybe he had had trouble with O. Henry in his time; he looked old enough. Max asked him how long it had been since he had had a good lay. The waiter had one of those smiles that seemed to say, There, there. Max told him he'd have all the pussy he could handle if he stayed around until America got into the war, but before that happened he wanted another drink.

I stopped arguing about it; I hoped another double Canadian Club would make him pass out. It didn't; he started on Fitz again.

"I really ought to be grateful to you," he told him. "You've taught Carol a lot. Before I went to Canada, when Carol and I were shacked up on the West Side, she was pretty passive. Not exactly frigid, but inexperienced, you know. I come back and she's not only put on a little weight, got nice round tits and a great ass, she's terrific in the sack. An absolutely world-class fuck. You've even taught her to —"

I couldn't stand it any longer. I pushed out of my corner and squeezed past Max.

"I'm sorry, Fitz." I felt so ashamed I couldn't bear to look at him. "I'm sorry," I repeated and hurried blindly to the door.

Max caught up with me on the sidewalk.

"Where are you going, Carol?" He looked concerned, but his voice was still cold with that quiet, frightening anger.

"Home." I started to walk away from him toward Gramercy Park. He walked behind, then beside me; he clutched my arm.

"I'm sorry. Maybe I did go a bit too far. But you can't blame me. You. Don. That guy Fitzpatrick. You all ganged up on me, trying to humiliate me. You did humiliate me. You —"

"Fitz had nothing to do with it." I was shouting as I stopped and faced him on the corner of the square. "Fitz didn't know."

"Don't call him Fitz." Max was shouting too. "How much do you think I can take? Sitting there, looking at him. He's a pretty good-looking guy, isn't he? Even if he is thirty years older than you are. I could *feel* the closeness between you two. No one could miss it. I kept thinking of him touching you. Kissing you —"

"Shut up."

"Fucking you."

"Shut up."

I turned and ran away from him across the street, around the corner of the gardens. A taxi was approaching. It stopped. I wrenched the door open and yelled "Tenth Street" to the driver. I was off, safe, away from him before Max could catch up with me.

Home in my apartment, I bolted the door and put up the chain. I was no longer angry; I was confused and shaken. But most of all I felt ashamed. As I sat in the chair by the window, I kept remembering everything Max had said in the restaurant. I listened to it, like a record, over and over again in my mind. When I thought of Fitz listening to it, I felt naked and guilty, unbearably ashamed — not exactly of myself, not even of Max. Somehow *for* Fitz. He was so kind, so decent. It was horrible that he had been subjected to accusations like that. There had never been anything sexual between us. He had never touched me, only once kissed my cheek. Max's attack on him seemed such a violation of his decency.

I must have sat there for two or three hours before I even began to think about the present. About Max. He was probably out in some bar getting drunker and drunker. Sooner or later he would come stalking wildly back here, beating his fists against the locked door, demanding to be let in. The thought of it scared me. I wasn't physically frightened of him — I did not for a minute believe he would hit me — I just knew I couldn't take it, that cold, still rage in him, that quiet voice going on and on the way it had that night in the Trotskyist apartment. I couldn't bear it.

Okay. I wouldn't open the door.

It was two o'clock when I heard his footsteps on the stairs. His key clicked in the lock. The catch snapped back. Thank God for the bolt and chain that the previous tenant had installed to protect herself. I would never have had the foresight to do it myself.

"Carol."

I didn't answer.

"Carol, please let me in."

I didn't move.

Now the hammering would start. It didn't. I listened to the silence, puzzled at first, then after a while concerned. I tiptoed to the door, slipped back the bolt as quietly as I could, leaving the chain on, and peered out.

Max was sitting on the stairs. He was holding his cap, turning it over and over in his hands in a thoughtful way. He looked up at me and smiled.

"Hello," he said.

I let him in. He sat on the couch, still fiddling with his cap.

"Where have you been?" I did my best to sound severe. "What have you been doing all this time?"

"Walking around. I had a hamburger and some coffee and then I walked around some more. I wanted to sober up before I came home. I figured we didn't have too much time left to talk and I wanted you to understand about tonight, and I knew I couldn't even understand it myself if I was drunk."

I sat down on the edge of the bed.

"You see," he said thoughtfully, as though he were explaining it to himself, "you're the only person in the world I care about, Carol. I guess you're the only person I ever have cared about. I don't even remember my parents. And that makes it difficult for me to think about you reasonably, rationally. When I was in Canada, when I didn't even know where you were, before I managed to get your address out of Mrs. Hainert, I kept thinking about you as something wonderful that had been given to me" — he looked up at me — "and I'd thrown it away, running out on you like that." He went back to his cap. "Then I found you again. And this last week together — all the time I've been scared of losing you again. I guess that's why I've been drinking too much. I couldn't handle that fear, the fear that you'd betray me, leave me, the way my parents did — at least, that's the way a kid feels when his parents die. And then tonight with that guy Fitzpatrick. Okay, Fitz." He smiled. "I felt you *had* betrayed me. I know it doesn't make much sense. But that's the way it was. Do you think you can understand that?"

I didn't answer. Nothing Max had said fitted in with my image of him, the way I saw him, thought about him. For over a year, ever since I first met him in that hotel off Times Square, Max had seemed to me indestructible. The quiet, confident Westerner of my fantasy-fed imagination. It had been childish of me to see him like that, as childish as my hero worship of Buffalo Bill when I was seven. Now with his talk of fear of "betrayal" he had revealed an aspect of himself that distorted, shattered, that image forever.

I realized for the first time how deeply complicated he really was. It didn't make me love him less; it made me love him differently.

I went over and sat beside him and took the cap out of his hands. I felt helplessly confused. I knew I should hold him, comfort him, and I didn't know how. I had never comforted anyone in my life.

"We'd better go to bed, Max," I said. "We've got to get up awfully early tomorrow morning."

It was terrible in the morning, rushed and desperate and sad. I made us both coffee and packed his bag and we scurried about, seeing if he had forgotten anything, trying to find something to say that would reach beyond our parting, keep us together after he was gone.

We couldn't find a cab. We had to run all the way to Fifth Avenue before one would stop for us. They were calling his bus as we hurried into the station. I went with him to the boarding exit. He put down his bag. We clutched each other's hands.

"Are you still my girl, Carol?"

It hadn't really hit me until then. He wasn't just going away. He was going to his base, his plane, his turret gun. He was going to war.

"Oh, yes, yes, Max." I was crying. "Yes, I am, Max, always."

There was a note on my desk at the office. Fitz wanted to see me. I walked down the long corridor, past the silent typists. He was standing by the window.

"Sit down, Carol."

I sat down, waiting. I felt shy with Fitz after what had happened, but not worried for myself. I never for a moment expected him to fire me. I didn't even expect him to be angry. It was as though there were a complicity between us which I sensed even then.

"Did your sergeant leave?"

"Yes, I put him on the bus."

"Everything all right between you?"

"Yes." I felt I ought to explain. "I'm terribly sorry about last night. I'm terribly sorry he was so rude to you, Fitz. But you see —"

"There's no need to feel sorry, Carol." Fitz moved away from the window and sat on the corner of his desk. He leaned forward, so close I thought he was going to touch me. He didn't.

"It's not your fault," he said gently. "It's the way things are. The people we love. We don't choose them. And we have to accept them."

Fitz's eyes were understanding, a little sad. "I ought to know. I've been in love with the wrong people all my life."

Eight

After Max left I saw even more of Fitz.

Although we never talked about it, there was a new understanding between us. We were both in love, both bereft in our different ways. Sitting listening to the phonograph in his apartment, we nursed our yearnings separately. I thought about Max, and Fitz thought about . . . I had no idea whom he thought about. Sometimes, when he was playing a Chopin record, I imagined a married woman. She and Fitz had loved each other for years, but she would not, could not, leave her husband. Sometimes Mahler would start me imagining an estranged wife, another Zelda, her nerves shattered by saxophones and champagne, writing him pleading, adoring letters from a private mental home somewhere. Berlioz, and she was more Byronic, mad, bad, and dangerous to know; she lacerated Fitz with her passion and her infidelity. Whoever she was, Fitz still loved her. That was the point, of course; he would always be faithful to his lost, "wrong" love.

In all the evenings I spent with him, Fitz himself never mentioned her.

Soon after Christmas I was promoted again. Fitz made me his personal assistant. It could have been awkward, seeing so much of him in the evenings and working so closely with him during the day. It never was. We would go straight from the office to dinner, then on to the theater or back to his apartment, without my having to make any change in my attitude, any distinction between Fitz my boss and Fitz my friend.

With a raise in salary, I finally did something to realize the possibilities of my apartment. I threw out most of the old junk, had the whole place painted, and refurnished it with things I liked. One of the few pieces I kept was the old double bed.

By the spring of 1941, living in an attractive apartment, having money to buy new clothes, eat in pleasant restaurants, I had a whole new sense of New York. It was a much freer city than the one I'd known only a year before when I was rushing up to Forty-second Street for a potato knish on my lunch hour. Certain places became my places. Lee Chumley's in the Village, and a bar called Julius's on Tenth Street, where Pee Wee Russell and the other musicians from Nick's hung out, and most of all Tim Costello's on Third Avenue. If I was working late, I would often go to Costello's alone for a drink or dinner. I was on nodding terms with most of *The New Yorker* people who went there, and the German waiter, Emil, adopted me. If Thurber or McKelway or any of the others was exceptionally drunk and started to pick on me, Emil would patiently shoo him away.

Looking back, that March, when I was twenty, I felt everything in my life had changed since my last birthday.

Everything except Max.

We wrote to each other two or three times a week. In June I had eighteen days of vacation coming to me. I planned to go up to Toronto; Max would be able to get overnight passes while I was there. He had found a motor court near the base where we could live together. All through May I felt an actual physical excitement at the thought of being with him again. At spare moments in the office I indulged in erotic daydreams about us.

And then, at the end of May, Max called late one night. He had been put on overseas alert and restricted to base; he expected to be shipped out before the end of the week. I cried after he had hung up. It might be years before I saw him again. He might be killed. Please, please, don't let him be killed. By midnight I had decided to rush up to Toronto the next day; surely we would be allowed an hour or two together before he was sent overseas. When I woke the next morning, I thought it over more realistically. An hour together on an air force base. Holding hands in a canteen. I couldn't stand it. I would weep with desire for him and make it desperate for both of us. What could we say to each other that would make another parting bearable. I love you? I said that in every letter I wrote him.

When my vacation came, I went up to Provincetown. I was there that Sunday when the German armies invaded Russia. I had been out sailing all day and I didn't hear the news until I turned on the radio that night. Later in bed I couldn't get to sleep; I kept thinking about it. Until then the war had been England and the Commonwealth countries and occupied Europe against Nazi Germany. Now the Soviet Union was in it. In it on *our* side. Churchill's speech had been on the news. "Anyone who fights against the Nazis is our friend." I was shocked by it. To me the German invasion of Russia had made the whole war senseless. There was no longer any right or wrong to it. The Stalinists imprisoned, tortured, murdered anyone who disagreed with them as savagely as the Nazis did.

I felt differently about the war after that Sunday. When I returned to New York, I no longer read each cable or transcribed each overseas call with the sense that my own life was at stake. The fact that Hitler's attack on Russia took the pressure off England, halting the air raids on London, had a lot to do with this. But beyond that, I no longer felt it was *my* war in the way I had since the fall of France. I followed the advance of the German army, the fall of Kiev, with the objective horror of someone watching two wild animals tear each other to pieces. For the next five months, I no longer felt personally engaged.

I was alone in my apartment that other Sunday, in December, when the Japanese bombed Pearl Harbor. Fitz called me with the news. I went to the office at once. Most of the others, the news writers and reporters and secretaries, were already there. They had come straight from their radios, grateful to be among the lucky ones in America that day who at least had something they could do.

We worked through until midnight, breaking in on the regular programs with special news bulletins as the reports came in from Hawaii, the Philippines, Washington, Singapore, Hong Kong, Wake . . .

In spite of the wildness of some of these reports, there was no confusion in the office and very little talk, only the usual compelling curiosity, the need to know more, that infused us whenever a big story broke. It was all the more compelling now because, for the first time in the war, the story was *ours.* It was the United States that had been attacked. People later told me how angry they had been that day. It seemed to me we were too startled to be angry; we were so surprised, we didn't quite believe it yet.

Fitz was less surprised than the rest of us. I was in his office soon after midnight with Lee Hearn, one of the announcers, and several of the news writers. Fitz brought out a bottle of Scotch and we all had a drink.

"Well, what I mean, this whole thing . . ." Lee Hearn's hesitancy expressed what we were all thinking more clearly than any words he could have found. "What do you think, Fitz?"

"I think it serves us damn well right."

Lee and some of the others stirred protestingly, but no one contradicted him.

"Look, Lee," Fitz went on, "we've all known for months this was going to happen. The Nazi-Japanese pact wasn't exactly kept secret, nor was our oil embargo and what it would do to Japan."

"Yeah, but, well . . ." Lee was still fumbling for words. "Why do you say it serves us right?"

"Because we kept telling ourselves it was going to happen to someone else. We knew the Japanese would attack the British and the Dutch sooner or later. But we just couldn't believe those funny little yellow men would ever have the guts to attack us. So we left our planes sitting on the ground and our battleships at anchor and they knocked the shit out of us."

One of the news writers asked him how bad he thought it was. "First reports are always exaggerated, Fitz," he suggested hopefully.

Fitz didn't agree. He thought the truth was worse than the first reports. Off the record, he had talked to people in Washington during the day: his understanding was that almost half our Pacific fleet had been wiped out in the first hour of the war. "And that's only the beginning. We're going to lose most of our bases, too. Guam and Wake and the Philippines. And it'll be a hell of a long time before we're in any shape to fight back."

Lee Hearn wouldn't believe it. "No one's announced it was that bad."

"Lee." Fitz shook his head. "You know the old saying. In any war the first casualty is the truth."

Fitz was right, as it turned out, about the immediate course of the war; for months one defeat followed another.

He was right about the truth, too. It wasn't only the wartime censorship. After that Sunday our whole attitude toward news changed. Our responsibility to the war effort made us strangely irresponsible. We announced rumored victories, like the battle of Lingayan Gulf, and then hushed our denials when our announcements turned out to be untrue. We ignored reports from our own correspondents. We suppressed bad news. Ten hours after Pearl Harbor, every plane at Clark Field was caught sitting on the runway and MacArthur lost half his air force in a few minutes. That news was suppressed on the grounds that it would give comfort to the enemy. "Don't you think the Japanese papers print things like that?" Fitz asked an official in Washington. We surrounded every disaster with a vengeful, bragging fiction. The Japanese were featured alternately as an irresistible phenomenon, like a tidal wave, and a bunch of suicidal, yellow fanatics. "We're going to have to slap the dirty little Jap" was on every jukebox. We invented comic-book heroes like Colin Kelly. We made up comic-book stories like the "Send us more Japs" message from Wake Island.

When Wake fell a week later, Don represented our defeat as a lesson to the Japanese. "Let Tojo learn from this," he announced in his most evangelical tones. "America is not going to be tricked into wasting its capacity to strike back."

Don seemed to be everywhere at that time. He was on the air six evenings a week now. He no longer stood out as a wishful fraud. It was as though we had all been swallowed up by him: we were all seeing with his eyes and speaking with his voice. Fitfully we knew we were insulting our audience, our country, with our lies. What I don't think we ever fully realized was that we were lying as much to ourselves as to our listeners. Like lunatics, we were unknowingly distorting the unacceptable.

Fitz stayed saner than the rest of us. "What worries me," he told me one night in his apartment, "is the way the war's dividing America. There are two wars. Admiral King's war in the Pacific and General Marshall's war in Europe. King's war is the patriots' war, the America Firsters', the old isolationists'. The way they look at it, the Marshall people are traitors. They're insisting on fighting a war in Europe that we never should have got involved in anyway. Never would have got involved in if it hadn't been for Roosevelt."

It was always a relief to be alone with Fitz in those days; he was the only person I felt I could talk to. "I wish I could feel more patriotic," I admitted to him. If I'd said that to anyone else it would have made me uneasy; I might be reported to the authorities.

"Sometimes I feel the whole war's become an advertising campaign," I went on. "I know the reality's still there — Bataan, occupied Europe, the concentration camps — but it keeps getting lost in the ballyhoo, the gup about our *boys* in the service, fixing them up with a date at the Stork Club on that radio show, using them to sell cigarettes. All the swindles that get packaged as part of the war effort. I wish we'd just shut up about the war and get on with it."

"The trouble with you is you've never been comfortable on bandwagons."

"I know." I remembered the store, that woman with the sad, pockmarked face. "I've got absolutely no team spirit."

"The only honest thing you can do in a war is get shot at." Fitz was lying on the sofa with his jacket off. I was in an armchair with my feet on the coffee table. I felt wonderfully easy there with him. We were like fugitives, safe in each other's acceptance. "Yesterday in the control room, listening to Don go on about Midway — 'The tide has turned. Our forces are on the offensive' — I thought, Goddamn it, it was the navy who won the battle, not you."

"I wish I had the guts to join the WACs."

Fitz sat up and looked at me. "That's just guilt. We all have it. Every civilian. All those overage men buying soldiers drinks and telling them how much they envy them. It's a lot of bullshit.

When they get home, they thank God they're not out in some foxhole."

"I wouldn't be any use to the WACs anyway," I admitted. "The first time some officer started giving me a pep talk about my duty to my country, I'd desert."

Fitz laughed. "Your duty to your country is to help me keep Don on the air so he can win the war for us."

Thank God for Fitz.

Although Midway *was* the turning point in the Pacific — the Japanese advance was stopped there — 1942 went on being a terrible year. It was the year of waiting and frustration, of confusion and hysteria, of ludicrous air raid panics in the Middle West.

In our guilt and frustration, we wanted so much to believe we were all in it together. And we knew we weren't. The soldiers on Bataan were in it. And we couldn't send them anything except words. The British forces in the Lybian desert were in it. And we couldn't help them either, as Rommel kept pushing them back, because the U-boats were sinking our supply ships in the Atlantic faster than we could build them.

The only Allied country whose forces were fighting with any success was the Soviet Union. And it was terrible to feel such a debt to the Russians. "Ah, there's good news tonight," Don kept saying all that summer whenever the German armies were halted. Don didn't really think it was good news, and neither did most of the rest of us. Suppose Russia won the war without us?

Still, we *were* getting on with it. We were building thousands and thousands of planes and tanks. We were inducting millions of men and training them. And then in November we landed in North Africa. In spite of the endless stories the network was asked to suppress about de Gaulle, and then Giraud, and then finally Darlan, it did seem like a tremendous step forward.

The landings represented the close of that terrible year. Nineteen forty-three would be better. It had to be better.

I worked late that New Year's Eve and then went back to his apartment with Fitz. He said he had something to tell me. He made me wait until midnight.

"You're swell, Carol." He kissed my cheek and we drank to each other.

"What's the news, Fitz?"

"I'm going overseas. Maybe not for a couple of months yet, but Elmer's finally agreed to send me over on a job for the OWI."

"I'll miss you." That was the first thing I thought of; then I started to congratulate him.

"You're coming too."

"Me?"

"I don't think I can get you on a plane." Fitz poured me another glass of wine. He was drinking wine himself now; it was hard to get whiskey. "But I've put in for you to be sent over on a ship, so you can work for me there."

"Where?"

"England."

"England?"

"Don't you want to go?"

Of course I did. I had been away almost four years. I could see my father and my mother and Sylvia and Daphne.

And then I realized with a sudden yearning excitement there was someone else I would be seeing in England.

Max.

Nine

I still don't understand why you're in uniform."

It was the fourth time Laurie Sue Maytag had said that to me since I had come on board the SS *Parkwood* two days before.

The first three times I had tried to explain it to her: although I was still being paid by the network, I was under the authority of the U.S. Army. This time I just shrugged and tried to get back to my book. Being in uniform seemed sensible enough to me: if they were going to let American women loose in England, they wanted to retain some control over them. They wanted to send them to army hospitals if they got sick. They wanted to send them home if they had a nervous breakdown or got pregnant.

"I don't see you've any right to be wearing that uniform."

Laurie Sue wasn't wearing a uniform. She was an employee of the State Department. She had been "with State" since the beginning of Roosevelt's second term. This was her first overseas posting. She was about thirty-five years old, blond, unmarried, tired looking, from Richmond, Virginia. At the moment she was wearing a yellow cotton robe and a shower cap as she lay on the opposite bunk in the tiny cabin we would be sharing until we reached Liverpool. She had a nail file in one hand and the fingers of the other hand were clenched against her palm. She wasn't actually filing her nails, she was only frowning at them.

"It isn't as if you were in the army, is it?"

The hammering had started again on deck. I put down my book and, pushing aside the canvas blackout curtain, opened the door.

"If you're going out there, you're supposed to wear your life jacket."

The cabin faced aft. I leaned on the rail overlooking the hatches and the seamen's quarters in the stern with the gun on top. Below me on the deck, nine men in soiled dungarees, sweaters, and knitted caps were sitting on wooden boxes. Each of them had a hammer and was solemnly, methodically striking the square foot of iron deck in front of him.

We were lying at anchor in the bay, the sea gray and sleek, the sky gray and woolly, the thirty or forty other merchant ships anchored around us gray and disparate and homely looking, like floating bric-a-brac. It was easy to pick out the American ships: they were the ones with guns mounted forward. The cheery petty officer had explained that when he brought me out to the SS *Parkwood* in the launch. It was a holdover from the First World War, the British insistence that merchant ships were not armed vessels, that the stern guns on them were defensive weapons. "They're bloody useless, anyway," he said. "What are they supposed to do, pot at bloody submarines with them? The Jerries've got too much sense to surface this time. Woop-woop. They come through the lines in packs. Woop-woop. Let off their bloody torpedoes and run like hell. They got half the ships in the last convoy we sent out."

Kang-kang-kang, went the little hammers. It was like a smithy.

Fitz was already safe in England after the dog-leg Lisbon flight. I had talked to him a week ago.

"When are you coming over, Carol?"

"I'm waiting now. I'm waiting for orders. I've been cleared and I've had all my shots and I've got my uniform. They told me to be ready to leave any time."

"I'm sorry I couldn't get you on a plane."

Kang-kang-kang.

That morning I'd wondered what they were doing, hammering the deck like that. What was the point of it? Lunch had cleared up that question. Laurie Sue and I, the only passengers on the small British freighter, ate in the officers' mess. We sat together at one end of the long table. The captain, the deck officers and engineers, came and went at the other end. There was little conversation.

"Are you going to get that afterdeck chipped before we sail?" the captain asked one of the officers in a brief moment of contact.

"Try, sir."

"I want every speck of rust off that deck before we dock in Liverpool."

"Depends when we sail, sir."

"Tell that to the owners."

I didn't understand that last part about the owners until several days later, but at least now I knew why they were hammering.

Kang-kang-kang.

One of the seaman had put down his hammer. When he saw me looking at him, he stood up and waved. He was tall and Italian looking with a smooth oval face and beautiful eyes, and I liked the way he moved. I waved back.

"Lofty." A man was yelling at him from the stern. "Never mind the Yank Judy, get the fuck on with it, Lofty."

"Jerk off, bosun," the seaman shouted back. He didn't sound Italian.

It was the middle of April 1943. I was on my way at last. In less than three weeks I would be with Max.

We sailed the next day. I was up early, watching the forty ships slowly and confusedly sort themselves into lines as they moved out into the open sea. A big freighter kept blinking a signal lamp at us.

"Bloody commodore," the radio officer told me, blinking back from the wing of the bridge. "Bloody navy bugger."

I asked him what the signaler was saying.

"Usual bloody nonsense. 'Get into line.' When we're at sea, it'll be, 'Make less smoke.' Every bloody ten minutes, 'make less smoke.' "

"Have you been at sea all through the war?"

He didn't answer. After a while I gathered from his silence that I wasn't supposed to be on the bridge.

Half a dozen small, dark men in dirty civilian jackets with padded shoulders were sitting around on the afterhatches washing their shirts in buckets. They slopped them up and down in the water, wrung them out, and hung them over the cargo booms to dry. Every few minutes, one of them walked over to the winches, opened a valve, and ran steam into his bucket with a fierce rattling sound. They were part of the engine crew, Arabs from the Persian Gulf, one of the officers had told me. It was hard to get British stokers to work on a coal-firing ship. "They're hard-working buggers, those Arabs," he said. "Tight as Jews. They save every bloody penny they earn." When they saw me watching them, they grinned and beckoned to me with their middle fingers. One of them unbuttoned his trousers and showed himself to me.

The seamen on watch were all over the foredeck. They had stopped hammering and were scraping away at areas of paint with long, bulb-handled chisels. The bosun hurried around, looking busy and shouting at them occasionally. The first mate walked out onto the wing of the bridge from time to time and shouted at the bosun. The bosun punctuated every sentence with obscenities; the first mate didn't. None of the seamen paid any attention to the bosun or to anything that was going on at sea around them as we edged into place in one of the lines.

Outside the estuary, two destroyers and some smaller escort ships joined us, circling around the convoy like horsemen around a herd of cows and blinking their lamps at the navy bugger. None of the seamen showed any interest in the destroyers either. The good-looking one called Lofty noticed me standing by the rail under the bridge and waved to me. He got shouted at by the bosun again.

I walked up to the raised deck outside my cabin. I felt less in the way there, but after a few minutes I was littered with soft black smuts. We were making a lot of smoke. Laurie Sue was lying on her bunk in the cabin, frowning at her nails.

"You're going to get that uniform all messed up," she told me. "And if you're going back out there, you're supposed to put your life jacket on."

And then I discovered the monkey island. It was a square of open deck on top of the wheel house, forward of the funnel and protected from the wind by a canvas railing. It was wonderful up there. I could see all over the ship and all over the ocean. No one ever seemed to use the monkey island except me. I began to spend all day up there. Sometimes I took a book and sat on the wooden deck out of the wind; more often I stood watching the ships around us.

Listening to Don talk about convoys on the air, I had built up a picture of long, orderly lines of sleek merchant vessels, every man on the alert, as the ships raced across the deadly Atlantic with their vital cargoes. Our convoy wasn't like that. It was more like a group of unruly children straggling to school. Hardly any of the ships seemed to be able to sail at the same speed for more than a few minutes at a time. An American tanker behind us kept creeping up on us. Again and again it would overtake us altogether and pull alongside before dropping back. A lot of the ships did that; sometimes the lines became so confused it was hard to tell there were any lines. At that point, the signal lamp would start snapping at us from the commodore. I wished I'd paid more attention to the Morse code in my Girl Guide days at school. I did remember the code for *m* and *a.* Whenever I caught two dashes and then dot-dash at the beginning of a message, I remembered what the radio operator had told me. The navy bugger was telling someone to make less smoke.

There was one pathetic Belgian freighter with jeeps all over the deck that became a part of my daily life, like a continuing serial in a newspaper. It couldn't keep up at all. As the day passed, it would get farther and farther behind until it disappeared altogether. The first time this happened, I felt terrible about it until I went up to the monkey island the next morning. There it was again at the end of the line next to us. It had somehow managed to catch up during the night. After that, it was the first thing I looked for every day. I became very fond of it. It had a row of blacked-out portholes along its prow that gave it the look of a sightless elephant, its tall, straight-up funnel swaying from side to side like a howdah on its back as it lumbered along. I never did figure out why it could go faster at night than it did in the daytime.

No one seemed to be particularly alert on the SS *Parkwood.* The seamen scraped despondently away, and then red-leaded the patches they had cleared, and finally slapped on a coat of gray paint. For all the attention they paid to the convoy, or to the sea, they might have been restoring a tenement in the Bronx. After the first time, they didn't even raise their faces when our planes flew overhead. The planes came every day for the first few days, morning and afternoon, sometimes one, sometimes two or three, circling maternally over the convoy and then disappearing into the gray sky ahead of us. Catalinas, I think they were. The only officer who ever mentioned them was the radio operator.

"That's the last we'll see of those buggers," he told me one day at lunch, squinting up at them through the porthole of the mess. "They'll stay home after this. Lucky sods."

There was still little conversation in the mess. The captain and the first mate were still going on about the rust on the afterdeck. "When are you going to get that deck chipped?" the captain asked him at least once a day. "When we sight the Fastnet lighthouse," the mate told him several times. After a few days he stopped answering altogether.

There was little eating in the mess, either. The steward despondently dragged in various pots and pans containing pieces of charred meat and watery stew or, at breakfast, congealed porridge. They sat on the table, ignored. The officers brought their own food to meals with them, cans of corned beef and hams and cold cuts. They only came to the mess for cups of tea and bread and condiments for their sandwiches. They stood around the end of the table, piling things together as though they were packing suitcases, and then took them away to eat in their cabins. I had a ham in my Valpack, a whole smoked ham I was taking to my mother. After a few days the temptation to eat it was becoming irresistible. Luckily for my mother, I found I could eat the potatoes the steward brought in if I mashed them up with butter. The *Parkwood* had put in to Norfolk, Virginia, and though the steward had been gypped on the meat — or maybe it was just the way it was cooked — the mess was rich in hard-to-get-at-home items like butter, sugar, strawberry jam, different kinds of pickles. I lived on these luxuries with bread and potatoes and endless oranges the steward had also picked up in Norfolk.

Laurie Sue wanted to complain about the food.

"Who are you going to complain to?" I asked her.

"The captain, of course."

"It's just as bad for him as it is for us."

"How can you eat those terrible potatoes? They're fattening."

I stayed out of the cabin except to sleep. I started going up to the monkey island in the evenings as well as during the day. It was peaceful up there in the dark, silent except for the throb of the engines down below and the constant, weary creaking of the ship. The convoy vanished at night; we were alone on the Atlantic except for the occasional wash of the American tanker as it came up too fast and pulled alongside for a moment.

One night as I climbed the companionway from the bridge, I heard a movement in the darkness above me. One of the seamen was on the monkey island. I didn't know whether to go on or turn back. I could just see him, leaning over the foreward rail. Something, a grace in the way he stood, made me recognize him; it was the seaman they called Lofty. I went on.

"That you, miss?" he greeted me.

"Yes."

"Haven't seen you about the deck since we sailed."

"I come up here."

We stood, leaning over the rail, side by side.

"Are you on watch?" I asked him.

"Yeh, but I'm farming."

He had to explain that to me. It had something to do with the extra watches — the field days, as they called them — the British merchant seamen worked on deck. To compensate for their sixty-four-hour week, they took turns goofing off at night. They called that farming.

"The Yanks don't have field days," Lofty said. "They get better pay than us, too."

"I'm sorry."

"Not your fault. It's the owners. They don't know there's a war. Don't care anyway. All they care is keeping their ships posh for after the war. All the captain cares about, too." He sounded quite cheerful about it.

I said the owners had lost a lot of ships in the war.

"That's all right, isn't it? Get a brand-new ship from the government then. Take those lifeboats." He pointed to them, vague, creaking shapes on the deck below. "That's wartime regulations, having them slung out like that in convoy. The captain didn't want to let us do it. He's afraid the sea might damage the davits. If a davit gets bent, that goes against him with the owners."

He had a curious way of talking, pausing between words. I thought he might be trying to hide a stammer, and then I realized the reason for the pauses. He was carefully suppressing all the *fuck*s and *bugger*s that were a part of his natural speech. He was doing it out of chivalry, respect for the Yank Judy. Me. I was glad he didn't suppress his natural opinions; he was a hot spring of cheerful rancor. He hated the bosun. "He was in the navy, see? That'll ruin any man. They break their spirits in the peacetime navy. Make them suck-ups. See the way the bosun sucks up to the mate?"

He hated all officers in every service. "They're having a good war, they are. Lots of Judys to bring them tea. They'll be glad if the war never ends. Have to go back to being clerks in offices. Sucking up to the manager."

He hated Churchill. "Think we've forgotten the way he carried on in the general strike? That's the first thing we're going to do when this war's over. Get rid of that —" There was a long pause. "Churchill."

He hated, or at best disliked, all doctors, lawyers, politicians, bank managers, policemen, civil servants, clerks — almost everyone in England, in fact, except his own family and his "mates," the people he called "we." And kiddies. Lofty had a deep sympathy for them. "But it's hard on the kiddies," he said about the bombings, as though that was the only drawback he could think of to blasting the whole country flat. The whole country except Bradford. Lofty was a Yorkshireman; Bradford was home. He spoke of the town with a fierce provincial patriotism. "New York's all right," he told me. "I like those juke boxes and the beer in cans. But it isn't like Bradford, you know."

He had been at sea for seven years, since the age of fifteen, sailed all over the world and found none of it a "patch on Bradford." He still lived there when he was ashore, with his Mum and Dad and so many brothers and sisters I couldn't get them all straight. Three of his brothers were in the army, one of them a deserter. "Ted's on the run," was the way Lofty put it. "He'll be all right if he can hang on till the end of the war."

By this time I was beginning to have disturbing feelings about

Lofty. As my eyes got used to the darkness, I could see his face when he looked at me, his beautiful eyes with their feathery lashes, the smooth oval of his cheeks. He had a beautiful mouth, too.

Although I'd been brought up in England from the age of twelve, he was the first working-class Englishman I'd ever really talked to. I say "really" because of course I had talked to bus conductors, milkmen, servants; but none of them had ever treated me as an equal. Lofty showed me an England I had never caught sight of before. The England I'd known was full of rigid rules, ordered conventions of behavior; I remembered it mainly for its stuffiness. There was nothing stuffy about Lofty's England. It was as natural and spontaneous as a wood full of larks. There were no rigid rules for Lofty and his mates either. They acted only on their own anarchic impulses.

The more he talked, the more disturbing my feelings about him became. One touch, and I was afraid I would lose all sense of reality, all resistance; he would have me right there on the monkey island. Thank God for the darkness. He wouldn't be able to see the awful government-issue khaki underpants I was wearing.

He didn't touch me. The watch ended. He went below to the seaman's quarters. I lay in my bunk, thinking how dishonest I'd been with him.

The trouble was, I would have to keep up the dishonesty. So long as he thought I was a Yank Judy, a foreigner, he would continue to trust me and be friendly. If I told him the truth about my middle-class English parents, I would join the bank managers and the police — the enemy.

Three feet away from me, Laurie Sue was snoring. Not loudly; she snored the way she spoke, delicately, chidingly. It brought me out of my fantasy. What was I thinking of? Had I really been prepared to get laid by a merchant seaman on the monkey island? A few minutes ago I had imagined myself snatching off my khaki pants before he could be turned off by them. The thought of that made me laugh. I had to pull the blankets over my head to muffle the sound; I didn't want to wake Laurie Sue.

The truth was, I suppose, that the whole experience of being at sea had unhitched me. I was like a pendulum stopped dead between the rush of my life in New York and Max. The worst part of this

arrested condition was my present uncertainty about Max. I knew
I still loved him, wanted him as much as ever. But recently I had
begun to have gnawing doubts about *his* feelings. Over the last
six months, his letters had become less and less communicative,
more and more evasive. He still ended them the same way — *All
my love* — but they were like letters from an acquaintance, full of
small talk about some movie he had seen, a book he had read.
Even about the weather. I was beginning to be almost sure he had
taken up with someone else. I could hardly blame him if he had.
We hadn't seen each other for two and a half years. England must
be teeming with attractive, lonely young women. All those Wrens
and Land Girls must be hanging around his neck.

I could hardly blame him, but the thought of it made me sick
with fear. Please don't let him have fallen in love with anyone
else. Please.

Well, in two weeks I would know. One way or the other. For
another two weeks I just had to live in the present, and there was
nothing in the present to hold on to.

Except Lofty.

I only glimpsed him the next day. He was painting one of the
vents, but he was there on the monkey island two evenings later.

He didn't have to say "That you, miss?" The sky was still half-
light when I joined him at the rail. It was lovely being able to
see his face, to watch him as he talked. In the grace of his movements,
in the natural way he wore his work clothes, his small knitted
cap, he had extraordinary panache. It sounds crazy — maybe I was
a little crazy with anxiety about Max — but I hadn't been with
Lofty for ten minutes before I began to feel, even more disturbingly
this time, that if he suddenly grabbed me, I wouldn't do a damn
thing to stop him.

"That bloody seaman's union," Lofty was saying. "It's a joke.
Half the men don't belong to it, and the ones that do couldn't
stick together . . ."

I was wondering what it would be like. What would *he* be like?
Hungry and urgent like Max? Or like the Max I loved best, the
"Ah, Carol" Max, whose sweet wonder made me feel I was such
a lovely surprise to him?

". . . Then they got this rule, even in peacetime. Can't strike in a foreign port. That means any bloody strike's useless before it begins. Stands to reason three-quarters of the ships're going to be in a foreign port any time . . ."

Or it might be completely different, not like Max at all. I couldn't believe after that week in New York that anyone could do anything new to me. But the intimacy of another man would be new. Different.

". . . You should hear my dad talk about the general strike back in twenty-six. He says that taught him who his mates were, who his enemies were, too."

It sticks in my mind as one of those insignificant coincidences that Lofty had just said that about enemies, meaning people like my parents, when it all began. Most of the convoy, the escort vessels, had vanished into the darkness by then, but there was still enough twilight to see the ships nearest to us as gaps in the dusk. The American tanker had caught up with us again. Its bow was level with our bridge when it exploded.

It didn't go up, bang, like a bomb. It exploded like a gas oven when you take a match to it too late. *W-o-o-f.* A bright oval of flame, billowing out, hurling heat and a shock wave of pressure at me. It seemed to light the whole sky.

The alarm bell was ringing all over the ship. It was the loudest sound I had ever heard. I had bruised my knee when I fell down. I rubbed it as I sat there on the wooden deck. My stocking was torn; there was so much light from the burning tanker that I could see the ends of the broken threads. I worked my way back to the rail and pulled myself upright. The tanker had fallen back a little, but it was still only thirty yards away. It was burning with a peculiar blue and yellow brilliance, as though that were its true function, to burn, like a flare. Two men were clinging to the forward gun. Two naval ratings. I could see their American pea jackets and their bell-bottoms. I could even see they were young. The long, tapering barrel of the gun and the two men hugging it were at the blue center of the flames. I stared at them, two brilliant figures in a miniature. It wasn't until hours later that I thought of them as men who were being burned alive.

There was another explosion. I was back on the deck, sitting up. My arms were wrapped around my shins. I thought how silly it was to be squatting there like that. Then I thought of Lofty.

He wasn't there.

The alarm bell had stopped ringing. By the time I got back to the rail, the American tanker was far astern. A whole area of sea around it was burning, too.

I saw a flash out of the side of my eye. As I turned my head to it, I heard the explosion. More of a bang this time. A ship ahead in the next line had flared up briefly, like a match head, then settled down to burn, steadily, modestly.

All my observations until then were as aloof as that. Until that moment I was a spectator. What made me understand for the first time that I was a participant was the sudden realization that I wasn't wearing my life jacket.

I had left it, as usual, under my bunk in the cabin. I felt terribly guilty; I had broken the rules. It was up to me to go and get it. Oh, shit, Laurie Sue might see me. "I told you, you were supposed —"

Another flash behind me. I saw the whiteness of my hands on the rail. My thoughts were becoming a little more coherent. I understood that another ship had been torpedoed. I hadn't thought of what was happening so explicitly before. That made three so far.

Flash. I pushed myself away from the rail and ran to the other side of the monkey island. I had missed a flash somewhere. Three ships were burning in the lines on that side. One of them had broken in the middle. Its prow and its stern stuck up clear of the water, flames trailing from them like streamers. Another American ship.

I was beginning to feel now as well as think. I felt helpless. The only certain thing in my bare, exposed world was the deck I was standing on. Any second that was going to give way. I was going to fall. I was going to fall through fire and breaking beams. I was going to plunge down into the icy water. I didn't even have my life jacket on.

The surprising thing was that I wasn't exactly frightened. That feeling of helplessness was astonishingly sexual. It reminded me of dreams I had had of being naked in public. But the sensation of being exposed was much more pointed than that. It was concentrated between my thighs. I couldn't rid myself of the conviction that a torpedo — *something,* anyway — threatened me there. Only there. There was nothing I could do except wait for it.

For some time I had been hearing a distant, rhythmic thudding. I paid attention to it now. Somewhere out in the night the escort vessels were dropping depth charges. I don't know how I guessed that from the sound. But I did. At once.

Someone was doing something, anyway.

Someone was doing something much closer to me. Below, on the boat deck, two of the seamen were hacking at the securing ropes around the lifeboat. It lurched away from the ship and hung clear on the davits out over the sea. Were they launching it? Was I supposed to go down there and climb into the lifeboat before they lowered it? Was that what the rules said for passengers to do?

I didn't move. I was afraid of making a fool of myself. At least the two seamen weren't lowering the boat yet. They had several packages wrapped in oilcloth on the deck beside them. They were picking them up, one by one, and tossing them carefully into the lifeboat.

Another seaman joined them. There was less light now: the broken ship had gone, but I recognized Lofty at once by his walk. He was carrying a duffel bag over his shoulder and had another package under his arm. He threw the duffel bag into the boat. The package he kept cradled against his chest. I could see what it was now. A whole ham. Like mine, the one I was taking to my mother. I understood why he had left me on the monkey island when the attack started. He had gone down to his cabin to fetch that ham.

Another flash. Far ahead to the right. Six. It was a tanker again. It took a long time for the sound of the explosion to reach us.

"You better eat that fucking ham, Lofty."

I didn't see which of the seamen said it, but that's what he said. It reminded me instantly of that day in Fitz's office, the Spitfire pilot. "Would he really say that, 'a piece of cake'?" Of course he would. It was the only thing you could bear to do, behave casually, make jokes.

"You men there." The captain was on the wing of the bridge below me. "You men there," he shouted down to them again. I couldn't see the captain's face. I saw Lofty's as he looked up. The hatred in it startled me. He didn't say anything.

"Get that boat hauled in," the captain shouted at him. "Get that boat hauled in before we lose it."

None of the seamen answered him. No one said "fuck you" or "jerk off." They didn't swing the boat in, either.

The captain was standing just below me, holding onto the rail. I wished I could see his face.

"If there's any damage to that boat, when we get to Liverpool, I'll dock your pay, all of you." He didn't sound angry. He was stating his position. Like the Spitfire pilot, he had escaped into a role. He was the responsible captain, defending the owners' property. He slapped his hand on the rail, affirming his decision. He would dock the seamen's pay when we got to Liverpool. Not *if* we got to Liverpool. If was unthinkable. He walked back into the wheel house.

It didn't occur to me at the time, but I had escaped into a role, too. I had become an observer again. Watching. Interested. Lofty and his mates sat down on the deck. Lofty sat under the afterdavit, the other two under the forward one. Lofty never once glanced up at the monkey island. He was still hugging his ham against his chest.

I was busy watching him; I must have missed another flash. When I walked back across the monkey island, I could see a ship in the far right lane, way behind us, palely burning. The flames lit one of the destroyers for an instant as it passed, churning up the sea like a speedboat. A little later I heard the rhythmic thudding again. It sounded very distant, miles astern.

"Woop-woop. They come through the lines in packs." I remembered the cheery petty officer in Halifax. "Woop-woop. Let off their bloody torpedoes and run like hell."

I hoped the destroyer had caught one of them. I hoped there were German sailors trapped and drowning down there under the black ocean. That's the way I felt.

There were no more flashes after that. After a while I heard the seamen moving about on the deck below. They were taking their packages out of the lifeboat. They hauled the boat in and lashed it back in place before walking away, back to their cabins with their treasures.

I stayed on the monkey island. I kept thinking about that American tanker. If it hadn't happened to be alongside, the torpedo that sank it would have hit us. We would have been the first to go. Without any warning. In the middle of a sentence. While I was thinking about being laid by Lofty.

I was standing at the rail with the boat deck below me. I just had time to drop onto my knees and get my head over the scupper before I started to vomit. I brought up everything I'd eaten for dinner, and probably for lunch, too. I went on retching and heaving long after there was nothing left in my stomach. I squatted there for several more minutes, the perspiration soaking through my underwear and chilling my neck and forehead, until I felt steady enough to get off my hands and knees and sit down. I leaned back against a stanchion and waited for the shivering to stop. There was a handkerchief in the pocket of my jacket. I scrubbed my mouth and my chin with it, then I scrunched it up and stuck it down the drain hole of the scupper. I hoped nobody would find it there.

I tried standing up, then walking a few steps, holding onto the railing. It was okay. I went down to my cabin.

Laurie Sue was lying on her side with her knees drawn up. She was wearing what I knew was her best suit under her life jacket.

"Have you been here all this time?" It seemed to me an act of extraordinary courage to have stayed enclosed in that small cabin through all those explosions.

"Catch me going out there," Laurie Sue said disdainfully. "It sounded just awful."

"We lost seven ships. At least seven."

"Serve you right if you'd drowned. I told you to wear your life jacket."

I reassured her it was all over. She didn't seem to hear me; she was staring at my face.

"My goodness, what did you do to your eyebrows?"

I went over to the mirror above the small sink. My eyebrows looked like a clown's, painted on. When I rubbed them they came off on my finger. My eyelashes were all frizzled up, too. I wondered if they'd grow back again.

"I'm just thankful I stayed here and minded my own business," Laurie Sue told me as I started to undress.

Lofty never came back to the monkey island. He didn't wave when he saw me on deck. A week later I woke to a familiar sound.

Kang-kang-kang.

I dressed quickly and left the cabin. Half a dozen seamen were sitting on wooden boxes, striking the square foot of deck in front of them with their hammers.

We had sighted the Fastnet. The mate was keeping his promise to get the rust off the afterdeck before we reached Liverpool and the owners came on board to inspect their property.

The Belgian ship got in safely, too.

Ten

What happened to your eyebrows?"

Fitz held me at arm's length, looking at them.

"It was nothing. A gas stove."

After one night in England, I'd made up my mind not to talk about the U-boat attack. Nobody wanted to listen. When I tried to tell Sylvia about it on the phone from the hotel in Liverpool, she interrupted me at once.

"Yes, I'm sure you had a terrible time. Everyone has. Now, darling, when are you coming to London?"

It was the same when I called my mother in Brighton. "Well, you have to expect that sort of thing nowadays," she said crisply the moment I mentioned the convoy. "Carol, have you picked up an American accent?"

I didn't know whether Max would have been interested or not. I couldn't get through to him at his base that first night. He was on a mission. I would have to wait another twenty-four hours before I found out how Max felt about anything. Everything.

"A gas stove?" Fitz asked.

"You know how they go *w-o-o-f.* It was my own fault. They'll grow back."

"You look swell in uniform." Fitz was still holding me by the shoulders. He wasn't looking at my singed eyebrows any longer, he was looking at my legs.

"Aren't you going to introduce me to your Judy?" A squat, florid-faced man in an American correspondent's uniform had come out of Fitz's kitchenette with a drink in his hand.

"This is Carol Clavering, Vince. I told you about her. You know Vince Campion, Carol."

"Hello." I didn't know him, but I recognized him. That fan of crinkly hair, those small, puffy eyes, had been all over American magazines since 1940. He had "stuck it out" in London during the worst of the blitz, writing "Britain can take it" pieces from his suite at the Dorchester.

"You didn't tell me she was such a piece of crumpet."

"Would you like a drink, Carol? Scotch?"

"Can you still get Scotch?"

"You can get anything if you know the right people. Stewed, screwed, and tatooed." Vince Campion drew me over to the window as Fitz went to make my drink. "This your first time in Britain?"

"No, I was at school here."

"Since the war, I mean."

"Yes."

"You'll find a lot of changes."

If Fitz had said that to me I would have questioned him about it. I was longing to talk to him about my first impressions of England after four years away. The thing that had astonished me in Liverpool, on the train, arriving at Euston and taking a taxi to the Dorchester, was how little had changed. I had no inclination to discuss it with Vince Campion.

"The whole country's worn out, on its knees. They've got nothing left but their pride. That's a bitch of a thing, pride."

"Jane Austen didn't think so."

"Screw Jane Austen." He was still holding my arm. Up close, his face had a grossness that was obtrusively carnal. I tried to pull away. "Britain today's like the South after the Civil War. They hate the Yanks just the way the South did because we're the ones with the know-how and the hardware. They think we're trying to turn Britain into an American colony."

"You still on about that, Vince?" Fitz handed me my drink. "Why don't you write it and sell it to *Collier's?*"

"*Collier's* doesn't want to know. This crumpet of yours doesn't want to know either, do you?" At least he had let go of my arm.

"It's great to have you here, Carol." Fitz raised his glass to me. "Have they fixed you up with a hotel yet?"

"Daphne, my sister, has an apartment in Earl's Court. She said I could stay with her."

"Isn't that going to be a little awkward?" Fitz was looking at me in a strange, jaunty way.

"Why?"

"Well, rather crowded?"

Did he mean because of Max? "Daphne's away a lot," I told him.

"That's good." That same jaunty look; it was like a wink. What had gotten into Fitz? He seemed different in London, and not just because of his smart uniform. He kept putting his arm around my shoulders, and when I left a few minutes later and he told me to get settled in, he'd see me in the morning, he didn't kiss my cheek in his usual brotherly way. He patted my behind.

A line of taxis stood outside the Dorchester. A huge commissionaire in a Ruritanian overcoat was wafting American officers into them, palming his tips with the lofty discretion of an ambassador receiving a note from a secretary. That hadn't changed.

I walked down toward Piccadilly. Hyde Park was full of young men and women sunning themselves in promiscuous huddles. A surprising number of people, not in uniform, were strolling along Park Lane, apparently not engaged in any work of national importance. Perhaps they were taking a well-earned day off. The men's clothes had changed more than the women's. Their lapels had narrowed, their jackets were shorter, and their trousers had lost their silly cuffs. Along Piccadilly some older Englishmen were still posh in prewar Mayfair tailoring, waistcoats, bowler hats, the lot.

There *were* reminders of what Don used to call "the bright nights of terror," great gaps in the rows of houses, but except for the absence of bulldozers they didn't look any more like wounds than the building sites in New York. Everywhere among the rubble grass was growing, weeds. Flowers. A lot of the shops and houses did look shabby, but that was the way I remembered England from the thirties, in need of a coat of paint.

Piccadilly Circus had certainly changed; this was a new world. The statue of Eros had been boarded up and around it hundreds of GIs squatted and sprawled in the May sunshine. They were all over the West End, some of them spruce and lithe with that rangy American walk, but many of them loutish in rumpled uniforms. For the last two years New York had been full of American servicemen. There they seemed vital and sure of themselves; here they looked aimless and forlorn. The pubs were closed and London couldn't absorb them the way New York did. They slouched about, bored and dispirited. It was impossible not to feel sorry for them; they seemed so poorly equipped to adjust to displacement.

I had left my luggage at the station. I decided to pick it up before meeting Sylvia at Daphne's apartment, off the bottom of the Earl's Court Road. I paid off the taxi at the entrance to the short, narrow mews and struggled up the outside stairway with my bags. Sylvia opened the door to me at once.

"Carol. Darling. What are you doing in that uniform?"

She didn't expect me to answer that. She didn't help me haul my things into the apartment, either. She just stood there, waiting for me to react to her in her pale blue knitted silk dress.

"You look absolutely wonderful, Sylvia." I meant it. She looked just as elegant and intact as I had hated her for being when I was a scruffy fourteen and she was in her first year at Cambridge.

We hugged each other. For a moment all the childhood indignities she had imposed on me as the baby of the family, all the resentment I had hurled back at her, all the differences that had grown between us out of our separate ways of competing for Daddy and Mummy's approval, and, later, struggling free from it, were as irrelevant as dreams. For a moment we were sisters and we loved each other.

"You've changed," she told me as we moved apart. "You've changed a lot, Carol."

"If you mean my eyebrows, they'll grow back."

"I don't mean your eyebrows. It isn't just that you're older, either. God, you were only eighteen when you went off, weren't you? You've really changed." She smiled at me approvingly. "Have you been having lots of lovely affairs over there?"

If I tried to answer that, there would be no end to it. I would have to explain everything that had happened to me in the last four years. I would have to explain Max.

"Is it really all right for me to stay here?"

"Daphne suggested it herself as soon as she heard you were coming. She sent me the keys." Sylvia handed them to me.

"How is she?"

"You know as much as I do."

"We've hardly written to each other the last couple of years."

"God, you've got a sort of American accent."

"Please tell me about Daphne."

"I hardly ever see her." Sylvia was moving away from me, her voice assuming the deliberate flippancy I remembered as her way of dealing with insistence, anything that bored her. "She works in one of those radar alert places, you know — or perhaps you don't. They have underground map rooms and move pins about. That's what Daphne does, somewhere miles underground in Kent. I don't think she comes up for air very often, at least not to London, and when she does that's all she can talk about, pips and scrambles and things like that, so there's no point in inviting her to dinner or anything."

I was laughing by then; Sylvia laughed with me.

"I've never even been in this flat before." She looked around at the dusty, perfunctory furniture in the living room. "It's pretty grim, isn't it? Are you sure you don't mind staying here?"

I told her it was my idea of luxury, having a place to myself instead of being in a hotel.

"I would have asked you to stay with me, but even with Nigel away I'm afraid it would be rather a squeeze for you sometimes."

"How is Nigel?"

"Being bloody-minded and self-important and diplomatic in Alexandria and having the nerve to complain to me about the food there. If you ask me, he's having a jolly good war." She opened a door and peered into the room beyond it. "My God, look at this."

I looked. The double bed was covered with a pink silk spread. One of those long-legged French dolls was propped up against the satin cushions on it. The whole room was like that, all frills and flounces and intimate lamps.

"It's like a tart's dream," Sylvia said. "What on earth do you suppose Daphne does in here?"

"How do I know?" I felt as though Daphne had caught me spying on her. But perhaps inviting me here, letting me see her bedroom, was her way of telling me she was no longer the rather prim little girl I had shared the nursery with.

I found the other bedroom and put my bags in there. Opening the Valpack on the single bed, I took out the silk stockings I had brought for Sylvia. She was still in the tart's dream, eagerly exploring it. "Look at this." She showed me a transparent black nightdress she had found in the closet. "Can you imagine little plump Daphne?"

I gave her her present.

"Oh, you are a darling." She forgot Daphne at once, opening the package and pulling the stockings over her long, slender hand. "*Six* pairs."

I hung the black nightdress back in the closet — it was rather like the one I had bought for Max's leave in New York — and steered Sylvia into the living room while she was still admiring the stockings. On a table in the corner were several half-filled bottles. "Gin, sherry, or whiskey," Sylvia announced. "Bourbon whiskey. Daphne must have an American lover. What would you like?"

"I don't think we ought to drink her liquor, do you?"

"Daphne won't mind. I'll say that for her, she was always a generous child. Don't you remember how she'd let us borrow her things? Even her lipstick."

"I never borrowed her lipstick."

"Let's have some sherry." Sylvia filled two wine glasses and handed me one. "What do you think of our father running off with a faith healer?"

"He didn't tell me she was a faith healer, exactly. He said she was a very fine woman and a wonderful support to him in his work." I was trying to remember his letter. "And there was nothing sexual between them."

"I know. He wrote and told me the same thing. I think it's disgusting."

"What?"

"All that celibacy. It's so bloody self-righteous."

"Have you seen him?"

"He's living in Bath."

"That's not so far."

Sylvia sat down on the arm of the sofa, crossing her beautiful legs and looking down into her sherry glass. I remembered that attitude: she was poising herself to deliver a judgment. "I rather think we owe it to our mother not to go and see him now that he's living with that woman." She didn't think anything of the sort; for some reason of her own, she didn't want to see her father.

"But, Sylvia" — I couldn't keep the protest out of my voice — "he must be so hurt. He must miss you so. He loved you so much. Much more than Daphne or me."

"I know." She raised her eyes and looked at me. It wasn't quite defiance I saw in her face — she was too sure of herself to feel defiant about anything — it was closer to disdain. "And don't imagine it was such glorious fun being the favorite either. He was terribly possessive. I mean, actually physically jealous of me. He always held it against Nigel, not just for taking me away from him, but for sleeping with me."

Families. Instantly I was eighteen again, still caught in that web of family emotions, love and need and guilt. I thought I had escaped it all by going to America. It made me realize I had no right to blame Sylvia; she was trying to escape it by not going to Bath.

"How does Mother feel about it?" I asked.

"Humiliated and furious and terribly relieved."

"Sylvia." I was trying not to laugh.

"She'd been bored stiff with him for years. Always having to play up to him. Now she can have her own friends and say what she likes. She can hate the Labour party and wogs and Jews without having Father make her feel she shouldn't."

"She never hated the Jews." But I knew what Sylvia meant. In that complicated English way, Mother had certainly never believed they were quite "our kind." God, it was awful being back in England in some ways. Suddenly I longed to see Fitz, to sit down and talk it all out with him.

Sylvia finished her sherry. "I've got to run. Can you come to dinner tomorrow evening?"

"I'd love to. Unless I have to work." I meant, unless I can be with Max.

"Call me in the morning."

At the door we hugged each other again.

"It's so wonderful to see you, Sylvia." And again it was true. I loved her.

As I walked back into the living room, I could still feel her presence, her scent, the cool softness of her cheek. They were replaced immediately by a sharp anxiety when I looked at my watch.

Max.

The operator at his base had told me I could reach Sergeant Ludlow in the NCOs' canteen any time after six this evening. It was 6:12 now. In a few minutes I would know how Max felt about me. One way or the other. I gulped down the rest of my sherry before I called.

The phone was in Daphne's bedroom. After I got through to the base, there was a whole series of men's voices, then someone calling, "Max, phone, Max." After that, a long wait and the sound of a piano and men singing.

"Fuck 'em all. Fuck 'em all. The long and the short and the tall," they sang.

"Hello."

"Max?"

"Carol." There was a pause. "Carol, where are you?"

"In London. I just got here today."

"When can I see you?"

"Whenever you say."

"Tomorrow. I can get off tomorrow. I don't have another mission till Friday. I had one last night. Where will you be?"

"I'm staying in Earl's Court." I gave him the address. "I'll be home by six. Can you meet me there?"

Another long pause. I could still here those men's voices. "There's a Lancaster leaving the Ruhr," they sang.

"Max," I said. "What the matter? Max?"

"Of course I'll meet you there. Oh, shit, some bastard's waiting to use the phone. I'll see you tomorrow, Carol."

He hung up and I was alone with the pink silk spread and the French doll. I shifted the doll and leaned back against the satin cushions. The tart's dream of a room, with its blatant, tacky eroticism, seemed to be jeering at me. When I had first seen it with Sylvia and she had shown me Daphne's nightdress, I had instantly

imagined Max and me together on this bed. "Get up them stairs."
He had sounded so far away on the phone, so private and controlled.
But he *had* sounded glad to hear from me. He had.

Or had he just sounded relieved? He had been bracing himself
for my arrival, the inevitable, painful confrontation. "I met her
last year, Carol. She's in the Wrens." No, surely he would have
written me about her. Wouldn't he? "I didn't want to write you.
It seemed so cold. A letter."

No. He hadn't sounded like that. He had sounded, okay, not
exactly excited. But . . .

I couldn't stand the tart's dream any longer. I went back into
the living room, closing the door firmly behind me before I poured
myself a long sherry. Another twenty-four hours to get through
before I knew. One way or the other.

At least I would be busy all day tomorrow. Thank God for Fitz.
Dear, kind Fitz. I could tell him about it. He would listen to me.
It would make me feel better, just talking to him about Max.

It didn't work out quite like that.

"I hope you're free tonight, Carol" was the first thing he said
to me after I'd taken off my cap and sat down.

"I was going to see Max."

"That sergeant in the air force?" Fitz sounded not only surprised
but annoyed.

"Yes."

"Is he stationed over here now?"

"In Suffolk."

"Why didn't you tell me?"

"I did."

Fitz shook his head.

"There's no reason you should remember. But I did tell you
Max was in England. I told you that night in your apartment,
New Year's Eve, when you first mentioned my coming —"

"Never mind all that." Fitz turned brusquely away from me.
"The point is he's here." He stood by the window, looking out
over the park.

"Are you still in love with that — that young man?"

"Yes." Yes, yes, yes.

He was still staring out the window. He had been so obviously relieved the last time I had told him I was in love with Max. He didn't look relieved now. When he turned and faced me, I could see the anger in his eyes.

"I was hoping we could spend as much time as possible together while you're over here, Carol." Although he was smiling, the anger was still there. "It doesn't matter about this evening. The Free Poles are giving a party and I hoped you could come with me."

"I'm sorry. I should have asked you before making —"

"I told you, it doesn't matter." Fitz took out a cigarette and put it in his mouth. "It'll probably be a terrible party anyway. All the usual Americans. Vince Campion and the rest of those second-front warriors." He lit his cigarette with a Zippo lighter I had never seen him use before. "I won't be sorry to miss it."

"Can't you go without me?"

Fitz didn't answer. He opened a drawer and pulled out some papers. "Just don't make any more dates without letting me know first."

"I won't. I'm sorry."

"And don't say you're sorry. You're not sorry. You're dying to see that sergeant of yours and I can't say I blame you."

It was better after that; we managed to recapture some of the easy, working companionship we had shared for so long. Fitz dictated several letters, then gave me a long handwritten report on the projected radio news coverage of the second front he had prepared for Elmer Davis.

"Is there any chance of a second front this year?" I asked him.

"Not if Churchill has anything to do with it. He wants to go into the Balkans. 'The soft underbelly,' he keeps calling them."

"How do you feel about it?"

Fitz shrugged and picked up his cap from the table. "Can you get that report typed before your date?"

"Of course."

"Okay. I've got an appointment. Just leave it for me with the letters and I'll see you tomorrow." He put on his cap. It made him look younger and very impressive.

"You asked about the second front, Carol. I think if we try to cross the channel and get thrown back, it could lengthen the war by several years." He started for the door and then paused and smiled at me. "But don't tell Vince Campion I said so. Vince and his buddies think that's sissy talk."

Working on Fitz's portable, I had everything finished by four o'clock. I went over the report carefully, collating and correcting the pages. It was still only 4:30 when I left the hotel. The London buses were faster than they had been before the war; there was less private traffic. If I went straight home, I'd have an hour to wait for Max. I decided to walk through the park to Knightsbridge and take the bus from there. It was 5:10 when I reached Harrods. I thought of walking on along the Old Brompton Road.

Then I realized what I was doing. I was afraid Max was already there; I would find him waiting in the mews outside the apartment. I was scared of seeing him. I didn't want to hear what he might have to tell me.

I took the bus from Harrods. He wasn't waiting in the mews. I climbed the outside stairs and let myself in. The phone was ringing as I opened the door.

Oh, God, he had changed his mind; he wasn't coming. I ran into the bedroom and snatched up the phone.

"Hello, Max?"

"Carol. Darling. At last." It was Sylvia.

"Oh, Sylvia, I'm sorry. I promised to call you, didn't I?" I'd been sitting next to a phone at the Dorchester all day.

"It's just that I have to know. Are you coming to dinner or aren't you?"

I began to explain, this man in the Canadian air force, I'd known him for years, and I hadn't seen him . . .

Sylvia's annoyance softened at once. "You mean it's someone you fancy, darling?"

"Yes." God, yes.

She thought that over for a second. "Is he an officer?"

"No, he's a sergeant. He's a gunner on a bombing plane."

She thought that over, too. "Well, I suppose it's all right if he's a Canadian. I mean it's different somehow if they're not English. I met a marvelous Free Dutchman the other day and he isn't even a corporal. So why don't you bring him?"

Maybe. It depended. If Max had fallen in love with someone else, it might be the only way I could bear to get through the rest of the evening together. Being with other people.

"I'll have to see. He isn't here yet. I'll have to ask him. I'll call you as soon as I can."

"That's what you said —"

"I promise."

"You promised yesterday."

"Stick a needle in my eye." The old oath popped up out of our childhood. Sylvia accepted its solemn finality at once.

I went back into the living room. I wanted a drink. I stopped halfway to the table in the corner. A man was standing at the top of the outside stairs; I could see his shoulder and part of his arm through the window. He was leaning against the door.

It might be someone looking for Daphne. I turned the light on; if he saw it wasn't Daphne in the apartment, maybe he would go away. I waited a minute. He didn't move. I went to the front door and opened it. The man stumbled, half falling into the living room.

"Max."

He straightened, holding out his hands to me.

"Are you all right, Max?" Oh, God, he was drunk.

"Yes, it's okay. I'm fine."

He wasn't drunk. His hands were still stiffly raised toward me. I went to him. Please let him kiss me. Please let him fondle my behind. His arms remained rigidly around my shoulders.

We stood there, neither of us saying anything, until I stepped back.

"How long have you been out there? Why didn't you ring the bell?"

Why was he behaving like this? Why was he so tense and awkward with me? Because he had something difficult to tell me? Something he knew was going to hurt? I glanced at him quickly, trying to discover if that was it. He looked terrible, tired and much thinner, and his uniform was all rumpled and needed cleaning.

"I don't know. I saw you get off the bus and come up here and I was going to call out to you and suddenly I got scared."

"Oh." It *was* that. I realized I was still wearing my cap; I took it off. "It's been such a long time, hasn't it?"

"Yes, it has." Max took his cap off, too. We stood there six feet apart, like two duelists. "It's been almost three years. You look wonderful, Carol. When I saw you get off the bus, I thought how wonderful you looked."

"There's nothing like a sea voyage. All that fresh salt air." God, I was talking like Sylvia, being flippant. "Come and sit down, Max." I moved toward the unlit gas fire around which Daphne had arranged her more comfortable furniture. As Max followed me, I noticed how wearily he moved. He slumped down onto the sofa; after a moment's hesitation, I sat beside him. He reached out instantly and took my hand.

"It's incredible. I never thought I'd see you again, Carol."

"Why not? I wrote you — I wrote you months ago I was hoping to get sent over."

"I know." He fumbled a cigarette out of his jacket pocket. "You still don't smoke?"

"No."

"God, you look beautiful."

It was all right. Oh, thank you. Thank you. There wasn't anyone else. I knew that now. Whatever was making him so tense with me, it had nothing to do with another girl.

"I guess I look awful, Carol."

"No."

Now that I was close to him I could see how lifeless his skin was. That dear, familiar face: the angular chin, the slightly arched nose, the gaunt cheekbones; they might have been carved out of cold clay.

"You do look tired, but —"

"Tired?" He smiled for the first time since he had come in; at least, his lips turned up at the corners. I expected him to say something more; he didn't.

"What's wrong, Max. What is it? Please tell me."

"Nothing. There's nothing. I'm fine."

"Is there anything you'd like to do?" I pressed his hand. "Oh." I remembered Sylvia. "My sister asked me if we'd go to dinner there tonight. We don't have to . . ."

"Where?"

"She lives in St. John's Wood. I said I'd call her and let her know."

"Will there be other people there?"

"I expect so."

"I look so bloody awful." He managed that perfunctory smile

again. "It's all right at the base. Everybody looks terrible at the base. But I don't know about other people. We don't have much to do with people off the base."

I was already on my feet. "I'll tell her we can't make it." I went into Daphne's bedroom, leaving the door open behind me. I sat on the bed and called Sylvia.

She was surprisingly agreeable. "Darling, I know exactly how you feel. Everybody seems to be the same these days. Nobody wants to *talk* anymore. I don't blame them, but you've only been here a day, and you do seem to have caught it awfully quickly."

"Caught what?"

"Sweets, it's become an absolute national epidemic. My Dutchman says people are even doing it on buses. And what goes on in those bomb shelters. Every time I pass one, I expect to be turned into a pillar of salt."

"What are you talking about?"

"Some of my friends go wandering around Hampstead Heath in their mackintoshes. I suppose you call them raincoats. It's like a recognition signal. As soon as they see someone else in a mac, they go off into the bushes together. They call it macking, and you wouldn't believe —"

"What?"

She said she had to run. Her Dutchman had arrived. I hung up.

Max was standing in the doorway.

My wishful fantasies of the day before, imagining Max's response to the pink silk spread, the satin cushions — he didn't appear to notice them as he walked heavily forward and sat on the bed beside me. He put his arm stiffly around my shoulders. I moved the doll and lay back against the cushions. Max's arm fell across my breast; he didn't try to slip his hand inside my uniform. He didn't say anything. His face was pressed against my neck.

He was crying.

I held him for a long time; he was as passive as an exhausted child. Then I made him sit up and look at me. I took his hands. "You've got to tell me what it is, Max."

"I don't know if I can. Even at the base, if we do talk about it, we never say what we mean — we pretend. If someone doesn't come back from a mission and some bloody fool . . . if someone asks where he is" — that meaningless smile again; it was like a tic — "we say he's gone for a Burton."

"What's a Burton?"

"It's a beer. It's a kind of beer."

"Oh, God."

I was back on that monkey island: "You'd better eat that fucking ham, Lofty."

"Go on," I told Max.

"It's the odds. You don't think about it at first. But every time you go out the odds get worse. You've got less chance of coming back. I've done twenty-eight now. You're supposed to be able to stop at thirty, but like goddamn fools most of us signed on for sixty. So I did too."

"*Sixty* missions?"

Max nodded. "Only about one guy in ten ever even finishes thirty. And it's getting worse all the time. Jerry's got night fighters now. They come up underneath you. You can't even see them from the *rear* turret of a Lancaster, and where I am on top . . . They can fire straight up at us. All they have to do is get out of the way when we blow up."

He stopped while he lit a cigarette and found an ashtray. When he came back to the bed, he sat facing me again.

"They keep telling us we've got a better and better chance all the time. We're experienced crews and experienced crews . . ." He shook his head. "It's a bloody lie. Anybody can see it's a bloody lie. As a matter of fact, it's just the opposite. The new crews are given easier missions. And when you've done about twenty, you *know* — you just know, Carol — you just know the next time or the time after that . . ." He turned his face away from me. "I'm sorry. I can't explain how you begin to feel. You can't understand unless you're in it."

I thought I could understand. A little. At least I could remember that terrible feeling of helplessness during the U-boat attack. But that had only been once. And it had only lasted a few minutes. Max was going through it hour after hour. Time after time. Twenty-eight times so far. Thirty-two more to go.

"Oh, Max."

"I'm sorry." He was facing me again, that tic of a smile at the corners of his mouth.

"Can't you get out of it, Max? Can't they see you're not you can't go on?"

"It's almost impossible to get grounded. A friend of mine, he'd done forty-six. Forty-six. He tried to bail out over Stuttgart. Get taken prisoner. Except he couldn't get out through the goddamn escape hatch. You can't — even when the plane's all right. You'd have to be a fucking Houdini if it was on fire. They transferred him, finally. Do you know what for? Lack of moral fiber. That's what it says on your record. Lack of moral fiber. It means you're a coward."

"It's better than being killed."

"I don't know." He put out his cigarette. "There are all the other guys. You feel you ought to stick with them."

"Would you like a drink, darling?"

"Have you got any beer?"

"No. But there's bourbon. And gin."

He shook his head. "I don't want any liquor. It gives me a hangover. And I can't — I can't take hangovers anymore. I get the shakes so badly, I can't control myself." He put the ashtray on the floor. "Can I — can we just . . . It's so incredible to have you here."

I pulled him down onto the bed. He lay against me, one arm locked around my back.

I touched his damp, cold cheek. "Would you like me to take my uniform off?"

He didn't answer. I started to unbutton my jacket. He stopped me. "I don't know, Carol." He was hiding his face against my neck again. "They give us a lot of Benzedrine. It sort of peps you up for a while, but it doesn't . . . It's no good for sex."

"It doesn't matter. We could just lie in bed."

I kept my slip and panties on. Max took off his jacket and tie. We lay under the silk spread together. I held him quietly; I didn't want him to feel I expected anything of him. After a while he kissed me and stroked my hip, then slipped his hand inside my panties. I raised myself slightly to take them off.

"Don't, please. It's useless. I'm no use, Carol."

After that we lay there side by side, holding hands. And we talked.

We talked until the long May twilight began to fade. About ten o'clock we got dressed and went out and found a pub that had some stale cheese sandwiches. Max drank two pints of beer. He said it helped him sleep.

It seemed to work. He woke me several times in the night, clutching at me, but each time I managed to soothe him back to stillness before he came fully awake. He had to go back to his base in the morning. We left the apartment together; I waited with him at his bus stop.

"When can you get leave again, Max?"

"Do you really want — I mean — last night."

I grabbed him by the shoulders and shook him.

"Now, you listen to me. I want to see you every moment I can. I want to be with you all the time. And don't you ever say anything like that again."

"After Friday night — I mean, I can probably get the whole weekend after my next mission if I, I mean, if I . . ."

He was trying to say, if he was still alive.

"Why don't you come straight to the apartment as soon as you get back," I told him quickly. "What time can you be there?"

"They have to debrief us. But I can be there by ten. Probably before ten."

His bus was waiting. I kissed him and watched him file on board. He was standing on the rear platform as it ground away. Suddenly he straightened and smiled at me. For a moment he was the old confident Max again. I watched him until he was out of sight.

Fitz was holding the report I'd typed when he opened the door of his suite. I sat down while he finished reading it.

"You've done a perfect job, as usual, Carol. What did you think of it?"

"It's clear and it's honest. It is important to give people at home an eyewitness report of the landings. But tanks are more important than broadcasting vans. I'm glad you said so."

"Good." Fitz smiled at me. "How's your sergeant?"

I wasn't sure how to answer that. He's terrified? He's on the verge of cracking up? I love him more than I thought I could ever love anybody?

"What do you know about Bomber Command, Fitz?"

"Victory through air power."

"Do you believe that?"

"Not altogether."

"It's a lot of deliberate, bloody lies."

"Is that what your sergeant says?"

"Their bombing patterns are hopeless. More than half the time they can't get within miles of the target. So Command just fakes the photographs. They turn in bomb plots that show a five-mile circle and palm them off as three-mile pictures. And if anybody at the War Office questions what they're doing, they talk about the effectiveness of area bombing. Do you know what that means, area bombing? It means it doesn't matter who you kill, hospital patients, refugees, anybody, just so long as you bomb something. And those new planes, those Lancasters — the gun turrets are in the wrong place. The German night fighters come up underneath and they can't even see them, let alone shoot at them. They'd be better off if they didn't have any gun turrets at all. They could fly a lot faster and get away. And everybody in the squadrons knows that and nobody at Command will listen to them. And the escape hatches on those Lancasters —"

I stopped because I didn't want to cry in front of Fitz. It wasn't his fault.

He didn't say anything; I wished I smoked.

"I've already heard a lot of that from our people over here," Fitz admitted presently. "But it's not exactly the kind of thing we can broadcast, is it?"

"Is it as bad in the American air force?"

"Some of it. We're making daylight raids, so our bombing's probably a little more accurate and a lot of our guys do manage to bail out if their planes get hit. But our losses over Germany — I've seen some of the figures. I mean, the real figures, not the ones we publish."

"And it's all absolutely useless, isn't it?"

"How?"

"Max says he knows, the way they send them back over the

same German cities again and again, they're not doing a thing to stop German industry. The factories and the freight yards just start up again the next day."

"He's probably right."

"Then why don't they stop it?"

Fitz thought about that before answering. "War's like anything else, Carol. Making automobiles, running any kind of business. Once you start to do something, make any decision, a lot of people's careers are riding on it. By the time you see the whole program's a mistake, it's too late. There are too many other guys' ambitions involved. Those guys will fight you any way they can. They'll fake figures, tell lies about you, anything to advance their own careers. That's always been true. It was probably true when they were building the Parthenon. You can't expect war to be any different."

"It is different. People don't get killed running a business."

"Don't they?" Fitz smiled. "They get ground down. I'll tell you that."

The phone was ringing; Fitz answered it. Vince Campion's voice was so loud I couldn't help hearing everything he said. He wanted to know why Fitz had missed the bash last night. The Free Poles were a great bunch of guys. They had real balls, those Poles. A lot of them were getting together in Campion's suite that evening. "And bring that tight-assed little crumpet of yours with you, Fitz."

Fitz said he'd try.

"It's okay," I told him when he'd hung up. "I'll go with you, if you want me to."

"I don't *want* to go." I was startled by the pained resentment in Fitz's eyes. It reminded me of Max the evening before when he'd told me about that sentence, lack of moral fiber. "But I'm afraid we have to, Carol."

"Why?" I couldn't see why he had to do anything for Vince Campion.

"Vince is trying to get the network to take him on."

"God, you're not going to let them, are you?"

"Not if I can help it. But he's flying to New York next month and he's got a lot of pull with Bill. His old-buddy circle includes several of the major stockholders."

"He'd be ghastly on the air. Worse than Don. He'd make the war sound like a football game."

"I know." Fitz opened his briefcase. "Let's get to work, Carol. I've got a stack of letters to answer."

There were over twenty people in Campion's suite by the time Fitz and I got there at six. I saw them as I always saw people at a party when I first arrived, the way I saw clouds when I was going sailing and was trying to guess what the weather would be like. This group put me on my guard at once. I stayed close to Fitz, hugging the lee shore, as we made our way to the bar.

Only four other women were there, two ATS, a Wren, and a tall girl in a frilly dress who looked, at the most, eighteen. All of them were surrounded by men who were giving them the eager attention of their hands while ignoring everything they said. Two British naval officers were having a private conversation by the mantlepiece. A Free French captain was sitting on the window seat, alone, watching everything with amused tolerance as only the French can.

Fitz handed me my drink. "Let's go over and talk to the French captain," I suggested.

It was too late. Vince Campion had his arm around my waist. "You win, Fitz," he said. "No bloody second front this year. We're going to play it the way that pansy flit Montgomery calls the shots. Sicily next."

"Where did you get that?"

"Sources." Campion's hand moved down over my hip to my behind, groping between my buttocks. I pulled away from him and walked over and sat down beside the French captain.

"Mademoiselle," he welcomed me.

"Do you speak English, Captain?"

"Un tout petit peu."

"Well, it doesn't matter. I just want to sit here to guard my rear."

"Votre rire?"

"Mon derrière."

"Vous parlez francais?"

"Un tout petit peu."

I would have been happy to leave it at that, to sit there without saying another word. The French captain wanted to talk. He had a lot on his mind. He told me at length and in sardonic detail how stupid we were being about de Gaulle, the lunacy of our involvement with Giraud and our toadying to Vichy pigs like Darlan. If we ever did open a second front, which he doubted, we would soon find out how much we needed de Gaulle. De Gaulle was the only man who could keep France together and lead her away from the Communists, and we were doing everything we could to make an enemy of him.

I don't think he expected me to understand his rapid, invective French; he was talking to himself, letting his anger out. I didn't tell him Daphne and I had always spoken French together until I was twelve; it was easier than English. I nodded and looked sympathetic, lapping it all up and feeling like Mata Hari.

My captain had only recently joined the de Gaulle forces, contacting them when the Americans landed in Algiers. Before that, he had been in the underground and he knew a great deal about present conditions in France, the political shadings of the various resistance groups. *"C'est imbécile,"* he kept saying. One could not imagine how *imbécile* it was, the way we were treating de Gaulle.

I nodded sympathetically again and then suddenly looked up. Fitz was standing over us.

"Fitz." I was glad to see him. "This is Captain —"

"Are you ready to go, Carol?"

"Already?"

I looked around the room. The girl in the frilly dress had passed out on the sofa. One of the ATS was slapping her face. In the open doorway to the bedroom, the Wren was struggling with two Free Poles. She wasn't struggling very hard. The second ATS was sitting on the floor with Vince Campion; he had her jacket and skirt off and was working on her bra. The two British naval officers had vanished. It did seem to be time to leave.

The French captain left with us. I tried again to introduce him to Fitz in the elevator.

"Never mind, Carol." Fitz ignored him.

Outside the hotel he pushed me into a taxi and got in beside me.

"Where do you want to go, Carol?"

"Wherever you like."

"Give the driver your address."

After that, Fitz was silent until we reached Knightsbridge; he was sitting back in his corner with his hand over his eyes.

"Please don't ever do that again, Carol."

"What? What have I done? What's the matter?" I felt so innocent it made me indignant.

"You were sitting flirting with that Frenchman for almost two hours."

"I wasn't flirting."

"You were practically sitting on his lap."

"He was giving me a lecture about de Gaulle."

"It's the way it looks." Fitz lowered his hand. I was shocked by the unhappiness in his eyes, confused by it, too. I couldn't understand what was going on.

"I'm sorry," I said lamely. "I'm sorry, I was just trying to get away from Vince Campion. He's always touching me, feeling my bottom."

"Don't you like to be touched?" It struck me how objectively and yet sadly Fitz asked that.

"Not by Vince Campion."

"Of course. You've got that sergeant of yours, haven't you?" Fitz leaned back again, looking out the window until we stopped at the entrance to the mews.

"Would you like to come up?" I hoped he would. I wanted to talk about the friction between us, whatever was causing it.

"I'd better get back before the blackout."

"It'll be light for hours yet."

"You go home, Carol." He obviously didn't want to talk to me; he didn't even want to look at me.

I got out of the cab. "What time do you want me in the morning?"

"Why don't you take the day off?"

I closed the door. The cab turned around and went back toward the West End. I climbed the stairs and let myself into the apartment. It was still light in the living room. I threw my cap on the table and was going to stretch out on the sofa when I heard a sound from the bedroom.

"Daphne?" I went over and tapped on the door. "Daphne?"

"Don't come in." It was a scream of panic.

I went back and sat on the sofa with a glass of sherry, feeling like an intruder and trying not to listen to my sister's ecstatic cries through the thin door. Halfway into my second sherry, I had a relieving fit of giggles. "It's an absolute national epidemic." I remembered Sylvia's ironic, amused voice. "My Dutchman says they're even doing it on buses." Everybody in England was getting laid every minute. Everybody except me.

I was thinking of having a third sherry when the bedroom door opened. Although that was what I'd been waiting for for almost an hour, I jumped up, startled.

"Hello, Carol."

"Hello, Daphne."

There were only eighteen months between us. We had splashed together in the bath, fought over dolls, shared slightly shocked information about the facts of life, neither of us quite believing that Daddy and Mummy did "that," and both of us indignantly certain that *we* never would, anyway. Now here we were. Both grown-up. Women. We were stiffly shy with each other.

"I'm afraid I've been drinking your sherry."

"That's all right. I left it for you. When did you get in?"

"Three days ago. Four. Three or four."

"Did you fly?"

"No, I came by ship. It's awfully nice of you to let me stay here."

We were searching each other with our eyes, seeking the changed and the familiar. Daphne had always been the odd one out, physically, dark while Sylvia and I were fair, small and plump while we were tall and thin. She looked sweetly buxom in her navy uniform. Good God, she was an officer, a first lieutenant.

"Ullo." A soldier had come out of the bedroom, buttoning his khaki blouse. "I 'speck you're Daph's sister."

"Carol, this is Pat."

"I'm glad to know you, Pat."

"Ow are you, then?"

We shook hands. I couldn't help staring at him. I'm not sure what I'd expected Daphne's lover to be like, some hearty Old School Tie, RAF type, perhaps. Pat was awkwardly thin, with a hard, bony face and pale eyes that were never still.

"In the Yank army, are you, Carol?" He was certainly not Old

School Tie. He had what my mother called an accent you could cut with a knife.

"Yes, in a way. Yes, I am."

"Good pay and all you get, don't you?" His pupils kept darting about like the steel balls in one of those puzzles you have to shake to get them into the right holes.

"Yes, I suppose we do."

"Better than us limeys, eh?"

"I'm really sort of a limey myself, aren't I, Daphne?" I was trying hard to sound cordial, to show her I wasn't a class-conscious little snob, that I'd outgrown all that in my four years in America.

"Well, you've been over there all through the war, haven't you?" Daphne reminded me.

"Lucky you," Pat told me. "What they got you doing in the army, then?"

"I'm not really in the army. I'm just a sort of secretary."

"Lucky you," Pat told me again. "This army lark's no bloody good. All shit and shine and standing in fucking line. Unless you're an officer, of course, that is." He looked at Daphne for the first time since he had come out of the bedroom. I saw a brief, furtive arrogance in his darting eyes. I could imagine him taking it out on Daphne in bed because she was an officer.

"You'd better start, Pat. You'll miss the last bus." Daphne was looking at him the way as a child she had looked at pictures of the royal family.

"Oh, yeh, well, ta, then." He put his cap on and turned and saluted her, snapping his hand down with mock respect. She laughed and walked with him to the door. I sat down with my back to them as they stood whispering together. "Next week," I heard Pat say, and then the sound of a slap and a pleased giggle from Daphne.

She was flushed and smiling when she came back to me. She poured herself some gin before sitting down.

"He seems very nice," I said quickly. "I can see why you like him."

"Mother would have a fit, wouldn't she?"

"She'd have a fit if she met my young man, too."

There was no way Daphne and I could recover our past intimacy; it had been based too precariously on childhood and innocence.

But at least we had that in common, we both had lovers our family would never approve of.

I started to tell her about Max. "I've got a sergeant —"

"He's as common as dirt. I can hear Mother saying it."

She didn't want to hear about Max. She wanted to talk about herself, to make me understand and respect the person she had become in the past four years. "That's why I like him. They're the only honest people left in England, people of that class. They hate Churchill. They think the whole war's a swindle. But they're not going to go on being swindled after the war's over. They've made up their minds. They're going to take over the country." She went on about that, what Labour was going to do when they got rid of Churchill and his lot.

I listened to her with surprised approval. It was what I had been vaguely searching for ever since I'd landed, that other England that had intrigued me so much on the monkey island. Lofty's England. Now here was my sister passionately defending it.

"Coming over on the ship —" I started to tell her excitedly.

But she didn't want to hear about that either. "Have you seen Father yet?" she asked.

"I haven't seen either of them."

"Sylvia's been rotten to him. I wish you'd talk to her about it. She won't even answer his letters."

"Why don't you —"

"Sylvia and I were never really friends. It was always you two. And I can't talk to her at all now. She doesn't seem to care about anything except sleeping with officers. Are you going down to Brighton to see Mother?"

"I thought I'd go tomorrow. I've got the day off."

"Don't say anything to her about Father. She gets wild if you even mention his name." Daphne finished her gin and stood up. "I've got to go back to the base."

"Tonight?"

"I'm on duty in the morning."

I went with her to the door.

"Please go down and see Father. It would mean so much to him." With her round face and her frown and her black hair still cut in bangs across her forehead, she was at that moment the little

Daphne I remembered, earnest and affectionate and naive. "It's awful for him to think his own children don't care about him."

And then she put on her cap with the silver Coastal Command badge and she was once again someone I hardly knew. I wondered if she had polished that badge herself or whether as an officer she had someone to do it for her.

"I will, Daphne. I promise I'll go down to Bath as soon as I can."

"And when you see Mother tomorrow, give her my love."

"I will."

It was disconcerting, arriving at Brighton station the next day. After our wandering life in Europe, my family had settled in Brighton when I was twelve. Brighton was the place where I had lived longest in my life. The same number seven bus still ran from the station to the top of our street in Kemptown. Daphne and I had scrambled to its upper deck to go to Woolworth's and the cinema; later I had taken it every day to that dumb commercial art college I had used as an excuse for leaving school. When I climbed to the top of it now, I could almost feel myself sitting there in the front seat, thin and leggy and restive, with my drawing things on my lap. Every street, every building, affected me like that. Past and present were overlaid in my mind like a silk-screen process, coloring every impression.

The tall, bow-windowed Regency house in Eaton Place needed painting, but the brass knocker on the door was as brightly polished as I remembered it. My mother came to the door herself. We kissed each other's cheeks in the dark hallway and she led me up the stairs to the living room. It wasn't until we were there among the familiar, slipcovered furniture that I was able to see her clearly.

I didn't know whether she had aged and changed much in four years, because instantly in that unchanged room she was the sum of every memory I had of her. She was simply, overwhelmingly, my mother.

"Have you had your eyebrows plucked, Carol?" That assured, slightly critical, English voice. "Is that an American uniform you're wearing?"

I gave her the ham I had brought across the Atlantic for her.

"That's lovely." Putting it aside at once, she tapped one of her cork-tipped cigarettes on the back of her hand before lighting it. "I suppose they don't have rationing in America."

"Some things."

"I must say I'm glad we don't have any American soldiers in Brighton. The Canadians are bad enough."

Four years ago I would have flared up at that. Now it struck me as only a quaint eccentricity. It made me smile.

I had come struggling out of this woman, red and shriveled and helpless, twenty-two years ago in a hospital in St. Louis. She had cared for me physically, fed and clothed me, seen that my teeth were straight, my bones strong, and my lungs sound. She had succeeded admirably in all that; I had every reason to be grateful to her. At the same time, she had tried for eighteen years to make me see the world, people, God, exactly as she saw them. In that she had failed hopelessly. I did not know why. The unpredictability of natural selection? Some strength of character inherited from her? It didn't matter; the important thing was that she *had* failed. I could listen to her most outrageous prejudices now with an easy tolerance that proved her failure. Nothing she said could any longer affect my independence.

"I do hope now you're home again, Carol, that you will try to lose that accent you picked up in America."

We had lunch in the dining room downstairs. An elderly servant waited on us. I was introduced to her. "This is my *youngest* daughter, Mrs. Bignal." Three elderly ladies ate with us. My mother had explained to me that they were paying guests. "I don't know how I'd manage without their ration stamps." Their presence seemed to mellow her attitude toward me a little.

"Carol knows Edward Murrow," she told them. "Carol's got a very good job in New York." "Carol was sent over to London specially by the American wireless people she works for." "Carol's brought me the most lovely ham."

They all seemed cheered by that last announcement.

She even found a good word to say for America. "That President Roosevelt, or however you pronounce it. I must say he does seem like a very decent man."

"Yes."

"He's not really Jewish, is he, Carol?"

"No."

She went up to her room for a nap after lunch. I walked down to the sea front and along the Marine Parade. Gun emplacements and barbed wire instead of people in swimsuits littered the beach below. I thought about Max. His mission that night. Please, don't let anything happen to him, please. Let him come to the apartment at ten o'clock tomorrow morning. Please, let me spend the weekend with him, please.

My mother and I had tea alone in the living room.

"Have you seen Sylvia in London yet?"

I told her I had.

"And Daphne?"

"Yes, last night. She sent you her love."

"Daphne's doing awfully well. She's a first lieutenant. The next thing above that in the navy is a commander."

"It's wonderful," I agreed. I remembered Daphne's ecstatic cries. "She certainly sounded very happy last night. She seems to be having a good time."

"I wish Sylvia was happier."

"Why? What's wrong?" It was almost the first thing she had said that had aroused my full attention. "Is there anything wrong with Sylvia?"

"It's not much fun for her with Nigel away in Alexandria. I asked her to come and stay with me down here. But she's got some sort of war work she has to do in London."

"Yes, I know. She's taking care of the Free Dutch."

"This beastly war. Still, we've all got to do our best to back him up, haven't we?"

"Who?" I must have missed something; was she still talking about Nigel?

"Winston."

"Oh."

"We should all thank God for that man, Carol. A fine mess we'd be in without him."

I waited. Did she mean we might be an occupied country?

"He's the only one who knows how to stand up to the Labour party."

After tea I said I had to go back to London. We kissed again in the downstairs hall.

"Thank you," I told her. "Thank you for everything." I meant my good teeth, my sound bones and lungs, whatever strength of character I might have inherited from her that had made it possible for me to break away from everything she stood for.

"Thank *you,* darling, for the lovely ham."

I caught the number seven bus at the top of the street. As I climbed to the upper deck, I no longer felt myself sitting there, seventeen and scuff-kneed and angrily rebellious. The past seemed to have less hold on me than it had a few hours earlier.

I was only just back in the apartment, putting away the food I had bought for the weekend, when the phone rang. I looked at my watch. Half past eight. It was all right, it couldn't be anything terrible, Max wouldn't be taking off until ten. I went into Daphne's bedroom and answered it.

"Carol?" It was Fitz. "Where have you been? What are you doing?"

I told him I had been to see my mother in Brighton; I wasn't doing anything much. He was at a party at the Connaught; he wanted me to join him there. I said I'd take a taxi.

The suites at the Connaught were bigger and darker and the furniture was shabbier than in the suites at the Dorchester. Apart from that, it might have been the same party: two ATS and a Wren, a girl in a frilly dress, and a crowd of not-so-young men in various uniforms. I wasn't sure if they were *all* the same people — the girl in the frilly dress looked plainer and shorter than I remembered her — but they were all behaving in exactly the same way. The women were there to be handled but not listened to; the men were there to fight the war at the top of their voices. This time there was no French captain to sit with to protect my rear. I got three wet kisses, two slaps, and a tickle before I found Fitz. He gave me a dry peck on the cheek and kept his arm around my shoulders while we pretended to listen to an American colonel explain why the British were shit scared of the second front.

I had two drinks rather quickly and thought about Max. Where would he be going? Stuttgart? Frankfurt? Cologne? Please, don't let it be Berlin, please. Berlin was the worst; it was the longest flight and the night fighters were thickest there. Please, let it be an easy mission, a piece of cake, please.

Someone was feeling my behind. It wasn't Fitz; he still had his arm around my shoulders.

"Come and dance," Vince Campion said.

For the first time I noticed the upright piano in the alcove. An American navy commander was sitting at it. I looked at Fitz. Do I have to?

"Go ahead, Carol."

The commander was playing "The White Cliffs of Dover." I had always loathed that song. It was hell to dance to, too, especially with Vince Campion. He didn't move his feet when he danced. He moved everything else, his hand on my bottom, his thighs against mine, the buttons of his uniform back and forth across my breasts. I had to arch my neck like a horse to keep him from rubbing his hot, damp face against mine.

After a while he stopped trying to nuzzle me and started to talk. "Why are you always so tight-assed? Is it because of Fitz?"

"What?"

"Are you trying to get him to marry you or something?"

"What?" I could hear him all right; they could probably hear him in the street. I hoped if I kept saying "What?" he'd stop talking.

"Are you scared Fitz'll can you if he catches you playing around?"

"What?"

The commander had exhausted "The White Cliffs of Dover" and was playing chords, feeling his way into another song. I stopped pretending to dance and tried to ease myself away from Vince Campion. He wouldn't let go of me. As I pulled back, he lurched forward, pinning me against the wall.

"Why don't you loosen up like the rest of the gash in this town?"

"What?"

The commander had the right chords now and was thumping out a tune. The girl in the frilly dress, standing behind him with a group of American army officers leaning all over her, started to sing the chorus. The others joined in.

"Fuck 'em all. Fuck 'em all. The long and the short and the tall."

It was the song I'd heard over the phone from the NCO canteen at Max's base.

"Damn right," Campion said. "Fuck 'em all while you can. How'd you like to go down to Hurley tomorrow?"

"What?"

I tried to slip away to the side. I wanted to hear the song. He raised his arm holding me there.

"I know a hotel where you can still get —"

I ducked under his arm. Turning toward the piano, I listened to the next verse.

> There's a Lancaster leaving the Ruhr,
> Bound for old blighty shore,
> Heavily laden with terrified men,
> Shit scared and prone on the floor.

"Fitz doesn't have to know." Campion had his mouth against my ear. "Tell Fitz you're —"

"Fitz has nothing to do with it."

It was that damn song. I was furious. Those safe, drunken American army officers had no right to sing it. Only Max and his crew mates had the right to mock themselves like that.

"If you want to know why I'm so tight-assed, I'll tell you." I was yelling at Campion. "I've got a sergeant in one of those bloody Lancasters. I love him and he's up there now over Germany somewhere. And I'm terrified for him. I'm terrified he won't come back."

I started to walk away. Campion grabbed my arm. I slapped his face.

It was extraordinary. There had been so much noise in the room, the piano and the singing and all those raised voices fighting the war. The sound of that slap was like a gun going off. Everybody heard it. Everybody stopped moving and talking and looked at me and Vince Campion.

I had a quick impression of his gross face, his small puffed eyes, the shock and anger and hatred in them.

Then everybody started moving and talking again and I went over and found Fitz. I slipped my hand into his.

"What happened?" he smiled at me.

"Nothing. You know. Vince Campion."

Fitz squeezed my hand. "Want me to go over and take a poke at him for you?"

That made me laugh. I couldn't imagine Fitz taking a poke at anyone. "I'd sooner you got me home," I told him.

It was the first time I'd been out in the blackout. Everything had seemed so little changed in London. There had been no air raids, not even any warning sirens, since I'd arrived. That night, feeling our way along the edge of the sidewalk, the railings, the windows of the shops, was the first time I felt I was in a city at war.

We reached Park Lane without finding a taxi. Earl's Court was beginning to seem as far away as New York. I thought of asking Fitz if I could sleep on his sofa at the Dorchester. I wasn't sure what stopped me. Maybe it was an indefinable sense of Fitz's privacy. I felt he'd hate the intrusion, the forced intimacy of having me undressing and sleeping in his suite.

In the end I didn't have to intrude on him. Some American M.P.'s came along in a jeep before we reached the Dorchester. Fitz managed to flag them down and asked if they'd take me to Earl's Court. They agreed at once; I climbed in with them. They were friendly and talkative and touchingly respectful as they drove me home. They kept calling me ma'am.

I stopped at the top of the stairs and looked up at the sky. It was after midnight now. Max was up there somewhere in his Plexiglas turret. He'd told me how cold it was even in a fleece-lined jacket. Please, let him be all right, please.

I woke early the next morning. I got up and opened the door into the living room so I'd hear Max's footsteps on the outside stairs, and then went back to bed.

I didn't mean to fall asleep again but I did, and when I woke up the second time it was 10:15.

I remember that very clearly. Ten-fifteen. And a sudden uneasiness growing slowly into panic. I don't remember much else about that weekend. I know I never left the apartment. I kept wanting to run down to the end of the mews to look for Max but I was afraid I would miss the phone if it rang.

The phone, that actual Bakelite object with its smooth, cold feel and its stale cigarette smell, became the focused center of what was otherwise not a focused experience.

Sometimes I was in the kitchen putting the kettle on to make coffee, and then forgetting it and wondering what that whistling sound was, and then turning it off because any sound except the phone ringing made me want to scream. Sometimes I was in bed with the sheet over my head, trying to shut out the light, as though the light were my thoughts and that would shut them out, too. All that is still vague in my memory. Everything is vague except the phone. I dialed the same number again and again, and sometimes I got nothing but silence, and sometimes I got meaningless bleeps and static sounds, and sometimes I heard men's and women's voices saying they couldn't tell me anything yet, they'd call me.

I got angry with those voices sometimes, but not for long because I knew it wouldn't help; they must be used to hysterical people asking them what I asked.

Each time I hung up I promised myself I wouldn't call again, I'd do what they told me and wait for them to call me, and then I'd wait and wait and they didn't call me.

They didn't call me until late Sunday night. This time it was a man's voice, and he said he was awfully sorry, but they really couldn't be sure and it was always best to hope for the best, wasn't it, and of course as soon as they heard anything definite they would let me know.

"Anything definite either way," I begged him. "Please don't keep anything from me. Please tell me the truth."

"Naturally, of course, although it may be weeks actually, and if it's bad news I'm afraid it may be even longer than that before we hear from the Red Cross, if we do hear from the Red Cross."

After that I started to talk to myself aloud. It was the best thing I could have done because what I said to myself most of the time was, "Stop it."

"Stop it. You're not the only person who's going through this. There are all the others every night. Night after night. And some of them have children. And the worst thing you can possibly do is feel sorry for yourself. Stop it."

I didn't have any sleeping pills — I had never had any — but I found some aspirin in the bathroom and I took two and then two more and sometime after midnight I fell asleep, sweating.

I got up very briskly on Monday morning and said "Stop it" several times very loudly while I had a shower and made coffee and even ate a piece of bread and margarine. After that I dressed and took a bus to the Dorchester. I felt numb when I arrived there, as detached as a sleepwalker, and when I entered the elevator I couldn't remember the number of Fitz's suite.

I did remember it, though, and I knocked and walked in, determined not to say a word about what had happened.

Fitz was sitting on the sofa with a cup of coffee and a cigarette. He wasn't wearing his jacket or his tie, and his shirt was unbuttoned; I could see the gray hairs on his chest. I wanted to go over and put my head on his lap and cling to him. I sat down facing him across the coffee table.

"You got home all right the other night?"

"Yes."

He was looking at the end of his cigarette as though there was something wrong with it. I knew that preoccupied frown. It meant he had a difficult situation to deal with.

"It isn't going to work, is it, Carol?"

"What?"

"Why did you tell Vince Campion about that sergeant of yours?"

I had forgotten all about that. I tried to explain: that song; I had blurted it all out without thinking. I didn't feel defensive telling Fitz what had happened. It didn't seem important, especially now.

"He came running up here to spill it all out to me the next morning." Fitz still wasn't looking at me. "I had to pretend I didn't know. It was all news to me you had a young man in the air force."

"Why?" Why did he have to pretend?

"Can't you understand, Carol. It's the way it looks. The way it looks to someone like Campion. Particularly now. The war. You know what our people are like over here. We're all swaggering around, beating our chests, to show what he-men we are compared to the British."

"I know. It's awful."

Suddenly Fitz looked at me. There was no anger in his blue eyes. They were pleading with me.

"Can't you see, I've got to go along with that. It's the way it looks. I've got to be one of the guys, one of that locker room crowd, too. Especially with people like Campion. I can't have him saying things about me to his buddies at the network in New York. Saying I haven't got any balls. You know what I'm talking about . . ." He moved his hand in a helpless way. "You've been to my apartment. You've met my friends. And from things I've told you, you must have guessed."

I never had. It had never crossed my mind. I felt as if I had opened a familiar door and found myself in an utterly foreign place. I couldn't think of anything to say.

"I'm in a hell of a sensitive position. That's one of the reasons I wanted you over here with me. So we could be seen together at parties. People would think we were —" He shrugged with distaste. "We were having an affair."

"I'm sorry."

I was. Desperately sorry. For Fitz. Why hadn't I understood?

"It's too late to be sorry now. Vince Campion kept saying he knew what he'd do if *his* girl . . . He said if *he* found you were having it off with a sergeant in the air force, he'd send you home on the next bloody ship."

It was strange, I didn't feel indignant or upset. I felt cold. It reminded me of that lonely time at the store in New York. I decided with the same bleakness with which I'd reacted to things then that I wouldn't ask Fitz if he was going to take Campion's advice. I would wait until he told me.

"It makes it very difficult for me because I'm very fond of you, Carol." Never mind all that, get to the point. "If Campion starts talking about this in New York — and you can bet he will — if he says I had a girl in London and she was just using me, she got me to ship her over so she could sleep with her sergeant . . ."

"I didn't."

"It's what Campion says, Carol. The way it looks." That was the third time Fitz had used that phrase. "And if I don't do anything about it, if I don't —"

"If you don't behave the way a drunken, loud-mouthed bully like Campion would."

Thank God I was finding a little indignation at last.

"If I behave as though I didn't *care*, I didn't care what — what any woman . . ."

Poor Fitz. I'd noticed at once when I arrived in London how differently he behaved here. Like those GIs in Piccadilly, he had been displaced. In New York he had his life so well under control, admired and respected in public, remote and discreet in the privacy of his home. The two lives always kept separate. Among the Dorchester mob, he was in a strange country, trying to understand the customs and morals of the people, to behave as they did, hoping they would mistake him for one of their own. Poor Fitz. I couldn't hold it against him. As he had said, it was the war, this town, those middle-aged warriors who would never be shot at, taking their pick of the women and the Scotch. If they discovered the truth about Fitz, they would cast him out with contempt. In their army, homosexuals were automatically rejected by law.

"When would you like me to leave?"

He smiled at me gratefully as he opened his briefcase. He was an excellent organizer and he had had the whole weekend to arrange things. I was booked on the *Queen Mary,* sailing the next morning. I would have to take the afternoon train to Glasgow, then the branch line to Greenock. He had my railroad passes. They had been issued by the U.S. Army. That made me smile in spite of myself; I remembered how I'd explained to Laurie Sue Maytag why I was in uniform. "They want to be able to send you home if you get pregnant or have a nervous breakdown."

"I'd better go and pack."

I stood up and put my travel papers away in my pocket. Fitz patted my shoulder. He looked desperately relieved.

"You're swell, Carol. You're being swell about this."

"It's all right. I don't mind going home."

It was true. I was sorry only that I couldn't keep my promise to Daphne, to go down to Bath and see my father. Apart from that, I was glad to be leaving.

"You sure, Carol?"

"Quite sure."

Fitz was still smiling at me, that grateful, relieved smile. His gratitude annoyed me; I wanted to punish him for it.

"There's nothing to keep me here now," I said curtly. "Max, my sergeant in the air force, got shot down over Berlin on Friday night. Somebody managed to bail out of his plane, but they don't know who. They don't know if it was Max or somebody else. He's just listed as missing. That means he's either dead or he's been taken prisoner. Either way, that's the end of it for now. If I ever do see him again, it won't be until the war's over."

Eleven

I wrote a letter to the network, quitting my job the day I got back to New York.

The crossing on the *Queen Mary* had been quick and uneventful. Conditions on board were very professional and efficient compared to the old SS *Parkwood*. The stewards served continuous cafeteria meals: we ate at two set times a day, 9:00 and 4:00, 10:00 and 5:00, whatever, the same menu for breakfast and dinner. The food was quite good.

There were five four-tier bunks in my cabin, sleeping room for twenty. But the ship wasn't full on the Western voyage. There were only three other women in the cabin with me, so we all had lower berths. Two of the women were on special assignment to Washington; they were self-important and mysterious. The third was pregnant. The mysterious ones disapproved of her and kept to themselves. I made friends with her at once.

Her name was Genevieve and she was a Catholic from New Orleans. I told her about Max and she said she was sure he was all right, he had bailed out safely. She was like that about everything, naturally optimistic. There was a boy she had known in high school, a 4F insurance salesman, who had a cute house at Lake Pontchartrain. He had been crazy to marry her for years; now she was going to make him the happiest man in Louisiana. "Why, goodness, Carol, it's well known all the women in my family have seven-and-a-half month babies." Everything was going to turn out just fine, in fact. "And it will for you, too, honey, you'll see." Like me, she was glad to be going home.

I didn't say good-bye to anyone in the radio news department. When I went to the network building for my pay, I took the elevator straight up to the accounting department on the fourteenth floor. They had been in touch with London and had arranged everything. All I had to do was sign some forms and they would mail me a check. I was there only five minutes. I took the elevator straight down to the street floor when I left. I didn't want to see anyone I knew.

I did stand around in the lobby for a minute. It was all so familiar, the echoing sounds and the smell of mopped floors and cigar smoke, and the candy stand at the entrance to the drugstore where Fitz and I sometimes went for coffee in the morning. It was over three years since I'd first gone to work in the typing pool of the news department. I knew it was trite to stand there feeling so much had happened in those three years, but it had. So much had happened in the world since 1940 and so much had happened to me. I wasn't a different person now, but a lot of my attitudes had changed. I wasn't so eager about everything.

When the check arrived from the network two days later, it was for over twelve hundred dollars. I knew I had Fitz to thank for that; he had arranged for me to receive full severance pay and per diem expenses on overseas assignment, even for those three weeks on the *Parkwood*.

Whatever Fitz's motives, his natural kindness or his discretion, I was grateful to him. The money meant I could afford to do nothing for a while. I could take a deep breath and try to sort out my own feelings before I decided what I was going to do next.

It wasn't easy for me to sort out my feelings. Emotionally I was hanging in space. I still didn't know if Max was alive or not.

There must have been thousands of other women in the same situation at that time. I was luckier than some of them. Their husbands, lovers, sons had been reported missing in the Pacific. From what we knew after Bataan, they had much less chance of surviving in a Japanese POW camp than in a German stalag. At least if Max had managed to climb out of his burning plane, he was probably safe now. He would come home at the end of the war. Please, let him be safe, please.

The end of the war still seemed far away in the future that summer of 1943. We invaded Sicily and bombed Rome, but even if we managed to knock Italy out of the war, nobody thought it would shorten the war much. The Germans would probably be glad to see the last of their volatile ally. The Russians counterattacked around Kursk and regained lost ground, but there could be no second front to help them for at least another year.

New York was crowded with soldiers waiting to be shipped out. The bars resounded with a strained heartiness as the soldiers and civilians, milling and yelling for drinks, insisted on their right to a good time. Nobody seemed to be having one. The civilians were defensive, telling anyone who would listen how hard they'd tried to get into it. The strange thing was that many of the servicemen were defensive, too. One evening, sitting in Julius's, trying to dissuade a young corporal from buying me a drink, I thought I understood why. Everybody felt more or less guilty. The civilians felt guilty about not being soldiers; the soldiers about not being overseas; the ones in England about not being in the fighting. It was like a ladder, narrowing up out of sight. Even the infantrymen in the front line probably felt guilty about someone who was in more danger than they were. Or maybe about the dead.

It made me realize something I needed to be told: I felt guilty about Max.

I could live with that guilt. I could even try to talk myself out of it. What I couldn't live with was constant grief, the minute-to-minute, day-to-day sense of loss, the realization that I might never see Max again. I would never touch him again, never hear his voice. That thought was unbearable. And because I couldn't bear it, I could not go on getting out of bed in the morning, having a shower, and going out for the paper unless I found some escape from it.

I suppose people who have been told by a kind, trusted doctor that they have a dangerous illness must behave a little the way I did. They walk out of the doctor's office and they get in their cars and they drive away and they remember to stop at the drugstore and buy a toothbrush and a bottle of nail polish remover. Doing these things is a small act of faith. Living in New York that summer was an act of faith to me. I was ignoring the central fact of my life. I was walking around it like a blinkered horse circling a bottomless pit. It was the only way I could keep going.

With practice I learned to forget, for several minutes, then an hour, then sometimes for three or four hours at a time, that Max might be dead.

I began to call the few people I knew in New York who had no connection with the radio news department. The one thing New York social life didn't need that summer was another unattached female. Some of my friends invited me to parties anyway. One more, they probably figured. With so many single women for every man under sixty, one more wouldn't even be noticed.

They were pretty desperate, those parties, but they were better than the ones in London. At least they were different. No one patted my behind, no one sang those awful songs, very few of the men in uniform ever talked about the war. If they did, it was only in a personal way, where they were stationed, how soon they hoped to be shipped out. The girls hung around them like clusters of flowers, or perhaps more like wreaths. Their feminine attention had a certain sadness: they seemed to be sighing for something they had lost, a promise that had been made to them and then cruelly broken by the war. They wanted to reach out to these young men in uniform, to claim them. After all, that was their right, what they had been brought up to expect. They hung back, withdrawing at the promised moment when the young men tried to claim them. Many of them used almost the same words to explain their feelings: "So you fall in love with someone and he gets sent off to God knows where and you don't know if he's ever going to come back, and if he does you've missed all that time together and you have to start all over again. I'm going to wait until they *all* come back."

So they went to the parties and listened and smiled and were fragrant and beautiful. In that they conformed to a popular convention of the times: we all owed that to our servicemen; it was our duty to look good and smell good. It was supposed to give them something to fight for, like blueberry pie. At the very least, it would make those awful girls in England look bad. Everybody knew *they* smelled terrible.

The dusk seeped in through the windowpanes, and the city looked sullen and uninviting in the brownout, and the parties went on and on until there was no gaiety at the bottom of any bottle, and the half-dozen girls and the two young men who were left decided to go to Manny Wolf's or the Stage Door Canteen in a group, in the safety of any number larger than a couple.

I usually left before that happened. In that way I was fortunate; in my dangling state over Max, I had no interest in any other young men. I couldn't even sigh over them. I was eager to go home and look in my mailbox for a letter: *We have been informed by the International Red Cross that Sgt. Max Ludlow, RCAF, is a prisoner of war . . .* I don't know how many times I imagined myself reading that letter.

One evening at one of those parties I saw a woman I thought I knew. She obviously had the same feeling about me; we kept glancing at each other in a tentative way, trying to remember where we'd met. Finally we introduced ourselves. Her name was Sally Morrison. That still meant nothing to me, but she recognized my name at once.

"Of course. It was before I was married. I used to be Sally Grant. We met at . . ."

I knew where we'd met then, and I almost ran away from her. She had been one of the regular guests at Fitz's apartment.

I didn't run away from her. I had had two dry martinis and I was damned if I was going to go on avoiding anyone who knew Fitz. I didn't care what stories they'd heard about my behavior in London. I knew I hadn't done anything to be ashamed of.

We sat on a sofa together. She told me about her husband. He was a lawyer, a major in the Judge Advocate's Corps. "He hates it, but at least he's safe, he won't get killed."

When she said that, I remembered something I'd always liked about her: her honesty. We started to talk about Fitz.

We agreed he was one of the sanest, kindest men we'd ever known. And then she smiled. "It's so sad about him, though."

Her smile reminded me of my own sentimental fantasies about him, his lost, doomed love. It was sad about him all right, but not in the way she thought. I felt like that character in the fairy story, the barber, who couldn't keep his secret to himself any longer, "The Emperor has goat's ears."

I told her the whole story of my week in England, the reason Fitz had sent me home.

She listened, and when I'd finished she touched my hand. "I know. He's like that. He lashes out when he feels threatened in that particular way."

Apparently I wasn't the only one who had seen the Emperor's ears. One of the young professors who was also a regular evening guest had given Sally a ride home one night. "He asked me to go out with him." She shrugged. "It was all perfectly casual. There was nothing between us. But I made the mistake of telling Fitz about it. It was terrible. He behaved as though I'd betrayed him. And of course, it wasn't me Fitz was angry about. It was the young professor. I was never invited to the apartment again."

"Did you realize . . . When you went out with that young man, did you know?"

She shook her head. "No. I never even thought about it. I never would have thought about it if Fitz hadn't made such a fuss about my seeing his boyfriend."

"Poor Fitz."

I had been so engrossed that it wasn't until Sally had gone that I noticed I was among the last people at the party.

"Come on," someone said. "We're going to Tim Costello's."

Well, why not? It was a Sunday night. There couldn't possibly be a letter about Max waiting for me at my apartment. Maybe it was partly the drinks I'd had. Maybe it was the relief of finally talking to someone about Fitz and finding I wasn't the only one who had felt close to him and trusted him and then been angrily, ruthlessly, shut out of his life. I felt more cheerful than I had for weeks. Did I really want to go back to my solitary apartment and lock myself in and try not to think about Max? Why not have a little fun for a change? I was only twenty-two. I *didn't* have a dangerous illness. I had a lover who was missing in action. It was high time I stopped behaving like a Hindu widow determined to throw herself on the funeral pyre. It was time I stopped being morbid and learned to laugh again.

"Okay," I agreed. "Let's *all* go to Costello's."

The bar on Third Avenue was crowded but not loud. Unless James Thurber was there, the people at Costello's tended to be argumentative but not quarrelsome. I recognized my favorite *New Yorker* writer, A. J. Liebling, by his bald head, and that marvelous cartoonist of the macabre, Charles Addams, by his ears. Addams was wearing the sloppiest private's uniform I'd ever seen; he looked like a KP in the Bulgarian army.

There were too many of us to fit into one booth. Even after Emil, the waiter, had brought over extra chairs, I was left standing on the fringe. I was going to slip away and go home after all when a soldier in the next booth stood up and touched my arm.

"Why don't you spill over into my party?"

He was alone. It seemed sad, a young soldier, eating roast beef alone. I sat down with him.

He didn't look sad. He looked brand-new, like a birthday present. His uniform was clean and pressed and beautifully tailored. Were enlisted men allowed to have their uniforms made for them?

"Private Stone." He held out his hand. "My friends call me Private."

"Carol Clavering."

We shook hands. He was about twenty-five, I thought. He just missed being handsome: his nose was too flat and his chin too blunt. But he had beautiful eyes, dark brown with feathery lashes. Like Lofty's. He had nice hair, too, soft and shining as an Indian's. I liked him for looking so young and bright and cheerful; these were all scarce qualities in New York that summer.

"May I offer you a drink, Miss Clavering." There was a bottle of wine on the table. He turned it so I could see the label. Nuits-St.-Georges.

"I'd love some."

He beckoned to Emil and asked for another glass. Emil brought it and poured the wine for me himself. I hadn't seen him since I'd been back, and he fussed over me in his mournful, dignified way. I did my best to make him feel I'd missed him, too, and ordered roast beef.

"You're obviously one of the honored guests here, Miss Clavering."

"Please eat your dinner."

"You're not drinking your wine."

"I'd sooner have it with my roast beef."

He ate in silence for a minute. I buttered a roll and nibbled it. We kept glancing at each other, not in the least shyly, but with suppressed amusement.

"Where are you stationed, Private?"

"It's a military secret but I'm with that bunch of clowns in Astoria."

"The Signal Corps?"

"That's what they tell me."

"Are you allowed to talk about it?"

"I don't see why not. Our activities are in the gossip columns every day. We're as famous as the Lost Patrol." He was funny about it, about the eccentrics and celebrities the army had sent to Astoria to keep them out of the way, the chauffeured limousines lining up to collect the actors and directors and playwrights in their privates' uniforms every evening while the brass headed for the subway, the special order that had been issued threatening to restrict the men to base if they didn't collect their army pay.

He was candid about it, too. Private Stone was having a good war. "I'm making some great contacts," he said. "Astoria's better than Skull and Bones for meeting the right people. But then I never made Skull and Bones. As a matter of fact, I never made college."

Emil brought my roast beef. Private Stone asked me about myself. I was less candid than he had been. "I'm out of work at the moment," I said. "But that's the way it goes; something'll turn up any day now."

"You mean you're in the theater?"

I shook my head. "Are you?"

He had finished his dinner; he took out a cigarette and lit it, deliberately pausing before he answered.

"I'm Jason Stone."

The name meant nothing to me. I felt easy enough with him by that time to admit it. I was going to ask him what he did in the theater.

I took a sip of the Nuits-St.-Georges first.

"What's the matter?"

I hadn't meant to make a face. "It's a little — Well, it's *off.* "

"This?" He looked at the bottle in an injured way. "It's Nuits-St.-Georges."

"I know. But it's corked or something. It's been kept standing up and the air got into it."

"You mean that tart bouquet?"

"That vinegar taste."

Jason Stone looked at me for several seconds in silence. Oh, God, I'd hurt his feelings; I'd offended his dignity.

"I thought —" The corners of his mouth trembled; was he going to be angry? He had too much bright humor, that spontaneous inclination to laught at himself. "I thought that was the way it was supposed to taste."

"No."

I caught Emil's attention. We were both laughing as he came over to the table.

"Emil, would you mind tasting this, please." I handed him my glass.

Emil took it with his usual solemn dignity. He held it under his nose and then touched it against his lips. "Oh," Emil said.

He picked up the bottle and the other glass and took them away.

"Where's he going with my wine?"

"To get you another bottle."

"You're kidding. Just like that?"

"Of course." I didn't mean to imply that was the kind of service I was accustomed to, only that Emil was a nice man and a good waiter. Jason misunderstood me.

"You've been around, haven't you, Miss Clavering?"

When Emil brought the new bottle and two clean glasses, he made me taste it before filling Jason's glass. I told him it was delicious. Emil hardly ever smiled but I could see he was amused. *"Prost, Hauptman,"* he said to Jason as he walked away.

"What does that mean?"

"Good health, Captain."

Jason sipped his wine in silence; he kept glancing at me in a hesitant, mystified way.

"How did you know?" It came out suddenly like a confession.

"I had to learn German in school. And anyway —"

"No." He finished his wine and poured us both more. "About this. How did you know about it's being corked or something and standing up and the air getting into it? Where are you from, anyway?"

"St. Louis."

"St. Louis? Where Budweiser comes from? How do you know about wine?"

How did I know? What did I know? Very little. We had drunk wine in France, and sometimes later in England, and after Sylvia was married and I went to dinner with her in St. John's Wood, Nigel used to go on rather about the claret he had decanted.

"For heaven's sake, anyone can tell when something tastes sour."

"I couldn't."

"Maybe you smoke too much."

"What's that got to do with it?"

"It's supposed to dull your taste buds."

He shook his head, slowly, solemnly. "You're a very mysterious girl, do you know that? You've got a funny accent and you learned German in school and you're a wine connoisseur, or however you pronounce it. You've probably got a title or something. You're the Duchess of Clavering, or Lady Carol, aren't you? Tell me the truth."

"I'm a researcher." I was laughing again. "And I just got fired for immoral behavior, if you want to know. Now tell me more about Jason Stone."

"What kind of immoral behavior?"

"Are you a famous actor?"

"Was immoral behavior part of your research?"

We went on like that for a while, being silly, but enjoying it. Then we settled down and did tell each other about ourselves. Jason had had the second lead in a Broadway play that had run for two years; there had been agents' talk about Hollywood. "But I knew I was going to get drafted and I didn't want to end up in a foxhole on some godforsaken atoll, so I beat them to it and joined the Signal Corps." He wasn't going to get maimed in Astoria, but he'd still be a returned veteran after the war. "One of our brave boys we owe so much to. I won't have any trouble getting into another play, or I might even get to direct one. That's what I'd really like to do, direct."

As I listened to him making fun of himself but being shamelessly honest about his own self-interest, I found myself liking him more and more. Jason Stone wasn't seeing the war from any of the rungs of that ladder of guilt; he didn't feel guilty about being safe in Astoria, in a cushy job, making useful contacts. He didn't see any reason why he should; it was refreshing to find someone that summer who didn't.

"I'm in the film unit," he told me. "And I'm learning a lot about editing, learning it from masters, some of the top directors, guys who wouldn't even talk to me on the phone if I wasn't in uniform. Besides, I've got plenty of time. I'm too young to be a director yet."

"Why? How old do you have to be? How old are you?"

"Twenty-two."

We were the same age. I rather liked that.

He had an overnight pass. We sat drinking coffee and then brandy and then Scotch and soda. It didn't make me drunk; it only made me feel more and more comfortable and full of goodwill. I told him quite a lot about myself, my childhood, the time in Hollywood, at the store, the three years with the network. I left Fitz out of it; by that time I was too full of goodwill toward Fitz to want to explain that whole messy situation in London.

I didn't leave Max out of it. I said I was in love with an air force sergeant overseas. I didn't tell Jason that Max was missing and might be dead; I didn't want to think about it myself. I had made up my mind not to think about it. Not for a whole evening.

We neither of us noticed the time until it was three o'clock. Emil was looking accusingly mournful, and Jason had to go home to his parents' apartment in Brooklyn. "My mother's probably calling the hospitals by now." I insisted on paying for my own dinner; Jason finally agreed if I'd let him drive me home.

"Drive me home? What in?"

He had a car parked outside on Third Avenue. God knows where he got the gas for it, from the Signal Corps probably.

He drove slowly and carefully, stopping at every orange light, and when he dropped me at my apartment on Tenth Street, he didn't ask if he could come up.

We stood for a moment on the sidewalk.

"When will I see you again, Carol?"

I wasn't sure I ought to see him again. Because of Max? What did Max have to do with it? I'd had fun with Jason. The first fun I'd had since I'd been told Max was missing. Was I going to slip back into that Hindu widow suttee frame of mind I'd finally managed to talk myself out of? How would that help Max? Or me? Or anyone else?

I agreed to have dinner with Jason on Friday night. He wanted to pick me up, but that seemed a waste of the Signal Corps' gas. I said I'd meet him at Costello's.

That was how it went on for several weeks, into the heat of July. The summer was particularly brutal that year. Tim Costello's wasn't air-conditioned; only the more expensive restaurants were and I wouldn't let Jason take me to those.

So we sat in Costello's and drank Tom Collinses and held the cold glasses against our foreheads, and Jason took off his jacket and loosened his tie, and I wore sleeveless cotton dresses, and we dabbed at our faces until our handkerchiefs were soaking wet. Or sometimes I made salads with hard-boiled eggs in them, or bought sliced ham at the delicatessen on the corner, and we lolled on the couch by the window in my apartment and drank chilled white wine from upstate New York, and fanned ourselves with sections of the Sunday *Times.* And the hotter it became and the more we frowned with stupefied disbelief at how hot it was, the easier and more comfortable we were with each other.

I knew one of the reasons I enjoyed being with Jason so much was that he flattered me. He didn't keep telling me I was beautiful or clever; he looked up to me. He kept asking me what I thought about books, painters, music, and he listened to my opinions with studious attention. He made me tell him about France and England, the cathedrals, the best hotels in Paris and London, European history. He sought my tastes in food and furniture. He asked me to repeat *porte cochère, boudoir, chaise-longue, Jean Gabin,* until he had the French pronunciation right. He had a good ear and he was a fast learner, so he was never a bore about it. I often felt rather a fraud as an instructor — it's only when someone asks you questions that you realize how ignorant you are — but I enjoyed being looked up to; it was a new experience for me.

The change between us came on one of the hottest nights of all. Jason had brought over some cold roast beef his mother had cooked for him. He was in a T-shirt and suntans. I had taken off my bra under my cotton dress. We were both barefoot, sitting on the couch, doing the Double-Crostic in the *Saturday Review.* When I got up to get another bottle of white wine from the icebox, the seat of my dress stuck to my behind. I peeled the damp cloth off my skin and flapped my skirt, trying to waft a draft up the back of my thighs. Jason was holding his T-shirt away from his chest and blowing into it.

"I don't care," I said. "I'm going to take my dress off."

"I care."

We looked at each other and I forgot about the wine.

Since I'd told Jason I was in love with someone overseas, he had been understanding and considerate about it. He had never tried to persuade me to sleep with him. I had never suggested it, either. I had hardly even thought about it. Perhaps it had been too hot. It didn't seem too hot now. I was suddenly aching to be touched. More than that. My body craved that extraordinary, compatible, ecstatic, indefinable, and slightly comic feeling of being fucked.

I pulled off my dress. Jason turned out the lamp. In the glow from the street, I crossed to the bed and lay down beside him.

The heat was all at once our friend. Our wet skins slid smoothly over each other; our bodies made loving, kissing sounds as they met and clung together and parted. Dear Jason, he was cherishing and kind and intensely personal. He made me feel my body was me. Only me.

When it was over we lay side by side on our backs, panting and dripping and wiping our eyes with the backs of our hands.

The street lamp threw a rectangle of light on the adjacent wall. It framed the picture I had hung there, a reproduction of Manet's *Déjeuner sur l'herbe.* I had always loved it, the innocent self-possession of that naked young woman, picnicking with her properly dressed young men. At that moment it seemed to reflect my own mood like a mirror. That was how I felt, innocent and content.

"Carol . . ."

"Mmm?"

"That guy. That sergeant in the air force."

"What about him?"

"That's what I'm asking you," Jason propped himself on his elbow. "What about him?"

I dragged myself away from the picnicking Eve in her calm French Eden. It was time I told Jason the truth about Max. I still couldn't think about Bomber Command without pain and anger, so I didn't go into any details. I just said Max's plane had been shot down over Germany. "And I don't know whether he's alive or dead."

"Jesus." Jason lay down again.

I tried to think myself back into the Manet but the mood had passed. I felt like talking now.

"Please don't worry about it, Jason."

"How can I help it? You're in love with him, aren't you?"

"Yes."

"All the way?"

"Yes."

"Suppose he is dead?"

"Then I'll have to get over it — like a lot of other people these days. I'm not going to carry on like the Widow of Windsor."

"Who's the Widow of Windsor?"

"Never mind." For once I didn't feel like explaining English history to Jason.

"If he was alive, wouldn't you have heard by now?"

"I don't know. It's only been a little over two months" — it had been seventy-two days — "and the man at Max's base, his flight officer, said it might be several weeks before the International Red Cross located a prisoner of war in Germany, and when they did, it would take another few weeks before Bomber Command heard from the Red Cross." I was talking as much to reassure myself as to explain it to Jason. "And then Max's flight officer would write to me at my sister's apartment in London and she'd have to forward it and that would take at least another month."

"I'm sorry. I didn't mean to grill you about it."

"I don't mind."

Jason wiped his face with the sheet.

"Are you sorry?" he asked presently. "I mean, are you sorry about letting me make love to you?"

"No." I wasn't. Not in the least. Maybe that was ruthless of me. Using Jason. But he had obviously enjoyed it as much as I had.

"Why did you?"

"Because I like you. I wanted you."

He was fidgeting, starting to get up. His lighter and cigarettes were on the night table beside me. I handed them to him and gave him an ashtray. I wanted him to go on lying there with me.

"Carol?"

"What?"

"Nothing."

"Go on, Jason, ask me anything you want to. It's only fair."

"If you haven't heard he's okay by, well, say, Christmas . . ."

"What?"

"Will you marry me?"

"Oh, Jason."

"Why is that so funny?"

I'd hurt him; I sat up and touched his shoulder.

"I wasn't laughing at you. I promise. It just startled me, that's all. Because I don't think I want to marry anyone for a long time yet."

"Don't you want to marry Max if he comes back?"

"No. I don't think so, anyway."

"Why not?"

Yes, why not? That threw me for a moment.

"I'd love to live with him. But the only reason I can think of to get married is because you want to have children, and I don't want to have children yet. I'm too young and too selfish and too frivolous. I'd be a lousy mother. I might even resent the poor kids and I had enough of that myself . . ." My voice trailed off as I thought about that.

"How?"

"I don't know. I didn't mean that really."

It wasn't fair to say my parents had resented me. What I felt was that they had never wholeheartedly welcomed me. They had both hoped I'd be a boy, anyway.

"It's just that's one of the things I feel so strongly about children. They have a right to feel welcome all the time. And that takes — well, you have to be absolutely sure you're marrying for life, don't you?"

"I want to have children. I'm crazy about children. *I'd* make them feel welcome."

"Oh, Jason, I'm sure you would. You'd be a wonderful father." I touched his shoulder again. "I'm sorry if I hurt you."

"It's all right. I'm not hurt. I'm quite happy. I'm very happy." He sounded surprised as though he'd just discovered that. "The only thing is, what are we going to do?"

"How?"

"Do you want to go on seeing me?"

"Of course I do." That made me sit up. "Don't you?"

"Yes. Jesus, yes. But do you want to go on —" He reached up, tentatively, and put his hand over my breast. "Do you want to go on sleeping with me?"

Yes, I did. I knew how that would look to most people: I loved Max and I was being unfaithful to him. But I didn't care how it looked. I thought that kind of convention was hypocritical bullshit. I had discovered John Stuart Mill that summer, and there were parts of *On Liberty* I had read over and over with delight. Mill thought abstract morality was a fraud. Only actions counted. A right action was anything that tended to produce happiness. Sleeping with Jason made me happy. It made Jason happy. How could it make Max unhappy? He would never have to know about it.

"Yes, I do," I told Jason. "I'd love to go on sleeping with you." I put my hot, damp hand over his on my breast. "So long as it doesn't get any hotter than this, anyway."

I applied for a job in August. Jason put me on to it. The agency that handled him as an actor was expanding its literary department.

"Expanding is a loose way of putting it," Jason told me. "They've had one woman stuck away in a cubicle for years. She was supposed to keep clients like Eddie Cantor happy when he wanted some ghost-written puff piece about himself published in a magazine. Then it suddenly occurred to some genius up there that people were staying home more because of gas rationing. What were they doing at home? They were reading. Magazines. Books. They were even *buying* books. So they moved their woman out of her cubicle and gave her an office and she's been doing so much business they've promised her an assistant."

I didn't think it over for a second. An assistant. A reader. An undemanding, frivolous job that had nothing to do with the war.

"What's her name?"

"Harriet Bach."

"Like the composer?"

"What composer?"

"Oh, come on, Jason. How do I get in touch with her?"

We were sitting in Costello's. Jason picked up his Tom Collins, using that deliberate actor's pause that meant he had a surprise line to deliver.

"You've got an appointment with her at eleven o'clock tomorrow."

"Jason. How did you ever manage that?"

"How can my agent refuse me anything? I'm a serviceman."

"Darling, come here." He leaned across the table; I kissed him. "You're a sweetheart, Jason. You're even more of a sweetheart than Sinclair Lewis."

"Sinclair Lewis? Don't tell me. I remember. *Babbitt. Dodsworth. Main Street.* First American to win the Nobel Prize for literature. He was a friend of your father's."

I dressed carefully the next morning.

"The trick is to play it halfway," Jason had advised me. "She'll want someone bright and reasonably attractive so the unimportant clients won't mind being fobbed off on you. But you mustn't be a threat to her in any way. If she thinks you're smart enough to do her job, she'll never hire you."

I knew that on that subject Jason was the master and I was the pupil. I would never understand as much as he did about how to handle people in business. I chose a prim but expensive linen dress with short sleeves, and pinned my hair back, trying to look serious but not mousy.

The agency was on West Fifty-seventh Street. I found out later it had been started in the early days of vaudeville. It still had some of that rakish, menagerie atmosphere; I always half expected to

find performing seals waiting in the lobby. As I followed Harriet
Bach's plump, rather sleazily dressed secretary through the opulence
of the radio department to a small office next to the mailroom, I
could see that writers were still considered very small cheese. Talent,
as performers were called, was where the money was.

I could also see, the moment I met Harriet Bach, that she was
determined to change that. She was in her late thirties, not pretty
or striking, but what my mother would have called a nice-looking
woman. Her hair was short for the feminine look of that time,
when shoulder-length hair, like fragrance, seemed to be part of
the women's war effort, but not short enough to be a statement.
She was expensively dressed, without style or distinction. Her eyes
were the most expressive and interesting part of her. They were
large and appealing in an I'm-only-a-helpless-woman way, and they
were as clickety-click busy as an adding machine.

She didn't greet me with any small talk. The first thing she said
to me when I entered her office was, "I've just sold a book to the
Literary Guild."

"That's wonderful," I told her. "What book was it?"

She never answered that. She gestured with her cigarette to the
chair in front of the desk and pulled a sheet of paper toward
her.

"You were recommended by Larry Owens?"

"Yes. In a way."

"How do you know Larry?" She gave me one of her soft, appealing
looks. "Is he a special friend of yours?" She was inviting me to
confide in her.

I realized from what Jason had told me that she was also asking
me a trick question. Larry Owens was more important in the agency
than she was; that was why she had agreed to see me. But being
on the talent side, he could do her few favors. If I was his girlfriend,
she would be very nice to me, but she wouldn't hire me. She wouldn't
want an assistant who might also be a pillow informer, full of sly
midnight tales about her.

"I've never met him," I said truthfully. I explained about my
actor friend in the service, and so on. She listened long enough to
get things straight about Larry Owens.

"Why do you want to be a literary agent?"

I realized just in time that was another trick question. Over Harriet Bach's dead body I was going to be a literary agent.

"I thought you were just looking for an assistant, a reader, and I used to be a reader for Jed Walker at —"

"Dove and Roberts. Yes, I know Jed Walker. When were you there?"

I had to admit it was a long time ago and that led us to what I'd been doing since. She seemed much more impressed that I'd been Fitz's personal assistant than she had been by Jed Walker. Perhaps she thought my experience with Fitz might mean I was competent and knew my way around, but not in her field. I would be a beginner there, no threat to her.

We had come to the end of my personal history. She lit another cigarette; she smoked almost continuously. I kept looking at her hair, her brown dress. They puzzled me. They didn't fit in with her knowing, assured manner. They were tentative. She had had her hair done that way, chosen that dress, without any conviction. I remembered the way she had greeted me, a stranger, with that announcement about the Literary Guild. For all her shrewdness, she was unsure of herself. She was feeling her way, trying to discover the person she wanted to become, guiding and encouraging her progress by the signposts of success. It made me feel much more friendly toward her.

"You started this whole department by yourself, didn't you?" I was genuinely interested. "It must have been a terribly difficult job."

"My mother told me I was crazy." She started to tell me about herself, her mother, a failed marriage. She had been a reader at Metro; she had wanted to be a writer; she had tried to get into publishing. She had grabbed at the wretched job at the agency because she had a feeling, a certainty, that was her real talent, working with writers and editors, negotiating between them.

"I grossed a hundred thousand the first year I started the department. And there's no reason why, in a few years time, I shouldn't push it up to —" She blew out a puff of smoke; the magic word, "million," floated in it between us.

"My mother says I'm crazy to talk like that. But I think —"

"Of course, you will. I'm sure of it." I wasn't trying to flatter her; I was as engaged as she was. I wanted her to gross her million and it seemed to be taken for granted by that time that I was going to be her assistant and help her do it.

Before I left we agreed I was to start on Monday.

"God," Jason said, "you're a real operator, aren't you?"

"I only did what you told me. I did exactly what you told me."

"I didn't tell you to feel sorry for her."

Jason was wearing his tailored uniform. His shirt was buttoned, his tie smartly knotted. He looked the way he had that first night in Costello's, young and shining and brand-new. I had insisted on taking him to an air-conditioned restaurant to celebrate my new job.

"I couldn't help feeling sorry for her. I don't mean like Tiny Tim, but —"

"Who's Tiny Tim?"

"He's the lame boy in Dickens's *Christmas Carol.* The Victorians were awful in that way. They loved to have a good weep over cripples —" I stopped myself; I was getting to be altogether too teachy with Jason. "Honestly, it was all thanks to you. If it hadn't been for you, I'd have made an absolute balls of it."

"Anyway, congratulations." He raised his glass to me. We were drinking a new cocktail he'd discovered, Gibsons. I loved their sharp, cold bite, with none of the oiliness of gin. I had never tasted Vodka before.

"Thanks, Jason. I mean it. I'm terribly grateful to you."

He shook his head at me, slowly, solemnly, the way he had that first night in Costello's.

"I don't know what I'm going to do about you, Miss Clavering."

"Why?"

"I'm in love with you."

"Jason —"

"No, don't stop me. I'm not in love with you just because you've got such beautiful legs and I like your aristocratic nose. And I don't think I'm in love with you because you know about people a hundred years ago weeping over cripples —"

"Oh, come on —"

"Yeah, I know what you're going to say. Everybody knows that.

They don't, Carol. Until I was seventeen I never met anyone who even thought about things like that. We didn't talk about Dickens in Brooklyn. Not in my neighborhood, anyway. We talked about the Dodgers and getting into girls' pants. Anyway, I'm in love with you."

"You're going to make me hide under the table in a moment."

"Just so long as you don't laugh."

"I won't."

"You see, I think the real reason I'm so crazy about you is that you're the first girl I can imagine spending the rest of my life with and not get bored."

"It's only because I'm a bit different you think that. I was brought up in Europe. Isn't that fascinating?"

"No, I thought about that, too. When I was a kid there was a girl on the block whose father was a doctor. It was during the Depression and he was just as broke as the rest of us. But he was a *doctor.* I used to hang around her house just to watch her walk down the steps. And then when I got out of high school I went to work for my uncle. My uncle the big shot. He gave me a job as an office boy at United Artists. And there were all those secretaries. Jesus, I'd never seen girls like that. They played tennis and lived in places like Manhasset and they didn't call it Long Giland. Then when I told my uncle to screw it and went into the theater, there were all the young actresses. I don't mean the kids hanging out in Cromwell's drugstore, I mean the actresses who'd already been in a couple of plays. On Broadway. So you're right, in a way. There's always another step up those god-damn stairs. But I never wanted to marry any of those girls, Carol."

"You will, darling. Listen, I know you will. I'm not the top. I'm miles from the top. When the war's over and you're a successful director, you'll meet women who make me look —"

"Cut that out, will you. All that modesty crap. What you're saying is that you're not in love with me."

I didn't say anything then. We ordered dinner and ate it and Jason was funny about William Saroyan, who was having trouble with his laundry at Astoria. He didn't want his collars starched. But later in my apartment, after we'd dried each other with the towels I'd learned to keep on the night table, and we were lying side by side, still a little breathless, but peaceful, I thought about it hard.

Dear Jason. I liked him so much. He was funny and kind and we never quarreled. We had so much fun together. But I didn't love him.

Not the way I loved Max. There was some mysterious, unfathomable relationship between Max and me, a recognition that seemed to go way back into my childhood. I knew him in some deeper way than I'd ever known anyone else. He was my intimate, my familiar. I could never love anyone else so long as there was the faintest hope that Max was still alive.

But there was very little hope now.

I couldn't evade that any longer. It had been ninety-one days. I had done those sums in my head so often: so many days for the Red Cross to locate him; so many days to send his name through to the embassy in Stockholm; it was true Daphne didn't go to her apartment very often; it might be at least a week before she forwarded the letter to me. But no matter how often I added it all up, it never came to as many as ninety-one days. I couldn't go on much longer believing Max was alive.

And if he *was* dead?

It wouldn't make me suddenly fall in love with Jason; but I knew how desperately I would turn to him then. There was nothing heroic about me; I had no more courage than most people. If Max was dead, I couldn't bear to lose Jason.

I tried to think that through, living with Jason after the war. He would be off like a streak then, chasing the "bitch goddess." She wasn't my goddess; I had very little interest in that kind of success. In that way I hadn't changed in the last four years. What I still wanted was that indefinable independence, to be what I was, to choose, to experience. To grow. When I asked myself what I meant by growing, the closest I could come to it was the idea of a runner, striving to improve his performance, but not giving a damn about winning any races.

Jason wanted to win races. That didn't make me feel superior; there was something endearing about his ambition. It would be fun to be caught up in all that energy and enthusiasm without having to emulate it. It would be exciting living with Jason and watching him get what he wanted.

I had an impulse to tell him so, then and there, to say that if he still wanted to when the war was over, he could move in with me. Some last, stubborn hope about Max held me back.

I found the letter in the mailbox on my way to work five days later. It wasn't the letter I had imagined myself reading so often.

It was from Max himself.

Dearest Carol, I made it. I made it. I don't know how I managed to squeeze out through that bolt hole in the dark with my parachute harness . . .

I was shaking so violently I couldn't hold the letter still enough to read it in the hallway. I went back to my apartment. For some reason the first thing I did was bolt the door. Then I sat down by the window and put the letter on the coffee table so I could lean on my elbows, holding my head still, and read it.

He had landed in a park somewhere and given himself up to the first German soldier he could find. *All that crap they told us about lynching flyers was horseshit.* They had treated him well; he had a broken ankle; he'd thought it was only sprained; a Wehrmacht doctor had set it for him. He was in a prison camp near —— ——. The name of the town was scissored out, the only censored word in the letter. It was boring as hell there. *But better bored than dead.* I could write and send him food packages through the Red Cross.

I'd stopped shaking. I read the letter again twice, then folded and put it away in my bag. I wanted to carry it around with me so I could look at it through the day and make sure it was true.

I was unbolting the door when I felt it coming; I ran into the bathroom and brought up my breakfast. The dry heaves only lasted a few minutes this time. When I was sure they were over, I washed my face and brushed my teeth again and went to work.

I sat in my small office and read manuscripts and wrote reports on them. I didn't call anyone. My joy was private. I wanted to keep it to myself, as long ago I had been careful to keep secret some rare object I had found, to preserve its magic. I was afraid others might intrude on my thankfulness, might disturb my euphoria with questions. I didn't want to answer any questions about Max. The only question that concerned me had already been answered. He was alive.

When I left the office at six, I walked up to Central Park South and across to the Plaza. It was like that day I had quit the store; I felt the same heady sense of freedom. I had been carrying anxiety like a malignant tumor for three months, trying to ignore it, at times even forgetting it, but always knowing it was there. Now it was gone, harmless as a nightmare.

I didn't take the Fifth Avenue bus this time. In my sudden liberation, I wanted to stroll. I walked, lingering, all my senses alive, down my favorite streets. Fifth Avenue as far as the library, then over to Third and under the antic El to Fourteenth Street, past the Academy of Music where I had once won five dollars at Screeno, back to Fifth Avenue, and down to the arch.

There were few people in Washington Square. I sat on the rim of the circle; the stone was still warm. I had said, Please, so often about Max. Please, don't let him be dead, please. I felt I ought to say, Thank you, now. To whom? Who was that nameless atavistic spirit I was always pleading with in my distress? I hadn't any idea. I tried to form, not a visual image — that was impossible — but some half-subliminal perception and understanding of who I thought it was. The closest I could get to it was that she was an ideal.

She?

Why had I thought that? The spirit's feminine gender had surfaced in my mind with the spontaneity of a dolphin. I welcomed this discovery. I felt an even closer trust in her now that I knew she was a woman. Kind, selfless, beautiful, loving. Then I felt, owing her so much, I should respect her as a voice of conscience, too. A spirit to try to live up to.

I suppose that evening, sitting in Washington Square, was the closest I ever came to a religious experience.

I strolled back to Tenth Street. There was a lock on the outside door now. I stopped under the streetlight to find my key. When I looked up from my bag, I saw a soldier sitting on the stoop. He jumped up and ran to me.

"Where have you been?"

It was Jason.

"I walked home."

"I've been waiting for you in Costello's since six o'clock."

"Why?"

"We had a date."

"Oh."

I hadn't thought about Jason once all day.

"What's wrong, Carol?"

"Nothing. I'm sorry. I'm sorry I forgot." Like someone coming out of a theater, still entranced, I needed time to adjust to this other world with its obligations and demands. "Let's sit down, Jason."

I walked over to the stoop. For the first time since I'd left the office, I realized I was carrying a folder of manuscripts. I put it down on the top step and sat on it. Jason crouched below me. The light was shining on my face and I must have been smiling in a helpless, idiotic way, because after staring at me for a minute, he suddenly understood.

"Oh, Jesus, you've heard from him. He's okay."

"Yes."

He walked over to the streetlight and thumped it, standing with his back to me and beating the metal post with the palm of his hand.

"I guess I ought to be happy for you," he said over his shoulder.

A woman was passing with a boxer on a leash. The dog was straining to get away; it wanted to stop and pee. The woman kept trying to pull it away from the streetlight.

Jason walked back to me.

"Christ, that's all I need, to get peed on. Couldn't we go somewhere and talk?"

"Why don't you sit here?" I moved a little to make room for him beside me.

"I feel like I've been sitting on those goddamn steps all my life."

I should have invited him in. Max's letter was in my bag; the longing to be alone with it in my apartment was irresistible.

"Jason, could you possibly call me tomorrow?" I was behaving like a selfish bitch, but I didn't think of that until later.

"I guess I can't blame you. You kept up your hopes for so long."

The woman with the boxer was gone. Jason walked back to the streetlight. This time he stood there, just holding on to it, for quite a long time before he came back to me.

"Okay. I'll see you on Saturday at six o'clock in the Sevilla."
It was the air-conditioned restaurant I had taken him to. "Do you
think you can remember that?"

I nodded and stood up. "I'm sorry about tonight. I'm sorry I
forgot."

I still had my key in my hand. I was halfway up the stairs before
I remembered I'd left the folder of manuscripts on the steps. I
went back for it. Jason was standing across the street, smoking a
cigarette. He dropped it on the sidewalk and ground it out with
his heel when he saw me.

I didn't wave or call out to him. There didn't seem to be anything
to say. I went upstairs to my apartment.

"Is he really all right?" Jason asked. "He's not hurt or anything."
"No, he's okay."

There was almost no one in the Sevilla that early. We sat in a
booth with our Gibsons. The restaurant was cool and quiet, and
it should have been easy to talk. I had had three days to think
over what I was going to say, and all I had been able to come up
with was a fierce resolution not to tell Jason I couldn't help the
way I felt.

"It's been fun knowing you, Miss Clavering."

I sipped my Gibson.

"I guess I always knew it was going to happen."

Jason lit a cigarette; I wished I smoked.

"Anyway, it has happened and I think the best thing we can
do is end it right now."

I nodded.

"There's no point in dragging it on until he gets back."

"Okay." I wanted to tell him how grateful I was; he had done
so much for me.

"You think I'm right, don't you?"

"Yes."

We ordered paella. Jason ate most of his in silence; I nibbled
the shrimps and the clams but I couldn't manage the rice. We
both edged our plates away from us.

Jason lit another cigarette. From the way he did it, I knew he
had something to tell me.

"I've volunteered to go overseas."

"No."

It was the first spontaneous thing I'd said since I sat down. "No, Jason." I wanted to grab him and hold him. "That's the stupidest thing I've ever heard."

"Why? What is?"

"Just because Max —"

"Don't flatter yourself. It has nothing to do with you or your fly-boy." I couldn't blame him for hitting out at me. "I've been wanting to get shipped out for a long time."

"That's not true. You never said a word —"

"I can go over with a film unit. You couldn't buy experience like that. There'll be a second front some day. I might even get to Paris. Shack up at the George Cinq. Did I pronounce that right? George Cinq."

"Yes."

Jason fiddled with his cigarette as though he were going to stub it out and then put it back in his mouth.

"Don't you think it's a good idea?"

"No, I don't. I told you, I think it's stupid."

"Why?"

"You might get killed."

"Wouldn't you like that?"

"Stop it, Jason."

"You know, Carol —" He leaned forward. He no longer looked angry, only serious and inquiring. "All the things we've talked about, we've never talked about the war."

"What about it?"

"It's not like the last one. It's important, beating the Nazis. It's got to be done. Don't you agree?"

"I suppose so."

"But you don't really believe in it?"

I had to think before I answered; I wasn't sure what I believed about the war any longer.

"I think maybe it isn't *what* you fight against, so much. It's *how* you fight against it that makes a war worthwhile."

I was thinking of Max, those "terrified" men, the official phrase used to describe them when they cracked, "lack of moral fiber," the safe, career-minded brass with their "acceptable" losses and their area bombing.

"I think maybe we passed that point some time ago, about *how* to fight so that it's still worthwhile."

"Yeah, maybe." Jason put out his cigarette and lit another one, taking his time over it. "But then I'm Jewish. I've got relatives in Latvia. A whole family of Steins. I used to have relatives in Latvia. They've probably all been murdered by now."

There was nothing I could say to that. It made all my arguments irrelevant.

We parted outside the restaurant. I walked home thinking about it, about Jason. I hoped it was true, what he'd said, that he wanted to get shipped out because of the film unit experience, the George Cinq, his murdered relatives, and not because of me.

I had a postcard from him a week later.

"I'm sorry if I was a shit the other night. I may get sent to London next week, and I want you to know I'm not mad at you. It's not your fault, Carol. You can't help the way you feel.

Twelve

The train to Montreal was crowded with American servicemen.

I hadn't expected that. Many high-point combat soldiers had been returned to the U.S. by then, July of '45, and millions of others were being redeployed to the Pacific. But I hadn't expected to find so many of them going to Montreal.

Some of the medium-drunk ones tried to make room for me on their seats in the day coach. They had bulky brown-paper bags tucked into their pockets. I didn't think they'd stay medium drunk long. I was afraid one of them might be sick on my new dress. I sat on my suitcase at the end of the aisle, where the conductor could trip over me.

After Newburgh two sober petty officers picked me up. They took me to a coach full of touchingly young sailors and found a seat for me. They were attentive and polite and called me ma'am, which reminded me of those M.P.s in London. One of them was from Iowa and the other from North Dakota, and they were going to Quebec for special sonar training. Why Quebec? They didn't seem to know, either. Later one of them fell asleep with his head on my lap. He slept the way dogs do, all relaxed except for his nose, which twitched now and then in a protesting way. At least, it did as far as Albany. After that I fell asleep myself.

Since the war in the Pacific hadn't ended yet, there was still official secrecy about troop-ship sailings. I wasn't allowed to meet Max when he disembarked. After a lot of cabling back and forth to the Canadian transport base at Le Havre, I had arranged to wait for him at the Windsor Hotel on St. Catherine's Street in Montreal.

The Windsor had been recommended in the list I got from my old contacts at the British Library. Their information must have been a little out of date. When I arrived there from the station that morning, the desk clerk didn't try to hide his surprise at seeing me.

"A cette heure?" he greeted me. *"Vous voulez une chambre à cette heure? Toute seule?"*

I had a little trouble at first understanding his Canadian French, but surprisingly he seemed to understand me. I told him yes, I did want a room at that hour, and I *was* all alone. I refused to be put off and sent to another hotel and when I explained why, *"Mon ami — prisonnier de guerre — nous avons fait rendezvous ici,"* and so on, he was sympathetic and fatherly and gave me a large front room with a private toilet on the second floor.

The Windsor was shabby in a way I liked and, until nine or ten at night, deserted. I had never been in a hot-pillow joint before and the first night I was intrigued by all the comings and goings. After that, the tramp of military boots on the stairs, the drunken singing, the shrill arguments about money in the corridors, became as routine and monotonous as the sound of traffic from St. Catherine's Street. I soon learned to sleep through them.

I had no indication what time of what day Max would arrive. He might walk in any moment. For two days expectancy kept me close to the hotel. I had brought some manuscripts from the agency; I stayed in my room and read them. When I was hungry I went to the café across the street and sat so that I could watch the hotel entrance.

The third day I decided I was being ridiculous. I couldn't keep it up. The feeling of anticipation was no longer exciting, it was just a constant strain. I was beginning to imagine Max's ship had been lost at sea; I would spend the rest of my life in that room, waiting for his knock on the door; I would become known in the neighborhood as the Widow of the Windsor.

I explored the city, climbed Mont Royal, found a street full of secondhand bookstores, went to the movies.

Newsreels of the German concentration camps had reached Canada by then and I saw them for the first time. There had been photographs in American newspapers and magazines, but the actuality of those films was overwhelming. Here was something one had only known about in theory before, as impossible to grasp as endless space. Infinite cruelty. For years in those camps men and women had been tortured and murdered with a routine callousness that added a different dimension to one's conception of the human character. I came out of the theater with a chill understanding that a certain security had gone out of my life forever. A barrier had been broken. The safe, cozy, middle-class illusion that there were limits, things *no one* would ever do, had been shattered. The thing that scared me, as I walked back to the hotel, was the suspicion that a precedent had been set. A license had been granted. The Germans had been the first, but they would not be the last. The quality of mercy had been strained and broken and left for dead now.

"Il est arrivé, Madame."

The fatherly desk clerk was smiling with pleasure when I entered the lobby.

I ran up the stairs and into the room. There was a duffel bag on the floor, an air force jacket on the bed. There was no Max. I stood there looking around like a child in a game of hide-and-seek that had gone on too long.

I heard a sound through the toilet door. I rattled the handle.

"Max?"

"Carol?"

"Max." I was close to screaming.

"I won't be a minute."

I sat on the bed trying not to listen to the strained, hurt sighs coming from behind the closed door. It was several minutes before Max came out. He was in his shirt and trousers and his belt was unfastened. I had my arms around him at once. I couldn't let go of him. He was trying to hold me and kiss me and do up his belt at the same time. Our impetuous confusion finally landed us on the bed.

We went on kissing until my lips felt bruised. It wasn't the sort of kiss that meant let's make love. All I wanted to tell him — I think all he wanted to tell me — was, You're here, you're really here, and the seeking of each other's mouths was the expression of our need to be sure that was true.

"Max."

"Carol."

We lay side by side like blind monkeys, touching and feeling and exploring each other.

"Are you all right, Max?"

We were sitting up at last. I looked at him, all of him. He was so thin. His hands were so delicate. There was no color in his skin except where the veins showed pale violet.

"Sure. I'm all right. I'm a hell of a lot better, anyway."

"Why? What's wrong?"

He told me about it gradually, in short, rueful admissions. He had had dysentery in the camp. It wasn't anybody's fault; German transportation had broken down completely toward the end; there had been nothing to eat except moldy turnips; a lot of the guards had had dysentery too. The U.S. doctors had given him pills at the base hospital he was taken to when the camp was liberated; they must have had opium in them; they had stopped the runs at once; he had even begun to put on weight; then on the ship it had started again, not so badly; he was all right now.

He wasn't all right. When we went out to dinner he couldn't eat anything except soup, and I kept waking in the night and hearing those sighs from the toilet. They sounded much louder to my ears than the drunken voices from the hall. Max would cling to me when he came back to bed. He would fall asleep for a while, then I would wake an hour later to those same hurt sounds.

He had to report to the air force base in the morning to start going through the process of being discharged. He could have taken a month's leave first, but that would have meant coming back to Canada later. We both felt it was better to get it over with now. He thought it would only take two or three days before he was through with the air force forever.

I had three weeks' vacation from the agency. Harriet had made me promise to keep in touch. I called her that afternoon.

Her secretary answered the phone with the usual rigmarole about Miss Bach being in a meeting. Could I hold —

"Never mind all that, Edna," I told her. "It's Carol. Just let me talk to Harriet."

The rigmarole was fairly new. It had been introduced at the time we had all been moved away from the mailroom into offices looking out over Sixth Avenue. It never worked very well because Edna couldn't learn to discriminate. She would keep Robert Penn Warren holding the line from Iowa when Harriet had been waiting all week to hear from him.

Harriet greeted me in the usual way. "I've just sold the Edward Heth book to Metro. Nat said I was crazy, they'd never touch it. Guess how much I got?"

I was calling from the desk; there was no phone in the room. In that alien lobby the talk about books and stories and prices was like news from home. Even the charade Harriet and I played with each other, about how brilliant she was if she sold something and how lucky I was if I did, seemed cozily familiar; we had been playing it for two years.

"*Il est maigre, votre ami,*" the desk clerk said as I paid him for the call.

Yes, I agreed. He was very thin.

Max was furious when he came back at five. The air force doctors had seen at once how sick he was. They wanted to keep him in the base hospital for a month or so before they discharged him.

"Well" — I thought it was a good idea — "isn't that — "

"The bastards. They're afraid if they let me go now, I'll put in for a partial disability pension."

I didn't believe him. The Canadians? Like many Americans, I had always had a shamed feeling that Canada was a gentler, more scrupulous country than the United States. I thought if the Canadian doctors wanted to keep Max in the hospital, it was only because they were trying to help him.

"I'll stay up here with you," I told him later that evening. "I'll just tell the agency I can't come back for a while. I'll find a room somewhere near the hospital."

Max wouldn't hear of it. He had had almost six years of barracks and restrictions and men. "Men," he said, lying with my arms around him that night. "Men's voices. Men's bodies. Their stupid jokes. Men's comradeship — that's a lot of bullshit. When men are together they're just a herd of mindless ids. I'm getting out of the herd this week if I have to desert from the fucking air force."

He didn't have to desert. He was right about the Canadian authorities: all they wanted was his signature on a release form. Once he had signed away all claims against them forever, they were glad to let him go. After that, it took only one more day to go through the rest of the processing and draw his pay. I met him at the base when he walked out through the gates.

"Free. Free," he yelled.

We went straight to a department store and bought a suitcase. Shirts, socks, ties, jackets, trousers, underwear — we wandered from department to department filling it. Max left his uniform with all its overseas ribbons and flight badges on the floor of the changing room in men's suits.

"Free. Free," he kept repeating as we drove back to the hotel.

We took the train to Boston the next morning. By some miracle we found a room at the Copley Plaza. We would have had champagne sent up to the room, but Max was afraid to drink anything except brandy and water. He had an idea brandy was "binding." So we had a bottle of Remy Martin instead.

He made love to me that night for the first time since he'd come back. He wasn't in the least like the urgent Max I remembered from his leave in New York; he was gentle and halting and made me feel a helpless tenderness for him.

I'm going to make it all up to him, I decided before I fell asleep. All those lost years and Bomber Command and the prison camp. I'm going to make it all up to him if it takes me the rest of my life.

The next day we took the boat to Provincetown. I'd spent three summer vacations there and my old friend and landlady, Judy Zora, let us have her best wharf studio. We woke every morning to the rippling pattern of light reflecting from the sea onto our whitewashed ceiling. We fell asleep every night to the ebb and flow of the tide under our wooden floor. I took Max sailing, until he admitted he didn't really enjoy it. He felt uneasy on small boats and had never learned to swim. We walked down Commercial Street to the main wharf to watch the fishing fleet come in. But most of the time we lay on the beach and talked.

We made plans. Or maybe I made plans and Max agreed to them. I caught an inkling of a question in his voice at times, as though he were qualifying what he said. Often he seemed to be thinking of something else, something beyond our immediate future together.

We decided we'd live in my apartment, at least for the present. Max would go to a New York hospital for tests and get rid of his damn bug once and for all. Later we'd start looking for a larger apartment. Max wanted to go back into film editing. He hoped he could find a job with a documentary film unit in New York. But there was no hurry about that; he had two years' back pay from the RCAF, over seven thousand dollars. He needed a long rest before he looked for a job.

And every once in a while, as we walked along the wharf or lay in the sand dunes, it would hit me with the force of a discovery: I'm happy. Not, Isn't this fun? or, I love it here. But a sudden wonder. I'm happy.

August sixth was our last-but-one day in Provincetown. I'd promised to be back at work before then, but Harriet had grudgingly conceded to let me stay away another few days. We were sitting on the sundeck of the studio when Judy Zora called out to us from next door. She'd heard something on the radio about a bomb.

"The power of the sun." I remember that phrase; it was in every newspaper we could find. "The U.S. has harnessed the power of the sun."

We sat up talking with Judy until midnight. She was a thirties radical who had married a Portuguese fisherman. She and I felt the same chill horror. We didn't think America could be trusted with so much power. We were full of sententious urgency about international control, handing the bomb over to the United Nations.

Max didn't argue with us, but I sensed he didn't agree. He sat and smoked and his cigarette ends were like small fireworks as he flicked them into the sea.

"What *do* you think?" I finally challenged him.

"You say you don't trust America. What you really mean is, you don't trust people."

I thought that was obvious. Neither Judy nor I had been singling out the U.S. as particularly irresponsible. I wouldn't even have trusted Norway with the atomic bomb, those clean, honest, civilized Norwegians. What Judy and I felt was that there had to be some absolute, irrevocable, international check on the ghastly thing.

"Why don't you trust people?" Max pressed his point.

I was beginning to see what he was getting at. I thought of the slave trade, the First World War, those concentration camp newsreels, our whole wretched history of slaughter and betrayal. Even when we'd started out with a good idea — Christianity, socialism — we'd always corrupted and perverted it: the sordid fanaticism of the Crusades, the Inquisition, Stalin.

"Do you think there's something fundamentally wrong with us, with humanity?" Max asked presently.

Perhaps I did. At the same time, there had been people of whom, I thought, that obviously wasn't true. Socrates, Tom Paine, my old friend John Stuart Mill. No one who wrote like Mill could be fundamentally flawed.

"We're stupid," I said. "Most of us, anyway. We're greedy and selfish and inclined to fanaticism, and we don't think —"

"No, we're not. We're not greedy or selfish. Part of us isn't."

I could tell from Max's voice he was saying what he had been wanting to say at last; he was no longer holding back something.

"Our whole trouble is that we don't know ourselves. We don't understand the conflicting forces inside us. Our subconscious processes . . ." He went on about that. A lot of it was familiar: the ego, the id, the superego, the suppressed sexual urges, the buried traumas. "Once we understand ourselves, rid ourselves of all that through abreaction, we'll become completely different people. We'll be able to handle things, even things like the atomic bomb, sanely and objectively."

"Okay, what are you saying? What's the answer then?" It was Judy who asked him.

"It's all in Freud," Max told her gently. "The answer is psychoanalysis, of course."

The night was so still; it was warm and untroubled, sitting there

on the sundeck. Max must have been reading Freud in the POW
camp, I thought. He's found something else to believe in, the way
he once believed in the Trotskyists. I would have to try to read
some of old Sigmund myself.

Thirteen

It's a fantasy," I argued to Maggie over the phone. "It's an *allegory.*"

"They're living together, and Mr. Hearst —"

"Oh, come on, Maggie, there's not a word about sex in the whole story."

"They're sharing a room, and Mr. Hearst won't stand for that unless they're married. I'm sorry, Carol, I like the story and I want to print it, but the writer will have to do something about that."

I knew it was no use arguing with her any further. It wasn't Maggie's fault; she was a good editor and a nice woman. She didn't make the rules, those weird, tangled relics of prejudice and superstition that decided what went into a women's magazine.

"I'll call him and see if he'll change it," I promised.

After I'd hung up I had my secretary bring me the carbon copy of the story out of the files. It was called "Cast the First Shadow." I read it through. It wasn't great or anything, but it was well written and it made its point. As I'd told Maggie, it was an allegory: A boy born without a shadow. It ruins his life; everybody who finds out his secret shuns him. He's sure he can't be unique; finally he does find a beautiful young girl who has no shadow either. Mutual outcasts, they fall in love and — this was where Maggie's problem came in — they move into a room together. They live there like hermits; she is even more of a recluse than he is; one night he persuades her to go to a dance hall. As they are leaving, they pass some mirrors on the stairs. Understanding at last why others have always been so repelled by him, he runs away from her in horror. She had been deceiving him, pretending they were alike. "She not only had no shadow, the monstrous, the unnatural girl had no reflection."

Okay. But it was better than most of the dross I handled. That probably said more about women's magazines than it did about the story. Those magazines sickened me — or would have if I'd read them. Their fact pieces, as Harriet called them, were worse than their fiction. Does your husband criticize your clothes? Do your children love you? They seemed filled with a sadistic determination to make their women readers squirm with abject guilt. Years later Betty Friedan wrote an interesting book about all that.

I called the writer.

"I'm sorry, did I wake you up?" It was noon, but I had only met him once; I didn't know what his sleep habits were.

"No. I always sound like that over the phone. What is it?"

I explained about Maggie, *Cosmopolitan,* Mr. Hearst.

"I don't understand. Can't you just put it in?"

"What?"

"Do you have a copy of the story anywhere?"

"In front of me."

"Read me the bit just before she moves into the damn room with whatever his name is."

I read it to him over the phone.

"Okay. Stop right there and write it in. Those three mumbling words. They got married."

"I knew you'd fix it," Maggie said when I called her back.

I checked with Harriet's secretary before going into her corner office.

"She can give you five minutes." The secretary was a shy, well-dressed young woman with glasses and a Bryn Mawr accent. We got along well and I hoped she'd last. She was the third new secretary since plump, sleazy Edna.

"Who's the writer?" Harriet asked when I told her I'd sold the shadow story. I gave her his name, Chris Deniken.

She called the business office at *Cosmopolitan* to settle the price; she still handled all the money side of the literary department. She asked for $1500 and settled for $1250. I congratulated her. She agreed to let me call the writer myself. It was the part of my job I enjoyed most, giving writers the good news that I'd sold something for them.

That summer I had been at the agency for five years. Most of the time I still enjoyed it, although some days the "needs" of the slick magazines, Harriet's unceasing demands for admiration and reassurance, made me want to scream. Luckily, they were far fewer than the days when I came across a manuscript I liked or sold something I thought worth publishing.

I no longer worked so closely with Harriet. She had long ago passed the million gross mark and now had time only for the big earners, the Micheners, the Taylor Caldwells, and an occasional prestige client like Justice Douglas. I took care of the rest, including the young and promising, until they became big earners. So long as my subdepartment paid its way, Harriet left me pretty much alone.

With this growing distinction between our jobs, Harriet's reliance on me was increasingly personal. She was still searching for Harriet Bach. *The* Harriet Bach, who had put Oscar Hammerstein onto *South Pacific,* who could pick up the phone and talk to Kazan. Just like that. Who *was* Harriet Bach? Was she charming and feminine like Claire Boothe Luce? Or butch like Maggie? Or all ice and diamonds like Fleur Cowles? After trying them all on for size, she was still unsure. I had seen Harriet through a hat phase, a severe black suit phase, a heavy silver bracelet and bangs phase. At the moment she was inclining toward pastel cashmere and a single strand of pearls.

Her mother thought she was crazy whatever she wore, so it was up to me to encourage her, to tell her *this* time she'd got it. By George, she'd got it. My personal opinion was that none of it, hats, bracelets, pearls, was going to make the faintest difference to the way she was or to the way others saw her. She was fast becoming the most successful literary agent in New York and she was still, she would always be, the same rather kind, shrewd, honest, and insecure woman who had greeted me with her news about the Literary Guild five years ago.

I was fond of her, and I think she felt safe and comfortable with me because she knew I wasn't essentially ambitious.

The little ambition I did have was identified with my clients. Like a schoolteacher, I wanted them to do their best. They were a maddening lot. I didn't mind them calling me at three o'clock in the morning to tell me they needed an abortion; what I did mind was that so few of them would write about anything that mattered to them. Even when they were writing for a "serious" market, they would desperately avoid their own convictions. Perhaps it was the times: Truman was still president, but Dewey was coming up like a smug brown cloud over the horizon.

The hours were good. I came in at ten, took a long lunch, usually with an editor or writer, and was away by six. I refused to meet any of my clients for a drink after work. Lunch, okay; but when Harriet went off every evening to the Plaza or "21," I went home.

Max and I were living in a duplex on Charles Street. "Duplex" sounds misleadingly grand; it was the top two floors of a red brick house and the rent was $115 a month. What I loved about it was that there was so much open space: the whole top floor was one big room, living room, dining room, and alcove kitchen, with no doors between them. On the floor below were two bedrooms and two bathrooms. The front bedroom was mine. I minded the street noises less than Max did. I didn't notice them, and I liked the light from the two big windows.

When I got home I made my bed, unless the cleaning woman had come that day and made it for me, and showered and changed and then went upstairs and had a drink. With all the lunches I was eating I was never very hungry, and I would fix a salad or a sandwich and take it back to the couch in the living room so I could read manuscripts in comfort while I ate.

Five nights a week Max didn't come home until after eight-thirty. He liked to stop by somewhere for his evening meal on his way downtown. He said the impersonal atmosphere of a drugstore or a cafeteria helped him focus. When he got home we sometimes talked; sometimes he was still focusing, and after we'd kissed hello and how are you, I went back to my manuscripts.

Around ten o'clock, unless I had my period, we made love on the couch in the living room. That couch — it was the cherished hub of my home life. Where my heart was. Around eleven we went downstairs to our own rooms.

We only slept in the same bed on the weekends. It was understood between us that this was only a temporary arrangement, but, as the French say, there is nothing more permanent than that. It had been going on for two years now. I missed Max sometimes in the night, his warmth and the familiar sound of his breathing; other times, if I had a lot of reading to do, I was glad to be able to keep my light on until one or two in the morning without feeling I was disturbing him.

We had started sleeping apart because of Max's dreams. He had to write them down. He kept a pen and a notebook beside his bed. I had told him it didn't bother me if he switched his lamp on in the middle of the night and started scribbling away; as a matter of fact, it never even woke me. But he said he could only concentrate properly if he was alone.

He had been going to the same analyst for two years now. At first he had switched about a lot, breaking with them suddenly and plaintively, the way my writers sometimes broke with me, and for perhaps much the same reasons. But he seemed to have found the right one at last. The right one for him. She was a woman in her fifties, a German refugee, Maria Schoenfeldt. She saw him five nights a week from 6:00 to 7:00 and she charged him fifteen dollars a session. This, and the fact that she lived on Central Park West, was all I ever knew about her. Max wasn't supposed to discuss his analyst with me.

He had settled into a "temporary" job as a cutter with a stock-film company that supplied special footage — airplane crashes, shots of Buckingham Palace — to the studios. He insisted on paying for Maria himself. That was essential, he explained. You would only value your analysis if you had to earn it; this was one of the reasons analysts charged so much. *One* of the reasons? I wondered what the others were. I didn't ask him.

Paying Maria left Max very little for anything else. I took care of the rent, and the cleaning woman who came in twice a week, and the other domestic expenses, phone and light — I've forgotten what else; I didn't think about money much. I was making a good salary and had no interest in acquiring expensive possessions.

One of my few personal extravagances was liquor. Max had stopped drinking since he'd been going to Maria. I liked to keep Scotch and bourbon and vodka and various mixes and French wines in the house. I enjoyed having a choice to come home to in the evenings. Scotch and soda, or bourbon on the rocks, or vodka and tonic, or a Gibson, or perhaps a glass of Beaujolais? I would think it over on the subway coming downtown from the office. By the time I reached Fourth Street, I had usually made up my mind. It seemed to me a small, harmless pleasure, that evening ritual of expectation and fulfillment. I was coming to value small rituals more and more.

I think a lot of people felt let down at that time, those first few years after the war. We had all been promised so much, such a fresh, exciting future when the war was over. Of course, we did have many wonderful new things. Frozen orange juice and ball-point pens and Birds Eye peas and cars without running boards and vitamin pills and disposable bottles and plastic everything-you-could-think-of. And DDT. Perhaps we were spoiled; none of these wonders seemed to keep us happy for long. Perhaps what we'd hoped for were new attitudes, new ideas. There were no "twenties" after the Second World War, no revolution in the arts or fashion. The New Look wouldn't have looked new to the Edwardians. The men came home and moved to the suburbs and started to worry about having to fight Russia. Except that the Depression was over, we might have been back in '39 worrying about Germany. It was exciting when Truman beat Dewey that November. I sat up all night listening to the radio. But morning brought the flat realization that nothing had changed; it just hadn't gotten any worse.

I tried to talk to Max about it sometimes. He said I was projecting, seeing my own malaise in others. Maybe he was right. I know I had an intermittent feeling that year that I was waiting for something. I could never quite define what it was I was waiting for.

I hadn't taken a summer vacation. Max had to fit his plans with Maria's so he wouldn't miss too many sessions with her. The month she chose to go to Vermont overlapped Harriet's three weeks in Southampton and I had to be in the office . . . Anyway, we couldn't work it out so Max and I could go anywhere together. He talked about flying to California alone, but in the end he stayed home and wrote down his dreams and thought of things to tell Maria when she came back.

I went down to Florida by myself for three weeks after the elections. Cedar Key on the west coast had once been a center of the pencil industry. All the cedar trees had been cut down years ago and it was more or less a ghost town now, with one hotel and a wharf and a few crab fishermen.

I rented a dilapidated sailboat for three weeks. The hotel would give me a box lunch and I went out, tacking up and down the coast, all day, every day. It sounds incredible now, but I used to find deserted coves where I could pull the little boat up on the beach and swim and lie in the sun with no clothes on. In Florida.

It was what I needed, time to myself. I thought about my job at the agency and about Charles Street and about Max.

I couldn't find anything wrong with any of them. Compared to most people's, my job was interesting, painless, and overpaid. If I could help a few young writers do some good work, or at least make a living, it even had a harmless purpose to it. The apartment on Charles Street was perfect. I loved the Village, its distinctive streets, its Italian groceries and Jewish delicatessens, the liquor stores that would cash a check for you even if you didn't buy anything. I never got tired of wandering around the Village with Max on Saturday afternoons, watching the chess games in the square and ending up having dinner in an Italian restaurant.

There was nothing wrong with Max, either. He was, understandably, self-absorbed at this stage of his analysis, sometimes "not there" when I wanted to talk to him, and there were many things we couldn't talk about at all. Maria, for one. But he was considerate, he never bored me, we didn't quarrel. He was amusing and fun to be with, especially on weekends when he wasn't seeing Maria. We had a wonderful, *ecstatic* time together on that couch.

Anyway, I loved him. And his analysis wouldn't go on forever.

It occurred to me *that* might be what I was waiting for, for Max to finish his analysis. One evening he would come home from Maria and he would be all adjusted to everything. He wouldn't mind the lipstick stains on my glass when he was doing the washing up. He would understand why the sight of lipstick on a glass upset him: that woman friend of his father's who had lived next door in Fresno when he was a child, and so on. He would understand everything about himself; it would make him tolerant and understanding of other people's faults, too. He would be unfailingly sane and wise and well-balanced.

Well, maybe. No. I didn't really believe that. Analysis hadn't worked that way with Freud: he had been a vain and jealous old grouch to the end of his life. It hadn't worked that way with any of the writers I'd known who had been analyzed, either: sometimes it had made them dull and self-righteous; sometimes it hadn't noticeably changed them at all.

I didn't think it had essentially changed Max in two years. He had become more self-controlled since going to Maria; he never lost his temper now no matter what anyone said to him. But he was still eager and passionate and given to unpredictable acts of kindness. He could still be moved to indignation over what had happened in Czechoslovakia or what would happen if we had Thomas Dewey in the White House.

One day, though, his analysis would end. We could go back to sleeping in the same bed every night. Max could turn his concentration away from himself. He could expend his enthusiasm and energy on some less internal pursuit, decide what he wanted to do with his life.

I still didn't think that was what I was waiting for. I still couldn't define or explain my intermittent sense of frustrated expectancy.

I was sailing home before the wind on the day before I had to leave, trying to judge my turn to the mooring so that I would drift to it smoothly and gently and be able to walk forward and catch the buoy without having to stretch for it. The tide was out and the bay smelled of dead fish. Nothing in any of that explains why it suddenly came to me. As I made fast and started to take the sail down, I knew exactly what I was waiting for.

I wanted to have a child.

For the rest of that Saturday and all the way back to New York the next day, I tried to plan it.

I would have to keep my job. Even without Maria, we couldn't live and bring up a child on what Max earned. If I was lucky, I could keep going to the agency until my seventh (eighth?) month. After that it would be best if I took a three (four?) month leave of absence so I could stay home with the baby and feed it. Breast-feed it? At that time, breast-feeding was regarded by some people as a solemn duty to one's children, like being active in the PTA. Okay. But there was no way I could both breast-feed my baby and keep my job. The poor, deprived infant would have to get along without its mother's milk. After all, a lot of my generation had survived on a formula. Breast-feeding had been considered unhygienic in the twenties.

I would start saving money for that leave of absence at once. The crucial time would come after I went back to work. I would have to have help. Surely, if I started looking early enough, I could find some kind, decent woman I could trust to take care of my child while I was at the office. Maybe it was racist of me, but I had a picture of a gentle, middle-aged black lady who had brought up children of her own. I decided I could pay her fifty (sixty?) dollars a week if I stopped drinking altogether and scrimped on everything else. Fifty (sixty?) dollars a week was quite an attractive salary. Plump, sleazy Edna had been getting fifty-five when Harriet fired her. There was no reason why I couldn't hurry home every day during my lunch hour to help with the bottles and diapers. My writers would just have to do without their free lunches. And weekends . . .

Ah, weekends, I would spend every minute of my time . . .

All the problems and the answers to them kept jolting through my head on the bus trip across Florida, the wait at Jacksonville airport. By the time I landed at Newark, I had run out of snags. I knew I could swing it.

I couldn't wait for the airport bus. Throwing away money I ought to be saving for my leave of absence, I took a taxi straight to Charles Street. Halfway up the stairs with my suitcase, I realized there was one aspect of parenthood I hadn't seriously considered yet.

Max.

Until that moment I had imagined myself bursting in on Max and telling him the good news.

"We're going to have a baby."

"Darling, you're pregnant."

Joy to the world.

"No, but I want to be."

And so to the couch, as Pepys might have said.

It struck me now that this bordered on fantasy. The phonograph was playing upstairs; Max was in the living room. I took my time hanging up my overcoat and combing my hair. The subject would have to be approached slowly, Max sounded out. It was only fair to give him time to think it all over as I had done. Max must be allowed to grow used to the idea of fatherhood.

I went upstairs.

We kissed, Ah, darling, and how are you, and I missed you, and how was the flight, and did you get my letters? On the phonograph Bessie Smith was wailing for a pig's foot and a bottle of beer. It was one of our favorite records; I waited, snuggling up with Max on the couch, until it was over.

"Are you hungry?" he asked in the silence.

"They gave us something on the plane."

He looked disappointed. "I made some stew. I thought I could heat it up for you."

Why not? It seemed like a good opening, Max being domestic, bringing me food. It would help create the right atmosphere for talking about home, families.

I went into the kitchen with him. He had obviously been eating the stew all weekend; most of what was left of it was stuck to the bottom of the pot. By pouring boiling water over it, he managed to get a few scraps loose and even warmed up a little.

I took my plate to the dining room table so Max could sit across from me in a cozy tête-à-tête. The singed smell of the meat and carrots made me long for a glass of wine to swallow them with. I had decided to give up drinking, hadn't I? But seven beautiful bottles of Beaujolais were lying on their sides in the bookcase I used as a wine bin. They were already paid for; what was I going to do, pour them down the sink? How would that help the baby? I opened one of them, filled a tumbler, and went back to the stew.

"Did you have a good time down there?" Max asked.

"It was very quiet. I did a lot of thinking." Now for the thin end of the wedge. "One of the things —"

"So did I."

"You did? What about?" Cross your fingers; he's been thinking about the same thing.

"I wrote a letter to the *New York Times* about it."

"Oh."

"They'll never print it, of course."

While I drank my wine and chewed the meat, Max told me about his letter.

"What this country, what every country, needs is a new elite. An elite of people who know and understand themselves. Who can make reasonable decisions based on the facts, without being influenced by a lot of neurotic, subconscious prejudices. Don't you see, Carol? It's only people like that who can ever be trusted with leadership, who have the right to be trusted with it."

"But, Max, who's going to decide?"

"What?"

"Who's going to decide who belongs to this elite, who those people are?"

He smiled that rueful smile he had developed lately. "I told you, I didn't expect them to print my letter."

I was fiddling with a burnt carrot.

"I guess that stew's awful, isn't it?" Max reached over to take my plate.

"No, it's all right. I'm just not hungry."

"Don't eat any more. I'll put it in the garbage. Would you like anything else?"

"No. Thank you, Max."

"What were we talking about?" he asked when he came back to the table. "You said you were doing a lot of thinking in Florida."

"Yes. All kinds of things. Mostly about . . . well, I mean, I'm twenty-seven years old and I . . . ." How could you lead up *slowly* to a subject like that? You either had to say it or shut up. "Max, have you ever thought about having children? About us having children?"

"We're not married."

"What's that got to do with it?"

"If we had a kid, it'd be a bastard."

I hadn't thought of that. Did it matter? Would it matter to the child? It all depended on the legitimacy laws in the state of New York. They were probably as archaic as the divorce laws were. Well, if they were going to be bigots about bastardy, we could always get married.

"Would you mind if we got married, Max?"

"Now?"

"Whenever we had to."

"I can't get married now, Carol."

"Why not?"

"It's a tremendous step. One of the most important decisions in anyone's life."

"We've been living together for three years. Why should getting married change anything?"

"It just does, that's all. It changes your whole attitude."

"I don't see why." Would it change my attitude toward Max? "We neither of us believe in that Catholic —"

"That has nothing to do with it." Max raised his voice slightly. He was always a little defensive about his Catholic upbringing, or maybe about having left the church. "It's all very well to say marriage isn't irrevocable, you can always get a divorce. But if you're going to have children, that's a hopelessly irresponsible way of looking at things. You're giving yourself an out before they're even born. They're the ones who are going to have to cope with the divorce — get along without one of their parents, or be shuttled back and forth between them. The children are the ones who are going to get hurt."

Darling Max. I loved him for saying that. He was absolutely right.

"Okay. What you're saying, then, is that the marriage part of it isn't the point. It's the children —" I only wanted one. "It's the child that matters. If you're going to have a child, you'd better mean it. No going back on it later, whether you're married or not."

"I guess so."

"Then how would you feel about having a child?"

We were back at the beginning.

"Jesus, Carol, you've been away for three weeks. You walk in here and you throw *this* at me. What do you expect me to say?"

That was fair enough; I had come to the same understanding myself while I was downstairs combing my hair. Max needed time to think about it.

"Darling, I'm sorry." I went over and put my arms around him. "I don't expect you to make up your mind right now, tonight. I just wanted to see how you might feel — sometime."

"I don't know how I feel." He smiled and kissed me before moving away. "I'll have to try and work it out with — with myself."

He meant with Maria. Well, why not? That was one thing about Maria, she wouldn't tell him what to do. Freudian analysts weren't there to give advice. It was part of the treatment — let the patient stew in his own juice, lie there and agonize about his decisions at fifteen dollars an hour. In the end Max would have to make up his own mind.

"We could talk about it next weekend," I suggested.

"All right." He came back and kissed me again. "You don't mind? You're not angry that I didn't just think it was a wonderful idea?"

"Of course not. No, of course I'm not angry."

It did make me a little angry that he wouldn't make love to me that night. He said he wanted to be by himself so he could think, but I felt the truth was he didn't trust me not to get pregnant on him.

By Wednesday, when he still hadn't made love to me, I decided we had to get that part straight. Celibacy wasn't helping either of us. It made me feel sad, not exactly cast off, but bereaved, as though a friend had died. I was absent-minded at the office because I kept thinking about it. When Max came home from Maria that evening, I insisted on having it out with him. I told him I was wearing my diaphragm. "I promise I'll go on wearing it, Max. I won't pull any sneaky tricks on you and then suddenly tell you I'm three months gone."

He did try to make love to me on the couch that night. It was my fault he didn't altogether succeed. I had challenged him to do it, making the situation strained, quite enough to debilitate any man. I did my best to make Max feel it didn't matter. It didn't; the important thing was we were back together.

On Thursday night everything was fine between us again. Max

was sweet and affectionate and I felt that physical, almost unbearable tenderness for him that I had missed so much for close to a month.

Saturday was one of those chill December days when you can taste the snow in the air even though it hasn't started to fall yet. We walked across Sixth Avenue — I could never think of it as the Avenue of the Americas — and then up to Eighth Street.

Neither of us had said a word so far. Like the snow, the subject of parenthood seemed to be hanging there, waiting to fall on us. We walked up Eighth Street to Fifth Avenue and then, because it was too cold to go into the square, back to Sixth. By that time my face was so frozen I couldn't have said an intelligible word if I'd tried. Not even "help."

There was a Bickford's on that corner then. I pulled Max into it and over to a table. After a minute my face had thawed out enough for me to be able to suggest coffee. Max brought it over on a tray. We sat across the corner of the table from each other, warming our hands on the cups. Dotted about us were the huddled, stone-silent junkies who made the cafeteria their hangout in those days, giving it a bad name and eventually driving it out of business. I tried not to stare at them, tried especially not to see them — most of them were quite young — as examples of what could happen to kids brought up in the Village.

"Have you been thinking about it, Max?" I asked him at last.

"Of course. All the time."

"I know. But how do you feel?"

"Do you really think you ought to have a child?"

The accusing way he said that startled me. "Why not?"

"Look at yourself. I mean, inside yourself. Do you think you'd make a good mother?"

I was damn well going to try.

"Why not?" I said again.

"Oh, for God's sake, Carol, you'd just be continuing that eternal cycle."

"What cycle?"

"You know that case of Freud's." He sounded impatient. "The mother's frigid, so the daughter's frigid, so the granddaughter's frigid."

"I'm not frigid." He couldn't possibly believe I was.

"You're neurotic."

It was extraordinary the effect those two words had on me. For quite a long time after that, for two or three months, they were like a verdict of guilty that had been rendered against me. It had absolutely never occurred to me that I was neurotic, that anyone else could think I was neurotic. I realized later that it showed how deeply, without knowing it, I was influenced by Max that I didn't protest; I didn't flare up and argue with him.

"Do you think I'm neurotic?" I asked meekly.

"Of course you are."

"How?"

I wanted him to tell me. I wanted to know.

"All kinds of ways."

"What?"

"Your insecurity, for one thing. If I don't make love to you for a couple of days, you feel rejected."

Maybe he was right about that.

"Go on," I said.

"Okay. You told me yourself, you feel disappointed, let down, all the time."

"Go on."

"You don't even try to understand why. It couldn't be anything to do with you. It has to be someone else's fault. The world. Truman. Your job. Me."

This time I didn't say, go on. I just waited.

"Your parents never really accepted you. So you overcompensated as a child. You decided you were special, an exceptional person. Never mind *how* you were special. You never even tried to define that. Because, inside, you were scared all the time that it might not be true. So how did you handle that? I'm talking about your subconscious, of course. You made damn certain never to risk that image of yourself, never to put it to the test. Look at that job you had in radio. You were absolutely safe there. You were Fitz's assistant. He was a father substitute for you. If anything went wrong, even when you got fired, it was Fitz's fault. It was the same when you were Harriet Bach's assistant. You could let her take the rejections and failures for you."

I still didn't say anything.

"Then Harriet forced you out on your own. She made you take the responsibility for your own mistakes and inadequacies. So now you're looking for another excuse. You want to have a child. Then you'll be able to blame everything on that. It won't be your fault you never managed to prove what an exceptional person you were. How could you? You sacrificed all that to have children. And the child will grow up just like you. With the same guilts and insecurities and neuroses."

He had been talking in the same quiet, urgent voice, almost without pausing. Occasionally I had moved one of my hands on the table in a gesture of denial, an impulse to protest, but that was all. I felt submerged in the flow of accusations. It was all I could do to raise my head above them for an instant, now and then, to keep breathing, to survive. I had no strength left to say any of the things I might have said in return. The impulse to shout "What about *you?*" was drowned before I could recognize it.

"You're probably thinking, what about me?" Max went on less urgently. "You could say you were doing better with your life than I am with mine. God knows, you're making more money. The difference is that I'm trying. I'm trying to understand my subconscious motives, so that one day I can be my whole self. I can stop rationalizing, stop making childish excuses for my failures, and do something about them."

I realized he'd stopped talking. He was standing up.

"I'm sorry, Carol." He was smiling in a confident way. He looked very commanding, standing there, leaning over me. "I didn't want to tell you all this. You forced me to. You have no right to have a child until you straighten yourself out."

I still didn't say anything.

"You're all fucked up, Carol. And you'll fuck up the kid."

He touched my shoulder. "Come on. Let's go home."

I shook my head.

"Come on, Carol."

"No."

He leaned over me still farther, trying to pull me up by the shoulders.

I hit him.

I hardly knew I was doing it. I slapped him across the face with the back of my hand, the one that was lying on the table.

Max shrugged. "That just proves everything I said."

"Shut up."

If he didn't shut up, I was going to hit him again.

"Shut up and get out of here."

I was shouting.

One of the huddled young men nearby stared at us. I thought he was trying to smile at me. He didn't seem to have enough control over his face; all he could manage was a rictus. When I looked away from him, Max was walking to the door.

Thank God he was gone.

I wanted to sit there alone with the empty coffee cups, the clogged sugar container, the junkies. I felt comfortable among those abject young people, passive as clay, at the tables around me. There was no blame, no accusation in them. They didn't condemn themselves. "I goofed," was the closest they would ever come to confession.

After a while I got myself another cup of coffee. It snapped me out of it a little.

You asked for it, I admitted to myself. Serves you right. Serves you right for feeling so superior to Max. You've been secretly criticizing him for a long time, haven't you? For his dependence on Maria. His self-involvement. His need for belief. Now you know what he thinks of you. You're a far more hopeless case than he is.

"You're all fucked up."

Without my thinking of it, a sentence formed in my mind. I whispered it into the empty coffee cup I was holding to my mouth.

"The monstrous, the unnatural girl had no reflection."

Fourteen

The extraordinary thing was that Max and I went on living together for another six months.

It was a grim time. That showdown in Bickford's was as irrevocable as an amputation. There was no going back from "You're all fucked up and you'll fuck up the kid." Not for either of us; we could only go on from there.

First of all, of course, I had to accept the fact that I wasn't going to have a child. Max and I weren't going to have one together, anyway. Forget my plan for a leave of absence, a kind black lady. Forget it at once. The rest was arguable.

And, God, how we argued about it.

For the first few weeks I didn't argue with much conviction. I was a little like a child who had been led to a mirror by a trusted friend. "Look, you're ugly," the friend had said. For quite a long time I kept peering into the mirror, seeking to find out if it was true.

It often dismayed me; sometimes it hurt; but I tried to keep an open mind about it. Had I been so happy in that job with Fitz because he had been a father substitute for me? Had that absolved me from the risk of failure? Was I trying to do the same thing now with Harriet Bach? Hiding behind her?

The insidious thing, as the B.O. advertisements used to put it, about asking questions like that is that you begin to examine every motive, every action. Even the most insignificant habits become sinister clues.

My evening drink.

Oral infant deprivation? That bloody bottle of formula that had been stuck into my mouth instead of my mother's comforting nipple?

That writer I wanted to drop.

Was it because I thought he was hopeless and I could never sell anything he wrote? Or some suppressed association, some restimulated childhood trauma, some pattern I was forever, compulsively repeating? Did he threaten me — he did once, literally, on the phone — in some way I didn't want to understand?

Not making my bed when I got up in the mornings.

The whole pattern, everything was a pattern, of my morning routine — my clothes set out the night before, on the *radiator* in the wintertime, staying in bed until the last possible moment and then wallowing in a warm bath — was a potential jungle of womb fixations.

It was difficult to believe a decade or so later, but I wasn't the only one asking questions of that kind in those years. Middle-class America was obsessed with them. Job questionnaires, schools, colleges, quizzes in magazines emphasized their importance. Psychiatrists — no one called them shrinks then — were the respected, the only undiscredited, authorities on everything. Plays, books, movies took it for granted that we all believed Freud's or Jung's or Karen Horney's theories were the explanation, the only serious explanation, of crime, murder, war, rape, alcoholism, and political chicanery. Of all human behavior. Psychiatry haunted every office, every living room, as New Deal politics had in the thirties.

I tried not to let my doubts about myself affect my behavior too noticeably. My secretary told me once or twice, quite sympathetically, that I seemed a little tense; but everybody in the agency was more or less tense. At least I never snapped at her the way Harriet snapped at her secretaries. The Bryn Mawr girl quit after only two months. "Miss Bach needs help," she told me her last day at the office. She meant psychiatric help.

On a wider level than my morning sloth was my relationship with everyone. Everyone. Past and present. Both my sisters, of course. Never mind my parents; it would take a lifetime to unravel that. They had both wanted me to be a *boy,* for God's sake.

There were friends, mostly couples, mostly in analysis, whom Max and I would invite for brunch on Sundays. Why did I like and feel comfortable with any given couple? Why didn't I? Why did I react in such a hostile way when one of the men made a pass at me? Because I *wanted* him to make a pass at me? Or because I didn't? And that girl who lived with a fashion photographer on Central Park South — how in Christ's name had we ever met *them?* Why did I want to get the hell out of there that Sunday evening when she insisted on taking me into the bedroom and modeling her clothes for me? All her clothes. Including her underwear. In my innocence I had thought at the time I was just bored.

And Max. Oh, God, Max. Why had I loved him so much, been faithful to him, except for Jason, for ten whole years? Where were the buried associations? What were the subtle dependencies, the neurotic needs that explained that?

In the end it was Max himself who cured me of my self-doubts. Most of them. Because I did start to argue with him. By the time February came, I was arguing more and more forcibly and with increasing conviction. At first my wrangling was mostly of the child-ish "you, too," kind.

"What about you?" I used to yell at him. "What about the way you hang onto that wretched job? Pasting pieces of film together. That's infantile if anything ever was. Nursery play. Snip and glue."

Max would explain it to me, calmly, patiently. Enforced routine — the word "structured" hadn't been discovered yet. Therapy of purpose. Means to an end.

I didn't have to ask what the end was. He was still going to her five nights a week.

"And your Trotskyism," I would accuse him ferociously. "It was nothing but a substitute for that Catholic church you feel so guilty about having left." I was on fairly solid ground there; several prominent Communists had recently defected to the church. "And now you're trying to find God in Freud."

He would dismiss that, too, still patiently. Associative tests. Rorschach. Dreams. Conclusive evidence: no psychological connection.

I didn't believe him.

"And when you tried to make love to me that time after I came back from Florida." I knew this was a foul blow, but I couldn't resist it. "If I ever saw a case of failing because you were afraid you wouldn't succeed . . ."

"I didn't trust you." His patience was slightly frayed by March. "It would have been just like you to take your fucking diaphragm out."

Soon after that, I stopped accusing Max and started to defend myself.

"I have a lot of responsibility in my job. I run that whole department by myself." I didn't even say, I'd like to see *you* do it.

"But why did you pick that particular job, Carol?" He regained his patience when I stopped attacking him. "You said yourself it's frivolous, unimportant. Do you really believe that? Or do you just want to protect yourself? So you can say it doesn't matter if you fail at it? If the job's a waste of time, why don't you quit? Why do you want an *unimportant* job?"

"I liked Fitz," I would say another evening. "I admired him and he was a good friend to me. I was terribly fond of him. Can't you understand a thing like that?"

"Of course you liked him. Of course you were fond of him. You felt safe with him. He was no threat to you. You knew he was homosexual."

"I did not."

"I don't mean consciously."

"I thought he was in love with another woman."

"That's what I'm saying. He was no threat to you."

Exchanges like this finally convinced me of one thing: I couldn't win. Max was in an unassailable position. Whatever I said only proved him right. If I actually insisted, "I am not neurotic," straight out, he could take that as proof I was. The fact of my saying it — or practically anything else — was a symptom of my neurosis. I was like Bertrand Russell's Indian, the one who lied all the time, even when he said he was a liar. That self-contradiction had bothered Russell. It didn't bother Max. By April it had stopped bothering me too; I could see the whole thing was ridiculous.

It didn't matter.

It didn't matter whether I had been fond of Fitz because he

was kind to me and I enjoyed talking to him, or because I subconsciously knew he was homosexual, a castrated father. What mattered was that I had worked hard for him, and if he asked me to do something he could rely on my doing it.

It didn't matter if I thought being the most successful literary agent in New York would be a strenuous bore, or if I only pretended to think that because I was jealous of Harriet. What mattered was that I read every manuscript I received that wasn't obviously illiterate and did my best to sell the ones I thought salable.

Finally, it didn't matter why I had loved Max for ten years. What mattered was that I had held him and comforted him that night in Daphne's apartment in London in '43, that I had sent him Red Cross food parcels, that I had paid most of the bills for three years without making a fuss about it.

I was back to good old John Stuart Mill and his decent sanity. He had had no use for casuistic arguments like Max's; he called them feelings and dismissed them. Actions were all that counted with Mill. A cruel action was wrong, however laudable the motive behind it. A kind action was okay, no matter how neurotic and fucked up you might be.

I stopped worrying about leaving my bed unmade in the mornings, my warm baths, my evening drink. They weren't harming anyone. I tried to stop arguing with Max. In practice that meant we virtually stopped speaking to each other.

What kept us together until June was sex. I can't explain it. Even at our most silent and most grim, with each other we still had a wonderful time on that couch. Our lovemaking — and it was still that, the physical rendering of love — seemed separate from everything else between us. He was still affectionate and generous to me then; I still felt that impetuous tenderness toward him.

Until June.

Harriet asked me to take my vacation early that year, the last three weeks of June. That suited me fine: Maria wasn't going away until August; I didn't want Max to come with me.

I called Judy Zora in Provincetown and she told me I could have the wharf studio. By the end of May, I was in a state of headlong excitement, crossing the days off my calendar at the office the way I had in boarding school. In eleven, ten, nine days . . . "No more Latin. No more French. No more sitting on this bench," we used to chant in school. No more grim silences, I promised myself now. No more fear that anything we said to each other would lead to another interminable argument. Three whole weeks of respite from all that tension between us.

I was leaving the second Saturday in June. Max and I went out to dinner on Friday evening. I ordered a bottle of Muscadet as soon as we sat down and tried to get him to share it with me. He finally let me fill his glass.

"What time are you leaving tomorrow?" He was turning the base of the glass round and round on the tablecloth but not drinking the wine.

"Nine o'clock in the morning. I'm taking the Cape Codder at nine o'clock."

I had gone out on my lunch hour and bought my ticket a week ago.

"I wish you wouldn't go, Carol."

"Why?"

Was he going to say something nice, he would be lonely without me?

"You'll start brooding up there, the way you did in Florida."

"I didn't brood in Florida."

"You know what I mean." He was still turning his glass; it had made a pale circle on the tablecloth, like the bloodless spot on your arm when you press your thumb hard against it. "You'll come back all steamed up about it again, about the idea of us having a child."

"No, I won't."

"You've been brooding about it all winter, haven't you?"

"Will you for Christ's sake drink that wine, Max, and stop fiddling with it."

"If it'll make you happy." He drank a whole spoonful. "You know, there's no reason you shouldn't have a child —"

I suppressed the start of excitement I felt; I knew from his voice there was a "but" coming in a moment.

"If you'd only be sensible."

"How?"

"Stop resisting it so much. Why don't you give it a try? Just for a year or two?"

"What?" As if I didn't know.

"If I get Maria to recommend someone, will you at least go and see him?"

I don't know why that was such a final moment for me. It wasn't as though we hadn't been through it all before, dozens of times. Perhaps it was the repetition itself that made me see at last what a hopeless situation I was in. Neither of us was going to give in. Ever.

I certainly wasn't. I wasn't going to spend a single hour, let along a year or two, talking to some creepy analyst about myself. It wasn't only that I didn't believe in it, didn't believe it *worked*. The whole idea sickened me. The impersonal emotionalism, the contrived intimacy of those naked hours of confession with someone you paid to listen to you — who would stop listening to you as soon as you stopped paying. It seemed so humiliating to me. Like paying a man to sleep with you.

Max wasn't going to give in either. The reason he wasn't — and perhaps I had never seen this so clearly until then — had nothing to do with Maria. Or analysis. Or my being all fucked up. Max would never give in because he didn't want a child.

Then what was I doing with him? What was I waiting for? Why go on like this?

I didn't feel angry. I didn't feel anything. I just knew it was over. Ten years and it was finished. The day had ended. The curtain had come down. The bottle was empty.

The waiter was ready to take our orders. I wanted red snapper; there wasn't any left; I asked for grilled trout.

While I ate it, I told Max. "I don't want to live with you anymore. What I want you to do is find yourself an apartment and move into it while I'm in Provincetown. I'd like you to be out of our place by the time I get back."

Max behaved admirably. I had to admit that much for analysis, it had taught him how to cope with rejection. He sat there eating his macaroni and cheese, nodding understandingly, tolerantly, the way I imagine Maria nodded through *his* hostilities, his sudden impulsive decisions.

We slept in our separate rooms that night.

I got up early on Saturday morning. I was all packed and ready to leave, when I heard Max cleaning his teeth in his bathroom.

He made a lot of noise over it, gargling and rinsing like a playful kid. I had always found it endearing. I suddenly felt I couldn't leave without saying something to him.

I tapped on the door and then couldn't think of anything to say except, "Good-bye, Max."

"Good-bye, Carol."

I caught the Cape Codder with thirty-five minutes to spare. I loved that train. Everybody on it was already dressed for the seaside, the women in halters and shorts or chino pants and shirts knotted above their navels, the men in Levi's or suntans and Oxford shirts with the sleeves rolled up. Once past 125th Street our vacation had started, the way a party starts when someone hands you a drink. We all kept changing seats and talking to each other and going to the snack car for hot-dogs and beer. By the time we reached Provincetown at six, I had three dates to play tennis and one to go sailing.

I might have kept those dates. I might have found out what it was like to have an affair with a Harvard man. But I went to the Atlantic House that night to hear Stella Brooks sing.

There was a party of people at a table near the piano and one of the men waved to me as I walked in. I didn't recognize him at first; I'd only met him twice, although we had been talking on the phone for a year. His name was Chris Deniken and he had written that shadow story I had sold to *Cosmopolitan.*

He made room for me at the table and introduced me to the others as a friend from New York. Not as his agent. I liked him for that. By the time I'd been sitting with him for a few minutes, I liked him very much. He was good-looking in a way I didn't usually find attractive. He had fair hair, almost white, and the kind of skin that would never tan. His eyes were pale gray, intense, and, with his light lashes, slightly startling, like a minor, interesting, not unattractive deformity.

From what Harriet had told me when she asked me to take him on as a client, I knew he was about thirty. He looked much younger in that fresh, smooth-skinned way that outlasts adolescence longer in some fair-haired people. He had nice manners; when he asked a question, he listened to the answer. I was very taken by that quality of attentiveness in him.

Stella Brooks sang "Little Bit of Leather" and told some jokes with her urchin charm that made them seem touching rather than funny. "If you're wondering why I'm so tanned" — enormous brown eyes, wide and unblinking — "H. L. Mencken says Americans will eat anything if it's toasted."

When she had finished her last song, she joined us at our table. "Carol." She settled in cozily between me and Chris Deniken. Where are you staying? how long? and so on. And then, "Carol" again in that wide-eyed way. "When are you going to grow some *boobs?*"

There was no malice in Stella; she could say things like that with the innocence of a child asking, "Why have you got a mustache, Granny?" But I understood she was telling me she was sleeping with Chris. I admired Stella's boobs in her low-cut dress: they were huge.

Around midnight I said goodnight to everyone and went home.

I was just going out for the Sunday *Times* the next morning when Chris arrived with it. I gave him some coffee and we moved out onto the sun deck.

He didn't try to talk. We sat there, dividing the paper between us and exchanging sections and moving our chairs in and out of the sun, as though we had known each other for years. He started with the book section. I shook my head, no, I didn't want it, when he offered it to me first. I hadn't brought any work to Provincetown with me, no manuscripts, and I wasn't going to think about new books for three weeks.

I picked out the "Week in Review." Chiang Kai-shek was still retreating in China and the usual congressmen were demanding more U.S. aid for him. The cold war was getting edgier and more threatening everywhere. I dropped the paper back on the deck with a sense of relief, duty done, and started to look for the magazine.

There was a photograph of someone I knew on the front page of the society section.

"Mr. and Mrs. Jason Stone," I read. Under the picture were two paragraphs about them. Some charity-tent do on Long Island. Mrs. Stone was the former Muriel Sideman. The department store Sidemans? Jason was described as a sales executive with United Artists. He looked a little heavier in the picture, but he was smiling in the bright, irrepressible way I remembered. I thought he looked healthy and he was obviously prosperous. Muriel *was* one of those Sidemans. The story mentioned her father, J.B. I wondered what had happened to Jason's ambition to be a director, but I was glad he was doing so well. Dear Jason.

"Do you like sailing?" It was almost the first thing Chris had said since we'd settled on the sun deck.

I told him I did.

"Would you like to go sailing this afternoon if we can rent a boat?"

I had already arranged with Judy Zora's brother-in-law to hire a boat for the whole time I was going to be in Provincetown. Trying not to sound like Commodore Vanderbilt about it, I explained that to Chris and said we could go together, if he liked.

One of the young Zoras rowed us out to the mooring. We clambered on board with our sandwiches and our beer and towels and bottles of suntan lotion. The boy rowed back to the shore and Chris and I looked at each other.

When two people are alone in a sailboat for the first time, there is always a question that has to be decided between them. Who's crewing? When the two people are a man and a woman, the question has a certain sexual freight. On top of that, I was Chris's agent. If I started taking charge, hauling up the sail while he cleared the runners, he could easily resent me.

I needn't have worried. Chris had already settled the question for himself. "Tell me what to do," he said.

I had always liked sailing out of Provincetown. It wasn't adventurous; there was nowhere to go except across the bay. You didn't even have to tack until you reached the beach there. You just flopped in the stern with your knee over the tiller and lifted your face to the sun and the cool crosswind.

Chris was lying on the forward deck in the shade of the jib. He was wearing Levi's and a tennis shirt and he kept rubbing suntan lotion on his arms and face. It was the nonoily kind that dried on the skin like vinegar and was supposed to screen out the sun's rays. Tartan, I think it was called.

Halfway across the bay I was close to dozing with contentment. I hardly moved when Chris came and sat beside me in the stern.

I was wearing a halter and white cotton shorts that buttoned at the side. Chris started to unfasten the buttons.

He did it so naturally, in such a helpful way, that it would have seemed unfriendly to stop him. Thank God I was still wearing my diaphragm. When he had the buttons undone, he slipped his hand inside, down between my legs, and played with me, very affectionately. I took my leg off the tiller and let the sheet go. The boat turned lazily into the wind. I lifted my hips slightly so that Chris could pull my shorts and panties off. I have an idea I took off my halter myself. I certainly helped Chris unfasten his belt and unzip his Levi's. The denim was so faded and soft it was almost as smooth as his thighs.

I was in such a sensuous daze by that time that I only noticed things like that. The duckboards we were lying on in the bottom of the boat smelled of salt and seaweed. There was a pleasant sharpness in the taste of Chris's suntan lotion when I kissed his skin. The sail flapped indolently above us. The bow made a sloshing sound from time to time, breaking into the lighter ripple of the tide against the hull. The frayed wood of the duckboards felt a little rough under my behind when Chris started to move on top of me — not painfully rough, no more abrasive than a rug. I suppose I noticed all these things because they were new to me. I had never been laid in a sailboat before.

I had never been laid by anyone quite like Chris Deniken before, either. It was like having a birthday party; everything was for me. Presents and cake and a conjurer, all to please Carol. I didn't feel it was forced; there was nothing calculating about the way Chris made love to me. It was a surprise party for both of us. He heaped every kiss and touch on me as if he had been saving them up all his life for this moment. He revelled in my shrill excitement; he soothed me out of it with grateful attentions. It was almost too much for me, in a way. I enjoyed it wildly, but later, when we were lying holding hands on the bottom of the boat, I had a lingering wish that he had been more demanding. I felt I hadn't done enough in return.

The boom was still creaking back and forth. I put on my clothes and untangled the mainsheet. Chris was zipping up his jeans.

"Stella's crazy," he said. "There's nothing wrong with your boobs."

It was the only reference he ever made to our abandoned behavior. He sat beside me in the stern and rubbed on more Tartan. We talked about writers, Nelson Algren and Carson McCullers. He admired Algren but he thought McCullers was the only young writer with any chance of being read in twenty years' time. I suggested Norman Mailer. Chris thought Mailer was too naive to be taken seriously. They had met several times in New York. "He's sort of embarrassing," Chris said. "He's got hips like a woman and those midget hands and he tries to come on like John Wayne."

Doing my best not to sound like his agent, I asked Chris what he was working on now. He was trying to finish a novel. He didn't seem to want to talk about it.

We ate our sandwiches and drank our beer. As we sailed on across the bay and back to the mooring, he didn't make a move to touch me or kiss me. But when we returned to my studio in the late afternoon, it seemed natural, inevitable, that we should take a shower together, that we should soap each other's body and cling together under the squirting water, that we should rub each other dry with a shared towel. I couldn't think of any reason to hold back when he took me to the bed. It all seemed as unexceptional as having a drink on the sun deck did after we'd put on our clothes again.

We had vodka and tonics and we talked, mostly about the Village. Chris knew it better than I did. Although I'd lived there for nine years, I had never been a part of it, going uptown to work, buy clothes, usually to eat. I had fewer friends there than most commuters do in their dormitory suburbs.

Chris belonged in the Village; it was his home, his family. He wasn't romantic about it; he didn't pretend it was the Left Bank. The students at NYU, where he had taught for a year, were a lumpish, conformist lot. Few of his friends claimed any particular interest in the arts.

"But they're the only people I can stand for long. The only people I feel comfortable with. They have no prejudices and no pretentions. They just live. And it's about the only place left in the United States that still has a center. Maybe some small towns in the South do, the courthouse square. But most cities have become such warrens of loneliness. The only link between people is the phone. You don't have to call anyone in the Village, make dates. You just go to the Minetta or the San Remo and there they all are."

Chris had to leave around seven; he had promised to cook dinner for Stella. "She's got some deal with one of the fishermen to give her lobsters, and she can't stand putting them in boiling water. She says they scream."

He didn't kiss me as he left. "Why don't you come to the Atlantic House later," he suggested.

I said I didn't think it was a good idea. Stella might not like it.

He didn't hesitate for an instant before answering. "That's Stella's problem, isn't it? It doesn't have anything to do with you."

And so with Chris Deniken I entered a new country.

It was a country whose customs and ideas coincided with many of my own. And with John Stuart Mill's. Its people were determined, as Mill was, to resist "the tyranny of the majority, the tendency of society to impose its own ideas and practices as rules of conduct on those who dissent from them." Their weapon was indifference. They regarded the rewards of ambition as worthless. They were stoics about poverty. They cared nothing about clothes or automobiles. Unlike their more self-conscious successors in the sixties, they had no uniform and no message. No anger. You couldn't recognize them by their hair or their jewelry, only by their ways. They were enthusiastic about sex, "making it," but they had an impulsive distrust of the word "love." They despised jealousy and possessiveness. "All that Who-shot-John," they called it. They were loyal to each other, sharing the one thing, after sex, that meant anything to them — liquor.

For the rest of my stay in Provincetown, Chris was my guide in all this. He initiated me, without a word of instruction, into the ways of his people. He came to my studio, sometimes in the afternoons, sometimes in the evenings, sometimes for the whole night. If I felt like it, we "made it." He never resented it if I wasn't home. He never asked me where I'd been. I soon learned that if he didn't show up for a day or two, it didn't mean he was with Stella. He was just as likely to be with Iris or Anne.

He was a fast learner in bed. He sensed that I didn't want it to be my birthday all the time, that I liked it better if it was his birthday occasionally. We talked a great deal, about all the things people were talking about that summer: the Brinks robbery, pyramid clubs, the Kinsey Report, Levittown, Alger Hiss. We never talked about "us." We avoided the word "relationship" as though it had a curse on it. We made no plans. When I went back to New York, we had no arrangement to meet there.

"I'll probably see you in the Remo," Chris said.

I paid off the taxi outside the house on Charles Street. No lights upstairs. But then it was scarcely dark yet. And Max had always liked twilight. I had always been the one to switch on the first lamp.

I opened the front door and stood listening, sniffing. No footsteps from upstairs. No smell of recent cigarette smoke.

"Max?" I called. "Max."

No answer.

I went into both bedrooms, both bathrooms, up the second flight of stairs, into the living room, dining room, and into the kitchen. I turned on all the lights.

"Max?" I kept whispering. "Max."

He wasn't there. His closets and drawers were empty, his bathroom cabinet bare. His favorite coffee mug was missing from the kitchen.

There was no note from him anywhere. Perhaps he had left one in the mailbox. I went down to the front door and collected the letters that had accumulated while I'd been away. I shuffled hastily through them under the light in the front hall. Nothing from Max.

There was no mail *for* him either. Perhaps he had stopped by and picked it up the day before.

I went back to the living room and made myself a drink. I sat down on the couch and started to put my feet up on the coffee table. There was a bunch of keys lying there. Max's keys. Two to the front door and one to the desk in his bedroom.

It looked as though he didn't intend to pick up his mail from now on. He must have left a forwarding address at the post office.

I glanced through my own mail. There was nothing in it that claimed my interest, nothing that could distract me from admitting the truth to myself.

For the first time I was alone in the apartment. Not just temporarily alone while I waited for Max to come back from Maria's or the delicatessen on the corner. I was permanently, all night, every morning, every weekend, alone.

I thought of phoning someone, inviting someone over for a drink.

Of all the people Max and I had met and become more or less friends with in the past three or four years, I couldn't think of one I wanted to see. They had always been more Max's friends than mine.

I tried to think of one of my writers I could call. I had never seen any of them after six. We had been lunch companions, discussing their manuscripts, contracts. I had never admitted any of them into my personal life. I had never wanted to. Never had to. My personal life had been Max. He had been all the personal life I needed.

I had another drink.

It wasn't only that I had no friends I cared about, who cared about me. For the first time in ten years, I had no one to love. How was I ever going to manage to live with the *emptiness* of that?

After three drinks I felt I'd better eat something before I got reeling drunk. There was nothing in the house. I would have to go out and have some spaghetti somewhere.

I walked across Seventh Avenue to Sixth and, without thinking, turned south. When I reached Bleecker Street, again without thinking, I crossed the avenue and walked up the block, past the funeral parlor, toward the neon light shining on the next corner.

When I think about the next two years, try to explain what I did with them, I remember what Sinclair Lewis once said when he was asked what happened to his marriage to Dorothy Thompson.

"Dorothy disappeared into the RCA Building," Lewis said.

I disappeared into the San Remo.

Fifteen

It's gone now.

The owner died. The place was turned into a Howard Johnson's for a while. I don't know what happened to it later. But at that time, on the corner of Bleecker and MacDougal, there was an Italian restaurant and bar. It was called the San Remo.

The restaurant was next door to the bar, though it always seemed to be in back, and the public phone was in a narrow, awkward space between them. In the bar were three tables, seven booths, and a large, shiny espresso machine. There were twelve bar stools, never enough. Five unframed oil paintings hung on the walls, mercifully obscured by time and dust and a patina of nicotine. The bar smelled terrible during the daytime until the steam from the espresso machine beat out the stale, almost palpable cigarette smoke and liquor fumes of the night before.

In other words, the San Remo was like hundreds of other Italian restaurant-bars in New York. And it was like no other place in the world.

It was our club, our asylum, our house of assignation, phone-answering service, mailing address, check-cashing bureau, and occasional employment agency. It was the place you could always be sure of finding someone to talk to, listen to you, buy you a drink, rub your back, lend you a dollar, tell you where Chris or Russel or Shane was, go to the movies with you on hung-over afternoons, and fuck you if you felt like it. In the way that an office is to some people and a home is to others, the San Remo was the center of our lives.

But it was even more than that to me. It was my refuge from the past.

For weeks I kept thinking about Max. Alone in the apartment, I would find myself waiting for the phone to ring. "Hello, Carol." That voice I knew better than any voice in the world.

He never called.

One evening in September I dialed information. Was there a new phone number listed for Ludlow, Max?

There wasn't.

Another day I called the stock-film company where he worked. He wasn't there. He had quit. They didn't know where he'd gone.

Had he left New York, returned to California? I looked up Maria's number. But I didn't call her. I figured she wouldn't tell me anything, anyway. It would be against her analyst's ethics to give out information about a patient.

I tried to forget Max, put him out of my mind. The only place I seemed to be able to do that was in the Remo. Unlike my apartment, it had no memories, no associations of Max.

I went there every day, on weekdays usually around nine, after I'd come back from the office and spent a couple of hours with my manuscripts, on weekends earlier, around five.

"There she is," someone would say as I walked up to the bar, and at once I felt welcome and celebrated and safe. We all did. All the desperate young people from all over America who had come to the Village for no reason they would ever be asked to explain. Where else would no one care what you did for a living, if anything, how much you drank, who you went to bed with, what you wore, where you came from, what color your skin was, or even what your surname happened to be?

By the end of September, after three months of hanging out in the Remo, I knew I wasn't going to last much longer at the agency. I wasn't getting to work late; I saved most of my hangovers for weekends; I still read every manuscript that came to me and sold those I could. It was simply that my job seemed more and more irrelevant. Harriet was going through a fluffy hair, organdy, and cigarette-holder period. I couldn't get interested in it; my admiration was becoming noticeably perfunctory. I could feel she resented it.

I quit at the end of October. It didn't change my life much. I stayed on in the Charles Street apartment, working three or four days a week as a temporary secretary. Mostly in legal offices: the pay was better there and the work was sometimes quite interesting. I had less money, but I didn't seem to need as much money as I had living with Max. I didn't go to uptown restaurants; I ate a lot of minestrone. I cleaned the apartment myself; I went to the Laundromat; I ironed my dresses instead of taking them to the French cleaners. I had more time. It was a relief not to have to take work home with me. It was wonderful reading only what I wanted to. For pleasure.

Even more than before, the Remo was the center of my thinking, feeling existence. The people I saw there were my only friends. Some of them were my lovers. I wasn't all that promiscuous; I didn't sleep with a different man every night. Usually when I made it with someone we went on making it for two or three weeks. Until one night I would be standing at the bar and I would feel a sudden, overwhelming physical awareness of some other man standing near me. Then he and I would make it for a while.

Some of my lovers wanted to move in with me. I was that most sought-after creature, a chick with a pad. If a man in the Village had a chick with a pad he had it made. He had a base, a source of toasted cheese sandwiches, security. He could quit moving furniture or painting other people's apartments or whatever he had been doing for drinking money. His chick would leave him a dollar when she went to work in the mornings and he could lie in bed until noon. He could spend the whole, idle, undemanding afternoon in the Remo, seeing what other chicks were around until his own ball-and-chain met him there around six.

There were certain customs he was expected to conform to. A permanently out-of-work actor named Duffy explained them to me once. "It's okay if you ball someone else now and then. But you mustn't do it in your own chick's pad. She'll always know if you do. It's weird. You can make the bed, open the window, clean the ashtrays — she'll always know you've been balling someone else there. And there isn't a chick in the world who'll stand for that."

I made a lot of toasted cheese sandwiches that year. But I resisted all offers to shack up with me. I clung to the luxury of being alone, of sleeping alone when I felt like it. There was no longer any danger of loneliness. All I had to do was walk five blocks and "There she is." All the welcoming friends anyone could ask for.

Most of the men I went to bed with were like Chris Deniken in one way. Fucking was their sport, it was what they did best, but they weren't studs. They never made me feel they were acrobats, putting on a performance for me. They were explorers. Not necessarily in the sense of trying new positions or "other things"; they were usually fairly straight, hooked on one-to-one copulation. Their explorations were into the realm of feelings, their own and mine. They liked to talk about it afterward in bed.

"Do you ever feel," they would ask, "do you ever feel when you're coming like you're really the person you're making it with? It's just an illusion that you're different sexes?"

I did. Almost. Sometimes. That was, I think, what we were all constantly seeking. The infinite, timeless reaches of intimacy.

Some of my lovers were disarmingly frank with me, confessing unsuspected insecurities. Many of them were afraid, each first time, that they wouldn't be able to make it. They couldn't get it up. That first moment of nakedness in bed with a new chick was each time a harrowing test. Years later, when women were going on about male sexual aggressiveness, I used to remember those confessions.

Chris Deniken was in and out of my apartment, in and out of my bed, all that winter and spring. I had a different kind of intimacy with Chris. It was the time of national security risks and loyalty oaths and "who lost China?" We talked for hours about those things. Chris talked about them with a despairing resentment, piling words on each other as though he were trying to construct a way of escape from his own thoughts.

I think I would have let Chris move in with me. He never suggested it. He had his own cold-water flat on Christopher Street. He was often broke, but he was also sometimes suddenly rich when *Cosmopolitan* or *Collier's* bought one of his stories. Over the year he managed, just, to make a living as a writer.

He finished his book. It got some good notices; it was reviewed in several magazines and in the *New York Times* book section. It didn't sell; it was forgotten and remaindered.

Chris pretended he didn't care, but he obviously did. He would get unbelievably drunk. I never knew anyone who could get as drunk as Chris could. It didn't make him hostile or aggressive, it made him helpless. Still wide awake, those pale gray eyes staring at nothing, he would lose all control of his motor system, become incapable of speech or movement. Getting him out of the Remo and home to bed was like trying to lift a corpse out of a well and lug it to the graveyard.

We all drank too much. It was the other, darker aspect of that bright, free, *Déjeuner sur l'herbe* life in the Village. There was a strain of desperation in our casual ways.

"Jesus, did you hear about Roberta?" someone at the Remo would say. "Roberta's in bad shape." That could mean almost anything: that Roberta had tried to slash her wrists, that she was in the alcoholic ward at Bellevue, that she had been busted for taking her clothes off on the subway and we had to take up a collection to bail her out.

I was lucky because I had a good constitution and always just enough sense of self-preservation to eat. I ate something hot every day. Even on weekends. Even when I started drinking at noon.

In spite of that, there were times, usually on Sunday mornings, when my hangovers were so bad I couldn't get out of bed. I was held there, gripped, immovable, as though bound in a dank winding sheet. I didn't have headaches or nausea, I had sweats. Sweats and terrors, surges of remorse. I would remember something I had said to Max during those awful, quarrelsome months before we parted. I would lie there questioning myself, perspiring with panic. *Why* had I said that? What had I been thinking of? How *could* I? I would want to cry out in protesting denial. I did cry out. "No. No. No." And, "I didn't. I didn't say that. I didn't." Finally I would start repeating phone numbers aloud, or the words of some nursery rhyme, trying to drown out my own guilty memories.

Nothing helped. Aspirin, coffee, Alka-Seltzer, Coke, prairie oysters. Nothing. Robert Benchley was right: the only cure for a hangover is death.

But then, if I managed to live through the next couple of hours, and especially if I could get out-of-doors somewhere, I found myself quite enjoying my hangovers. My senses were unnaturally acute, a little distorted. I would walk down a street I had walked down a thousand times and see things I had never noticed before — the shape of a windowsill, the color of a chimney pot. Look, I would think, it's red. How red it is.

By the middle of the afternoon, my skin would start to itch. Not unpleasantly. It would feel unnaturally tight all over, prickling, as though I'd been pickled in salt. I would resist it for a while, but I knew what I wanted then. I wanted to get laid. There were Sunday afternoons when I felt I would do absolutely *anything* to get laid. I didn't have to do much. Walk down to the Remo.

A few dollars at a time, I saved enough money to spend a month in Provincetown that summer. I had one of Judy's wharf studios again, a smaller one. I sailed and swam. Several of the Remo people were there, living in a three-story frame house down by the station. In the evenings we couldn't afford the Atlantic House; we all used to meet in the Pilgrim Café.

I drank less; being out in the sun all day made me sleepy quite early. I didn't go to bed with anyone all month. I'm not sure why. Perhaps it was simply that I didn't run into anyone I wanted; perhaps I was changing.

It was the summer of Joe McCarthy's squalid rise and the beginning of the Korean War. I wanted to talk to Chris about it all; I kept thinking of things to tell him, to ask him. He was in New Hampshire, at the MacDowell Colony, working on a new book.

When I returned to New York at the end of July, I needed money for the rent, for the electricity and phone bills. I went to work for a law firm on a weekly basis to get everything paid up. The firm was handling a complicated damages suit against the city. It dragged on and on and there was a lot of overtime and weekend rush typing.

It wasn't until September that I started to go to the Remo again. It was like coming home. A warm night, and the street doors were wedged open and everyone I knew or cared about drifted in. By ten o'clock, when Chris joined me at the bar, I felt I had never been away.

I saw more and more of Chris that fall. We were beginning to count on each other. When I went to the Remo in the evenings, it was no longer to see who was there, it was to meet Chris. He began to keep a few things at Charles Street, a razor, a toothbrush, shirts and underwear. I gave him a key to the apartment. By October I wasn't sleeping with anyone else.

I knew Chris was. There was a beautiful, long-legged girl named Iris, who talked about studying to be a dancer and who sometimes answered her apartment door in the nude; sometimes she wore panties. Chris would disappear for a night or two and I would know he was with Iris. To make an issue of it, me or Iris, would have been against the conventions we lived by. Chris would have resented it and I would have felt in the wrong.

So *what* if he fucked Iris occasionally?

Christmas was a community feast in the Village. No presents, but a dozen of us would each chip in a few dollars for a turkey, and whoever had an oven big enough would cook it. I cooked it that year. The top floor of my apartment was ideal for a party. At least twenty people showed up in the late afternoon. We ate the turkey and we drank and we danced to records.

I remember a sudden feeling I had that evening. I was momentarily alone, coming out of the kitchen with a gallon of wine. I put the wine on the table and I saw all those young people, as different from each other in looks and speech and background as subway travelers, talking and dancing together in that room.

They really care about each other, I thought. It was a discovery and a conviction. All of them. Every single one of them cares about every other one.

Chris got drunk, but not helpless. We sat on the couch and I told him my discovery. He didn't think it was silly or sentimental. "I explained that to you a long time ago," he reminded me. "In Provincetown."

I lost sight of him for an hour after that. People left and others came. Around midnight I went looking for Chris. He was gone and so was Iris.

I was still in bed, only slightly hung over, when he showed up at noon the next day. I wasn't going to say anything. I wasn't even going to ask him, although I wanted to, if Iris was a better lay than I was. Maybe she was just different.

It was Chris who insisted on talking about it. "I've decided something." He sat on the end of my bed. His fair hair was damp; he had evidently just had a shower at Iris's apartment. Probably with her. "We'll never make it if we stay in the Village. It never works. I've never seen anybody make it together for more than a few months if they keep going to the Remo."

I knew he was right. The whole atmosphere of the place discouraged monogamy. There was too much casual affection, too many opportunities.

"Do you want to go on making it together?" I asked him. "Are you sure?"

He said he was. He was sick of living like a bum. He wanted to settle down. He actually used those words. He said he wasn't a kid any more.

It struck me that I wasn't a kid any more either. In three months I would be thirty. *Thirty.*

I didn't agree to Chris's suggestion at once. We talked about it for the rest of the day. I didn't want to make conditions, but I did think Chris ought to know exactly how I felt about settling down with him. In the first place I wanted to keep on working. I went into detail about that, because I was afraid to tell him what the second place was. "Not as a literary agent again . . . maybe in publishing . . . or some decent magazine like *Harper's.*"

Chris thought that was fine. He was all for having me out of the house all day. He had to be alone to write. "But we've got to stop living in the Village."

In the second place . . . It was late in the evening before I had the courage to get to this.

"Not right away, or anything, Chris, but if it seems to be working out, in a year or two, say . . ."

"What?"

"I want to have a child."

Okay. That was fine with him too. "But we've got to stop living in the Village."

We decided on Murray Hill. We looked at several apartments around Thirty-sixth and Lexington. We almost took one of them, but it had only one small bedroom. We thought we could do better, maybe in Chelsea.

And then at the beginning of February everything seemed to

fall into place for us. Paramount bought an option on Chris's book. They only paid five hundred dollars for it, and they didn't hire Chris to write the screenplay, but it seemed like a good opening for him.

California. Living was cheaper out there. If Chris didn't get taken on at a studio right away, we'd get by. I wouldn't have any trouble finding a job. After all, I'd worked for one of the biggest agencies in New York for five years.

And Los Angeles was three thousand miles from the Village.

It all seemed perfect. We talked eagerly about a house on the beach.

The only, minor problem was that I had never driven a car in my life. How could I even look for a job in California without being able to drive, Chris asked. I would have to learn. We decided that Chris should go ahead first. I would stay in New York, sublease the Charles Street apartment, take driving lessons. Chris would send for me as soon as he was settled.

He left at the beginning of March. I enrolled in an auto school; I listed the apartment with several agents; I stayed home every evening waiting for Chris to call me.

After three weeks I began to worry. Chris hadn't phoned, hadn't written. I had no address for him in California except General Delivery, Santa Monica. I sent him a telegram. No answer. Chris had left Harriet when I quit; I called his new agent. His new agent was as vague as I would have been two years ago if some shrill woman had called me wanting to get in touch with Chris Deniken.

It was Duffy, the out-of-work actor, who finally gave me my first news of Chris since he had taken off.

I ran into Duffy one Saturday afternoon in the square. He looked surprisingly prosperous and pleased with himself. He had it made, he told me, a great pad, and he was working as a waiter at Nick's. I listened without much interest as he went on about his good fortune. He was living in Iris's apartment on Horatio Street. I congratulated him. I asked him if Iris made good toasted cheese sandwiches.

"I'm not shacked up with her. She just let me have her pad. Iris is in California. She went out there with Chris."

I didn't hate Chris. He hadn't done anything I hadn't done, several times — left one person for another on a physical impulse. He had probably never wanted to settle down, anyway. He had only been playing with the idea of it. The thought of having a child must have scared him senseless.

I didn't love Chris. I liked him, we had a good time together, but I had never loved him. I kept telling myself that. It didn't seem to do much good. I was lost, crawling around in despair. When someone rejects you, you are temporarily robbed of the sense of your own worth. You lose your immediate belief that you are worth loving. I felt scared all the time. I was scared of going out on the street, to the delicatessen. I stayed in bed, afraid to run into anyone I knew. They would see at once how despicable I was, how unlovable. I had no defenses against their contempt. I felt like an eggshell with nothing inside it.

I spent my birthday in bed. I was thirty years old. Thirty. And I had nothing to show for it. No child. No one I cared for. I had done nothing with my life. Dribbled it away. I was a mess.

I had to do something about myself.

If I went on like this I would become an old lush. The Village was full of them. You could see them in places like Schrafft's and Goody's, prissily dressed women with jobs in travel agencies, calling the bartender Dear and asking for another drinky.

I had to do something about myself.

The driving lessons were paid for in advance; it was silly to waste the money. I finished them and passed my test. I put in an application at *Harper's*. They said they'd let me know. I worked for a week as a temporary researcher at a news magazine. They called me back the next week and offered me a permanent job. I turned it down. The writers never seemed to pay any attention to the researchers' facts and the magazine had a policy of not promoting women.

I had to do something about myself.

I started going to the Remo again. The second night I was there, I ran into a man I had had an affair with the year before. I took him home with me. At least he made me feel there was something inside that eggshell. Not exactly me; but not an old lush, either.

I was in bed with the same man one morning a week later when the phone rang. I groped my way into what had once been Max's bedroom and answered it.

"Miss Clavering?"

"Yes."

"I've got Harriet Bach for you."

It wasn't true; it was the rigmarole. I stood there with nothing on but a T-shirt, looking at my feet and deciding I *must* cut my toenails, until Harriet finished another call.

"Carol?"

"Yes."

How are you? what are you doing these days? and so on.

I was rather short with her. "What is it, Harriet?"

"Jason Stone wants you to call him."

She couldn't keep the surprise out of her voice. Jason Stone of United Artists. He had left his phone number for me, both of them, office and home. Harriet kept me standing there for another two minutes, trying to find out what my connection with United Artists was. I didn't know any more about it than she did. We agreed we must have lunch together soon. We both knew we never would.

I didn't call Jason until the end of the week. Saturday morning. I was alone. No hangover. I had just finished cleaning the apartment. I must do something about myself. I cut my toenails before calling Jason.

"Carol." He answered the phone himself. That irrepressible confidence, the bright pleasure in his voice. "Carol. It's you."

"How are you, Jason?" I could imagine him sitting there at home in some Park Avenue apartment, looking brand-new in a tailored silk dressing gown.

"I'm great. I'll bet you're great, too."

"I got a message from Harriet Bach."

"Yeah, I called her. I wondered if you were still working there." For a moment he didn't sound sure of himself. "Listen — I'd like to see you, Carol. I keep thinking about you and I want to see you."

"Okay." I wanted to see him too. Dear Jason.

"What are you doing tonight?"

"I don't know." It depended on who was in the Remo.

"I know what I'd like you to do. If you feel like it."

"What?"

"Meet me in Costello's."

Sixteen

For the next three months, until the end of June, I divided myself and kept the two halves separate.

I saw Jason three or four times a week. He wasn't living on Park Avenue; he had an apartment on East Fifty-seventh Street, one of those gloomy, expensive places with a lot of uniformed hall porters who expected to be tipped for whistling up a taxi for you. It was furnished with odds and ends left over from his marriage, presumably the things his wife hadn't wanted.

He told me about his marriage that first night in Costello's.

"She was a nice girl. She was dull, mind you, and as predictable as a bagel. But she was a very nice girl."

Jason hadn't changed. He was a little heavier and he looked older than thirty, but then he had looked older than twenty-two when I had first met him during the war. His hair was still black, no gray, and it was still thick and soft and shining. He still had that wry humor, that tendency to make fun of himself that had made me like him so much eight years ago.

"Muriel. That was my wife's name. Muriel"

"I know. I saw it in the Sunday *Times.*"

"Then it must have been Muriel. The *Times* checks things like that. She thought I was pretty dull, too. But we would probably have gone on boring each other to death for the next thirty years if we'd had a family. I don't mean her family. All those Sidemans. We had them the way some people have horses. I mean a family of our own. Kids."

"Why didn't you?"

He lit a cigar — that deliberate, actor's pause I remembered. He no longer smoked cigarettes; he smoked short, square, Swiss cigars.

"It was bad luck and very tough on Muriel. She couldn't have children. There was something wrong with her whatever-it-is."

He said they had thought of adoption, but Muriel's parents had talked her out of it. "They wouldn't buy the idea of having to leave all that money to kids who weren't really Sidemans. And that was one thing about Muriel, she always did what her parents wanted."

After that, there had been nothing to keep them together. A trial separation had led to a divorce. "She took the house on Long Island and the apartment in New York and a few other little things like that, but she didn't ask for alimony. It's like I said, she was a very nice girl."

Jason always talked about his marriage that way, as though it were a casual incident, a little absurd. A few days later in his apartment, he showed me a photograph of Muriel, a pretty, soft-looking young woman with rather heavy legs. The softness ended at her mouth: it had a determined set to it.

That first evening in Costello's, he asked me about Max. I said we'd broken up two years ago.

"What have you been doing since?"

"Having a ball."

"You?"

"Why not?"

"You were always so serious."

I hadn't remembered myself that way.

"Well, maybe not serious. Not *solemn* serious. But you always seemed to know what you wanted."

I didn't know what I wanted now. Not immediately, anyway. The fourth time I went out with Jason I slept with him in his air-conditioned apartment. It was friendly and there was a grateful, old-times'-sake contentment in the way our bodies remembered each other. But I had changed, learned so much physically since those breathless summer nights on Tenth Street. All those exploring young men had made rather a bitch out of me. I expected too much.

I only took Jason to Charles Street once. One Saturday morning, after I'd stayed at his place, we decided to drive to Connecticut and I wanted to change my clothes.

"My God," he said when he saw the living room. "Why don't I have a layout like this?"

"There's no air-conditioning and you have to whistle up your own taxis."

"I could park my car in the dining room and I wouldn't need any taxis."

I never took Jason to the San Remo.

It still had a hold on me. It wasn't just the drinking and the getting laid. It was the sense of belonging I felt when I walked into that shabby bar with its smell of espresso and smoke and cheap whiskey. Belonging and expectancy. I would come home from one of my temporary jobs and take a shower and change into tight jeans and a T-shirt. And something would pull at me; it was like a wanderlust. If I went to the Remo, something exciting would happen.

That illusion was always so much more persuasive than the experience. I would walk down MacDougal Street, past the Minetta, and turn in through those familiar doors. And nothing exciting, nothing new, anyway, would happen. Someone would be glad to see me. I would sit at the bar and a quality of fond despair would settle over me. I would find myself remembering Chris and Roberta and all the other ghosts who haunted the place for me. After a couple of drinks the nostalgic sadness would be replaced by restlessness. I would start looking then, moving from group to group, wildly aware of anyone eyeing my ass. Then sometimes, late, I would go home with someone. I never once thought of Jason when I was in the Remo.

In this way, until the end of June, I divided myself and kept the two halves separate.

At the end of June, Jason asked me to marry him.

I didn't decide right away. I made up my mind to think it out reasonably. Why and why not.

In the first place, why not, I wasn't sure I was in love with Jason. I liked him enormously. At times I felt love *for* him, but never that single-minded passion I had felt for Max. But then maybe that was a good thing. Looking back, I could see there had been folly in the way I had loved Max, a strain of obsession. Maybe it would be better to marry someone for whom I felt a saner affection.

Why did I like Jason so much? Well, he was fun and sweet and kind — yes, but there was more to it than that. Jason admired me. I had to admit that was an important part of it. He still looked up to me in the way he had when I first met him. He still believed I knew more than he did about food, wine, books, paintings, decorating an apartment, that I had inborn taste, some esoteric information he would never have. To put it crudely, he thought I had class. It was a fantasy, but it was flattering.

The strongest reason, why not, was Jason's job. In his business no one was concerned with quality, whether the product was vicious or silly or just plain shit. How much did it cost? How much did it gross? What was the net? Those were the only questions that mattered. The people Jason had once cared about most — actors, writers, directors — were factors, pluses and minuses, inanimate and dispensable, like playing cards. I had brushed up against that attitude for five years with Harriet. I wasn't eager to live with it. As Jason's wife I would have to live with it quite a lot, entertaining his friends and associates.

Another reason . . . But I was wasting my time. In the end I didn't decide rationally at all.

Jason had taken me to a party in the East Seventies one evening. An Industry party. Men in dark suits, with the anxious, capable look of dentists. A few name actors. Wives. The men talked grosses and the women talked hairdressers. I found an elderly writer I'd known through Harriet. I got her to a sofa and held on to her, as I had once held onto that French captain at the Dorchester, while she told me about her garden in Maine.

She left around midnight and I went looking for Jason. He was with a group of men near the bar. I recognized one of the men: he was a young lead who had made an enviable reputation for himself as a serious, talented actor. I held back from joining the group, partly because I admired the young actor so much and I felt he must be sick to death of admirers, partly because I could see at once how drunk he was.

He was a leaner. He was leaning helplessly against Jason now, clutching at him while he told the others a story. "Jason and I were at a party in Washington. Listen to this. It was a Washington party. They had these waiters in tail coats. So Jason stops this guy in his fancy tails and he says, 'Bring me a vodka and tonic, please.' And the guy says, listen to this, he says, 'I'll try, sir, but I'm afraid that's not strictly in my department. I'm the Swedish ambassador.'"

The men laughed; their laughter had an ugly sound. They were laughing at the actor because he was drunk, and there had been too many stories about his drinking, and the insurance companies were becoming uneasy about taking a chance on him. And they were laughing at Jason because he was important in the Industry, but maybe only because of his uncle, and if he started slipping, it would be a nice item to give to Vince Campion for his slimy little column.

I was watching Jason. The actor was hanging on to him now with both hands. I could see Jason understood all about the laughter.

"Now, you listen to this," Jason began. He was gripping the actor by the shoulders. For a moment I thought he was going to wrench him loose, let him fall on the floor, humiliate him. Then I saw the gentleness in Jason's eyes, the sad admiration for the man's great talent. He put his arms around the actor, holding him.

"That story's a goddamn lie, Mr. Montgomery Clift," Jason said. "He was the Norwegian ambassador."

Dear Jason. Going home in the taxi I held his face between my hands and kissed him. "If you still want me to, I'd love to marry you, darling."

"It's okay with me, if it's okay with my mother."

I had never met Jason's parents. Sometimes he talked about them with a streak of self-mockery, but always with real affection. "I don't deserve my parents," he once said. "They did everything for me and nothing worked." Now that Jason and I were engaged, he said I had to meet them.

I said I'd love to, and why didn't we take them out to dinner one night. But that wasn't the way it had to be. We had to go to their home and it had to be arranged at least a week ahead.

We settled on a day and took a cab out to Brooklyn. Jason was nervous in the cab, smoking his small Swiss cigars, throwing one out the window and lighting another. The cab driver lost his way on some ghastly concourse that seemed to go on forever. We finally stopped in front of a small two-family house that reminded me, with its tiny, neat front garden, of one of those suburban Victorian villas in England. The kind that had names like Bide-A-Wee.

When Jason paid off the cab, he kept dropping bills on the sidewalk and then scrambling around to pick them up. He was still trying to brush the grime off his knees as we climbed the stairs to his parents' apartment.

The moment we walked into the small, over-furnished living room, I understood why it had taken a week to arrange for my visit.

Everything in that living room shone — the windows, the floor, the tables, the bonbon dishes, the frames of the photographs, even the cushions. There were vases of flowers; there were plates of canapés, chocolate mints, plain mints, and a mound of chopped liver as big as a cottage loaf. There was Scotch and bourbon and gin and vodka and, in case I had a taste for it, Tio Pepe sherry. There was roast beef and string beans and two kinds of potatoes and, so help me, there was Yorkshire pudding for the visiting Englisher.

I did my best. I tried to refuse nothing. I helped myself to horseradish as well as mustard. I ate as I had never eaten before.

Jason's father smiled at me shyly and Jason's mother offered me things and Jason said nothing and kept lighting cigars and putting them down and forgetting them. And while I ate I tried to think of something to say besides Thank you.

What made it easier was that I liked Jason's parents at once. His father was a pharmacist. He had come over from Latvia, at eighteen, before the First World War. He was a quiet man, reluctant to talk about himself, but from the little he did say I gathered there had once been dreams and night school and an interest in socialism. Then, quite soon, there had been responsibilities, a younger brother, Jason's uncle the big shot, who had failed at everything and had to be repeatedly rescued until he happened into the movie business in the twenties. For the last thirty years, Jason's father had worked in the same drugstore two blocks away.

Jason's mother was a gentle, rather nervous woman, who had once wanted to be a schoolteacher. She had been brought to America very young, at four or five, and she had no trace of a European accent. Her dreams, I suppose, had been submerged in Jason, the only child; but she also suggested, in things unsaid, that a certain timidity had handicapped her all her life, a feeling that the world outside her family was a dangerous and hostile place.

Over the roast beef she asked me, hesitantly, about *my* family. I said I had two sisters, who were still in England. "In the old country," Jason explained sardonically. And my mother was still there, too, I said, and I had to admit I hadn't seen any of them for eight years. "But we do write," I added apologetically.

I was hoping they wouldn't ask me about my father. He had died, three years ago, while I was living with Max. I hadn't seen him since 1939, and he had almost never answered my letters. I knew how shocked Jason's parents would be if I admitted I hadn't even known about his death until I saw his obituary in the *New York Times*. I didn't think they could understand a family like ours. They would feel we were inhuman.

I needn't have worried. Jason's father changed the subject. They were both very sensitive people.

"They're wonderful," I told Jason, going home in the cab. "You look like your father. He must have been a very handsome young man."

"Did you like my mother's chicken liver?"

"I liked everything about them."

"My mother's very proud of her chicken liver."

"She's very proud of you, too."

I went home to Charles Street alone that night. For the next few days, I didn't see Jason; we only talked on the phone. It began to worry me. I wondered if I'd said something to offend his parents. On Friday he asked me if I'd come up to his apartment. I went there straight from my temporary job.

Jason was edgy from the moment he let me in. He seemed angry and at the same time inexplicably apologetic as he made me a drink and talked about some movie I hadn't seen.

After five minutes I couldn't stand it any longer.

"Okay. What is it? What have I done?"

"You haven't done anything. It isn't your fault. You just picked the wrong parents."

"Whose parents? What are you talking about, your parents or mine?"

"Both."

At least the anger was gone. He sat beside me.

"It's a lot of crap, Carol. I don't believe a word of it, and I don't think my father really does, either. But my mother does. She called me five times today. Five times so far."

"About me?"

"Us."

"She doesn't like me?"

"Of course she likes you. She thinks you're sweet. She said you had very nice manners. Such an educated girl, my father told her."

"Then what the hell's wrong?"

"Oh, for God's sake, Carol, I'm Jewish. You know that." He said it so solemnly I couldn't help smiling.

"What do you expect me to do about it?" I asked him.

"Convert."

Jason wasn't smiling. He still had that grave, apologetic look in his eyes. It reminded me of his father when he had mentioned socialism.

I leaned over and kissed him. "What does that mean, Jason? What do I have to do?"

"You have to go to a rabbi and take instruction. You have to promise to bring up the kids in the Jewish faith."

I thought about it for a minute. It was no use pretending I was going to experience any genuine religious conversion. The closest I had ever come to believing in God was my trust in that tenuous female spirit I pleaded with in moments of panic, and I had always thought of her as existing somewhere inside me, not at the top of Mount Sinai. But our children were sure to be exposed to *some* church, sometime. And at least the Jews didn't believe in hell.

"All right," I told Jason, "I don't mind."

He was so grateful he made me feel like a fraud. "It's just for my mother," he kept saying. "She couldn't stand it if her grandchildren weren't brought up as Jews. She'd feel they were lost to her. It's difficult to explain . . . It's just for my mother."

Reform Rabbi Hoffman lived on Central Park West. A brisk businesslike man in a double-breasted dark gray suit, he treated me with an offhand indifference in which I sensed a trace of contempt. Perhaps he thought I was doing it for the money. Jason's money. I went to him four times. He gave me some books and pamphlets to read. They aroused my interest, but nothing I said aroused his.

I tried hard to find out from him exactly what Reform Jews did believe. I wanted to know about the coming of the Messiah, their concept of an afterlife, the soul, Judgment Day. Rabbi Hoffman was evasive and finally impatient with me. He seemed to think that was none of my business. He explained the importance of women, the mother, in the continuity of the faith. He made me take a solemn oath that my children would be raised as Jews.

The only time he ever showed a gleam of interest in me was when I mentioned that I had once been a literary agent. He asked if I still had any connection with publishers. He had written a book; he had the manuscript in the drawer of his desk. Perhaps I could help him place it.

I gave him Harriet's phone number.

That was on my fourth visit, after I had taken my solemn oath. I walked out into the park. Well, I thought, I'm Jewish. I looked at the mothers in the playground. Some of them must be Jewish too. I felt a certain kinship with them that was almost pride. But I didn't really feel any different.

With that problem out of the way, Jason and I could go ahead and plan our life together.

I didn't want to make an issue of it, but I wasn't crazy about the idea of living in that gloomy apartment on Fifty-seventh Street. Jason was more than willing to meet me halfway on that. He detested the place. "Anyone would think I was a stockbroker," he said. "That dump's wall-to-wall square. It's got Vote Republican written all over it."

I didn't understand what he was leading up to at first. Then he scared me blue. He wanted me to redecorate the apartment on Charles Street. "New furniture, anything you like."

"Oh, no," I told him. "Oh, no. No. No. No, I'm not going to live in the Village. I'm getting out of all that." I was more firmly determined than Chris had ever been. I had stopped going to the Remo when Jason and I became engaged. I was never going near the place again. Like a reformed junky, I was going to cold-turkey that shit. I was going to sever all those connections forever.

We found a place in the East Seventies, two floors in a brownstone. Jason opened an account for me at his bank. He was naturally generous and he wanted me to have anything I liked. I got decorators' cards. I went to furniture auctions, rug sales, art galleries. I didn't really know what I was doing, but it was fun trying to live up to Jason's fantasies about my impeccable taste. I made one rule for myself: never think about how anything would look to other people. How were we going to like living with it?

We moved in a few days before the wedding. When I looked around at what I had done with all that money, I didn't feel too guilty. The apartment was bright and warm and comfortable; it had a welcoming look. I had been careful about the lighting: you could sit and read in every chair in the place; you could talk to anyone without having a light in your eyes.

Jason was delighted with it. "Jesus," he said. "Wait till those bastards at Metro see this."

Rabbi Hoffman married us in his study. I had trouble finding any friends of the bride to invite to the wedding. In the last two years, I had lost touch with everyone except the Remo people and I wasn't going to ask any of them. I finally managed to dig up three women friends from the agency days. Jason kept his guest list down to twenty by excluding all business associates. He invited only his relatives and a few people from Brooklyn he had known all his life. His uncle the big shot was on the coast, thank God. He sent us a silver chafing dish, which we returned to Hammacher Schlemmer's.

We didn't have a canopy, but Jason stomped on a glass, forswearing all his household goods for mine. I repeated some Hebrew words that I had learned like a parrot. Jason kissed me. Rabbi Hoffman, rather surprisingly, read a few lines of Robert Browning. "Grow old along with me . . ." Jason and I were man and wife. After thirty years of being Carol Clavering, I was Carol Stone now.

We all went to dinner at the Plaza. I was sadly aware that none of my family were there, but Sylvia had sent a gift and a telegram.

Charles Laughton was at the next table, amiably drunk. He stood up at one point and did a sweet little dance like a hornpipe. Jason and I danced. Everybody kissed me. We went back to our new home.

Lying in our double bed that night after Jason had made love to me, I knew how lucky I was. With Jason's approval, I had thrown away my diaphragm. Dear Jason. We would make a family together.

I felt wonderfully peaceful falling asleep beside him.

Seventeen

L unch? What time?" I asked warily.

"You've got a run-through at two," Sara, my secretary, reminded me.

I lowered the phone and put my hand over the mouthpiece, looking up at her and shrugging with exaggerated helplessness. "It's the Gestapo."

Sara shrugged back.

"Could Mr. Campion possibly make it earlier, say at twelve-thirty?" I said into the phone.

After some mumbling at the other end, his secretary said he could. I asked her where, hoping it wouldn't be "21" or Toots Shor's. I didn't want to be seen in public with Vince Campion.

She suggested a small French restaurant on Tenth Avenue. Apparently Campion didn't want to be seen in public with me, either.

"Shit," I said after I had hung up. "What in hell does he want?"

Sara didn't answer; we both knew what Vince Campion might want with me. I was the script editor on a successful network television show. If Vince Campion had decided that one of our writers was a Commie-fink, as he called them, he would try to force me to drop him. If I didn't drop him, both the writer's name and mine would appear in Campion's column. I might or might not get fired; the writer would never work in television again. "Going My Way," Vince Campion's syndicated column, was only slightly less powerful as a blacklist than Red Channels.

"We've been lucky so far," Sara reminded me. "Look at some of those soaps. They've lost almost everybody."

She was right; I had been lucky. I had been working for Studio One for almost two years, and although every time I wanted to hire a writer, his name had to be sent up to the fifth floor for clearance, had to be sent up *each time* he worked for us, I had so far managed to remain blithely uncontroversial, as the current jargon put it.

I called Jason. "I can't have lunch with you, darling."

"Why not? No, don't tell me. I know. Something's come up."

"Yes."

"I think that's the most loathsome expression in the world. Something's come up. It sounds like a nurse who — "

"Tell you about it later. Okay?"

"Okay."

I don't know if I really thought my phone was tapped. But like many people in New York at that time, I never said a word more than I could help over any phone.

I hadn't seen Vince Campion since those ghastly parties in London during the war. He had sickened me then; he disgusted me now. His face had always been porcine; it had become grosser with age. As he sat across the checkered tablecloth from me, drinking Scotch and soda and nibbling cheese sticks, while I tried to eat a Dover sole, I felt a physical revulsion every time I looked at him.

"Must have been forty-three," he was saying. He was one of those long-time-no-see conversationalists. "You were working for that faggot, Fitzpatrick. Whatever happened to old flitty Fitz?"

"I don't know."

"I heard he was teaching at Berkeley."

"I don't know."

He went on about Fitz, probing and picking to see what I could tell him. I couldn't tell him anything. I hadn't heard a word from Fitz in ten years.

"You're married, huh, Carol? Jason Stone of U.A.?"

"Yes."

I knew, if I looked at him, I would find him exploring me with his piggy eyes, the way he had in London. He had been imagining me in bed with Fitz then; he would be imagining me in bed with Jason now.

I pushed away my Dover sole. "What did you want to talk to me about?"

"There's a certain pinko bastard. I'm going to get his balls. And you better help me, Carol, because he's a friend of yours."

"Who is?"

I made myself look at him. He was watching my face.

"A guy named Max Ludlow."

It was so unexpected I almost laughed. I had been going over my writers' names, hoping it wasn't this one, that one.

"You want to talk to me about *Max?*"

"You knew him, didn't you?"

"Of course I knew him."

"When?"

"In London, in forty-three. He was a sergeant in the RCAF. He was shot down over Berlin. He spent two years in a German POW camp."

Campion waved his fat hand impatiently. He wasn't interested in all that crap; Max's war record was irrelevant. We had reached a point, at that time, where favorable evidence was always irrelevant.

"You shacked up with Max Ludlow after he came back to the States, didn't you?"

"Yes."

"What was he doing then?"

I told him about Max's dreary little job with the stock-film company. He wasn't interested in that either.

"What else?"

"He was being psychoanalyzed."

"Politically. What was he doing politically?"

"Nothing."

"Don't give me that shit."

"I never knew anyone less involved in politics. He didn't even vote."

"He's involved in politics now, all right. He's working for the Voice of America."

"I don't know anything about that. I haven't seen him for five years. Since the summer of forty-nine."

The waiter brought Campion another Scotch. I thanked him for the lunch and said I had an appointment. He reached across the table toward me. I sat back, putting my hands in my lap.

"Okay, Carol. One more question. When and where did you first meet Max Ludlow?"

That was a dangerous one. How much did Campion, how much did *they,* know about Max's activities in California? Was Mrs. Hainert still alive? Had she become one of those breast-beating ex-radicals denouncing all her old friends? Did they know I had first met Max in his Trotskyist period?

I decided to risk it. "Well, if you insist, if I have to tell you . . ." I stared down at my hands in my lap, trying to look embarrassed. I was hoping to leave Campion with something more raunchy and congenial to think about than Max's politics. "I met him in New York in 1940. He was on leave from Canada. It was in a bar in the Village. He picked me up and I took him home with me. Just like that, if you must know. The first night. And we shacked up together for the rest of his leave."

I glanced at Campion. His piggy eyes had moved down from my face.

"Jesus." He was looking at my tits. "How old were you then?"

"Nineteen."

In the cab going down to the rehearsal hall on Second Avenue for the run-through, I kept compulsively repeating every moment with Campion, the questions, the answers. Had he believed me? Had I managed to protect Max at all? Campion's prying malice, his grubby prurience, seemed to pursue me; I could actually feel him there, just out of sight.

I loved run-throughs. I looked forward to them all week. There was a childish element in my enjoyment. Twelve years old, at school in Switzerland, "Let's put on a play. Can we put on a play, Fräulein?" But there was more to it than that. All those weeks of going through words typed on paper; now I would hear them. It was like developing a negative, seeing what would come out. It fascinated me every time.

I looked through the script I had brought with me. *"Fade in: Int. Hotel Room. Day. Edward Cowan is unpacking his suitcase. He takes out his bathrobe and crosses — "*

"Hello, Carol."

"Hello, Chris."

Chris Deniken had become one of the dozen most successful "new" television writers. He had written for Philco-Goodyear, Kraft, Hallmark — all the top dramatic shows. This was his first play for Studio One.

He sat down beside me. "Are you happy with it?" I asked him.

"Sure."

He had taken to wearing dark glasses. Concealing his pale, strangely naked gray eyes, they gave him a tough, aggressive look.

"How's Daly?" James Daly was the actor who was playing the lead.

"He's all right."

"Don't you like him?"

"Sure."

I had had a dozen meetings with Chris since the producer had told me to try to get him to write a play for us. I didn't feel any resentment toward him any longer. I had been married for two and a half years; that whole world of the Remo seemed as insignificant and improbable to me now as some movie I'd once seen. It was Chris who seemed resentful. Every time we met, there was a tacit reproach in the way he looked at me, spoke to me.

"What are you going to be working on next?" I asked.

"I'm supposed to write something for Playhouse Ninety."

"Will you be going back to the coast?"

"You wish to hell I would, don't you?"

"What? Why?" Why did he think that?

"You want me out of your life."

He *was* out of my life. He had walked out of it when he went to California. Lucky break for me that he had.

"You know something I've noticed about you, Carol?"

"No, what?"

"You never once asked me about Iris. You've never mentioned her name. Not once."

What did he want me to say? Iris. Iris. Iris. Would that make him feel better?

People were getting up, moving toward the center of the hall where the outlines of the various sets were marked out with white tape on the parquet floor.

"Come on, Chris. Let's see what they've done to your play."

We joined the small audience, the producer, the director, the key camera and sound crews. The script girl was the only one of us with anything to do except watch and listen, clicking her stopwatch, timing each scene, noting the minutes and seconds on her script. I always admired the script girls. They had none of our "creative" pretentions; they did an essential, difficult job, expecting and getting no credit for it.

From the moment James Daly started unpacking his suitcase and crossed to the closet to hang up his bathrobe, the whole play went like the Eighth Avenue Express. It was clever and tricky, but it worked. The direction and Daly and Chris's dialogue made it work.

We all gathered around the script girl's desk afterward. Felix Jackson, the producer, congratulated everybody. "Good, good," he kept saying. He was a sweet man, a European refugee from the thirties with years of experience producing movies in Hollywood. He never got excited, never criticized anyone. If he really disliked something, he would look hurt and shake his head like someone suffering from an earache.

Felix had no reason to look hurt that afternoon. We all knew that, so long as we didn't have any terrible, unpredictable screwup during the live broadcast on Monday night, we had an exciting show. Maybe even one of those golden hits that made people all over the country call in and send telegrams.

The script girl finished adding her figures. "We're twenty-eight seconds over."

We all looked at Chris. It was up to him to suggest cuts.

His dark glasses looked back at me. "Okay, you fix it, Carol."

The indifference in his voice reminded me of that phone call years ago, when I was working at the agency and I had told him about *Cosmopolitan*'s objections to his shadow story. He had used almost the same words then: he didn't care what changes I made, "just go ahead and do it." He wasn't lazy; he had worked hard and conscientiously, making revisions up to the last day before the run-through.

I had one of those flashes of understanding. It was an integral part of Chris's character. In everything he did, he would reach a certain point. It was like a wall; he would stop, make no effort to go any further. He would just give up. And when he did, he would blame other people for it. He would hold it against them, privately and forever.

I opened the script and found a scene, a few moments of light relief when Daly was talking to a woman at a bar. We had both felt the play needed the contrast and Chris had put some wonderful, funny dialogue into it. It had gone beautifully at the run-through. I felt like a vandal as I drew tentative pencil lines around it.

"Carol."

Felix was looking hurt. He would start shaking his head presently.

"Fine. That's it."

I couldn't see Chris's eyes when he said that, but he was smiling. He looked relieved, as though I had just proved him right, confirmed something he had known all along. We were all shits who had intended to screw up his play from the beginning.

I could usually get away from the office at five. I took scripts home with me, as I had at the agency. Thank God Jason and I weren't going out that night. We had to spend several evenings a week entertaining and being entertained, usually in restaurants; there was no way Jason could get out of it.

The evenings at home were a luxury for both of us. I had become interested in cooking. I would make a ragout or a goulash or, if Jason insisted, an English steak-and-kidney pie, over the weekend and take it out of the freezer before I went to work.

Jason had given me a pair of pale blue velvet toreador pants. He was a born sybarite. We would sit on the couch together after dinner, reading or listening to music. Lightly, almost absently, Jason would stroke the blue velvet, stroke me. After over two years of marriage, I was still eagerly discovering fresh intimacies with Jason. There was little of that yes-stop-oh-please-I-can't-stand-it-I'm-going-to-die-please-don't-stop madness in our lovemaking. I had had enough of that in my Remo days; I didn't miss it, ever. Jason could make me purr for hours, which made me much happier.

I changed into the toreador pants and a silk shirt when I got home that evening, skimmed the fat off the *boeuf bourguignon* I had taken out of the freezer that morning, and put it in a very low oven. I opened a bottle of Moulin-à-Vent to drink with it later and settled down with a sherry and a script to wait for Jason.

I was halfway through the second act when I felt it, that first unmistakable physical intimation I always had.

"Damn. Shit. Hell. Fuck."

All week I had been thinking I had finally made it.

"Oh, shit. Oh, goddamn it." Oh, please. Why can't I? What's wrong with me? Please, let me. Next time. Please.

I was in the bathroom when I heard Jason downstairs. I decided not to tell him. Not until after dinner, anyway.

He was taking off his overcoat, blowing on his hands, his face white from the February wind.

"Couldn't you get a cab?" I hung up his coat for him. "What happened? Poor Jason. You're frozen."

"I am?" He gave me one of his what-else-is-new looks. "I'll tell you what happened. My uncle the big shot wanted to talk to me, so he drove me home. In his limousine."

I made him a drink.

"He drove me to *his* home. Eightieth and Park. Then he told his chauffeur to put his car in the garage so it wouldn't get chilled, and left me standing there on the sidewalk. There was a poodle peeing on a hydrant and it came out solid. An icicle. Did you ever see a poodle-piss icicle? It looks — "

"Why didn't you take a cab?" I rubbed his hands. They weren't all that cold. He had probably kept them in his pockets. He wouldn't wear gloves; they reminded him of policemen.

"Eight blocks. You can't take a cab for eight blocks. They hate you."

"They don't. They like short rides. They get the starting fare and the tip. They —"

"You really want to warm my hands?"

"Sure."

"Let me put them . . . yes, there."

I shifted slightly on the couch beside him.

"God, you're warm, Carol. God, you're lovely."

"What did your uncle want to talk to you about?"

"The goddamn Industry's on the skids. That's the only thing he ever wants to talk about these days. Do you know how many people went to the movies last year? Do you know how many people *didn't* go to the movies? Lift your hip a little."

"All right?"

"Yes. Jesus. Yes."

I kissed his ear; it was quite warm now.

"You're so *soft* there. It's incredible."

"I'm supposed to be soft there. It's only ballet dancers —"

"How was your run-through?"

"That was all right. That was fine."

"What's wrong?"

I told him about my lunch with Vince Campion.

"That bastard."

"There are a lot of them around these days."

"Would you mind if you lost your job?"

"I'm not going to lose my job. I didn't refuse to answer Campion's questions. I was a friendly witness."

"Would you mind if you had to quit?"

"Why?"

"Don't move away. Please come back. Just the way you were sitting before with your —"

"Why should I quit my job?"

"You really are the loveliest girl. You don't seem to have any bones at all."

"Nobody has bones *there*. Hardly anybody. Now go on, tell me."

"Because I think I ought to quit *my* job. That's why."

Yes, I did too. He would come home sometimes after one of those afternoon meetings that lasted till eight o'clock, looking as though he had just escaped from the Château d'If.

"What would you do if you left U.A.?"

"Go to Europe."

"What would you do there?"

"Make movies." He explained it to me. Independent productions, international financing, the Anglo-French-Italian deals that were being made now; even the Germans were coming in on some of them. He was sick of deprecating other people's work so the company could buy it cheap. He was sick of touting crap so the company could sell it dear. He wanted to make movies; he had had that itch, that bug, ever since the Signal Corps. London or Rome was the place to go.

It didn't take me long to make up my mind. I would miss the

apartment — it was so comfortable, it had so many happy associations for us. But I wanted Jason to be happy in the other side of his life, too.

"Okay. We'll go to Europe and you'll make movies."

"You're a sweet girl, Carol. God, you're a sweet girl."

"You'll make good movies."

"How do you undo this goddamn zipper?"

"Wait, Jason. Please —"

"The girl in Lord and Taylor's said it was easy."

I was going to have to tell him before dinner after all. "I can't. I'm sorry, darling. I've got the curse."

He had his face against my neck. I felt the sudden stillness in him. "Shit," he said softly.

"That's what *I* said. Shit. Damn. Hell. Fuck." I stood up and buttoned my shirt. "I don't know what's wrong with me."

He was leaning forward on the couch, his head lowered. "It isn't as if we didn't try, Carol. How many times have we tried this month?"

"I didn't count. My mother told me never to count my blessings." I started toward the kitchen to take the casserole out of the oven. "Do you think I ought to go to a doctor, Jason? Maybe it's something quite simple. Something my ovaries are doing wrong. Something that can be fixed."

He didn't answer.

He was smiling, bright and eager again, when he joined me in the kitchen.

"Wait till we get to Europe. Siestas. Love in the afternoon. Everybody gets pregnant in Europe."

We made plane reservations to London for the end of May. Felix gave a small farewell party for me in his office, the script girls and three of our regular directors and Sara and a few writers. I felt sad and sentimental and grateful and for about ten minutes I didn't want to leave.

The last week was a mad rush. We were subletting the apartment to one of Jason's colleagues. I had lists and lists with things like "clean freezer," "dental check," "return library books," "stop milk," scribbled on them. I left the shopping to the last day. I needed a suitcase. Jason wanted calf-length socks and jockey shorts and blue Oxford shirts, things he believed were unobtainable in Europe.

I was in the men's department in Bloomingdale's, checking the shirts off my list, when I saw a woman I thought I knew buying handkerchiefs. It took me a moment to remember who she was. And then I decided I must be mistaken.

I knew I wasn't mistaken. I remembered that soft, pretty face, those rather heavy legs, that determined mouth, too clearly from the photograph Jason had shown me.

I waited until she left and then asked the salesgirl. I was right. Mrs. Carl Brauer. Her husband was a well-known attorney with political ambitions.

Before being Mrs. Brauer she had been Muriel Sideman most of her life. Then for four years she had been Mrs. Jason Stone.

It didn't bother me that she had once been married to my husband. What had confused me at first and then left me feeling slightly sick was that Muriel Sideman Stone Brauer was unmistakably, conspicuously pregnant.

Eighteen

In the winter of 1956 we were living in London, in a furnished house in Chelsea, five blocks from the King's Road, ten minutes' walk from Harrods.

It was a pretty little house, three floors and a basement. As a special privilege, we had a key to the private gardens in Cadogan Square. "It's nice to have somewhere you can be sure of meeting only people like yourselves, if you know what I mean," the real estate agent told me when he gave me the key. "Specially if you have children."

We didn't have children. We weren't going to have any children.

Jason and I had faced that two years ago, soon after we came to England. When I told him about seeing Muriel in Bloomingdale's, he admitted it *might* be his fault. He reluctantly agreed to see a doctor in Harley Street. After the tests, he conceded it was *probably* his fault. I was relieved to find I wasn't barren; the possibility of that had made me feel secretly incomplete. But it didn't seem to me to matter whose fault it was.

I wanted to adopt a child.

Jason went through several phases in his reaction to that idea.

"We can't do it over here," he said at the beginning. "They'd never let us adopt an English kid."

I found they would. Like most things in England, it could be arranged if you knew the right people. Sylvia knew everybody. Her husband, Nigel, was now an undersecretary at the Foreign Office. Although Nigel and I couldn't stand each other, he was willing to talk to a chap at his club who was at the Home Office. Sylvia talked to a Lady Somebody who was honorary governor of a home for orphaned Jewish children. The day I came home and told Jason it was all fixed, he shifted his ground slightly.

"We don't have to do it now, right away, do we? I'm just getting started . . . We don't even know if we're going to stay here . . . If things don't work out and we have to go back . . . It makes much more sense to do it in New York. Then there won't be any hassle about the kid's legal nationality."

I let that ride for a few months. When Jason got his first production together and it was obvious we were going to stay in England for at least another year, maybe indefinitely, I suggested making an appointment at the orphans' home and putting our names on the list.

That brought us a little closer to the truth.

"It would kill my mother . . . It would be like admitting there was something wrong with her son . . . She'd be so ashamed . . . She'd blame herself . . . You don't understand how Jewish people feel about things like that. About sterility in the family."

I didn't think Jewish people had anything to do with it. After several evenings of trying to talk it out with Jason, I realized his mother had very little to do with it, either. It was Jason who would feel ashamed. He must have told so many people the same story about his first marriage: Muriel couldn't have children. If he and I adopted a child, it would be an open admission that it was Jason who couldn't have children.

He refused to believe that. Never mind the tests. Never mind the fact that Muriel was suddenly, miraculously pregnant. He clung stubbornly to the conviction that he *could* have children. It was just a question of time. If we went on trying long enough, we *would* have children. We would have children of our own.

It was illogical. It was absurd. He could not bring himself to admit he was sterile. Perhaps in some complicated, atavistic way he associated sterility with impotence. Whatever the explanation, it was the one subject on which there was no reasoning with him.

We had our first row about it. Jason accused me of trying to castrate him in public. He called me a ball-breaking bitch. He said I didn't give a shit how he felt. He said I only wanted a child so I'd have someone to boss around.

At that point I got hysterical, too. I called him a selfish prick. I said he was pathetic. I told him he was the most dishonest, self-deluding jerk I'd ever known. If I hadn't abruptly seen that he was crying, I might have walked out on him that night. His silent, grieving tears brought me to my senses.

Dear Jason. He couldn't help it if in that one area of his character he was absurdly insecure. It was worse for him than it was for me. I began to understand his pain. He wanted a child so much. A child to take home to his parents. "See, you will live on through me." Maybe the logical answer *was* to adopt a child, but in that realm of raw feeling, logic had no persuasion.

After that night I stopped pressing Jason. We never talked about it now.

Jason's first production, a medium-budget British picture with some U.S. financing, was a fair success. It was the story of a twelve-year-old girl who befriends a young American wanted for murder. It was shot on location in Liverpool. The scenes between the man and the child were both touching and frightening. It did well in England and was playing art houses in America, when Jason got lucky. Walt Disney put the young actress who played the girl under contract and spent a lot of money publicizing her. Jason's film moved out of the art houses into general release. Jascar Productions, as he called his company, was solidly in the black.

He was sensible about it. "The trouble with this business," he explained to me, "is that half the money is spent on a lot of crap that never gets on the screen. Nobody wants to go to the movies to pay a producer's hotel bills or his goddamn limousines or his office rent. They fork out two dollars for two dollars worth of entertainment." He converted our basement into offices. A small brass plaque indicated the separate entrance: *Jascar Productions, Ltd.* I was all for it; it meant he was home more.

Jason's second production, which was in the planning stages that winter, also started modestly. It was an idea we both liked. Omar Khayyám, the Persian tent maker. "He's one of the best-known poets in the world," Jason told anyone who would listen. "His verses are on *greeting* cards."

Very little was known about Omar's life, but we thought an interesting story could be built around his character as it came through in the Rubáiyát. We wanted Robert Newton, an English actor who had made an international success in *Treasure Island,* to play Omar. Even half-drunk he was a superb performer with an unforgettable voice. We could shoot the picture in Spain against the Moorish architecture. Jason and I and a young English director spent evenings going through the verses and putting them together to make a story. It was one of those ideas that acquires a momentum of its own. Some evenings we were helpless with admiration at our own wit and ingenuity as we invented plot twists and situations and bits of comic business for Newton. It was fun at that stage.

Jason got a tentative commitment from Newton's agent and hired a writer to prepare a draft script from the outline we had put together.

And then one of the studios showed interest. That seemed a lucky break at first. They were willing to put up a million and a half, almost three times as much as we had decided we needed. Naturally, there were conditions. There were always conditions. One of them was a thirty-six-year-old actress who had once made a lot of money for the studio. She had retired; she had married an Indian rajah; she had divorced him; the studio had her back under contract. The way they looked at it, they had a lot of money tied up in her. She was an investment. She would be perfect, or as Jason put it, ripe, for the Persian princess in our story. Naturally, the part would have to be built up a little.

By November the projected budget on the picture had reached three million-five. There were four existing scripts, none of them acceptable to the Investment. Omar Khayyám — Vincent Price now, not Newton — was a minor character in the subplot. Jason was flying back and forth to the coast, to New York, to Madrid, every week.

I had lost interest in the whole bloody project.

At the beginning of December Jason told me he had to go to Rome.

"Rome?" Where did Rome come into the story? "Do those illiterate nits at the studio think Omar was a friend of Nero's or something? What's in Rome they can't find in the Persian Room at the Plaza?"

Jason let me go on like that for a while before he told me what was in Rome.

"Tyrone Power."

"For *Omar?*"

"No. There's this Arabian prince who kidnaps the Investment. So they want to get Power. He's the only American actor who can say My Father the Caliph without making it sound like the punch line of a Jewish joke."

Jason flew to Rome the next day.

I was growing used to being alone in the Chelsea house. I saw a lot of Sylvia. She was thirty-nine now, still as beautiful and immaculate as she had been at twenty. We had fun together so long as we stayed clear of Nigel. That wasn't difficult: they had one of those marriages in which they treated each other with polite affection and avoided ever being alone together in the same room. "Nigel has his club," was the way Sylvia put it, "and I have my macking. That's why we get along so well."

I couldn't get along with Nigel for a minute. He hated Americans; he had become paranoid about them since the Suez. I found him pompous and overbearing and essentially stupid.

They had one child, an eleven-year-old, Timmy. Sylvia had refused to let him be sent away to boarding school. "Remember?" she said. "Remember the food? And those hellish, *dank* dormitories. And it's even worse for boys. They cane them. I'm not going to let some bloody pervert cane Timmy."

He went to a private day school in Kensington. Sometimes when Sylvia was busy macking with one of her young men, I used to pick Timmy up there in the afternoons. He wore a gray flannel suit with the school crest on his breast pocket and a little gray peaked cap. I would take him to tea at Harrods or to the movies or the zoo. He was an intelligent boy, with beautiful manners and a sudden, perky sense of fun. He called me Aunt Carol and always shook hands with me when I dropped him at his house. "Thank you for a very nice time, Aunt Carol."

I paid visits to my mother in Brighton. She was living in what she called a guest house, a nursing home for elderly ladies. The place had a genteel chintziness that made me want to yell Shit, just to see what would happen. Resisting that impulse, I had very little to say to my mother.

She had plenty to say to me. The postwar changes in England, the welfare state, the slight social leveling, had left her in a state of perpetual outrage. Her anger kept her alive; it seemed to be all she had left to live for. "That awful little man Atlee" and "That awful little man Bevin." She could go on about them for hours. "Our British post office was the envy of the world," she told me once. "Until *they* got their dirty hands on it." I spent a lot of time wandering around Harrods trying to find things, peace offerings to take to her. Whatever I gave her always seemed to be the wrong kind or something she had just bought for herself.

I hardly ever saw Daphne. She wasn't married and according to my mother had become a Red. She worked for the Central Office of the Labour party. We had tea once or twice in a canteen in Whitehall. She had grown earnest and overweight and not in the least interested in me. Daphne hadn't spoken to Sylvia since my father's death.

Jason called every day. He couldn't get Tyrone Power. The studio wanted Yul Brynner. Brynner was coming to Rome. Jason had decided to wait for him there.

"How does Yul Brynner sound when he says My Father the Caliph?"

"Shaky."

I was getting a little shaky myself. Jason had been gone for over two weeks. I missed him terribly. I told him so. "When are you coming back?"

"As soon as I've seen Brynner."

"It's only eight days to Christmas."

"You mean Hanukkah?"

"Okay, I'll put a Star of David on top of the Christmas tree."

Five days before Christmas-Hanukkah he suggested I join him in Rome. He sounded slightly unsure of himself when he said it.

"Do you really want me to, Jason?"

"If you can stand all these studio pricks here, I can."

I was met at the Rome airport by a uniformed chauffeur. He

was holding a sign that said "Mrs. Jason Stone." He almost missed me because he was looking for me among the first-class passengers.

He drove me to the Excelsior on the Via Veneto. Jason had a suite there. He had left flowers and a note for me. *Welcome to Rome. I'm sorry, darling, I'm sorry I couldn't be at the airport . . ."*

He had a meeting with the studio pricks at Cinecita; he would be home by five. I took a shower and changed. The phone kept ringing. I told a number of nameless women Mr. Stone was at Cinecita. Maybe they were secretaries. None of them left a message.

There was a script with a lot of different-colored pages on the table beside the bed. *FINAL* SHOOTING SCRIPT, it said on the cover. I opened it at random and counted seven exclamation points on a single page, four of them in the stage directions. *"Fatima recoils from him!"* is a line that sticks in my memory.

I put on a coat and walked up the Via Veneto to the Borghese Gardens. Children were watching a Punch and Judy show, screaming with delighted terror in their shrill, tuneful Italian voices. When I found myself watching only the children, wanting to touch them, I decided it was time to move on. I had a sandwich somewhere and was back at the hotel by five.

Jason came home at six. He seemed glad to see me. We kissed and he took his coat off and we sat on the couch and kissed again. He put his hand up under my skirt, reaching for what he called his favorite place, the inside of my thigh just above the top of my stocking. For a minute or two I thought he was going to make love to me. He had been saying, "Oh, God. Oh, Carol," in his fond, wondering way. The third time the phone rang he said, "Oh, shit," and I knew he had given up on the idea.

He ordered ice and I made drinks and we talked between phone calls.

Yul Brynner was unavailable. The studio wanted Jack Palance. They had decided to shoot only the locations in Spain and the interiors in Rome. They had frozen lire and they were fucking well going to use them.

"I guess frozen money looks just as good on the screen as any other kind," I said.

"I know. I know. A limousine and a hotel suite and all that crap. But the studio's paying for it. And we might as well get something out of this dog-eared picture besides grief."

I did my best to go along with that. The studio's paying for it, I told myself when a group of people arrived an hour later and Jason ordered up champagne. The studio's paying for it, I told myself again, when we all moved on in three limousines to a restaurant two blocks away, and then to a nightclub, and finally to a wine cellar in Trastevere.

The wine cellar was full of men with cropped blond heads. "They're Cisalpine Gauls," Jason explained. I didn't believe him. I thought they were Swiss. Europe was full of Swiss at that time. Most of them from Hamburg or Munich.

Swiss or Gauls, they were better behaved than the people in our crowd, anyway. I got used to it later, but that Christmas in Rome was the first time I understood that movie people have a special, awful self-importance of their own. They are like colonialists. Their attitude toward any country where they are making a movie is that the natives are a bunch of ungrateful, ignorant sloths who are out to screw them.

For the next few days we seemed to do everything in a crowd. The people at the tables for twelve or sixteen or twenty at the restaurants and nightclubs weren't always the same, but they might as well have been. They said the same things about wops in the same carrying voices and made the same in-jokes and were rude to the waiters in the same godalmighty way. At first they were just cuff links and Charvet ties and monogrammed shirts to me, but after a day or two I learned to recognize some of them and even to remember their names.

There was Mario, a gray-haired cameraman with tired eyes who spoke fluent Italian and was the only one who ever listened to anybody. I always tried to sit next to Mario in the limousines. Any time after midnight was open season on women in those limousines. Unless I managed to squeeze in next to Jason or Mario, I had to keep saying, "No," and "Don't," and finally, firmly, "Cut that out."

There was Harvey, a studio prick in his fifties who kept telling me long, pointless, obscene stories. He never touched me; he was a verbal flasher. He would watch me, watch my eyes for any gratifying signs of shock. I felt sorry for him at first, but something creepy about his voice reminded me of Senator Everett Dirksen and I began to avoid him.

There was a girl named Jill, Jill Ashton, with a put-on English accent. She had short blond hair, artfully tousled in the windswept look that was just coming into fashion. She began every sentence with "I say." "I say, look here," and, "I say, how smashing." Jason explained that the studio was interested in her. He also told me, with far more reverence, that she was related to Anthony Eden, a second cousin or something. She was always hopping into the limousines at the last moment and sitting on Jason's lap. "I say, do you mind awfully?" Jason didn't seem to mind at all.

On Christmas Eve I wanted to go to midnight mass in Saint Peter's. Not because I had any religious feelings about Jesus; on the whole, I thought the Christ cult had done more harm than good, and I didn't believe he had been born at that time of year anyway. I just wanted to watch the pageantry in that beautiful cathedral and hear the choir singing in Latin.

Jason tried to arrange it for me, but you had to belong to one of the right Italian families or have a friend at the Vatican. Around eleven o'clock that night, we were all leaving a restaurant near the Spanish Steps. I told Jason where I was going and let the limousines roll off without me.

The night was bitter cold with that special stony Roman chill that seems to seep up out of the streets like the cruelty of history. Fewer than a hundred people had gathered outside Saint Peter's. I stood close to the main door where I could hear the choir and see the lights through the stained glass windows. After the gregarious rowdiness of the last few days, the stillness, the echoing Latin responses, had a severe innocence. It made the vulgar wastefulness of the way I was living seem inexcusable. Someday I would be punished for it. In the depths of my mind, where that helpful spirit had her subliminal existence, I still retained those contradictions acquired in my childhood. I didn't believe in the last judgment, but I was afraid I would be judged; I didn't believe in hell, but I was scared I was going to be sent there.

The cold was becoming unbearable. I decided to stay there, bearing it, for another two minutes, as a penance. As I glanced at my watch, I noticed a man standing a few yards away. His head was bowed, his face hidden by the collar of his shabby overcoat. I saw him cross himself. He straightened, looking up into the light from the windows.

It was Max.

My first impulse was to escape, to walk away without speaking to him. But then, I don't know, he looked so alone. I went over and touched his arm.

"Hello, Max."

"Hello, Carol." It was obvious from the lack of surprise in his voice that he had seen me standing there, had been wondering, perhaps, whether I would want to speak to him.

I was glad I hadn't walked away. "It's good to see you, Max."

"Is it?"

"What are you doing here in Rome?"

"Oh, that. That's a long story."

It was difficult to see his face clearly in that light, but he looked thin, and not so much pale as gray. His hair, his cheeks, even his lips, had a dull gray tone.

"What have you been doing all this time, Max?" It had been over seven years since I'd seen him. "Are you married? Tell me about yourself."

"No, I'm not married. I know you are. You're Mrs. Stone." There was something in his voice, a flatness, that was hard to define.

"I heard you were working for the Voice of America."

"Did you?" I recognized that flatness now: it was resignation.

"Are you still with them?"

"No. Of course not."

I was so cold I didn't think I could bear it any longer. I touched his arm again. The sleeve of his coat felt as thin as cotton. "Couldn't we go somewhere, have a cup of coffee?"

"I can't leave here yet. Not until the mass is over."

I could have smiled, nodded. I could have said I was glad I had seen him and left him there. I couldn't make myself do it. We had had such a long history together. For ten years of my life he had been the most important person in the world to me. Now here he was, thin and gray and obviously poor, with that terrible resignation in his eyes. It reminded me of that moment at the bus stop in London when he was going back to his base and he had started to say he would see me over the weekend if he was still alive.

"Well, will you meet me —" No, not tomorrow. Tomorrow was Christmas Day. "Can you meet me the day after tomorrow, Max?"

"Meet you? Where? I don't —"

"Why not here? In the afternoon. At two o'clock?"

"I don't know."

"Please." The cold was driving me to get it settled quickly. "Please. Two o'clock. The day after tomorrow. Promise?"

"All right." He said it in the same flat way as he had said everything else, as though it didn't matter.

I started away.

"Carol."

I stopped and turned my head. He was still standing in front of the great door of Saint Peter's. The stained glass windows were behind him and I couldn't see his face.

"I'll say a prayer for you, Carol."

I walked on.

It didn't surprise me that Max had gone back to the church. I had always thought it was the security of his lost faith that he was pursuing in Trotskyism, in Freud. Maybe in those bloody Lancaster bombers. That had always been the decisive difference between us: I was willing to accept immediate answers to immediate questions; Max couldn't. When I rejected his panaceas, he had accused me of frivolity.

I took a taxi back to the hotel. Jason wasn't home yet. I ran a hot bath and, feeling rebelliously frivolous by then, lay in it for a long time with a Scotch and soda. It was a new pleasure I had discovered in Europe, the tart contrast between the hot water and the cold drink.

Jason still wasn't home by two o'clock when I put down Edmund Wilson's *Scrolls from the Dead Sea,* turned off the light, and fell asleep. He was lying beside me when the phone rang at nine. I let it ring and went to the bathroom. It was still ringing, or maybe ringing again, when I came out. Jason had his head under the bedclothes and was making fretful sounds. I answered it.

"I say, is Jason there?"

"He's asleep."

"I say, I don't want to disturb him, but I thought he might be worried."

"Why?"

"He left one of his gold cuff links at my flat last night and I was afraid he might think he'd lost it. I say, I do hope you don't think —"

I hung up.

I called the switchboard and told them nobody, *nobody* was to be put through for the rest of the day. Jason stopped making fretful sounds when I got back into bed. He turned over and put his arm around me. I lay there trying to figure out how I felt about him fucking that bloody girl.

I felt disappointed, resentful, angry, and slightly humiliated. But not jealous. It was impossible to feel jealous of Jill Ashton. She was one of those joke people, as contrived as a trick glass or a laughing cushion. I couldn't believe Jason could have any serious feelings about her.

She was also one of those crowers. She had proved that with her phone call. From now on she wouldn't miss a single chance to let me know my husband had laid her. She would rub my nose in it. When I was around, she would be clinging and possessive with Jason. "I say, do you mind awfully if Jason takes me home. I've got a frightful headache and you'll come back *immeejitly,* won't you, Jason?"

I wasn't going to stand for that. I was going to have to make it clear to Jason that from now on any group that included me did not include Jill Ashton.

That still left me feeling angry. I tried to figure out why.

"So *what* if he's fucking Iris?"

I had said that about Chris so often. Why was it different with Jason? For one thing, of course, I had never loved Chris. For another, I hadn't been faithful to him. I hadn't even necked with another man since I had agreed to marry Jason. I had to admit I hadn't wanted to.

Had Jason wanted to? Had Jason —? All those trips to the coast and New York and Madrid. How many other Jill Ashtons had there been?

At that point a wish, a regret, came to my mind that I was to

remember again and again later. It was to become a secret understanding with myself, almost a principle. It was to influence the
most important decision of my life.

If only I didn't know.

That wish was no use to me now. I did know. It was no good
trying to pretend I didn't, either. I was going to have to have it
out with Jason.

Now? As soon as he woke up? On Christmas morning? Oh, hell.
No. Not now. Later. Maybe tomorrow. I wasn't going to let Jill
Ashton spoil our Christmas together. She wasn't worth it.

Jason awoke mumbling and reaching for the glass beside him.
He had a funny way of mopping his lips with his tongue when
he sipped water in the mornings. Like a cat. He looked like a cheerful
cat now as he put the glass down.

"Happy Christmas, Carol."

"Happy Hanukkah, Jason."

He jumped out of bed with a wait-and-see smile and went into
the living room. While he was gone, I took his presents out of
the closet and piled them on the bed for him. He came back and
piled mine beside them.

We each opened a present and kissed. It became a ritual. We
kissed after opening each present. We went on kissing after we
had no more to open. Presently we were back in bed and my nightdress was all bunched up under my arms and I was thinking for
perhaps the thousandth time that Jason had the kindest, most loving
hands of any man I had ever known.

We had breakfast sent up and ate scrambled eggs in the living
room with the windows open so I could wear the new vicuña coat
Jason had given me. I loved that coat. He had wanted to give me
a fur, but I wouldn't let him. I didn't want a fur coat. Ever.

The phone didn't ring, but the doorbell did, constantly. A succession of bellhops bearing gifts. Presents for Jason with cute cards
about the movie. "One man's meat is another man's Persian" was
on five of them. Presents for me from people I hardly knew, wouldn't
have recognized on the street. Expensive presents. Silver and porcelain things and kid gloves that were the right size.

I tried to feel grateful as I stripped off the fancy wrappings and
tied the cards to the gifts so I would know who had sent what

when I wrote thank-you letters. By noon I had run out of gratitude. There were presents all over the room and every one of them was like a reproach, a reproach for being rich and privileged and spoiled. I wanted to gather them all up and take them over to Trastevere. A lot of people in Trastevere could feed their whole families for a week on what one pair of those kid gloves cost.

"Can we, Jason?"

He knew how I felt. "No, darling, I'm afraid we just can't."

"Why not?"

"They'll be coming here for drinks. They'll look to see if you've got their what's-its-name on the mantlepiece. Where everybody can admire it."

"Who's coming here for drinks?"

"Most of them. Most of the people who sent these —"

"Today?"

"Not until seven. I wanted to keep as much time as possible to ourselves. Be alone for a change."

I was going to have to have it out with Jason on Christmas Day after all.

"Is Jill Ashton coming?"

"Why?"

"You know why." Now that we were talking about it, my anger had returned.

Jason lit one of his small Swiss cigars. He didn't usually smoke that early.

"I haven't been snooping on you. She called. You left one of your cuff links there, so she called. She wanted me to know you'd screwed her. And I do know. And I'm not going to pretend I don't."

"Yeah." He found an ashtray. "She's a little bitch, isn't she?"

"Yes."

"Do you mind very much?"

"Yes. Yes, I do. I hate it."

"It was just a — Nothing."

"I know it was just a nothing. But how would you feel if I went to bed with — with Mario?" I didn't want to go to bed with Mario but he was the only person I knew in Rome I could imagine even holding hands with.

"That's different."

"What's different?"

"With men. It's much more casual with men."

"That's a load of bull. It's the kind of crap men tell each other to make themselves feel better."

"It doesn't mean anything to a man."

"It means exactly the same thing whether you're a man or a woman." If there was one thing I'd learned in the Remo, it was the truth of that. "I know exactly what it means. It means curiosity and desire and — and excitement and physical closeness and discovery and — and pleasure and feeling gratified afterward."

"Is that what it means to you? With *me?*" He sounded a little shocked.

"We're not talking about you and me. We're talking about casual fucks."

"Jesus."

"What?"

He put down his cigar and went over to close the windows. "I'm not going to ask you how you know so much about casual fucks," he said when he came back to me. "I guess I know how you know so much. You told me. All that time you were having a ball in the Village. And maybe you're right. Maybe it isn't all that different with men or women."

He picked up his cigar again. It had gone out.

"The point is, Carol, people think it's different. It looks different. If I screw that little bitch, nobody thinks anything about it. But if you go to bed with Mario, with my cameraman, I'm a stand-up comic. I'm a joke. I'm that schmuck whose wife is putting it over on him. You know that's true."

I was afraid it was. It was ridiculous and unfair, but it happened to be true — at least among the people we knew in Rome that winter. Maybe that was one of the reasons I didn't like them much.

"I don't care how it looks, Jason. Especially to this movie crowd. The trouble is if you go to bed with someone else, it makes me feel inadequate. Maybe it's just vanity. But it hurts. And I'm not going to stand for it."

"Haven't you —" he picked up his lighter — "haven't you ever wanted — had one of those urges? Jesus, how did you put it? Curiosity and desire. Haven't you ever felt that about anyone else since we've been married?"

I had already thought that out in bed.

"No, to be honest with you, Jason, I haven't. Not for a moment."

He relit his cigar. He took his time over it.

"Christ," he said. "I guess that's quite a compliment. It's a hell of a nice Christmas present, being told that, Carol."

"Good. I'm glad you like it. But the point is, what are you going to do about it? What are you going to do about that phony little slut?"

"It's all over, I promise you, Carol. I promise you I won't ever see her again. Okay?"

"Okay."

We went for a walk in the Borghese Gardens. When we came back we arranged our presents, displaying them like objects in a museum. Thirty people came in for drinks and Jason was right, they all made a point of identifying their own gifts. I exclaimed gratefully over them to all the right donors.

Jill Ashton was not among the guests. Jason had called her. I don't know what he had said, but she didn't show up at the restaurant, either, or pop into any of the limousines that night.

The next day Jason was busy at Cinecita. I had not told him about running into Max. Since that night on Tenth Street, when I had stood him up at Costello's, had almost forgotten he existed in my joy that Max was alive, he had had a special sensitivity about my whole involvement with Max. We never talked about him. I didn't want to make Jason unhappy by mentioning him now. "If only I didn't know." Okay. I was only going to have a cup of coffee with Max, talk to him for a few minutes. There was no sense in having a lot of Who-shot-John about it.

It was a bright day, cold, but lovely in the sun, and I was all wrapped up in my new vicuña coat. There were more people in the square than there had been Christmas Eve, tourists conscientiously admiring the perspective of Bernini's colonnades. I was a few minutes early. I stood outside the great door of Saint Peter's, repressing the desire to slip inside and wander around the cathedral. I was afraid of missing Max. He might think I had changed my mind and didn't want to see him.

The clock tower boomed every fifteen minutes. I waited until half past three. By then, I could rule out the possibility of a mistake, a last-minute delay. Max wasn't coming.

I felt a little sad. I felt a little relieved. I had done my best. What more could I do? Best of all, I had nothing to hide from Jason now.

He left for Madrid the next day. When I returned from seeing him off at the airport, I told the desk clerk I wouldn't take any calls from anybody except Mr. Stone. I missed Jason as soon as I walked into the empty suite, but it was lovely having Rome to myself, to be away from that damn crowd, to go to all the places I had wanted to see — the Coliseum and the Piazza Navona — to be able to loiter alone and in silence.

My box was always stuffed with messages when I came home in the evenings. I went through them all in case there was anything I ought to pass on to Jason when he phoned, but I didn't call any of the callers back.

When Jason had been gone three days, I found a cheap blue envelope among the message slips. It was addressed to CAROL STONE in block letters. It had obviously been delivered by hand.

I didn't open it until I was upstairs. The single flimsy page of the letter was not written in block letters, and I recognized the handwriting at once.

Twice in my life the sight of it had filled me with such happiness it was like suddenly regaining one's sight: once in that furnished room on Perry Street, and then again later when he had written from the POW camp and I knew he was still alive.

My only reaction to it now was mild concern. He was ill. That was why he hadn't come to Saint Peter's. If he needed help, I would have to do what I could for him.

I read the letter.

Dear Carol, I'm sorry I didn't meet you as I promised. It wasn't because I'm angry or blame you for my being fired from the Voice of America. I know you were in a very difficult position — that job at Studio One — they must have forced you to give them information against me. But you see, there's never been anyone else for me, and I'd like to go on remembering you as you were, without any regrets or reproaches between us. Under that he had simply signed his name. *Max.*

I put the flimsy sheet of paper back in the envelope. Well, if he thought that, if he thought I'd informed on him, gotten him fired from the Voice of America, I didn't care what he thought.

I went through the rest of the messages. I made notes on two of them I thought might be important to Jason.

Goddamn it, I hadn't given anyone any information against Max. I had done my best to protect him. I had deliberately lied to Vince Campion, made him think I was a randy little pushover, picked up by a serviceman in a bar, so I wouldn't have to say a word about the Trotskyist party. It was probably one of Max's old Trotskyist friends who had given information against him.

The hell with him. Forget it.

I had a drink and tried to read.

I couldn't forget it. The injustice of it kept gnawing at me. Ten years old and my mother sending me to my room: "I didn't do it. I didn't do it." I felt the same indignation now. I wanted to fight back, prove to Max I didn't do it.

I picked up the envelope. No return address. None on the letter, either. That was that. I couldn't write to Max, tell him the truth, clear myself. I went back to my book.

Jason called; I gave him his messages. The Investment was in Madrid. He was funny and sad about her; she was on a diet and she cried all the time. We talked for half an hour, the studio was paying for it. I told him I wished he would hurry up and come back. He said he wished he could.

I still couldn't forget Max's letter. At odd moments during the next few days, in the Castel San Angelo, eating alone at a little trat' on the Via Giulia, I found myself talking to Max in my mind. I wanted to get it all out, make him believe me.

When I ran into Mario, the nice cameraman, on the Spanish Steps, I had no intention of unburdening myself to him. We went to the English Tearoom and talked about the movie. I told him how it had started as a modest British picture and grown and grossened like some crazy monster. He listened with so much sympathy and understanding in his tired eyes that I found myself talking more personally about it, about my distrust of the whole movie world. From that we went on to the way the studios had caved in to HUAC and the blacklists and then I was suddenly pouring it all out to him, Studio One and Vince Campion and Max's letter.

He didn't say anything at once; he was smiling in his patient way.

"I guess that man, Max Ludlow, must have felt the same way you do."

"Why?"

"He probably wanted to confront his accusers, too. But he didn't even know who they were. That's the one thing those people never told you. So he turned on you."

"Okay, Mario. I understand that. But I still wish I could talk to him. It's awful to have someone, anyone — it's awful to have Max blame me for something I didn't do."

"Then why don't you go and see him?"

"I don't know where he lives."

"It wouldn't be hard to find him."

"How? He's just one of thousands of Americans living in Rome. In a furnished room —"

"But he's not just one of thousands of Americans. He's an American who worked for the Voice of America and got fired as a security risk."

I didn't see how that would help me; Mario had to explain it to me. "He was lucky to be given a passport at all. The number's certainly on a list. They keep a check on those listed passports. Every time your friend registers at a hotel, a rooming house, anywhere, the Italian police pass the information along to —" He shrugged. "Well, to the embassy."

"Would the embassy tell me where Max was living?"

"No, probably not. Do you really want to find him?"

"Yes. But I don't see —"

Mario smiled; I was obviously being stupid; he had to explain himself again. "I've been in Rome for seven years now. I left Hollywood as soon as things started to turn ugly. I shot a documentary film for the Spanish Loyalists in thirty-six. But I still work for the studios when they make a picture over here. I've never been blacklisted." There was no apology in his eyes, only the patience of experience and acceptance. "That's because I have friends, Carol. I made friends." He lifted his hands, holding them above his head. "I surrendered."

The next evening when I returned to the hotel, I found a folded

note among the message slips. *Via Tusconi, 38. Apt. 22. Trastevere.*
It was unsigned.

Number 38 was a tenement building, four tall gray tombstones
sagging against each other around a small courtyard. Each of them
had its own narrow entrance. A small boy showed me which stairs
to climb when I scratched a 22 in the dirt of the courtyard. Each
floor had three doors; some of them had names or numbers written
in chalk on them. The stone stairs were slimy with something I
didn't want to identify. On every landing were piles of refuse loosely
wrapped in newspaper. Even in the intense cold there was a cloying
reek of urine. Apartment 22 was six flights up.

LUDLOW. The name was written on the torn flap of an envelope stuck to the door. I waited until I stopped panting and then
knocked.

No answer. I heard the twang of bedsprings, then someone moving
around inside.

I knocked again. The door opened a crack. Max peered out.
He looked gray and sick and frightened. He looked ghastly. He
tried to close the door on me. I pushed it open and walked into
the room.

There was an iron cot with a crucifix on the wall above it, a
wooden table and chair, a fiber suitcase open on the floor, a heap
of books and papers in the corner. A yellowish electric bulb hung
from the ceiling. No curtains, no carpet, no sheets on the bed.
The inch-thick mattress over the springs was torn and stained. A
dark, rumpled blanket lay on it. I couldn't see a pillow.

"Get out of here."

Max was wearing his overcoat over a sweater and he had a woolen
muffler wound under his chin. The room was so cold that his breath
misted between us with each word.

I closed the door behind me.

"Get out of here and leave me alone."

I walked over to the suitcase and started to pick up the clothes
on the floor beside it and fold and pack them.

"What are you doing?"

I finished with the clothes and began packing the books.

"Don't touch those things."

I spread the rest of the books and papers on top of the clothes and looked around.

"What else is yours, Max?"

He was sitting on the bed with his elbows on his knees.

"I told you to get out of here and leave me alone."

His voice was hoarse, pleading, without conviction. We knew each other so well; all the years of our past were in that room with us. From the moment I had walked in, every one of my actions had been as inevitable as time. I didn't have to think what I was doing or why.

"You can't stay here. It's ridiculous for you to be living like this. You're sick and you probably haven't had a proper meal for days and there's no one to look after you. And on top of all that it's freezing cold in here."

I closed the suitcase.

"Have you got your passport?"

He nodded. It was in his pocket. I put the rest of his belongings — a toothbrush, a razor, and the crucifix — into a paper bag. He followed me to the door.

"Where do you think you're taking me?"

I turned the yellow light off.

"There's a hotel called the Inglaterra near the Spanish Steps." We started down the slimy, reeking stairway. "It's clean and it's cheap and a lot of writers and painters and beatnik people stay there, so you needn't worry about your clothes."

"I haven't got any money."

"Never mind about that."

"I'm not going to borrow money from you."

"Oh, come on, Max, stop being so silly." I led him across the courtyard. "You paid for me often enough."

"When? When did I ever pay for you?"

We walked toward the river, looking for a taxi.

"You took me to the Copley Plaza once. When you had all that back pay from the air force. Remember? And lots of other times, too."

In the taxi I made him accept enough lire to pay for the room at the Inglaterra for a week in advance. It was a light, pleasant room with French windows and a balcony. Best of all, it was warm and there was hot water in the bathroom. I ordered up soup and an omelette while Max was soaking in the bath. He ate in his pajamas and overcoat; he didn't have a bathrobe. The food acted on him like alcohol: it revived him and made him slightly aggressive.

"I guess you do owe it to me," he said when he had finished the omelette. "After what you did."

It was time to get that straight. "I don't owe you a damn thing. I never told anyone anything about you and those bloody Trotskyists." I was off now, letting out my indignation. I told him what had really happened, what I had said to Vince Campion. "And that was all. He was the only one who ever asked me about you and that's what I told him."

Max didn't want to believe me at first. He argued. Who else could have informed on him?

"Dozens of people. Leda. Mannie. What about Mrs. Hainert?"

"Mannie's in jail."

I remembered that now. It had been in *Time* magazine. Emanuel Orville Lind. He had stood up to them and been given two years.

"There was Leda and all the others. The ones in New York, too. They didn't go to jail."

"You're probably right," Max admitted at last. "One of them could have turned informer if the bastards were after them."

"What happened to Mrs. Hainert?" I was curious about her; I had liked her so much. Later, when she didn't answer my letters, I had decided she had never liked me anyway and stopped thinking of her.

Max didn't know. He hadn't heard from her for years. He told me things about her past she had kept from me. "She was married to a prominent German Communist, Gunther Hainert. He was expelled from the party in thirty-six, at the time of the Popular Front. She came back to their hotel room in Paris one night and he wasn't there. She didn't find him until the next morning. He had hanged himself from the window ledge. His body had been dangling outside in the areaway all night."

It was Mrs. Hainert who had first brought Max into the Trotskyist group in Los Angeles. "She started talking to me in the library one day. Talking about Stalin, how he had betrayed the revolution."

By tacit agreement we had leapfrogged back into the past, over the bad times in New York to the summer of thirty-nine. We recalled the house above Laurel Canyon, the meetings, the community singing. We remembered the Eriksons on that drive to the coast, the afternoon in Joplin when they were selling their Bibles.

"You hated them," I reminded him. "You said you could never trust those religious freaks."

"I never said that. They were crooks, that's all. I never said anything about their religion."

Abruptly, jarringly, we were back in the present.

"I didn't mean it that way, Max." We had quarreled enough; all those bitter rows on Charles Street. "I'm glad you've gone back to being a Catholic. Is that why you came to Rome?"

"I thought —" He seemed embarrassed. "I thought of trying to become a priest."

I wondered if his analysis had led him to that decision. But then after the analysis there had been the Voice of America. I decided not to question him. Max brought up both subjects himself.

"I thought I could do something worthwhile through the Voice of America. Something to give hope to all those people in the Eastern bloc countries."

And then, later: "You see, the one thing I learned from analysis was that I could never be happy just trying to make an ordinary career for myself like most men. I had to feel I was involved in something more important. I'm not saying there's anything special in that. Some of us just naturally see our lives in terms of our influence on other people. We're sort of clan oriented."

He went on about that, about his discovery of himself.

Oh, Max, I thought. Did it have to take you all those years with Maria to find out what anyone who knew you could have told you in ten minutes? You never had a family. That's what you've been searching for all your life. Why couldn't you just create one of your own, let me have a child and make a family with you?

I didn't say it. Maybe he would be happy in the Catholic church. He would probably make a good priest; he had always had a gift for faith.

But the church wouldn't have him. "It's very difficult if you're my age. And I haven't any influence. I can't get any of the orders to accept me and train me for ordination."

"Can't you just enroll in theological college, or whatever they call it? Isn't it like becoming a doctor?"

I knew so little about it. Max lay on the bed and I sat in a chair beside him, discussing it, until almost ten o'clock. After a while, as I tried to think of people who might help, I began to sense a frightened reluctance in him. He had had such a hard time these past few years, being fired from the Voice of America, turned away by the church, living in that ghastly tenement in Trastevere, the little money he had dwindling away, pawning anything he could, until these last few weeks he had been slowly starving. I understood the resignation I had heard in his voice on Christmas Eve. He had been beaten down until he had lost hope.

When I left I promised to come back the next morning. I walked to the hotel through the cold, busy streets, wondering what I could do to help. I had a lot of the money I had earned in two years at Studio One; Jason had never let me spend my salary on the house-keeping. But money wasn't enough; it wouldn't help Max out of that despairing resignation. He had to be encouraged to regain his enthusiasm.

The usual sheaf of messages was waiting for me at the desk. I felt a slight start of guilt when I saw the top one. Jason had called at 9:30 as he did every evening. I had always been home for his calls until now.

Before I even took my coat off upstairs, I asked the operator to get me the Hilton in Madrid. The call went through in less than five minutes. When I gave her my name, the woman at the Hilton switchboard told me in English that she didn't think Mr. Stone was in his room.

"Please try him anyway."

"Mrs. Stone, I don't think —"

"Please."

The room answered at once.

"Hello. Hello. Hello? I say, who is this?"

Gently, rather furtively, I replaced the receiver without speaking.

Okay. You asked for it. And the moral of that is, don't call your husband at ten-thirty at night and insist on being put through to his room, when the tactful Spanish lady at the switchboard has warned you, in English, that it's a lousy idea.

Still. There it was. And now I knew. Jill Ashton was in Madrid with Jason. He had probably told her not to answer the phone, but she wasn't the kind of girl who would ever be able to let a phone ring.

What was I going to do now? I sat in a chair, still wearing my heavy outdoor shoes, thinking about it, remembering Jason's promises on Christmas Day — it was all over, he would never see her again — and hating him. Hating him as much for his promises as for breaking them. When the phone rang a half-hour later, I let it ring, nine, ten, eleven times, until it stopped ringing. It could only be Jason and I didn't want to talk to him.

I still didn't want to talk to him when the phone rang again, and again and again, the next morning.

I had breakfast downstairs in the restaurant, ignoring the boy who kept paging me, and walked back to the Inglaterra. Max was dressed, waiting in his room. I had cashed some traveler's checks before leaving the Excelsior and I made him accept the money.

"You've got to buy a new overcoat. You can't walk around in that one in this weather."

He responded with the same flat resignation. What did it matter? He didn't mind the cold. By the time I got him to the Via del Corso, I realized his indifference could be turned into obedience. In that hopeless, despairing mood, he would do what he was told. We went to the men's department at the Standa and I made him buy a tweed jacket and slacks, several shirts, two sweaters, and a pair of gloves, as well as an overcoat.

"Why don't you wear them, Max? Put them on now."

"What shall I do with my own things?"

"What you did with that bloody uniform. Remember?"

"When?"

"In Montreal." It had worked the night before; the only time he had shown any animation was when we were talking about the past. "When you got out of the air force, Max. We went straight to a department store and you left your uniform on the floor in the changing room with all those ribbons and flight badges and everything."

"That was different."

"No, it wasn't. Go on. Go and change."

He was silent and thoughtful when he came back in his new clothes and as we left the store with our packages.

"It *was* different," he said outside on the street.

"What?"

"In Montreal."

"Why?"

"You." He made a vague gesture with his free hand. "The way we felt. Us."

It caught at me like an inadvertently remembered dream. We had been so much in love then. The war was over. We were at a beginning together. We were so happy and we had so much hope. I stopped on the crowded sidewalk; suddenly I felt scared. What did I have now? I was thirty-five years old and I had a barren marriage and a husband who was screwing a starlet in Madrid.

"We'd better go back to your hotel, Max," I said, "and get rid of these packages."

I waited in the lobby while he took them up to his room.

"What do you want to do now?" he asked me when he came back.

What did I want to do? I wanted to go to Madrid and kill that bloody girl. That wouldn't help. She wasn't worth it. I wanted to kill Jason. Not really kill him. Hurt him. Hit him. Hard.

"Let's go to the Keats Memorial House," I suggested. "It's quite close."

We walked through the narrow-roomed house. In the library, earnest Japanese students were sitting over piles of books, making notes in their decorative script on the English Romantic poets. We saw the small room where Keats had died, in bitterness and despair, neglected by everyone except his friend Joseph Severn.

He was only twenty-five, I kept thinking. He was only twenty-five. I was glad we had come. It restored my sense of perspective a little. I was never going to write an "Ode to a Nightingale," or do anything else that would bring Japanese students to my shrine. But at least I wasn't dying of tuberculosis. I was still a young, healthy woman and I could feel grateful to Keats for the beauty and magic he had left us all.

The visit seemed to affect Max in the same way; over lunch he was earnest and purposeful.

"It makes you realize you've got to get on with it, do something. I mean, nobody has all that much time."

Then, for the first time, he asked me about my marriage.

I told him a little about Jason, the movie. He was surprisingly well informed about that already. There had been a lot of publicity in the Italian papers and he had obviously read it all studiously.

"Why didn't you ever have any children?" he asked presently.

It was a question I had been asked several times in the past two years. I was, usually, deliberately vague in my answers, careful not to blame Jason. For once, because I was so angry with him, I felt like telling the truth.

"He can't," I said. "Jason can't. I don't mean he's impotent. He's sterile."

Max nodded sympathetically. "You wanted so much to have children."

Yes, Max, I thought. That was what broke us up. I wanted to have children and you refused.

I asked him if he felt like going to look at some paintings. There was an exhibition of Renoirs at the Modern Museum in the Borghese Gardens.

We spent most of the afternoon there. The quality that I had always loved in Renoir was his affection for the commonplace. I was in that mood myself, that day. I wanted to appreciate simple things, a woman's dress, a tree, a room. When we left the Borghese I was only a few minutes' walk from the Excelsior. There would be messages waiting for me at the desk, and upstairs that too expensive suite, full of presents from strangers. Would the phone ring? Did I want to answer it if it did?

"For Christ's sake let's go and have a drink, Max."

"Where?"

Donay's was just down the block. I didn't want to go there or to any of the other places near the Via Veneto. They would be full of movie people, friends of Jason's. We stopped at a grocery store for a bottle of brandy and went back to the Inglaterra.

We drank some brandy, and didn't feel like going out again, and ordered sandwiches in the room. I took my shoes off and lay on the bed; Max sat in the chair. We talked. The present was uncertain and we had no future, so we talked about the past, not just do-you-remember, and I-wonder-what-happened-to, but trying to explain ourselves now in ways we had been too preoccupied to understand at the time.

"Why were you so mad at me, Carol?"

We were back in 1940, Max's leave in New York, that disastrous evening after Don's radio program.

"Of course I was mad at you. The things you were saying about me in that restaurant."

"What? Why did they make you so angry?"

"Because of Fitz." I could admit that now. "You were probably right, Max. You accused me at the time of being in love with Fitz, and I suppose in a way I was. I looked up to him so much. I always wanted to show him only my best side. I wanted him to approve of me. And then in that restaurant you kept going on about what a good lay I was." I sat up a little, leaning toward him. "You thanked Fitz for teaching me how to fuck. I couldn't bear it. I felt so ashamed."

"Because he was really your father, wasn't he?"

"I guess so." For once I didn't mind the Freudian explanation. "He was the father I always wanted to have. The father who was interested and paid attention to me."

"So you felt I was accusing you of incest."

"No, Max. It wasn't that simple. When I was a little girl, I wanted my father to pet me. I wanted him to hold me on his lap and kiss me. All little girls probably do. I never wanted anything like that from Fitz. I had no physical feelings about him at all. That's why I was so angry at you. I didn't feel ashamed of myself. I felt ashamed *for* Fitz. He was so completely remote from sex to me. Like a priest, if you like." I lay back on the pillow. "I guess I always knew he was homosexual, really. I just didn't want to think about it."

Max was silent for a minute.

"It was a wonderful leave anyway, wasn't it, Carol? I think it was one of the best times of my life."

"Yes, it was." Impulsively I stretched out my hand. "For me, too."

"Carol." He was holding my hand, kissing it.

I sat up and put my feet on the floor, started to fit them into my shoes.

"Don't go, Carol."

There was no longer any resignation in his eyes. For an instant I saw him as I remembered him best, eager, excited. It wasn't a sexual excitement. It was that old certainty and enthusiasm: this is what I'm going to do; this is right.

"Stay with me, Carol."

I wasn't drunk. I was angry at Jason. He had lied and broken his promise to me. And besides . . .

And besides, I didn't want to go back to that bloody suite at the Excelsior. Those extravagant, useless gifts all over the living room, reminding me of the extravagant, useless life I had been living in Rome. I had never wanted that kind of life. I had never wanted to be the kind of person I associated with it. All our talk of the past had done more than recall my memories of Max. It had recalled to me the image I had once had of myself, independent and rebellious. And so *hopeful.*

It wasn't that I believed there was any hope for me in Max, that we could ever recapture the excitement, the sense of "beginning" we had felt in Montreal. It wasn't that lost hope I was seeking in him. It was my own past, my suddenly remembered self. And anyway . . .

And anyway, I had once loved Max so much, and anyway, damn Jason, and in other words, why not?

I stayed with Max at the Inglaterra for the next four days. I went to the Excelsior every morning to change my clothes and pick up things I needed and cash traveler's checks. I hardly glanced through the messages. "Mr. Stone called." "Mr. Stone called." Let him call. On Thursday morning there was a cable from him. *Trying to reach you. Please call me. Urgent. I love you. Jason.*

I hesitated for half an hour. If it was really urgent, if he was sick or had had an accident, he would have said so in the cable. What was urgent to Jason was that he had guessed I knew about Jill Ashton. I wasn't going to talk to him about that on the phone; it would make me want to throw the receiver at the wall.

I cabled him back. *Will talk to you when you return to Rome. Carol.* It sounded cold and smug when I read it over. I sent it anyway.

Max was getting stronger, less resigned, day by day. There were subjects, whole areas, we had to avoid — there always had been —

but he was increasingly willing to talk about his own future, to make plans.

I had met a man through the movie people, a friendly, bouncy ex-college professor, who worked for UNICEF in Rome. He was a film buff; he had attached himself to our group one evening and listened to our vapid shoptalk like a courtier eavesdropping outside the royal bedchamber. He had thanked us all for a fascinating evening and pressed his cards on us. What made me think he might be able to help Max was that he was Canadian.

"After all, they owe you something, Max," I insisted. "You were in the Canadian air force for six years. You flew thirty missions. You were a POW."

"The Americans would never let me work for the U.N." He was still inclined to see the objections first.

"They can't stop you. Those bastards at the embassy, or whatever they are, can't tell the Canadians what to do. Wouldn't you like to work for UNICEF, Max? Isn't that the kind of thing you're looking for?"

He said it might be. I called the Canadian and the three of us had lunch together. Max behaved very well; he was frank about the Voice of America without sounding bitter or self-pitying and the Canadian was immediately sympathetic. He had friends who had been fired from American colleges and when it came to loyalty oaths and security risks and all that dreadful rubbish, as he put it, he was more than willing to stand up to the Americans and tell them to go to hell. He was obviously impressed by Max's war record, and as the lunch went on he became more and more bouncy and friendly and eager to help. He asked Max to come and see him in his office and bring his passport and his discharge papers. He couldn't promise anything, but the U.N. agencies in Rome were expanding every day and he would do everything he could to find Max a job.

That was on Friday. Max made an appointment with him for the following Monday. He was thoughtful as we left the restaurant. I didn't say anything; I had pressed him enough. We went to the movies. I spent the night with him. The next morning we rented a car and drove across the mountains and explored the Adriatic coast.

That Saturday evening at a pension in Pescara, I began for the first time to think objectively about what I was doing. Until then, because of my resentment toward Jason, I had been going along with Max like a sleepwalker, in a heedless, trancelike way, from hour to hour.

What was I getting into with him? Where was it leading me?

It was Max himself who forced me to consider this. Over dinner he began to talk, not just about his own future, but about "our" future together.

I tried to put a stop to that at once. "The thing that broke us up, Max, was that we have completely different ways of looking at everything. And that hasn't changed."

"The thing that broke us up, Carol, is that you stopped believing in me."

"I stopped believing in us."

"Do you remember that night you came back from Florida?"

Did he think I could ever forget it, all my excited plans for having a child?

"I tried to tell you that night about an idea I had for a new elite."

"You'd written a letter to the *Times* about it."

"You wouldn't listen to me. You made fun of the whole thing."

He reached across the table and grasped my hand. There was a sudden fervor in his eyes. It wasn't the old eagerness I remembered so well; enthusiasm had been warped by misfortune and bitterness. "I was meant to be one of those people, Carol. I know I was."

It was what the desperate, dying Keats was supposed to have said to his friend Severn. "I was meant to be one of the great ones." But Max wasn't Keats, and I didn't think he was talking about the same kind of greatness.

I pulled my hand away. "That's exactly what I mean about the difference between us," I told him. "I don't believe in elites. I don't believe —"

"Listen to me." The bitterness was in his voice now. "You think my whole life's been a failure, don't you. You think I've been beaten down and defeated."

"I think —" I was going to say I thought he'd had some very tough breaks, the war, the POW camp, the blacklisting.

"Just listen. What you don't understand, Carol, is that I haven't even started yet. My life so far has been nothing but a preparation, a time of learning and understanding myself. But I'm ready now. I'm ready to take the place I was meant to take. Be the kind of leader and teacher I was meant to be. And we're going to do it together. You believed in me as a leader once, Carol, you know you did." He grasped my hand again. "Didn't you?"

Yes, perhaps, in a way, I had. I had imagined him riding the western plains, leading the wagon train, competent and kind and trustworthy. It had been an adolescent fantasy. I had grown out of it.

"You're going to believe in me again. You'll see. I'm not going to let myself be ignored and turned away any longer. It's only a question of getting a start. Finding a few people who'll listen to me. A small group of followers. People who've been degraded and kicked around themselves, who are looking for someone to help them, tell them what to do. Who need someone to look up to and give them hope." He hadn't raised his voice, but his eyes were filled with passionate intensity. "I know I can make them listen to me. I can make them obey me. I know we can do it, Carol. You've got to believe that. You've got to believe in me. Promise me you do. Promise me. Now."

He was hurting my hand. I knew there was no point in arguing with him. I could see that the old rage, so carefully suppressed during the years with Maria, was still latent in him; it would explode in an instant if I opposed him.

"Okay, Max," I said. "I believe in you."

Thank God that, because of our passports, we had been forced to take separate rooms at the pension; provincial Italian towns were very stuffy in those days. When Max knocked on my door later, I wouldn't let him in. I told him I was exhausted.

We hardly talked at all on the drive back to Rome the next day. Max was self-absorbed and withdrawn. I didn't know whether he was brooding over what he had said the evening before or thinking about his appointment at UNICEF the next day. I was grateful for his silence.

I dropped him off at the Inglaterra and went to the Excelsior. It was the first time I had been inside the place since Friday.

The desk clerk started waving at me as soon as I walked into the lobby.

"Signora. Signora."

Signor Stone had arrived. He had come late Friday night. He had been very agitated not to find me. He had become more and more agitated when I didn't return. He had spent most of the weekend sitting in the lobby watching the door. The desk clerk was becoming agitated by this time, too. It was one of the things I liked about the Italians; they were never neutral observers. Whatever small dramas were presented to them, they became instant participants. As the desk clerk went on, describing Jason's behavior, acting it out, I began to feel he was on my side. Jason was only a stock figure in the drama, the husband who had flown in from Madrid to surprise his wife, surprise her, presumably, in bed with another man. I was the heroine. Not only had I put horns on my husband, I had gotten away with it, evaded discovery. The clerk did not say any of this, but it was evident in every gesture, every smile. It was in the smiles of all the other hotel employees who had gathered around the desk to listen and participate.

I found myself smiling back at them. However genuine Jason's concern about my absence, it had by this time been deprived of all seriousness. The situation had become entirely theatrical. If Jason had walked out of the elevator at that moment, he would have been greeted with a sigh of disappointment that he wasn't actually wearing his horns.

The theatricality was catching. "And my husband?" I asked. "Where is my husband now? Is he still waiting for me in our suite?"

No. No. The smiles became reassuring. There was a murmur of laughter. Signor Stone had stalked out of the hotel half an hour ago. He had taken a taxi to the airport. He had returned to Madrid.

I made my exit from the lobby to a rustle of approval.

There was a note from Jason on the mantlepiece in the living room.

Okay, you win. But please cut it out now, will you, darling. I've got to talk to you. I'll call you tonight. PLEASE LET ME TALK TO YOU.

I sat down, holding the sheet of paper. "Okay, you win." That made me wonder. What had I won? I had made a clown of my husband in front of the hotel staff. "If you go to bed with someone else," Jason had told me Christmas morning, "I'm a stand-up comic. I'm a joke." I had certainly proved the truth of that, anyway.

"Okay, you win." What did I want to win? A divorce? I hadn't, even once, thought about that. For almost a week since my call to the Hilton in Madrid — "Hello. I say, who is this?" — I had been acting impetuously, out of anger at Jason.

Mostly out of anger at Jason I had gone to bed with Max. Without thinking of the consequences, I had let myself get involved in his life again. Well, that was over. I had made up my mind to that in Pescara. For a week I had responded to his needs out of sympathy and nostalgia. Nostalgia was, at best, a self-defeating motivation, and I no longer felt sympathy for Max. What he had revealed about himself over dinner in the pension had sickened me. In his frustration and bitterness, his once-generous idealism had become twisted into a craving for power. Power and revenge. My strongest feeling about Max now was a determination to have nothing more to do with him.

What did I feel about Jason? He had behaved like a shit. There was no question about that. But for over five years he had been sweet and funny and kind and loving. For over five years I had felt so close to him, so happy, that I missed him if we were separated for a single day. I had sent him that cold, smug cable saying I would only talk to him in Rome, and he had flown to Rome at once to talk to me. He had sat around the lobby all weekend watching the door for me, while the desk clerks and the bellhops snickered at him. The very least I owed him was to answer the phone whe₁ he called.

He called at eleven.

"Carol? Jesus, is that really you?"

"Hello, Jason."

"It is you."

"Yes, it's me."

"Welcome back. I mean, you were away for a while, weren't you? You weren't in Rome the last time I was there, anyway. And I guess it's none of my business, but I sort of wondered where you were."

"Pescara."

"How was it in Pescara?"

"Cold."

"It was cold in Rome, too. Especially in the lobby of the Excelsior. Cold and lonely. Lonely as hell."

"How is it in Madrid?"

"Why don't you come and see for yourself?"

"Is that a serious suggestion or just one of those shipboard invitations?"

"When can you come?"

"When are you free?"

"All the time."

And suddenly I wanted to go. I wanted to be with him. I didn't want any explanations, any Who-shot-John about Jill Ashton or Max. I wanted to forget the whole bloody business and be back with Jason as though none of it had ever happened. I asked him about the planes to Madrid.

"There's a great one tomorrow."

"What time?"

It left Rome at two o'clock. I said I'd be on it. He said he'd meet me.

After I had packed my own things the next morning, I went around the living room collecting all those Christmas presents and putting them into a box. I called an organization called Caritas, which ran an orphanage in Trastevere and explained what the gifts were and said I would leave them at the desk. The Irish nun, or whoever she was I talked to, sounded pleased.

When I checked out of the hotel, I could feel the desk clerk's curiosity reaching out to me like a plea. It seemed mean to withhold the end of the story from him. I told him I was joining my husband in Madrid. He looked at me with that extraordinary understanding only Italians seem able to extend to strangers.

"Buona fortuna, Signora." He sounded as though he really meant it.

I kept the cab waiting at the American Express office while I got five hundred dollars in American bills. It was half past twelve when I reached the Inglaterra. I had made a deal with myself. If Max was back from his UNICEF appointment, I would not leave without seeing him and saying good-bye. If he wasn't, okay, I could leave with a clear conscience.

"Il signore, Signora?"

There was a long pause while the clerk looked for the key and I fidgeted with my handbag.

No, he wasn't in. I took the key and went up to the room and left the five hundred dollars in an envelope with a note for him. *Jason's stuck in Madrid and I'm going to join him there. Hope things work out well for you at UNICEF. I don't know when I'll be back in Rome, probably not for several months. Carol.*

When I read it through, it sounded not only curt but evasive. I felt I owed it to myself to give him some explanation.

I'm glad we went to Pescara, I added under the signature. *It brought everything out in the open between us again. What we want, the kind of people we are. That's why I don't think we should see each other again. Remembering our past together, I'm sure you understand this.*

I hurried crossing the lobby on the way out, afraid Max would walk in. I was safely through the door. The cab was waiting across the street; I started toward it.

"Carol."

"Hello, Max. I just left a note for you in your room."

"Where are you going? Can't you come up?"

Hastily I explained. Jason. Madrid. My plane left in an hour. I had to get to the airport.

"Don't you care what happened at UNICEF?"

"Of course I do. But I've got to catch that plane. I left you a note."

We stood there on the sidewalk, people eddying around us, while I tried to get away and Max tried to detain me. How long was I going to be in Madrid? That was all in the note. Where would I be staying there? Couldn't I at least wait a *minute?*

"Oh, come on, Max, come out to the airport with me. We can talk in the cab."

So that was what we did. All the way out to Leonardo da Vinci airport. Talked in the cab.

Suddenly, horribly, after I had made it clear I was going back to Jason because that was what I wanted, it was Max, only Max, who was doing the talking. He didn't explode in bursts the way he had in the past. This time his rage was steady, extended, and cumulative. A summing up.

"Ever since I've known you, you've been trying to tear me down . . . Sneering at the Trotskyists. At psychoanalysis. At anything

I believed in. Sneering at me . . . That's all you ever wanted. To destroy me. Get me down, right down . . . Hoping this time, at last, I could never get up again. I'd have to come crawling to you for help . . . So you could gloat and watch me suffer. The way you did in London when I had to keep flying those missions. And you pretended to be trying to comfort me. Taking your clothes off, forcing me into bed with you. Because you knew I'd be impotent. That's what you've always wanted, to make me finally and completely impotent. That night on Charles Street, challenging me to fuck you, knowing I wouldn't be able to . . . You loved it, didn't you, finding me broke and starving in that filthy tenement? You revelled in it. Masturbated with pleasure at my pain. That's why you came looking for me there. You hoped you'd find me half-dead, so you could poke me back to life, the way children poke a bird with a broken wing, watching it flutter, so they can beat it down again. Enjoying its struggles. Enjoying its agony . . ."

I didn't argue with him, didn't try to defend myself. There was no arguing with hatred like that. I could even understand it a little. I had seen Max at his most helpless several times in our lives together. From his point of view, I had witnessed his pain in what he must have felt were degrading and humiliating circumstances. Fear. Sickness. Destitution. He could not forgive me for that. He could only cover his own shame by hating me for it.

How could I argue with that? Halfway to the airport I stopped listening to him. Stopped listening to the words. I could not close out the sound of that quiet, monotonous, raging voice.

I kept glancing at my watch. In five minutes, four minutes, three minutes now, we would be at the terminal and I could step out of the cab and escape from him. And this time my escape would be complete. I would not let his accusations goad me into private indignation or protest. I would close my mind to them. Forget them. I would put this twisted, tormented creature out of my life forever. I would never feel another instant of affection or sympathy or concern for him.

The cab pulled to a stop at last. I got out. A porter took my luggage out of the trunk. I paid the cab driver. Max had followed me to the sidewalk. I did not look at him once. I started into the terminal.

"Carol."

I walked on.

"You've tried to destroy my soul, Carol. I'll make you pay for that if it takes me the rest of my life."

MRS. JASON STONE.

I saw the sign as soon as I came out of customs in Madrid. It was huge and had red hearts for the *o*'s. Jason was carrying it.

We kept grinning at each other and grabbing each other's hands in the limousine all the way to the Hilton. We hardly said a word until we were upstairs in the suite, and all he said then was, "God, oh, God, it's good to see you."

"You, too."

I meant it. And the only thing I said for quite a while after that was, "It won't unzip any farther. I'll have to pull it off over my head."

We had dinner alone together in a restaurant in the old part of the city. The food was terrible, but we were the only Americans there.

"I know you don't want to talk about it," Jason said over the stringy goat meat.

"No, I don't."

"Can I just say one thing?"

"Okay."

"She followed me here. She just showed up. And I kicked her out, and she'll never come back."

"Okay."

After that I never mentioned Jill Ashton again. And Jason never mentioned Pescara.

I made him tell me about the movie.

Everything was going wrong. The Investment had had hysterics at a costume fitting and gone off to Paris. Jack Palance didn't like the script. The horses the Spanish army had agreed to provide refused to pull chariots. Children kept stealing the hand-carved Persian tent pegs and taking them home for firewood. The director kept disappearing. "I wouldn't mind if I thought he was drunk. But I don't think he is drunk. I think he's sick."

The picture was scheduled to start shooting at the beginning of

February, in three weeks' time. The studio refused to set it back until spring, when the weather would be better. "They want to book it into the Music Hall for Christmas. They think it's the kind of gup that'll go big at Christmas."

Gup. Crap. Garbage. Sometimes, Shit. Every time Jason talked about the movie, he used one of those words. But his joking contempt for what he was doing had no effect on his day-to-day actions. He was always there, good tempered, patient, helpful, the one person everyone else could rely on to listen, to get things done. Shit or not, he was going to bring it in on schedule and make sure every dollar of the budget appeared on the screen.

There were no more of those crowd evenings, no more clamoring our way from bar to bar in a confusion of limousines the way we had in Rome. Jason suggested we move out of the Hilton. I found a gloomy but well-heated apartment two minutes' walk from his office. He gave the phone number to only a few key people — the director, Mario, the production man — who wouldn't waste his time.

He hired me as a gofer. I drove around in a rented VW, seeing caterers about box lunches, truckers about delivering them to the location, a construction company about building latrines. I spent one whole day buying safety pins for the wardrobe department. There was a shortage of them in Madrid and I had to go from store to store, buying a dozen here, a dozen there. Jason and I would meet for dinner around ten o'clock and talk about the next day's problems and be asleep by midnight.

The Investment came back from Paris. I became her gofer, too. She was one of those women with a passion for the insignificant. She could only use a certain kind of soap, drink a certain kind of gin, blow her nose and dry her eyes with a certain kind of tissue. I did my best to provide her with them.

We became friends. In a way. She would stop weeping when we were alone together and plaintively question me. Mostly about sex. She had been married to three of the most celebrated studs in the Western world, and some years ago a photograph of her in a white nylon nightdress had been the second most popular pinup for thirteen million GIs. In spite of this lavish self-exposure to desire, she couldn't understand what it was all about. In some stubborn, impregnable way, she was as innocent as a nun. "What do they want?" she would plead with me. "What do they want me *for?* Why in the world would anyone want to do *that* to me?" I don't think she had any lesbian tendencies. She was a natural celibate. To her men were like Oscar Wilde's horse, dangerous at both ends and uncomfortable in the middle.

I saw Mario almost every day. Our shared secrets hadn't made us shy with each other. I ran errands for him, too, seeing equipment through customs, finding accommodations for his crew. He was evidently still in touch with his "friends" in Rome. He told me one afternoon that Max had turned down the job at UNICEF and returned to the United States.

Good.

Shooting started on schedule in February. The first shot was a raid on the Arabian camp. The director got a good third take and printed it.

In the afternoon, the Investment's double, a French stuntman who looked remarkably like her, was snatched off his/her horse by Jack Palance's double. The Investment herself was tearless and cooperative in the close shots. The weather was kind to us, lighting the scene with pale sunlight.

Everything went well for three days. "Two minutes and fifteen seconds," Jason told me when we met for dinner the first night. "Two minutes forty," the next. And on the third, incredulous and excited, "Three minutes ten, Carol. We got three minutes ten."

On the fourth day of shooting, in the early afternoon, the director was walking over to say something to Mario when he stumbled, went down on one knee, grabbed at his left arm and collapsed altogether. The first-aid men got him into a tent. When Jason came out a few minutes later, he called off shooting for the rest of the day. After another half-hour, the director, his skin looking like wet paper, was helped to a limousine and Jason rode back to his hotel with him.

"It's his heart," Jason told me at dinner that night. "Angina pectoris. He's been having attacks for months. He says he's okay. He just sniffs some amyl nitrite and he's okay."

I didn't say anything. Jason spent hours every day answering questions, and when he was alone with me he liked to take his time, thinking things over out loud without being prompted.

"The hell it's okay. If we replace him now, we'll lose two or three days before another director can take over. If he croaks halfway through the picture, we'll have to find some hack who'll accept his footage. Any top director's going to insist on retakes. We'd be a million over before we were through."

I knew Jason wasn't being deliberately callous. He liked the director as a man and respected him as a craftsman. But Jason was playing with other people's money; he was responsible for it.

When he was silent for a minute, I knew he wanted to be prompted now. I asked him if he had talked to the director about replacing him.

"Jesus. He begged me. He pleaded with me. He said his whole life depended on finishing this picture."

His whole life.

The irony of it shocked me. If he went on with the picture, it would probably kill him. But he didn't see his life that way, as an alternative to death. He saw it only in terms of his reputation. A major credit. Death meant nothing to him. It was a vague unreality compared to the threat of being taken off the picture. Prevented from completing a piece of stereotyped rubbish. Gup. Crap. Garbage. Shit.

What *was* it about this movie business that could so possess a man's mind, distort his values so entirely? I never did understand it. The closest I could get to an answer was that there was a unique, rarefied snobbery about making movies. You were in the club. The thought of being excluded from it, to this director at least, was literally worse than dying.

Whatever it was, Jason evidently sympathized with it. He didn't replace him. The director was there on location every day. Jason made him rest and take it easy. The director consulted with Jason and Mario; they took over the actual process of completing the shooting in Spain.

They completed it, a day ahead of schedule, on March 14, 1957. I remember the date so clearly because I had a doctor's appointment that morning. He gave me the results of the tests he had made the week before. They confirmed what I already secretly knew and hoped for.

I was pregnant.

Nineteen

I waited until we were settled back in Rome before telling Jason.

We were out of the Excelsior, in a furnished house on the Via Giulia. The picture was going well: they had started shooting the interiors at Cinecita; the studio was pleased with the footage from Spain. I felt that, however shattering my news was going to be to Jason, he was in as secure a position as he could be to handle it.

I had made up my mind to accept his reaction whatever it was. If he wanted to know who the father was, I would tell him. If he wanted to divorce me, I wouldn't make any difficulties.

After that I would be on my own. I would get a job and bring up the child by myself. I would do everything I possibly could to make sure Max never knew of its existence.

I didn't want Jason to leave me. Dear Jason. His behavior in Madrid, his unfailing, kindly competence, had given me a new respect for him. I felt closer to him than I had at any time since our marriage.

What made it easier for me to be fatalistic about the future was my own feeling about my pregnancy. I was in a constant state of passive euphoria. After longing for a child for close to ten years, I had done it at last. Or almost done it. All I had to do now was wait, blissful and inert, for another eight months and a small human being would come into its own independent existence as a part of my life. It was a miracle, and I accepted it without question.

Jason could accept it or not as he chose.

We had eaten at home. We were in the living room. Jason was lying on the couch, I was sitting on a hassock. He was talking about the Investment. "She can't act. I don't think she knows what acting is. But all those years of experience, swinging her ass, have given her a kind of automatic professionalism. She just does it, and sometimes it works." He took out a cigar.

"I'm going to have a baby, Jason."

He was holding the flame of his lighter in front of his chin. It gave his face an artificial, gilded look. He closed his eyes. The flame went out. He took the unlighted cigar out of his mouth and rolled it between his fingers as though making sure it was a solid object. He opened his eyes and put it down in the ashtray.

He laughed.

"All those stupid tests. I knew they were crazy. I knew we'd do it if we kept trying long enough."

I had been expecting almost anything. But not that. I wanted time to think. He didn't give it to me. He was off the couch, dancing across the room. He was leaning over me. He took my face in his hands and kissed me.

"Carol, Carol, oh God, I love you. Wait till I tell my mother. It'll be all over Brooklyn in two hours."

It's so mysterious, the whole question of human will. You go along from day to day believing you determine this and that. But in times of crisis you so often determine nothing. I knew I was confronted with the most important decision of my life and it was like that time on the monkey island during the U-boat attack. I felt absolutely helpless. All I could do was watch and see what happened.

I watched Jason skip over to the phone to call his mother. I thought in a vague, protesting way that it would be three o'clock in the morning in Brooklyn. At the same time, I was thinking how excited and pleased she would be. And then suddenly I was remembering Christmas morning and my vain wish then. "If only I didn't know."

"Hello. Hello. Dad? This is Jason, Dad. Let me talk to Mom. Well, wake her up. No, nothing's wrong. Everything's great. Out of this world. Colossal. Wonderful. Hello? Mom? Guess what . . ."

He was laughing, shouting, possessed with happiness as he told his mother he was going to be a father. She was going to be a grandmother. Tanta Vera was going to be a great aunt. Uncle Bernard . . .

He wanted me to talk to his parents. Well, yes, I told them, and I thought probably in October, and I could feel the gratitude and affection pouring out to me from all those thousands of miles away, and I was in tears when I gave the phone back to Jason.

Please, I didn't lie, I kept telling myself while I listened to Jason bubbling on. Please, isn't it better this way? He'll adore the child and the child will love him, and I did promise to accept whatever he said, and please, he's so happy and proud.

It seemed to be okay with my familiar spirit. In her subliminal way, she seemed to be encouraging me. By the time Jason hung up I knew I wasn't going to tell him. Ever. Not unless he asked me outright, "Is it my child, Carol?" If he did, I would tell him the truth.

I don't think it ever crossed his mind. He was already making plans. I must go back to the United States, July, or August at the latest, so I could be in touch with a really good pediatrician there and the child could be born in a New York hospital and his mother could see it. "Having a grandchild's going to give her a whole new life."

Later I did think it all over more calmly, although my passive euphoria probably affected my judgment then, too. I should have known Jason would welcome the child as his own. He had never accepted the idea of his sterility. He had never asked me if I had been alone in Pescara. After my admission to him on Christmas morning, that I hadn't wanted any other man since our marriage, he had never doubted that I would continue to be faithful to him. It was part of his naturally cheerful nature: once he had come to believe anything, that was it; he wasn't going to wake up in the middle of the night and start brooding about it. He was going to be a father. Wasn't that something?

My own behavior seemed to me more difficult to understand. I had spent five nights with Max without once thinking of taking any precautions. It was true I had thrown my diaphragm away over five years ago. I had been sleeping with Jason night after night without conceiving. I had given up the idea of ever having a child. There still seemed to me something groping and deliberate about my carelessness. What disturbed me most was that it had been Max. That tormented, malignant creature, Max, was the man who had given me a child at last. That scared me a little. If I had been blindly, unconsciously trying to get pregnant, why hadn't I picked some healthy young stranger?

For a day or two I worried about it, then that concern, too, became submerged in my self-centered bliss. Thank God Max had left Rome. Mario told me he had heard he was in Santa Monica, California, living in some commune there. I hoped, I made up my mind to believe, I would never, never see him again.

Jason finished shooting in May. He had to stay on at Cinecita dubbing and scoring and editing. It was uncomfortably hot in Rome by the beginning of June. He insisted on my going back to London, to the house in Chelsea. I was in such a bovine, trancelike state by then, I didn't care where I was. Sylvia met me at Heathrow and helped me settle in. She was full of sympathy and cautions.

"It's hell being pregnant. It just deforms you. Specially at your age. I know. I was almost thirty when I had Timmy. And if you're not very careful and don't take lots of exercise, it'll deform you forever. You'll look middle-aged for the rest of your life."

She took me for long walks by the river. "There's something calming about flowing water. It'll help you forget all that ghastly agony ahead of you."

I didn't need calming. A lovely stillness seemed to surround me. I used the key to Cadogan Gardens and sat watching the children play. I no longer had any impulse to touch them. Soon I would be bringing my own child there.

Jason flew in for weekends whenever he could. He was endearingly solicitous, helping me up steps and out of chairs. "Sure you're not tired?" "Is there anything special you'd like for dinner?"

I wasn't tired. I ate anything anyone put in front of me. My back ached sometimes and I had an occasional craving for clams. Most of the time I was lost in a serene conspiracy between myself and my body, that life growing in it.

I went down to Brighton to visit my mother.

"Carol. Don't tell me you're pregnant," she greeted me. Later she told me it was a horrible world to bring a child into. "But I suppose it's not *quite* so bad if you're American. Churchill thought a lot of that man Eisenhower."

We flew to New York in September. We had given up the East Side apartment. For a while I stayed with Jason at the Meurice near Central Park. The suites were large and unpretentious, but I had never liked living in hotels, being supervised by uniformed strangers. When Jason had to go back to Rome, I moved in with his parents.

Brooklyn was strange to me, more foreign than Rome. I sensed an intensity of purpose in the people on the streets, an impetuousness, that penetrated even my vegetable calm. When a man was doing nothing, just sitting on a park bench, he seemed to be doing it so actively. With all his might. It made me understand Jason's energy and ambition more clearly. He had spent the first twenty years of his life in this restive world.

His parents were wonderful hosts. I was still something of an enigma to them. The Englisher their son had married. They accepted anything I did — the way I ate, my habit of reading in bed until midnight — as part of that enigma.

Tanta Vera died while I was there. I went to the synagogue with the family. Jason had flown over for the funeral. I was moved by the service, the chanting, the rabbi's straightforward eulogy of the dead woman. When we left the synagogue, Jason's father put his arm around my shoulders; he had never done that before. I felt I had become less of a stranger to him. I was "family" now.

"You'd better make a list of names beginning with *v,*" Jason told me on the way back to the house. "Just in case."

"In case what?"

"In case it's a girl. We'll have to call her after Tanta Vera. Use her initial. It's a custom."

"What happens if it's a boy?"

"Any name beginning with N. After my grandfather."

We walked on along the strangely archaic, stridently contemporary, Brooklyn street.

"Will you mind if it's a girl?"

"Of course not. I love girls. Besides, she might look like you. Either way, it's great with me. Whichever it is, boy or girl, it couldn't be better."

It was a girl. She was born in Doctor's Hospital on October 3. I had been advised that Doctor's Hospital was a great place to be so long as you weren't sick. I wasn't sick. Sylvia's warning about the ghastly agony ahead of me was a load of rubbish. I was given a shot on the way to the delivery room and when I woke up it was all over.

The nurses treated me like a visiting celebrity. They even let me see the baby for an hour or two every day. The rest of the time they were busy serving martinis to the relatives and friends and movie people who were allowed to crowd into my room anytime they felt like it. Except when I was actually holding the child, I felt I was there under false pretenses. I hadn't done anything to deserve being a mother. I decided that if I ever had to do it again, I would have the baby in private, in a field, and *bite* off the umbilical cord.

The pediatrician I had been going to had talked me out of breast-feeding the child. "It's not advisable at your age." What he really meant, I think, was that it was no longer fashionable and it might spoil the provocative pinkness of my nipples.

I regretted giving in to him almost at once. The third time I was allowed to hold the baby, she grabbed at my breast with a blind, pathetic instinct, trying to get her mouth to it. By that time it was too late. She was already on the bottle and I had been given medication so that I couldn't feed her anyway. It made me feel I had let her down. She was small and red and wrinkled, with a fuzz of black hair and deep, serious blue eyes. I thought she was beautiful.

So did Jason. He was luckier than me. He was allowed to see her more often. He spent hours staring at her through a sheet of plate glass as she lay with a dozen other babies in a sterile, temperature-controlled showcase.

"I feel so sorry for those other poor bastards," he told me, "the other fathers, looking through that window. She's so beautiful they can't take their eyes off her."

We decided to call her Vanessa.

"Vanessa Stone." Jason kept practicing the name. "Vanessa Stone. Don't you think she ought to have another name, too?"

"You choose one."

"How about Clavering? Vanessa Clavering Stone."

"After who?"

"Your father. Your family. You. It's funny, I still think of you, in a way, as Carol Clavering."

"Do you, darling?" That was rather flattering. After six years of marriage, I still held for him some of that exotic, fantasy quality that had first attracted him to me. I wasn't sure I wanted him to feel that way about Vanessa. I didn't want her to be Vanessa Clavering to him. And then I thought of my father with a sudden, unexpected tenderness. I remembered sitting in his lap on a balcony somewhere in the south of France. He was doing a crossword puzzle, probably the one in the London *Times*. He'd write in a word and then prod my cheek, gently, playfully, with the eraser end of the pencil. He *had* loved me sometimes, in his own absent-minded, English way.

"Okay. Vanessa Clavering Stone." I hoped it wouldn't upset my mother.

Jason's parents came to the hospital every day. The nurse allowed them to hold Vanessa. Jason's father handled her with an affectionate confidence that reminded me of an Indian chief celebrating an ancient birth ritual. Jason's mother seemed a little in awe of Vanessa, holding her with timid respect as though she were a priceless and unexpected gift. Jason held her firmly and possessively, a prize winner who was never going to let anyone take her away from him.

He was finished with his work in Rome. The picture was out of his hands for the final cut; it had been booked into the Music Hall for the first week of December. We were back at the Meurice. A hotel, however comfortable, wasn't an ideal place to look after a baby. We weren't supposed to cook in the suite — I had to use a smuggled-in hot plate to warm her bottles — and the phone kept ringing and waking her up. It was only for a few weeks, though. We would be going back to London after the picture opened.

I took Vanessa to the park in her baby carriage and consorted with the other mothers there. Their talk of formulas and three o'clock feedings and diaper rashes fascinated me; I couldn't get enough of it. I was like someone who has discovered an unexpected talent in herself. It seemed to promise enough interest and achievement to fill the rest of my life.

My life was full, too full, in other ways as well. Jason was worried about the picture. The studio's only interest in it was as a vehicle for the Investment, her future box-office drawing power. Jason was afraid they would butcher the movie in the final cut, emphasizing her footage at the expense of the story. To protect himself, he spent a lot of time cultivating the studio pricks, entertaining them, trying to win them over to his point of view.

I didn't believe it would influence their hidebound judgment if he set them all up to a weekend in Shangri-la. They clung stubbornly to the values that had worked ten years ago in the days of the big studios, the system. The Investment was a great star; the public would pay to see her; fuck the story.

Still, we had to try. We spent long evenings at Sardi's, at "21," at El Morocco, with faceless executives and their wives or girlfriends. When we went out Jason's mother came over and spent the night; we wouldn't trust Vanessa to anyone else. I acquired a reputation for having a weak bladder by sneaking off to the powder room every hour or so to call the Meurice and have long chats with Jason's mother.

The picture opened at the beginning of December. It played four weeks at the Music Hall to what *Variety* called so-so business and then it died. There just weren't enough people interested in seeing what effect being an Indian rajah's wife had had on the Investment's once-famous ass. The studio would eventually earn a small, carefully concealed profit out of foreign sales and television. The executive accountants were unhappy with the immediate gross.

They blamed Jason. It was no use telling them the picture would have earned more money if they had listened to him and cut it his way. Telling studios the truth was never any use. It was his picture, wasn't it? What was all this shit about what they had done to it? It was Jason's picture and it had laid an egg.

We went back to England at the end of January on a small French Line ship. For ten wonderful, storm-tossed days, Jason and Vanessa and I had each other to ourselves. Neither Jason nor I was seasick and Vanessa seemed to feel that every pitch and roll of the ship had been arranged especially for her benefit, to rock her to sleep.

Jason and I talked about the immediate future. His career wasn't in serious trouble; a lot of people in the industry knew it was only Jason and Mario who had saved the picture from total disaster. He didn't have what Stanley Kubrik called fuck-you money, but he wasn't pressed for cash. One of the studios wanted him to take over as producer on *William Tell,* another epic that was floundering at Cinecita. I didn't want him to do it. I thought he ought to make a picture of his own, something with meaning and content in it, something that really interested him.

Jason smiled. "Messages are for Western Union."

"I didn't say anything about messages. *The Wages of Fear* didn't have any message. And *Rebel without a Cause,* what was the message in that?"

"James Dean."

"Why don't you find some story you really like?" Something else had been on my mind for a long time, too. "And this time direct it yourself. You're too honest to be a producer."

"I'm not that honest."

A few days after we had settled back into the house in Chelsea and Jason had reopened his basement office, he gave me a novel he had been reading.

"It's got two strikes against it. Paramount had an option and dropped it. And the writer's supposed to be an absolute shit."

"He isn't. Not really. Not an *absolute* shit."

"You know him?"

"I used to. He was around the Village. And then he worked for us at Studio One." The book was Chris Deniken's first novel, *The Time of the Fire.*

Jason asked me about Chris. I admitted I had had an affair with him. I didn't go into a lot of explanations about Iris; I said we had broken up years ago, before I started seeing Jason again.

"Do you think I ought to have the bastard come over and talk? What do you think about him as the writer on the picture?"

"I think he's talented. He's conscientious. He works hard. But if it ever comes to a real crunch, he won't be there." I told Jason about the rehearsal at Studio One. "At a certain point, Chris will just cut off. You'll have to do it without him. And he'll hold that against you. He'll blame you for it."

"What have I got to lose? An airplane ticket."

Chris came to London in March. He was thinner, and, in his forties now, he had grown a little mannered, almost waspish. He stayed at a small hotel off Eaton Square a few blocks from the house. He and Jason spent hours together in the basement, laying out the story scene by scene.

"You're right," Jason admitted one night. "He's not an *absolute* shit. But he's not the guy I'd choose to be shipwrecked on a desert island with, either. There's something creepy about him."

I didn't see him often. Sometimes Jason would bring him up for a drink at five. We would talk about the book, the movie, other movies. Occasionally I would find Chris watching me from behind his dark glasses. Once when Jason was getting something from downstairs, he smiled at me in his waspish way.

"Why are you avoiding me, Carol?"

I wasn't deliberately avoiding him. Chris was busy with a girl in Fulham. He had found what he called a poor man's San Remo there, a pub named Finch's. I was busy with Vanessa.

We had an Austrian *au pair* girl, Heidi. She was sweet and responsible, in a Germanic way. Once when I was driving her and Vanessa to Regent's Park, I started to turn into a wrong-way street. "No. No," Heidi yelled at me. "It's *verboten. Verboten.*" She was helpful about the house. I didn't want any help with Vanessa; I spent every minute I could with her myself. She slept through the night now. She was beginning to crawl in her playpen. She was grave and inquisitive and beautiful.

Jason made a deal with Chris to write the screenplay. It was understood Jason would direct the picture. Chris decided to go to Spain to work on the script. Jason had offered to drive him to the airport and then found he had a meeting with some people in Wardour Street. I picked up Chris at his hotel.

"At last," he said as I headed for the Cromwell Road. "At last we can talk."

I didn't think there was much for us to talk about.

"Don't you want to know about Iris?"

Iris? Why? Why should I want to know about Iris? I hadn't thought of her for years.

He insisted on telling me anyway. She and Chris had lived together in California for a while. "Then I began to realize there was something weird about her. I always knew she was a kook, but this was something else. She kept disappearing. I thought maybe she was screwing another guy. But it wasn't that. You know what it was?"

"No." I could guess.

"She was on junk. Mainlining horse. She was hooked. All the way."

I said I was sorry.

"After that we split. I lost touch with her. Then when I was out on the coast last fall, I ran into her in Santa Monica. She was off the junk. Living in some kind of place out there where this guy has a new way of treating junkies. They all live together and have sessions about it. Anyway, it worked for Iris. She looked great."

I said I was glad to hear it.

"She kept asking me about you."

"Me? Why?"

"This guy who runs the place she lives in. They were talking about the Village and when he found out Iris knew you, he flipped. He never stopped asking her questions about you. He wanted to know everything she could tell him."

I turned off the M4 toward Heathrow.

"What was his name?"

I thought I could guess that, too.

"I don't know. Father something. She called him Father something. Father Max? Does that mean anything to you?"

"No."

I dropped him off at the European-flight building. The usual aimless construction work was going on at the airport, and I was stopped for a minute behind a bulldozer. Chris came back to the car and leaned in the window.

"You never should have left me, Carol. You should have married me."

A policeman waved at me and I pulled out around the bulldozer.

All the way back to Chelsea I could feel them, thin but tangible and clinging, like the skeins of a web, not holding me yet, no more than a warning. Those skeins had been spun so arbitrarily, and yet so inevitably, by such diverse people. Chris, who did not seem able to remember, or forget, that it was he who left me, and still resented me for it. Iris, coming to her door in the nude, grabbing at Chris, and then at drugs, and now at Max.

And Max, who hated me, prying, clutching at every chance source of information about me.

There had been several stories in the syndicated columns about Jason Stone, his double-header, as Earl Wilson put it, a picture at the Music Hall and a baby in Doctor's Hospital.

I would have to face the fact that Max knew all about Vanessa's birth, her name, the exact date, where she was now, everything.

Twenty

It took just over three years to put *The Time of the Fire* together.

The financing, the casting, everything was more complicated this time because it couldn't, like Jason's first independent production, be a British picture. It had to be shot on location in the Middle West with American actors. That meant most of the money had to come from one or another of what were now being called the Majors: Universal, Columbia, Metro; the Undertakers, as Jason referred to them.

As soon as he had what he considered a good draft script from Chris, he was off to the coast to talk to them.

He was gone seven weeks the first time. It was summer in London. Vanessa was learning to walk. Heidi and I took her to the gardens, to the zoo. One afternoon we went to the river at Richmond, where we rented a skiff. Vanessa sat in the stern with Heidi while I rowed. She was not a smiling child. She stared at everything with her dark blue eyes as though trying to see through it. She was fearless and adventurous. She wanted to put her hand in the river, and then her foot. If I hadn't stopped her — "No, darling, no more. No" — she would have dipped herself in up to the neck. I said no as little as I could. She would listen to me gravely and patiently when I did. She hardly ever cried.

When Jason came back from the coast, he was tired and edgy. He had always been a deep sleeper; now I would wake sometimes in the night alone and I would find him in Vanessa's room, sitting by her cot watching her sleep. "I woke up," he would say. "I just wanted to see if she was all right."

He spent as much time as he could with Vanessa. He liked doing things for her, giving her a bath, putting her to bed. He would sit her on his lap and tell her stories. They didn't end with "they all lived happily ever after," they ended with Jason hugging her, telling her he loved her.

Things had gone neither well nor badly on the coast. The trouble with dealing with the Undertakers, he explained, was that they almost never said no. They said show us and then we'll say maybe. The script was okay. It was a downbeat subject, but *Bad Day at Black Rock* had been downbeat, too. Of course *Black Rock* had had Spencer Tracy. There was no part for Tracy in *The Time of the Fire;* but if Jason could come up with a hot young actor to play the sheriff, the Undertakers would think about it.

So Jason was hunting for a hot young actor. I remember that time as a series of phases. There was a Newman phase, a Widmark phase. There was a Steve McQueen phase.

Steve McQueen's agent, William Morris, finally persuaded him to read Jason's script. There was a long wait for a phone call from the Beverly Hills office.

It finally came. McQueen was interested. McQueen had some questions about the script. McQueen was in Paris.

"Come with me, Carol. Please. His wife'll be there. She never lets him out of her sight. If I have to talk to the two of them, we'll get into one of those three-way situations where they're playing off some private grudge against each other. You can take her shopping. You can take her to the powder room. And anyway, I'm sick of going places alone. Please come with me."

I didn't want to leave Vanessa.

"It's only for a couple of days. You can call every day. Three times a day. You trust Heidi, don't you?"

I did trust Heidi, but I had never been separated from Vanessa for more than a few hours in her whole life. I wasn't sure how safe she would feel without me. I had images of her searching for me from room to room, grave and puzzled.

"Two days. Please."

We flew to Paris and went to the Raphaël. McQueen was at the George Cinq, almost next door. Jason had decided not to stay at the same hotel. "I don't want him to feel I'm crowding him."

McQueen was cordial on the phone. He even remembered who Jason was. Sure, they ought to get together. Maybe for dinner.

Dinner would be fine, Jason agreed. Tonight? What time?

"Yeah, maybe tonight."

McQueen would call him. We sat around the room waiting. Other people called, actors, writers, directors. They had heard Jason was in Paris; they had heard he was producing a new movie. Was there anything in it for them? Jason was patient and courteous. "It's not the people who call who bug me," he said, "it's the people who don't call."

McQueen did call. Usually around seven o'clock in the evening. He was out at Fontainebleau, he had to pick up a car in Neuilly, once he was in Le Mans. It took six days to pin him down for dinner. We met at the Brasserie Lipp. McQueen was alone.

He was smaller than I expected, with a curiously scrunched-up face, which he seemed to be constantly trying to make look even more scrunched-up by frowning, clenching his lips together. He drank only beer and managed to give the impression that he would sooner be drinking it out of the bottle. He had remarkably blue eyes and no apparent vanity. He was casually dressed but not casually enough to draw attention to himself.

Jason talked about the script. He didn't crowd him. He said he thought they could make a good movie; they could have fun making it; there might be some good hunting in Missouri in the spring. I don't think Jason had ever fired a gun in his life, not even in the army, but he had evidently heard McQueen was an outdoor type.

McQueen listened and nodded. He was a man who seemed always to be thinking about something else. He had nice manners in an old-fashioned way that made me feel he had been very strictly brought up. He asked me if I minded if he smoked.

Jason said he had heard McQueen had some questions about the script. "I'd like to hear them. Please go ahead."

McQueen had only two questions.

"What kind of car does this sheriff drive?"

Jason told him he could drive any kind of car he liked.

"Okay." McQueen came out with the second question. "How about putting in a sequence where he rides a motor bike?"

That was fine with Jason.

We parted on the Boulevard St.-Germain; McQueen had to pick up his wife somewhere. He was very "hot" in Paris at that time. People kept stopping and gaping at him — was that really *him?* McQueen stood there frowning and pressing his lips together. He seemed completely unaware of the people looking at him. He was evidently still thinking about something else.

We got a flight back to London that night. Vanessa was asleep, lying on her back with her arms straight beside her. I asked Heidi if she seemed to have missed us. Heidi thought it over in her usual serious way. No, no, she hadn't seen any signs.

When I woke at seven o'clock the next morning, Vanessa was standing beside my bed. She didn't come closer when she saw I was awake, she just stared at me. As I hurried out of bed to take her in my arms, she ran away. I cornered her at the top of the stairs. For a minute she was as stiff as a china doll, and then she started jumping up and down, stamping her feet with excitement. It was two or three days before she stopped following me every time I went out of the room.

I promised myself never to go away and leave her again.

William Morris called from the coast at eleven o'clock one night. McQueen was still interested, but he had one more question. Who was going to direct the picture?

"I am." Jason sounded definite about it.

Well, that was going to be a slight problem.

"Why?"

McQueen wanted Nicholas Ray to direct it.

"Why?"

Well, Nick Ray hadn't exactly discovered James Dean, but he had directed *Rebel without a Cause,* the picture that had made Dean a great star, and McQueen felt, or more likely the agent felt . . . and so on.

I watched Jason listening to all this. His face looked tired, his eyes a little bored. He had wanted to direct a movie since the Signal

Corps. His experience with the Persian epic had convinced him he could. *The Time of the Fire* was his very own; he had been planning every shot from the time of his first discussions with Chris.

He waited until the agent had stopped talking.

"Okay, I'll talk to Nick Ray."

He still looked a little bored; he hadn't hesitated for a second. So we were into the Nick Ray phase.

Calling Ray's agent, sending the script to him, persuading the agent to persuade Ray to read it. It was spring before the agent reported that Ray was interested. Ray would be calling Jason.

He called ten days later from the south of France. Yes, he was all set to do the picture. He would shoot it in Missouri. He wanted to start in September. Jason was holding onto the receiver so tightly he looked as though he were trying to crush it.

"There's only one slight problem."

"What?"

"I don't want Steve McQueen."

"Return to Go," Jason said after he had hung up. "Do not collect any money. Return directly to Go."

It went on like that, or more or less like that, for another two years. Several times everything seemed set, the director, the actor, the actress, the financing and distribution deal. Each time one of the key elements fell through at the final moment. The whole strategy collapsed. Jason had to start all over again at the beginning.

Except for these disappointments, and my concern for Jason, they were happy years for me. Vanessa was growing into a ravishing little girl. Even the English, who have always preferred dogs and budgerigars to children, would pause and look at her on the street. Once on a trip to Paris some American tourists in the Champ-de-Mars asked me if they could take her picture. "With the Eiffel Tower. Please. She looks so darling with the Eiffel Tower."

She was quiet and composed and private. She adored Jason. She had a way of coming into a room and claiming him. She wouldn't say anything; she would simply, confidently, take his hand and lead him away. Her own.

Heidi returned to Vienna to study hotel management. After a succession of other *au pairs,* none of whom I felt I could trust, I decided I would sooner manage alone with an occasional cleaning woman. If we had to go out in the evening, I would get one of the nurses from Brompton Hospital to babysit. Sometimes Sylvia's son, Timmy, who was fifteen now and had developed a surprisingly maternal devotion to Vanessa, would come and stay the night.

Sylvia still refused to send him to boarding school. He was at Saint Paul's. "Daddy wanted me to go to *Eton*," he told me once. He made it sound like Alcatraz. He didn't talk about Nigel much. When he did, he made *him* sound like Neville Chamberlain. "Daddy hasn't a clue what's going on anywhere," he confided to me. I thought Timmy was right. Nigel still referred to three-quarters of the population of England as the lower classes.

Jason's parents came for a visit. His mother still seemed in awe of Vanessa, a gift from God. His father was confident and friendly with her. He was obviously excited to be back in Europe. He went to the Tower, to Hampton Court, to Greenwich, to all the places he had read about as a young man. He visited Karl Marx's grave in Hampstead. Jason's mother sat in the gardens with me and never took her eyes off Vanessa.

I had heard nothing from Max.

For a few months after that talk with Chris, I sorted through the mail each day with a quick Please and then Thank you when there was no envelope with Max's handwriting on it. Gradually the apprehension faded. I stopped waking in the mornings to a sense of unease that defined itself a moment later as Them. I lost the creepy feel of that net binding me to Chris and Iris and Max. By the time Vanessa was a year old, I had stopped worrying, stopped thinking about it.

I worried about Jason; not only because of the repeated frustrations with the picture. He was good-humored, often funny, about them. Our Dog, he called the movie. I was worried about his health. He still wasn't sleeping well; he was often tired. He kept a bottle of heart-shaped pills in the medicine cabinet. In the San Remo days I had occasionally taken Dexedrine myself — it was an easier lift than coffee — but I had never taken more than half a tablet at a time, and even that sometimes made me jittery. Jason was taking two or three tablets a day. There was no point in nagging him about it. "That's what keeps me so cheerful," he said.

He was working on other projects besides Our Dog. He co-produced a half-hour series for television, grinding out thirteen episodes, back-to-back, at Elstree. He set up and supervised the European end of an international two-hour variety show for CBS. But he never gave up on *The Time of the Fire*. He flew out to the coast every two or three months. "I'm going to get Our Dog on the screen if it takes me the rest of my life," he said.

It took him just over three years.

In the end, time was on our side. The bland, cautious Eisenhower years were over at last. He had been the last prewar president. After fifteen years we were finally moving into our own Roaring Twenties, or a prickly version of them. Ideas, attitudes, were changing fast. Even the motion picture industry was struggling out of its hidebound torpor. A few executives were beginning to understand that a whole new group of moviegoers, under thirty, would pay good money to stand in line on Third Avenue, in Westwood, even in Indianapolis, if you gave them something to talk about.

In the summer of 1961, everything fell into place for Jason. The president of an independent theater chain came up with the money. Jason stopped chasing Widmark, Newman, Heston, Peck. He signed up a young actor who had appeared in one previous movie. The rest of the cast was equally nameless.

Chris had lost all interest; he had cut off as I had known he would. A twenty-two-year-old writer, who had had a play produced on Bleecker Street, wrote the final script, putting back all the scenes the Undertakers had thrown out as too downbeat.

Jason started shooting in Missouri at the beginning of August, with a tight budget and a seven-week schedule. He was directing the picture himself, and after all those years he knew exactly what he wanted in every frame of film.

Fulton was the central location of the picture, but he would be moving to Jefferson City, to Joplin, to the banks of the Mississippi, for individual scenes. He suggested Vanessa and I might find a place in Fulton, but I didn't want him driving back to be with us after a twelve-hour day. We decided it was more sensible for us to stay in London; we would all be together on the coast later while he was scoring and editing.

He called me every night, usually around 2:00 A.M. London time. I would sit up in bed and he would ask first about Vanessa. I would tell him what she had done and said that day. "Tell her I love her," he always said.

And then one night, "Tell her I love her no matter what."

"What do you mean, no matter what?" I was startled.

"I mean, just tell her I love her."

"She knows you love her, Jason, and she loves you, too. She talks about you all the time. She's so proud of you. Daddy's in America. Daddy's making a film. She misses you. She can't wait for you to come back so she can go to Los Angeles with you."

After I had finished telling him about Vanessa's day, he would tell me about Our Dog. It was going well; he was a day ahead of schedule; the young actor who was playing the sheriff was really something. "He's going to be bigger than Brando. He's coming across in the dailies like a thousand-watt bulb."

After that he would ask about me. "Are you wearing a night-dress?"

"Yes."

"Which one?"

I would tell him the white one, or the one with the ribbons.

"Jesus. You know something, I can feel you. I can feel that warm soft part just above your hip where I used to hold you before I went to sleep."

He finished Our Dog on schedule, spent a day on retakes, and flew to Los Angeles for meetings with the money man. He was coming back to London on Saturday, October 2, the day before Vanessa's fourth birthday. His plane was due in at eight o'clock in the morning. I took Vanessa to the airport to meet him.

It was one of those cold, damp London mornings. Vanessa was wearing red woolen tights and a light blue coat. Whenever I remember that day I see her in those bright clothes, happily expectant and looking like a Christmas present, brand-new, the way Jason had looked the night I first met him.

According to the board, the BOAC flight from Los Angeles was on time. We stood at the exit to the customs hall.

In ones and twos, in small groups, the arriving passengers emerged, the Americans often defiantly, as though expecting the worst, the English and Europeans with an air of discretion, like messengers bearing their private lives in their briefcases. A tall, good-looking, immaculately posh Englishman was met by a pretty woman in a fur coat and two boys of twelve or thirteen. He kissed the woman on the cheek, stared at her briefly, then pushed a strand of hair away from her face. He shook hands with both boys without looking at either of them. Oh, well, maybe the woman was his sister; maybe the boys weren't his sons.

"Where's Daddy?"

"Darling, you know how Daddy is. He always likes to get to an airport hours ahead of time. He's always the first one to check in his bags, so they're the last off the plane. Daddy's probably still waiting for them so he can go through customs."

"I saw Daddy's suitcase. A man brought it out."

"Vanessa. What man?"

"He had stripes on his sleeve."

"But a lot of people —" I was going to say a lot of people could have a suitcase just like Jason's. The public-address system stopped me.

"Mrs. Jason Stone," a casual English girl's voice was saying. "Mrs. Jason Stone. Will Mrs. Jason Stone please come to the information desk on the ground level."

"Suppose Daddy comes and we're not here." Vanessa had heard the announcement, too.

"He'll wait. He knows we're meeting him."

A man in uniform was standing near the information desk. I told the girl behind it I was Mrs. Jason Stone.

She didn't say anything. The man moved forward a step.

"I'm Captain Granger. I wonder if you'd mind coming with me for a few minutes, Mrs. Stone."

He had stripes on his sleeve, but he didn't look like a pilot.

Oh, hell, I thought, Jason's tried to smuggle something through customs and he's been caught.

"Of course. Come on, Vanessa."

The man gave Vanessa a brief, pained look. "Perhaps it would be better if your little girl stayed here."

"I'll look after her, Mrs. Stone," the girl said in her casual English voice.

"No." I wasn't going to leave Vanessa in that busy, impersonal hall. I took her hand. "We'll both go."

The man didn't move. He seemed to be considering me. Where did I fit into his experience of American women? Would I make a scene if he insisted on my leaving Vanessa?

He nodded. "Just as you like, Mrs. Stone."

He led us across the hall, up in an elevator, through a door, and down a corridor into a large carpeted office with windows overlooking the field.

There were two men in the office. One was about fifty, with a graying, bristly mustache. The other was younger, with receding hair and an insignificant chin. Neither of them was in uniform and they didn't look like customs men. They looked like the senior civil servants I had met sometimes at Sylvia's parties.

"This is Mrs. Jason Stone," the man named Granger said.

"Thank you, Captain."

The older man was looking at my shoes, my handbag, beyond me to the door. Anywhere but at my face.

"I'm sorry we had to send for you like this, Mrs. Stone."

Granger started out.

"Perhaps you'd better stay, Captain Granger," the younger man stopped him. "Or perhaps —" I was still holding Vanessa's hand. "Or perhaps it would be better . . . We have a very well equipped nursery. And there's a registered nurse."

"Oh, come on," I said. "She'd sooner stay with me. Why don't you just tell me whatever it is."

I was beginning to realize it was something bad. Maybe very bad.

"Is my husband ill?"

"Well, no, I'm afraid not."

Afraid not?

"Please sit down, Mrs. Stone."

I sat down holding Vanessa against me.

"I'm afraid the fact is —"

The older man was looking into my eyes at last, steadily, without blinking.

"The fact is, I'm sorry, but I'm afraid your husband's dead."

He stopped and then went on in the same reluctant English voice.

Jason had had a heart attack on the plane. A massive heart attack, evidently. Cardiac arrest. Unfortunately, there hadn't happened to be a doctor among the passengers, but the chief steward, who was, of course, thoroughly trained in first aid, had done everything he could. He had massaged Jason's chest. He had given him oxygen.

"But I'm afraid it was too late, Mrs. Stone."

I was holding Vanessa's face against my breast by that time, as though to keep her from hearing. I knew she could hear, of course. But how much could she understand? Your husband's dead. Dead. I wasn't sure how much that word meant to her. Whether it had any meaning in terms of people. Jason. Her Daddy. Dead was what wasps were, sometimes. "It's all right, darling, it can't hurt you. It's dead."

"Isn't Daddy coming?"

She had understood that.

"No, Vanessa. I'm afraid not, darling."

We all kept using that word. Afraid.

She didn't ask why. Her dark blue eyes showed no sign of tears. They were thoughtful. They had lost their expectancy.

"Our company did everything they possibly could, Mrs. Stone." The younger man sounded faintly accusing. "Our doctor who examined him on arrival said your husband must have died —"

"Where is he?"

Until then I had thought only of Vanessa. My whole concern had been for her, to protect her. The meaning of what I had been told was beginning to penetrate to me now. I didn't altogether believe it. I didn't think I had misunderstood what these men had said. I didn't think they were lying to me. Jason was dead. I believed that. What I didn't believe was that I would never see him again. It would be a long time before I believed that.

"Where is he?"

"Your husband's body has been taken to the airport infirmary, Mrs. Stone."

I knew what I wanted then. I wanted to get out of there. I wanted to take Jason away with me. Away from these men, this airport. I wanted him to myself in private so I could cry or scream or do whatever I might find myself doing as soon as I was alone with Jason with no one watching me.

"Will you please call an ambulance. I'll take my husband to a hospital."

The older man was still looking at me with those unblinking eyes.

"Will you please call an ambulance."

"Yes, of course, Mrs. Stone. But first . . ."

There were a great many things I would have to do first. He kept referring to them as "formalities." I would have to identify the body, I would have to sign for my husband's personal possessions, the contents of his briefcase, his passport, his luggage. I would have to answer questions about his medical history. I would have to absolve the airline of any responsibility for my husband's death. That was just a formality too, of course, but the younger man was insistently accusing about it.

I was still holding Vanessa. The uniformed man, the one called Granger, mentioned the well-equipped nursery again. Vanessa no longer had her head against my breast. She was watching me.

"It's all right, darling."

She understood at once what I meant. I would not leave her with strangers. She nodded as though she had thought it over and agreed with me. I would have to call someone she knew, someone she loved, to come and take her home.

I phoned Sylvia and asked for Timmy.

"Could you come out to Heathrow, Timmy. Right away in a taxi. I'm afraid something's happened to Jason and I'd like you to look after Vanessa for me."

He didn't ask any questions.

"Yes, of course, Aunt Carol."

I told him to ask for Mr. Granger at the information desk.

"Captain Granger, actually," the younger man corrected me.

Captain Granger disappeared. A hostess brought us cups of tea, a glass of milk and some chocolate biscuits for Vanessa. She wouldn't eat them. The hostess tried to persuade her.

"Don't you like chocolate, dear? Most children do."

We all talked about that for a while. The older man had a son who had eaten a four-ounce bar of chocolate every day until he was twelve and then suddenly gone off it. There didn't seem to be anything else to talk about. Planes kept landing and taking off. I led Vanessa to the window so she could watch them.

The passengers came down the ramps and walked to the waiting buses. Baggage was unloaded onto runabout trucks. Everything looked distantly small and tidy. Toy buses, toy trucks. Vanessa seemed interested only in the baggage. She shifted from one window to another so she could keep it in sight. It struck me with sudden pain that she was still worried about Jason's suitcase.

After the chocolate conversation no one said anything. It occurred to me much later how different it would all have been in America. I was asked no questions about Jason, his profession, where he came from. The two Englishmen were totally incurious about us. Perhaps it was their way of being tactful. Perhaps they were afraid that if I started to talk about my husband, about myself, I would lose control and make an embarrassing scene. At the time, I was grateful to them for their silence. I didn't want to chat with strangers. I felt safer concentrating tightly on Vanessa.

Timmy arrived in less than half an hour. Captain Granger had evidently explained to him what had happened.

"I'm so sorry, Aunt Carol," Timmy said. And then he gently and very capably took charge of Vanessa.

I gave him the key to the Chelsea house.

"Don't worry, I'll play with her and keep her busy, Aunt Carol."

"And if she asks you any questions, please just tell her the truth. As much as she can understand."

"I know, Aunt Carol."

I kissed Vanessa. She had had one of those abrupt four-year-old changes of mood. It was as though she had forgotten why we had come to the airport. She was excited by the idea of spending the day with Timmy. She walked out of the office in a bright flurry of color, holding his hand.

"All right," I said. "I'm ready now."

The identification came first. I had led a sheltered life, in some ways. I had never seen a dead body before. Forcing my eyes to look at Jason was like making myself jump off a high place. I was afraid his features would be all distorted, swollen, discolored. They weren't. He looked tanned and calm and indescribably empty.

"Yes, that is my husband, Jason Stone," I had to say, and then sign an identification statement.

After that we went on to the rest of the formalities. I glanced into his wallet, his briefcase. I put his keys and loose change away in my bag. I answered the doctor's questions. I signed more papers. I claimed Jason's suitcase.

It was all very efficiently arranged, in an English way. Nothing was improvised or spontaneous. Even the hostess who led me from place to place gave the impression she had been rehearsed.

Captain Granger came to the hospital in the ambulance with me. We rode in the back with Jason's body. It had been placed in a canvas bag and strapped to a stretcher.

Captain Granger seemed puzzled about something.

"Your nephew," he said at last, "Timmy, is that his name?"

"Yes."

"Is it his half term?"

I understood what was puzzling him. Why wasn't Timmy away at boarding school?

"He's a day boy," I explained. "He goes to Saint Paul's."

Captain Granger said he had heard it was a very good school.

There were more formalities at the hospital. Jason was certified as dead. His body was taken to the morgue. I had to agree to a postmortem. Captain Granger insisted on that. Perhaps he was afraid I might later claim my husband had died from something he had eaten on the plane. There were arrangements to be made with an undertaker. There were more papers to be signed.

It was early afternoon before I got home. Vanessa and Timmy were in the kitchen doing a jigsaw puzzle. I kissed the top of Vanessa's head without distracting her attention from it. I sat down and watched her.

"Where does this go?" she kept saying. She wasn't asking Timmy. She didn't want him to help her.

Suddenly everything around me had stopped. The stillness was unbearable, as insistent as pain.

Thankfully, I remembered all that still needed to be done. People to be told, calls made to New York. Jason's parents first, then, if I could reach them on a Saturday, his lawyer and the people on the coast.

It was eleven o'clock in the morning in Brooklyn. I felt a craven sense of relief when Jason's father told me Mom was out shopping. I wouldn't have to be the one to tell her. It was difficult enough telling him. Break it gently. How? How can you break it gently to someone that his son is dead? I got it out at last. Jason's father didn't say anything. I told him Vanessa and I would be flying to

New York with the body. He sounded quite calm as we discussed arrangements for the funeral. His voice was so quiet I could hardly hear him.

After that there was the airline, the reservations, the instructions to the undertaker to deliver the body to the plane, and then trying to reach the business people in New York and California.

I welcomed it all. Every time I remembered something else to be done, I was grateful. It wasn't that activity kept me from thinking. My mind seethed with spasmodic recall, Jason doing this, Jason saying that. It was simply that inactivity was intolerable.

There was one other moment of stillness that evening when I was putting Vanessa to bed. Timmy was staying the night. He had warmed her pajamas in front of the gas fire. She was lying on her back under the bedclothes with her arms straight down at her sides.

"Daddy's dead, isn't he?" she said suddenly.

"Yes, darling."

I couldn't leave it at that. If she was puzzled, the questions that troubled her now might leave her feeling abandoned later.

"What do you think that means, Vanessa?"

"It means he's gone away."

"Yes, but he —" I was trying to find some way of assuring her that he hadn't wanted to. He hadn't ever wanted to leave her.

"It means I won't see him again for a long time. Not until one day we're all together in heaven."

Where had she got that from? From Heidi? Not from me. I didn't believe in heaven, except fitfully, with that contrary part of my mind that was afraid of hell.

"Yes, darling."

I was glad Vanessa believed it. Bless Heidi or whoever had given her that hope.

We were met at Idlewild by a hearse, a studio limousine, and two reporters. I gave the reporters brief factual information about Jason's heart attack, the funeral arrangements. The business with the hearse took longer. It had never occurred to me that a corpse would have to be cleared through customs. The limousine drove us to Brooklyn.

Jason's parents were subdued, like punished children. His father retained that sensible fortitude with which he had met all the hardships of his life. His mother seemed bewildered. They both concentrated on Vanessa, as I had at Heathrow, offering her food, finding toys for her, cushions to sit on.

Gratefully I found there were still things to be done. Jason was to be cremated, the funeral service held at the synagogue we had attended together at the time of Tanta Vera's death. That was the family's decision.

Now the Industry people were crowding in. One of the studio pricks wanted a eulogy to be read by a well-known movie actor. I hesitated. Would Jason have liked that? It would certainly have amused him.

The actor called me. "It would be a great honor, Mrs. Stone."

Talking to him, I realized he knew nothing about Jason, had scarcely met him. It wasn't the honor he was after. He was a notorious cutup. The publicity of being associated with any sober event would be a welcome change. I thanked him and said no.

The rabbi made a brief, straightforward speech about Jason. He said he had been a devoted son. He said he had been a loving husband and father. He said Jason had been a good and kind man. He did not mention the Industry.

I made no effort to keep myself from weeping. In that close, cherishing community of Jason's family and old friends, I felt no constraint. I could cry at last. That was what funerals were for, I realized thankfully, not for the dead but for the living, to release their grief. I sobbed out loud. I didn't want anyone to hear me, but I didn't care if they did.

After the funeral there were even more things to be done. Lawyers and accountants, taxes. I had always liked Jason's lawyer, a serious family man with an office in the RKO building. "He's not brilliant," Jason used to say. "Anybody can be brilliant. The extraordinary thing about Arthur is that he's honest."

I spent hours with him, or alone in an adjacent office, going through Jason's papers, contracts, insurance policies, canceled checks.

"You're going to be fine," Arthur told me the fourth day. "Even when the IRS gets through with you, you're going to be just fine. He was a far-sighted man, Jason."

At the end of the week there were only personal files left to go through, some press clippings from Jason's early days as an actor, his army discharge papers, letters from friends.

In one of the files was an envelope on which Jason had written, "Vanessa Clavering." Had he left her a letter? I opened the envelope. There was nothing inside but a sheaf of canceled checks, clipped together with a sheet of paper folded around them. I unfolded the paper.

It is always so startling to see one's own handwriting on a forgotten letter.

Jason's stuck in Madrid and I'm going to join him there. Hope things work out well for you at UNICEF. I don't know when I'll be back in Rome, probably not for several months. Carol.

And then beneath the signature those words I had added as an afterthought, an attempt to explain myself. Words, I could see now, that were dangerously ambiguous.

I'm glad we went to Pescara. It brought everything out in the open between us again. What we want, the kind of people we are. That's why I don't think we should see each other again. Remembering our past together, I'm sure you understand this.

I looked at the canceled checks. The amounts varied from eight hundred to two thousand dollars. Around twelve thousand dollars in all. The dates covered a period of three years. The first was July 7, 1958, the time of Jason's first trip to California after Vanessa was born. The last was July 19, 1961, just before Jason left for Missouri to start shooting *The Time of the Fire.*

All the checks were made out to Max Ludlow and endorsed by him on the back.

Twenty-One

For the next year I was on the run with Vanessa.

I tried not to be melodramatic about it. I didn't look over my shoulder to see if Max was following us. I didn't walk into a hotel and expect to see him waiting for us there. I did feel certain he would try to find us. The meaning of that letter, those canceled checks, was too clear for me to have any doubts about that.

Max had gone to Jason back in '58, when Jason was on his first trip to the coast, trying to finance *The Time of the Fire.* He wouldn't have had any trouble finding him; Jason was seeking publicity at the time.

He had shown Jason the letter I had left at the Inglaterra. *I'm glad we went to Pescara.* And then Max would have told Jason about the other nights he and I had spent together just nine months before Vanessa was born.

Jason paid him two thousand dollars for the letter. Why? And why had he continued to buy him off again and again for three years?

I tried to understand that. Jason hadn't consulted his lawyer. When I did, Arthur assured me that Max had no conceivable legal claim on Vanessa. The explanation for Jason's behavior, I decided, lay partly in his insecurity about himself, his sterility. Whether he altogether believed Max was Vanessa's father, or not, his impulse would have been to push the whole subject as far away as he could, no matter what it cost.

But far more important than that, I think Jason had been trying to protect us. Our marriage. To insure us against the threat that one day Max would thrust himself into our lives.

"Ask her. Ask Carol who Vanessa's father really is."

It was a question that could destroy the trust and happiness between us.

Jason himself had never asked it. Only once, obliquely, on the phone, had he ever approached it. "Tell Vanessa I love her. Tell her I love her, no matter what."

Dear Jason.

I did not believe that Max would stop now that Jason was dead. The money he had extracted from Jason in return for his silence had been of secondary importance to him, I felt. It was the fact that he could make *my* husband pay that mattered. He would be after me now with his bitter vindictiveness.

"You've tried to destroy my soul, Carol," he had told me at the Rome airport. "I'll make you pay for that if it takes me the rest of my life." And I did not think he could be appeased by money from me. He could make me pay through Vanessa. He would feel no consideration, no affection, for her. He would be moved only by his hatred for me.

And it would be so easy for him to destroy Vanessa's security. He would corner her one day in the street or the gardens. "I'm your father. Your Daddy. Ask your mother if you don't believe me. Jason wasn't your father. Jason couldn't have children . . ." He would go on and on, insisting, arguing, frightening and bewildering her.

A child is so vulnerable. Any shock, any wound, may not be apparent until years later. A scar will reveal itself as shyness, anxiety, guilt. I wasn't going to let that happen to Vanessa. Jason had been her Daddy. She had loved him. She had accepted his death. In her own private way, she was a happy, self-confident child. No matter what I had to do, she was going to grow up that way.

I wasn't going to let Max find her. Ever.

I explained most of this to Arthur. As a lawyer, he thought I should take action against Max, turn the case over to the D.A.'s office in Los Angeles. Those canceled checks, the letter, were conclusive evidence that Max had been blackmailing Jason.

"And the whole thing'll be in the papers. And one day when Vanessa's a little older someone will blurt it all out to her. And anyway, even if they send Max to jail, he won't be there forever. I'll still have to keep Vanessa away from him when he gets out."

Arthur suggested a court injunction constraining Max.

"Oh, come on, Arthur. You think that's going to stop him? If he knows where Vanessa is, sooner or later he'll get to her."

As a friend, Arthur agreed with me. He wanted to help in any way he could. One invaluable way he could help was by letting me use him as a forwarding address. I would tell no one else where I was. I was traveling; I could only be reached through Arthur's office. I would keep in touch with Arthur and he would send any worthwhile mail on to me. Any letters I wrote I would send to him to be mailed in New York.

I hated taking Vanessa away from Jason's parents, telling them only we were going back to Europe.

"No, we won't be staying in London. I haven't made up my mind yet where we'll go. But you can always reach us through . . ."

Of all the people I had to say that to, Jason's father was the least inquisitive. "Don't worry, Carol. I understand." I think he meant I had to make a new life now, cut myself free from the lost past and get away on my own.

We went first to Spain, to Torremolinos, a small fishing village with a single hotel. It had not been discovered at that time. In November it was deserted by all but Spaniards and a few retired English people.

We stayed there six weeks. It was too cold to swim; we walked on the beach. I found a riding school outside Málaga and Vanessa took riding lessons. She was fearless and enthusiastic and soon wanted to go out on "her" pony every day. It was one of those small discoveries I kept making about her: she had a natural feeling for animals. In the evenings we played dominoes and I began to teach her to read. We ate at our own table in the dining room. The food was terrible; we lived almost entirely on eggs and rice and beans. We nodded to the few English guests at the hotel; occasionally one of them paused and stooped to ask Vanessa how old she was. It rained.

I received a large package of mail from Arthur. Most of it consisted of belated letters of condolence; there were a few business things I had to deal with. Among the letters I opened last was one that had been forwarded to Arthur from the house in Chelsea. The return address, printed on the corner of the envelope, was Genesis, Santa Monica, California. The letter was typewritten.

Dear Carol, I was so sorry to read about your husband's death. I never met him, but I have heard from people who knew him that he was a very fine man. I wonder how things are going for you. Do write and let me know . . .

I didn't read any further. Fuck him. I tore it in pieces. It wasn't difficult to figure out how he had found the Chelsea address. Jason's office in the basement, Jascar Productions, had been listed in the London phone book for years. All Max had had to do was go to the Santa Monica public library and look it up.

It didn't frighten me. It just made me see all the more clearly how careful I had to be.

Genesis. That was probably the name of the place Chris had told me about, where Iris had gone to be helped off heroin. Max was evidently still running it.

What sort of contacts would that give him? There was Iris, of course, and through Iris, Chris. It seemed to me Max's sources of information might be much more extensive than that. Running a drug-abuse center like Genesis would entail fund-raising, charity committees, probably contacts with the movie people on the coast. None of those people, of course, knew where I was. I must be careful to avoid places where I might run into any of them.

There was very little to do in Torremolinos in the rain. Just before Christmas we moved to Deyá in Majorca. Sylvia had told me about it. A number of English and American expatriates had followed Robert Graves there. From what Sylvia had said — "Darling, it's full of mothers who play the flute" — they were not the kind of people who would ever have heard of Jason Stone. To them I would be only one more American woman with money from somewhere and a child to bring up. If there were flute-playing mothers, there would be children. I thought it was important for Vanessa to make friends her own age. I imagined play groups and slumber parties.

Vanessa did make friends in Deyá. They came to the house I rented and some of them stayed, not just for slumber parties, but for days on end when their mothers were "busy." Some of them were the busiest women I'd met since the San Remo. Life in Deyá that winter was like a game of musical beds. Apparently one of the rules of the game was that if a flute-playing mother wanted to sleep with someone, she had to move in with him first. She had to make a permanent domestic arrangement with her new lover. Some of these permanent arrangements lasted all of a week. They ended in a lot of china getting broken and tempests of tears.

It was none of my business. I found a riding school in Sóller and took Vanessa there almost every afternoon in the tiny Fiat I rented from the local garage. She had learned the alphabet and was reading short words. She was playing checkers. She was picking up Spanish. I loved watching the sudden forward leaps she made. I enjoyed seeing her welcome the children who wandered in with their airline bags. "Mom says can I stay here till Wednesday because she's going to move to Simon's and Bruce and Alice are going to live in our house."

Several men invited me to join the musical-bed game, but I remained firmly celibate. That winter, three months after his death, was the time I missed Jason most deeply. I felt his absence and, in recollection, his presence all the time. I had no desire to exchange memory for experience, Jason's recalled tenderness for a casual affair. I said no, and meant it, to a succession of Bruces and Simons who were temporarily out of a place to live.

I was planning to stay in Deyá through the summer. There was a beach, a long climb down from the village, but calm and shallow, a perfect place for Vanessa to learn to swim. I could rent a sailboat in Sóller. Vanessa had found a best friend, a little girl of six whose mother had married a Spaniard and was still living with him.

Then one evening we were sitting on the café terrace. Vanessa was eating ice cream and I was drinking the local specialty, rum and chocolate milk. It sounds revolting, but I liked it. A man at the next table kept glancing at me in a puzzled way. He looked familiar to me, too. After a few minutes, he came over to my table.

"Aren't you . . . Didn't you used to live on Charles Street?"

It was Duffy, the out-of-work actor from the Village. He sat down without being invited and began to talk about himself. He was no longer interested in the theater, in acting. "It's such a phony world." He was writing now. That was why he had come to Deyá; he wanted to get to know Robert Graves and show him his work. He was planning to stay all summer.

Vanessa had finished her ice cream. I was going to take her home when it occurred to me I might get some useful information out of Duffy.

"Do you remember Iris?"

"Sure. We used to make it together. She had the greatest tits. I mean they weren't all that big —" He wanted to go on about Iris's tits. I interrupted him.

"Do you know what happened to her? Is she still in California?"

Yes, he thought she was, most of the time. She was at that Genesis place. But he had run into her in New York a few months ago.

"She was at the Minetta with that guy she used to make it with, you know, that Hollywood writer, Chris Deniken. Do you remember him?"

I said I did.

I took Vanessa home and put her to bed and read to her. After she had fallen asleep, I went into the living room and poured myself a glass of wine and sat in the only comfortable chair. I didn't want to be paranoid about it, although, as Delmore Schwartz said, even paranoids have real enemies.

I didn't think Duffy would sit down the next day and write to Chris or Iris about seeing me. I did think he was exactly the kind of garrulous limpet who would be sending off picture post-cards all summer to let all his old friends know where he was, he had met Robert Graves, and guess who else was in Deyá. One of those post-cards might be to Chris.

Or Iris.

I decided not to risk it.

A week later I packed up and took Vanessa to France, to St.-Jean-de-Luz. It seemed a good choice. We stayed in a hotel for a week and then I found a small villa overlooking the sea. The ocean was too rough for Vanessa to swim in but there was a sheltered crescent of beach beyond the port that was like a children's club.

The mothers were a different lot from the flute players of Deyá. They were firmly middle class, mainly French, with a few Americans and English. Most of them were women whose husbands came down for the weekend from their offices in Bordeaux or Toulouse or, in the case of some of the Americans, Paris. They talked about *au pair* girls and recipes for Basque dishes and de Gaulle and clothes and impeaching Earl Warren and *au pair* girls. It was a relief to be back in a country where I could speak the language without sounding retarded. When the French mothers discovered this, they stopped treating me like Typhoid Mary and some of them even invited me to dinner and introduced me to their husbands as *l'Americaine qui parle français.*

Almost every evening there was a half-hour of overwhelming beauty as the sun set behind the Pyrenees. Vanessa found a new best friend, a seven-year-old English child named Jennifer Sandwich, who wanted to be a champion show jumper when she grew up. She took Vanessa riding and was teaching her to jump three-foot hurdles until I stopped her.

Her father, Colonel Sandwich, thought this was a bit unsporting of me. Jennifer had already broken her collarbone twice and he couldn't see that it had done her any harm. I thought his wife, Molly, was on my side, but she didn't say so. Whenever I saw them together, she seemed a little frightened of her husband.

It was a quiet summer. No scares, no old friends from the Village, no movie people. Vanessa could swim a few strokes without water wings and was picking up French. It wasn't until the middle of August that I felt any concern about the life she and I were living.

"Jennifer's going back to Wiltshire next week," she told me one evening. A few days later on the beach, one of the American mothers looked up from *Rebecca,* which she was reading for the third time.

"Well, next Monday, I guess, we'll be back in Paris."

It struck me then. By the middle of September, they would all be gone.

That night after Vanessa was asleep, I sat on the terrace and tried to think it through. St.-Jean-de-Luz in the winter would be Torremolinos all over again. Cold and wet and empty. We could go farther south, to Morocco, the Canary Islands. Or we could go to the mountains, some unfashionable town in the Italian Alps or in Switzerland where Vanessa could learn to ski.

There were plenty of immediate answers. I was trying to look beyond them. Vanessa was reading Beatrix Potter now. She could add and subtract better than Jennifer Sandwich. At the rate she was going with just my help, there was no hurry about sending her to school. But could I go on like this, moving her from place to place, interrupting her friendships, erasing the familiar, every few months? Vanessa needed a home somewhere, a chance to make friends she could grow up with. She needed a settled base.

Where?

I got a pad and pencil and wrote down all the places to be avoided first, to see what was left.

Rule out anywhere near Paris, Rome, New York, London, Madrid, Cannes. Too many movie people. And they were the obvious places for Max to look for us. Arthur had forwarded two more letters from him. *Why don't you answer? Please write and tell me . . .* Fuck him. At the end of July there had been a third, overtly threatening letter. *I'm not going to let you take my child away from me. I'm going to find her and get her back.*

Rule out Majorca, Greece, San Francisco, Key West, Florence, Venice, Provincetown, Mexico. Too many Duffys, leftovers from the Village.

Rule out all the places I didn't want to live. Germany, South America, Belgium, the Middle West, Australia, New Zealand, Japan, anywhere in England except London, any tourist resort with a constantly shifting population where Vanessa would have to keep making new friends.

That still left a lot of possible areas. After a few days, I had narrowed them down to half a dozen. Scandinavia, Oregon, Unfashionable Switzerland, Holland, the Dordogne in France, and Portugal.

I was inclining more and more toward Switzerland — I had been particularly happy at school there — when Jennifer's mother came over one evening to say good-bye.

Molly Sandwich was a beautiful, soft-spoken woman, with dark, pensive eyes. She and I had spent a lot of time together because of our children's attachment to each other, but she had never told me anything about herself. We sat out on the terrace and had a drink. It was evidently not her first that evening. Halfway through it, she seemed to change all at once into a different person.

"You're so bloody lucky," she said, not softly at all, but with a shrill, accusing edge to her voice. "God and Jesus, you don't know how lucky you are, not being married to that bloody man."

I could see what she meant. Even at his best, Colonel Sandwich was an arrogant bore. I didn't say anything.

"All the hell I have to put up with. It's like living in a padded cell with no windows. I wouldn't stick it for a minute, only for Jennifer. And she's growing up to be as bad as he is."

In what way? I wondered. Jennifer had always seemed to me a placid child, not in the least like her choleric father. Perhaps Molly was upset by her show-jumping ambitions. "You mean the horses?" I asked.

"It's not the horses, for Jesus Christ's sake. It's the way he's taught her to look at things. Like a bloody cow staring into a lake and seeing only its own piss."

She finished her drink. I was afraid if I got up to make her another she would lose her impetus and I would never find out what she was talking about. I handed her mine.

"Ah, the blind, rotten English. They've no more life in them than a stuffed owl. That man can watch the sun going down over those mountains, and what do you think he says? He says, 'jolly good show.' Jolly good show. What in hell does he think God gave him a tongue for? There's one thing sure, God never gave him any feelings. And ten years from now she'll be as cold and dead as he is. Sometimes I think the only hope for that child is to run away with her and take her home with me where the people have a bit of life in them, a bit of poetry and feeling and laughter. Ah, you can't think what it's like back there. It's another world entirely."

She went on about that other world for almost half an hour. About the lakes and the hills and the skies. But mostly about the people. Their spontaneity and kindness, their wild, impulsive ways, their sudden dark grief and generosity and laughter.

She spoke in a longing, lilting voice that was now shrill, now soft, and was altogether more like music than speech, so that for minutes at a time I found myself listening only to the sound of it, gleaning its meaning more from its melody than its words.

"Ah, what can life promise you but the unexpected? And who'd ask for more? And that's where you'll find it. Only there. Where they're not ashamed to feel, and to say what they feel, and a woman can come out from behind her face and cry. Ah, God and Jesus, how I long to cry sometimes."

Molly's voice trailed away. She *was* crying. I didn't try to stop her. After a minute she put down her glass and pushed herself clumsily out of her chair. She stumbled and almost fell as she crossed the terrace. It was only a hundred yards to the Sandwiches' villa. I put my arm around her and helped her home.

The front door was open. The colonel appeared in it at once when he heard our steps on the drive, lean and angular against the lighted room behind him. I felt a quick apprehension. What would he do to her?

I kept my arm around her shoulders. She tore herself suddenly and fiercely away from me and ran to the house.

"Ah, darling," I heard her cry. "Is it you, my love?"

"Molly. My own Molly."

The colonel seized her. I saw his hands move over her shoulders, down to her waist. His hard, horseman's fingers were lifting the back of her skirt, thrusting beneath the elastic of her panties, gripping her behind.

"Ah, Molly," he kept saying. "My own Molly. It's me. There, there, it's all right, Molly."

I knew I was intruding on something secret and mysterious. Something I might never understand. I left them there, grappling in the doorway like wrestlers — no, not like wrestlers; there was nothing antagonistic in the way they were tearing at each other.

I went home and made myself a drink and sat out on the terrace again. I was a little confused by the last half-hour. I also felt strangely excited and alert. It was as though Molly Sandwich had opened an unexpected door in my mind and shown me what lay beyond it. I saw myself comfortable and safe in Switzerland, growing dull and middle-aged, more and more placid year by year, until, as Molly had put it, I was like a bloody cow staring into a lake and seeing only its own piss.

It was a depressing prospect. Worse than that, it went against my private nature, my attitude toward myself, what I thought I was and wanted to be. I remembered the way I had felt at eighteen, my excitement about escaping from the security of the familiar to a new country peopled with reckless, impulsive, eccentric Americans.

Why not? I was only forty-one. I wasn't too old to make voyages into the unpredictable, what Molly had called the unexpected.

Why not?

From a certain point of view, my mother's, for instance, Molly Sandwich was undoubtedly mad. But at that moment I was enchanted by her madness. I wanted to join her in it. That night, for the first time since Jason's death, I felt entirely alive.

When I woke the next morning, the madness was gone, but the impulse wasn't. What the hell, why not? What harm, as the Irish themselves said, if Vanessa and I spent a few weeks seeing if Molly Sandwich was telling the truth about Ireland, if it really was a country where the people still had a bit of wildness and feeling and poetry in them?

Clean, tidy Switzerland would still be there two months from now.

What harm if we tried to find that other world Molly had talked about? A world that was not a neat, safe place but a hope, and maybe a challenge.

Twenty-Two

1962–1971

We never found it, of course. That world existed only in Molly's drunken mind. But in the end we found something even better.

I risked two nights at Sylvia's on the way to Ireland. *The Time of the Fire* had opened at the Odeon and I wanted to see it. I wanted to see Sylvia, too. She and Timmy seemed to be all that was left of my family. The last time I had visited my mother, she had kept calling me Daphne and telling me I ought to be ashamed of myself working for those Reds.

There wasn't much risk; I could trust Sylvia to protect me.

"God, don't I know?" she said the first night at her house when I explained in a general way the need for secrecy about my whereabouts. "Old lovers can be absolute hell. They simply won't give up, will they? Just because you've done a bit of macking with them, they think they own you for the rest of your life." She would not tell anyone where I was or where I was going.

I saw Jason's movie the next afternoon. I went alone to the two o'clock showing. The Sunday critics had written excitedly about it and even at that hour the Odeon was two-thirds full. I sat through the interminable commercials for Campari and cigarettes, hunkered down in my seat and whispering to myself. Please, let it be good, please don't let those studio pricks have spoiled it, please let it be the movie Jason wanted to make.

It was. Jason had been clever; he had practically cut the film in the camera. Without resorting to a lot of expensive retakes, the studio had had very little choice about how to edit his footage. The climax, the fire, was a brilliant piece of staging. When the animals that had been trapped in the burning house escaped from their cages and attacked the lynch mob outside, the whole audience gasped with frightened approval. The young actor who played the sheriff had an understated sincerity that made you want to elect him secretary-general of the U.N. In spite of the years that had passed since McCarthy, the movie's indictment of guilt by association was as fresh and urgent as the current headlines from Oxford, Mississippi.

You did it, I thought as I walked out into the Haymarket. Dear Jason, you really did it. He had left a film behind him that, like *The Maltese Falcon* or *Odd Man Out,* would not be entirely forgotten for ten, twenty, perhaps even thirty years.

I wanted a drink. The pubs wouldn't be open for another hour. I took a taxi back to Sylvia's. Timmy was home from school. He came into the living room as I was settling down with a Scotch.

"Hello, Aunt Carol. I'm glad you're here. I wanted to talk to you."

"I'd love to talk to you too. But first of all" — he was seventeen — "don't you think it's time you stopped calling me Aunt Carol?"

"What would you like me to call you?"

"Carol."

He said he would try. I asked him what he wanted to talk to me about.

"About my father. I want you to tell me honestly. What do you think of him?"

I realized it was a compliment, being asked that, but I didn't feel I should be too candid. After all, I was a guest in Nigel's house.

"Probably just about what you think of him, Timmy."

He nodded. His hair needed cutting, or perhaps he was letting it grow on purpose. I thought it suited him.

"He wants me to go to university so he can wangle me into the Foreign Office."

"Don't you want to go to university?"

"It's what I do there. I don't want to do modern languages. I can already speak French and I'm not interested in learning German."

"What do you want to do?"

"Economics. Political science."

"Then Nigel will try to wangle you into the Treasury, won't he?"

Timmy smiled. "No fear of that. I want to study political science so I can help start a revolution and abolish the Treasury."

"Isn't it marvelous?" Sylvia said when she and I were alone after dinner that evening. "Timmy's an absolute anarchist. And he's not a bit stuffy about it like Daphne with her bloody Labour party. Timmy hates the Labour party as much as he hates Nigel's rotten lot. Well, almost as much."

Vanessa and I caught the Rosslare ferry the next day. We arrived early the next morning. The sea was as still as the cloudless sky when the comfortable, old-fashioned boat dawdled into the bay. We were on deck, watching for our first sight of Ireland. The coastline seemed to rise out of a mirage. After the precarious, smoke-stacked clutter of South Wales the evening before, the low hills beyond the shore had a look of timeless confidence.

The boat tied up without haste to a long, ancient stone jetty. A dozen men in baggy dark suits came on board. One of them asked me if I had any luggage. I took him to the lounge and pointed to our suitcases. It wasn't until he picked them up and started to carry them down the gangplank that I realized he was a porter. He didn't look like a porter in that dark serge suit. He didn't act like one, either. He acted like a man who had been expecting us for some time and was taking us to his leader.

There were no passport formalities. One customs man lounged behind a trestle table at the foot of the gangplank. He was eating an apple and hardly glanced at me as he waved us past. Our porter was carrying our bags toward a cluster of stone cottages at the land end of the jetty.

I asked him if I could rent a car somewhere.

"You can, of course."

He walked on. He still seemed to be taking us to his leader.

He took us to one of the stone cottages and knocked on the door. After a moment it was opened by a man in a green tweed suit. The porter said something to him I couldn't hear. The man looked at us, one quick, direct glance.

"You'll be all right with him," the porter told me. He had put down our bags and was waiting, with interest, but without impatience, as though to see what I would do next.

It occurred to me after several seconds of silence that he might be waiting to be paid. How much? I didn't feel I knew him well enough to ask. I didn't feel I understood anything about this whole situation. I took out an English pound note and handed it to him. He fingered it in his calm, interested way.

"Is that enough?"

"It's grand."

He put it away in his trouser pocket, then he knelt in front of Vanessa and pressed something into her palm. It was a small silver coin, an Irish sixpence. Vanessa accepted it without question. She already seemed better adjusted to this new world than I was. The porter walked off, away from the boat. He was apparently finished with his job for the day.

"You'll be wanting a car." The man in the green suit had stepped out into the street — there was no sidewalk — and was searching through his pockets for something.

I said yes, I did want to rent a car for a few days. Did he know where I might find one?

"I do, of course."

He led us around to the back of the cottage. A blue English Mini was parked there.

"Will that do you?" He had found some keys in his pocket.

I said it would do fine.

My memories of that morning are a little confused; I was confused at the time. I'm not sure whether I ever signed any papers for that car. I know I never showed the man in the green tweed suit my driver's license. I did not give him any money as a deposit. I did not produce any credit cards. He simply handed me the keys to the car and put our suitcases in the back. I drove off in it.

For a little while I was troubled by his casual trustfulness. It made me feel strangely guilty. But as I took the road to Wexford, I remembered that one direct glance he had given me, me and Vanessa. He had not really been hasty or naive. He had decided I was not going to steal his car. I was going to bring it back and pay for it. And he was right. I was. His trust had been in his own judgment.

I had intended to drive west, to Bantry Bay and then up into Kerry and Clare. As it happened, we never got farther than County Waterford. In the late afternoon, we came to a hotel outside Tramore. It didn't look like a hotel; I would have taken it for a country house if I hadn't seen the small wooden sign over the front door. Beyond the French windows was a vast overgrown lawn, a broken fountain, an apple orchard, a meadow with cows in it.

"Would you like to stop here?" I asked Vanessa. "Would you like to stay here for the night?"

She said she would.

We stayed there, that first time, for seven weeks. The hotel was run by a family, the Sutreaus. Descended from Huguenots who had settled in Waterford in the eighteenth century, they were more than a family; they were a clan. Irene, the mother, was the head of it. She and her two daughters, Ann and Catherine, were the day-to-day managers of the hotel. There was also a son who looked after the cows and the orchard, and another son who sometimes worked in the bar. There were daughters-in-law and cousins and aunts who helped out in the dining room and the kitchen when they were needed.

And there were the children.

Sometimes there were a dozen of them, tucked away in various rooms, sometimes only five or six. They ranged in age from two to sixteen, and they were the freest children I have ever known. They were free because they were unfailingly accepted. If they came into meals, they were fed. If they were still there at night, they were told which rooms to sleep in. They were never unwelcome and they were never questioned. They were not spoiled. They had beautiful manners and were always willing to help make the beds or pick apples or wash up if they were there. If they weren't there, no one ever seemed to question that, either.

In the same casual, unquestioning way, the children accepted each other. Even the older boys took it for granted that if they were going somewhere — to the village, to the beach — all the others, no matter how young, were welcome to go with them.

Our first evening at the hotel, Vanessa went out to explore the orchard. When she hadn't come back a half-hour later and I couldn't find her, I asked Mrs. Sutreau if she had seen my little girl.

"Oh, I expect she went into the village with Stephen. I asked him to get me some pork chops. I expect they'll be back presently."

They were. Stephen, all of twelve, came back pushing his bicycle. Vanessa was riding on the handlebars. He helped her down as though he had been looking after her all her life.

"Do you want to go pee-pee before dinner?" I asked her.

She shook her head. "Stephen took me in the pub."

The next morning after breakfast she went off to the beach with a whole covey of children. She was gone all day. I asked Catherine at lunch whether they had taken any food with them.

"Oh, I expect so. I wouldn't worry about it, anyway. Someone'll give them a sandwich and cup of tea if they're hungry."

When Vanessa came home that evening, I asked her if she had had anything to eat since breakfast. She had been freeloading all day. Bacon and eggs in a farmhouse where she and Susan, a little Sutreau girl of nine, had gone to help gather firewood; cold chicken in a pub in Tramore where they had delivered some eggs for the farmer's wife; a bag of chips from a man who had given them a ride home in his cart.

"And they gave her money, too," I protested apologetically to Ann. Sometime during the day, Vanessa had acquired another two sixpences.

"Oh, that's just for luck. It's supposed to be lucky to give a child a silver coin."

"Shouldn't I at least go into the pub and pay for the chicken she ate?"

"Oh, they wouldn't take it. I wouldn't worry about it, anyway. We all help each other out if we can."

During the next few days, as I let Vanessa go her own way with the children and drove around, exploring the countryside, I saw what Ann had meant. If I appeared lost, someone was sure to ask if they could help me. The friendliness of the people was overwhelming; it was as though there were a conspiracy of kindness in the country.

Reading books I found around the hotel, I understood at least part of the reason for this. Ireland had been almost completely cut off from the rest of Europe for the past forty years. The "Troubles," the economic war with England, neutrality during the Second World War, had forced the Irish to revert to a simple system of barter and mutual aid to survive. Naturally generous and hospitable, they had made a pleasure and a ceremony of necessity.

"The country keeps alive on hope, a feeling for the past, and Guinness," a man I met in the Waterford public library told me. "Not necessarily in that order."

I had gone there to find a book on the Easter Rebellion, and, seeing me shuffling through the card catalogue, he had asked if he could help. One thing had soon led to another in the usual Irish way, and we were having a drink together in the pub across the street.

He wasn't Irish. His name was Anton Krasny and he was a Czech. He had been living in Ireland for over twenty years.

"I was the Czech consul in Dublin," he explained. "I was fired when the Germans took over my country in thirty-nine. So I just stayed on." He had thought of going back after the war, during the brief Masaryk democracy before the Russians took over. "But I was interested in the Grattan parliament at the time. I was writing a book about it, working in the Trinity library. You know the Grattan parliament?"

I didn't.

"Never mind. It was dissolved by the Act of Union over a hundred and fifty years ago. But I often think Grattan saved my life. If I had gone back to Prague, the Russians would probably have shot me."

I asked him what happened to his book.

"I never finished it. I became too interested in the other side, the traitors, John Beresford, the Kingfish, and what came afterward. That led to Daniel O'Connell and Catholic Emancipation. I almost finished a book about Daniel O'Connell, but you can't understand him unless you understand the famine. And of course once you start on the famine . . ." He spread his hands on the table in a gesture of helplessness. He had beautiful hands.

We had finished our Guinnesses. I insisted on paying for the next round.

"How long have you been here in Ireland?"

"Only three weeks."

"And you're already up to 1916 and the Easter Rebellion?"

"I'm starting there."

He smiled. "I'd say you were safe for three months," he warned me. "After that you're done for. You'll be here for the rest of your life, like me."

I thought about Anton Krasny, his warning, when I was sitting in the lounge after dinner that evening. Vanessa, I knew, was already done for. When I had suggested, a few days before, that we might drive on to West Cork and Kerry soon, she had looked at me as though I were crazy.

"Why? Why do you want to go there?"

"There's so much to see, darling."

"I've got enough to see here."

She had her fifth birthday at the hotel. Ann made her a huge cake and she got dozens of presents, homemade things which she treasured because at her age they seemed more her own than things bought in a store. I stayed away from the party, sitting in the lounge where I could hear the children's voices.

"Next year," I heard Vanessa say, "next year we'll put the tables closer together."

If there was any one moment at which I decided to stay in Ireland, I suppose that was it.

It wasn't only that it seemed so cruel to separate Vanessa from those children, their unbounded private world. I had a personal reason for wanting to stay, too. I was seeing Anton Krasny almost every day. He was the first man I had felt close to since Jason's death. I could talk to Anton about anything, about Max, the movie people, Fitz, the war; he had a way of listening and seeing it all in relationship to a much larger design of human experience. He had read more, he knew more, than anyone I had ever met. He had an inexhaustible tolerance and a quick, humorous irreverence about everyone, including himself, that reminded me of Jason.

I didn't know if I was physically attracted to him or not. There was one thing about him that did intrigue me. Almost every other man I had ever known had smelled of tobacco. Jason had smelled of those small Swiss cigars. I had come to like it after a while; cigar smoke had acquired associations of intimacy for me. Anton didn't smoke. He smelled of soap and his tweed jacket and wool. I found this provocative.

He was in his middle fifties, thin, gray haired, untidy, shabbily dressed. He drank a good deal and he seemed entirely without ambition. He wasn't indifferent or aimless, though. There were times when he would make some simple gesture, hand me a drink or open a door for me, and I would glimpse a refinement in him, a tempered chivalry that was as incorruptible as steel.

I found a house for sale, a few miles north of Tramore. It was cold and drafty and the roof leaked, but it had nine large rooms, a huge barn, stables, eight acres of land, an old ruin of a carriage house, and a stream. The asking price was just over eight thousand dollars, which Irene Sutreau thought was too much. I took Vanessa to see it. She hurried around exploring all those rooms.

"We can have *everyone* to stay here."

That was exactly what I had been thinking. I bought it at the end of October.

There were things in storage in London: books, records, crockery, linens, clothes, a few pieces of furniture Jason and I had bought for the Chelsea house. I took Vanessa back to Sylvia's so I could sort through them and decide what to give away and what to ship to Waterford. Sylvia had a package of mail for me forwarded by Arthur. I looked through it quickly. Nothing from Max.

"Did anyone phone for me?"

No one had.

"Is he still after you, your demon lover?"

"I don't know."

"They do give up after a while," Sylvia said a little regretfully. "They find someone else."

I went down to the Harrods storehouse on the river the next day. It was a fascinating place, a museum of the ages.

"Some of this stuff's been here for fifty years. They still keep paying storage on it. They'll never want it again, but they can't bear to part with it," the elderly man in charge told me as he led me through the maze of trunks and commodes and clocks and stuffed animals to my own familiar possessions.

He checked the labels on them. "So you're Mrs. Stone, Madam." He sounded gently intrigued.

"Yes. Mrs. Jason Stone. Why?"

"There was a gentleman here last month inquiring about you."

"What kind of a gentleman?"

"An American, Madam."

He described him. In his forties. Gray haired. Well dressed.

"He said he had been stationed in England with the Canadians during the war, Madam. He was most interesting, but I knew he was only telling me about himself to try to get on the right side of me so I'd answer his questions."

"What questions? What did he ask you?"

"He wanted to know where you were. Then he asked where your storage payments came from. Which bank they were drawn on."

"What did you tell him?"

"Nothing at all, Madam, naturally. We don't give out information of that kind about our clients."

I thanked him and gave him a pound note. Arthur had been paying for the storage through a New York bank, but God bless Harrods and their discretion, anyway.

He must have gone to the Chelsea house, I decided. Neighbors had told him I had left. His questions about where I had gone and when I was expected back had prompted someone to remember the Harrods van taking my things away. It may have seemed like a long chance that Harrods would know where I was, but Max had always been persistent.

Why hadn't he called Sylvia? He knew I had two sisters in London, but it was possible, I realized, that he had never known Sylvia's married name.

I phoned Daphne at her office that afternoon. How are you, and let's have lunch sometime, and isn't Macmillan the end? And then she brought it up without my asking. A man had called her twice at home about me. He hadn't given his name, or if he had she had forgotten it, but he had said it was very urgent that he get in touch with me at once. He sounded American.

"And of course I couldn't help him, Carol, because I didn't know where you were. Where are you living now?"

I told Daphne I was living in New York, I was going back there the next day, but I would call her when I was in London again and we must have lunch then.

"Yes, do let's, and love to your — is it a boy or a girl you have?"

I said it was a girl and her name was Vanessa, but even if Daphne was still listening I didn't expect her to remember that.

I told Sylvia about Harrods that evening.

"He is a demon, isn't he? Do you think he's still in London?"

"I don't know."

He had been in London last month. "Well dressed." I knew Max had been prospering lately; there had been a column about Genesis in *Time* magazine. "The young addicts who come to Father Max for help are subjected to a discipline that seems harsh to many at first. But like a Victorian paterfamilias, Father Max believes that indulgence can foster the very weaknesses that led them into addiction . . ."

Max had found his followers at last and was working out his frustrations on them. What troubled me was that he had money now. He could afford to travel. He might even hire private detectives to look for us.

I called Arthur in New York and told him about the house in Ireland. He thought I had made a sensible decision. Ireland was a small, sparsely populated country; it was hard to lose yourself in it. But there was nothing in my past to connect me with it, no reason Max should think of searching for us there.

"But you'll have to start doing something about money pretty soon, Carol."

"I thought the insurance and Jason's investments, there was enough —"

Arthur interrupted me. He apologized; he hadn't meant it *that* way. *The Time of the Fire* was doing record business. Jason had been shrewd: he had held out for a percentage of the gross. A great deal of money would be coming in.

I arranged to have it put into a trust fund for Vanessa until she was eighteen.

"You'd better be good to her," Arthur warned me. "She's going to be a very wealthy young woman."

I stayed out of Chelsea, out of the West End, while I was in London. I got through at Harrods as quickly as I could. It was mostly the books and records I kept. I didn't want to put too much trust in Harrods' discretion; I had them crated and sent to Sylvia's. She would ship them on to Waterford.

"Don't worry, I won't give you away, darling. Not even if your demon kidnaps me and ties me to a bed and does *unimaginable* things to me." She sounded as though she rather hoped he would.

It was a rough crossing to Rosslare. The old boat wallowed around like a drowning cow, pulling itself out of the troughs with a shudder that rattled all her joints. When I saw Anton in his shabby tweed overcoat, waiting for us on the jetty, I felt as though I had come home after a long, perilous absence. We had only been gone five days.

We went back to the hotel, to the Sutreaus, the children. As I was putting Vanessa to bed that evening, she said, "I hope you're going to stop being so restless now."

For the rest of the winter I was busy with the builders, going to the house every day. I had them put on a new roof, strip and insulate and replaster every room, install a coal-fired central heating system, refit the doors, and double-glaze every window.

The builders thought I was eccentric. "What harm in a bit of damp?" But they took as much interest in the work as I did. I used to give them all a glass of stout before they left in the evenings. Then Anton would come by and we would go to the pub in the village.

"You know the house is going to be finished eventually," he said one evening in March.

"I hope so."

"What are you going to do then?"

I was planning to have a house party, all Vanessa's friends, as many as we could pack into all those rooms.

That wasn't what Anton meant. "You're not like me. You don't know how to putter."

"You think I'm one of those driving American career women, don't you, Anton? You're dead wrong. I've never had any real ambition in my life."

Anton shook his head. "You're intensely ambitious in your own way."

"Oh, come on. I was at that agency for five years, and I never for one instant wanted Harriet Bach's job."

"You had twenty or thirty writers dependent on you for their living. You took their manuscripts home with you and you fought to get them published."

"I never took *those* writers out for drinks in the evening."

Anton laughed. "All right, I'll pay for the next round. You're extraordinary, Carol. You don't know anything about yourself."

"Don't start on me with that Freud rubbish, please. I had enough of that —"

"I'm not talking about Freud. I'm talking about your character. You've set your mind on something all your life. Not the same thing, always one thing after another. To go to America, to get through secretarial school, to help that man Fitz. To get good scripts for that television show. To have a child. To see your husband's movie produced. You only imagine you're not ambitious because you're not the kind of person who thinks much about the future. And because to you most of the prizes that other people are after — to be powerful or rich or famous — are not worth having. But you have a very strong will and what you are interested in is *now*. Always the immediate objective. And I am afraid, Carol, that if you ever reach a time when there is nothing you want *now*, you will be very unhappy."

I wanted to tell him to go to hell because I was afraid he was right. Except for those two lost years in the Remo, I had never gone very long without a sense of immediate purpose.

"Okay. I'm going to retype all your manuscripts and get them published."

"The only way you'll do that is if you print them yourself."

"Fine. Then I will. I'll buy a printing press and set it up in the barn, and I'll start a company and publish all your books."

I was joking when I said it, but thinking it over during the next few days, I found myself more and more drawn to the idea. I would start cautiously, in a small way.

I went to the public library and took out some books on typesetting and binding. It interested me at once, spacing and design and all the different kinds of paper and the almost infinite varieties of type-face. When I saw a want ad in the *Cork Examiner* offering a printing press for sale, I drove over to look at it. It was a hand-powered press, made in England in the 1870s. The type had to be set letter by letter and then locked into the chase. It would take weeks to print a whole book on it, setting one signature of four pages at a time, running off the copies, then returning the type to the cases before beginning to set up the next signature.

I bought it and a week later two men carted it over in a truck and installed it in the barn for me.

"You see?" Anton said when I showed it to him. "Always the same Carol. First an idea, then a purpose. And then nothing can stop you."

"Oh, shut up. Look at it, Anton. Isn't it beautiful? The craftsmanship. The engraving on the lever. And that worm gear. It still works so smoothly, so precisely, after almost a hundred years."

"So will you, Carol." He touched my cheek. "You will always be beautiful."

It was the most personal thing he had ever said to me. The caress of his hand made me realize at once that I *was* attracted to him physically. My only reservation was the thought of going through all the preliminaries — the invitation, the acceptance, the rendezvous, the undressing. I wanted him to jump me right there in the barn. We would be lovers then, and we could go on being lovers without all those first-time formalities.

The grounds were full of children taking turns riding Vanessa's pony. One or even half a dozen of them might wander into the barn at any moment. The exhiliration of desire between us passed.

For a week I regretted the lost chance. I kept thinking of things I might have done. Why hadn't I just taken Anton down to the woods by the stream? Or into the old carriage house across the meadow? I was an idiot; I'd blown it.

Then one evening Vanessa had gone to spend the night with the Sutreaus and the woman who worked for me had gone home, but Anton hadn't. I cooked some pork chops and rice and we ate in the kitchen and then took our wine with us into the living room.

It was June and still light; the nights were like catnaps between sunset and dawn in Ireland in the summer. I was sitting on the sofa and Anton was in my chair, the one I liked to read in, on the other side of the fireplace. He was talking about Dublin during the war and I was only half listening. Well, this is it, I kept thinking, and I'm not going to blow it this time.

"Did you know I was married, Carol?"

I heard that all right. "No, I didn't."

"She was over twenty years older than I was and she had a house in Stephen's Green and she had been a friend of Yeats and George Moore and all those people. I was broke and it was very hard to find work in Dublin during the war, particularly if you were a foreigner. A lot of people said that was why I married her — her house and her private income and her connections. But it wasn't. I married her because I loved her. She was an extraordinary woman, shy and awkward in company, and there were a lot of stories about her, about the time she had gone to a ball at the Castle and had forgotten to take her overshoes off. Unkind stories. Because that was only one, unimportant side of her. When she was alone with me, she had a grace and delicacy of mind and of feeling, a quickness and a sensitivity — I loved her, Carol. It wasn't until she died that I ever had any thought about the money. I was grateful for it then. It was just enough to keep me in idleness, and" — he shrugged — "I wasn't like you. I didn't have your spirit and energy. I only wanted to be left alone to read and remember her and putter with my books."

I didn't know what to say. My earlier carnal thoughts seemed suddenly misplaced.

"I'm glad you told me, Anton."

"I had to tell you. I've been wanting to tell you for weeks because I was afraid you would hear about it from someone else and I wanted you to know the truth." He leaned forward in his chair. "You see, you're so beautiful to me, Carol. So infinitely beautiful and I have fallen in love with you."

I wished there wasn't so much light in the room. The sun through the French windows was like a spotlight on me. It was my cue and I didn't know my lines. I was on the wrong stage in the wrong play.

Anton lived in another, more romantic world than mine. A world of chivalry and troubadors and palely loitering knights. But I was not a faire and goodlye damsel, nor *La Belle Dame sans Merci.* It was no use pretending I was. I was a forty-two-year-old woman who wanted a friend and a companion and what Sylvia called a bit of macking. I liked Anton and I admired him and I cared for him, but I knew it would be hopeless to pretend I was anyone except myself.

I went over and closed the curtains. "Okay," I said. "Come on, Anton. I'm very fond of you and you can have me if you want to. But for God's sake let's not talk about it."

I had always known he was not a simple man. There were more sides to him than there were to me.

Anton laughed.

It was an unselfconscious laugh, filled with enjoyment. Then he came to me by the windows and held my face between his hands and kissed me.

I was wearing a loose woolen dress, fastened with a tie belt. There was no difficulty lifting that above my waist. But like an idiot I had put on tights. After I had kicked off my shoes, one of my heels got stuck in the damn things. Anton had to kneel and pull the tights off for me. I had expected him to be tentative, perhaps a little diffident. He wasn't anything of the kind. He had me on the sofa and he had me with a passion that surprised me. After the first minute my legs were up around his back and I was kissing him with an abandon that was part hunger and part gratitude.

He lay on top of me for a long time afterward and I didn't want him to move. When at last he stood up and put on his clothes, I turned on my side so that I could look at him, but I was still a long way from having the energy to stand on my feet. My contented exhaustion reminded me of something. It made me laugh.

"What are you laughing at?" He sat beside me and stroked my hair.

It was difficult to explain. I had remembered something Jason had once said about the Investment. "That poor klutz. All those experts who fucked her, but she never stayed fucked."

I had to tell Anton who the Investment was and what Jason had meant.

He still didn't quite understand. "What has that got to do with us?"

"Me. The way I feel this minute. I feel as though I'm going to stay fucked for the rest of my life."

*

Timmy came over in July and stayed for nine weeks. Together we printed the first book for the Connemara Press, as we called it. It was a short biography of Wolfe Tone that Anton had actually finished. Timmy was as interested in the printing process as I was. "It'll be a great asset in the revolution, being able to set type."

By the middle of August, we had three hundred copies in galleys. I bought a cutter and a press and we glued the pages and bound them in heavy mat paper. When Anton came over that evening, we presented him with a copy of his first published book.

"By Anton Krasny." He kept reading his name on the cover. "By Anton Krasny. I can't believe it. It's like a monument."

He would have been perfectly happy to leave it at that, three hundred monuments tucked away in the barn. I sent copies to the Dublin and Cork book editors with covering letters. I was afraid to sign the letters myself — I didn't want my name in the papers — so we invented an imaginary editor for the Connemara Press, Kevin Box, and carried on all our correspondence in his name.

Kevin Box got lucky at once. After all those years of isolation, Ireland had developed a familial pride about any local effort. The Irish *Times* gave *The Life and Death of Wolfe Tone* two favorable columns. A Dublin bookstore ordered fifty copies. The airports put it in their Books on Ireland racks. We sold out the first edition before Timmy left.

"I wish I could stay," he told me when I took him to Rosslare. "It's just the kind of thing I'd like to do, work with my hands at my own job like that."

"What about the revolution?" He was going to the London School of Economics that fall to prepare for it.

"I don't feel angry about anything here."

"You can come back at Christmas if you like," I told him as I saw him off on the jetty. "And at Easter, too, and of course next summer."

"I wish you weren't my aunt. I'd ask you to marry me."

I didn't want to marry anyone. Anton didn't press me. "It would look terrible if I married another wealthy woman," he admitted.

Although Vanessa was so occupied with her own friends that she would scarcely have noticed Anton's presence at breakfast, I was shy about letting him stay the night. We would go to his cottage outside Waterford or make love on the sofa in the living room after dinner when Vanessa was asleep. There was a lock on the barn door now and several times Anton did jump me there. He still surprised and delighted me with his willful passion.

Vanessa was six that October. Anton agreed with me that there was no point in sending her to school unless she insisted on going. I was teaching her French. Anton was teaching her history and mathematics, and she asked so many questions about everything, I had to buy a secondhand encyclopedia in Waterford to try to answer them.

One thing that did concern me a little was her religious education. I had promised to bring her up in the Jewish faith and I felt I owed it to Jason's parents to keep that promise. There was a small community of Jews in Waterford. I began to take Vanessa to the synagogue occasionally to say a prayer for her grandparents. One day she asked me if we were Jews, and when I said yes she wanted to know what a Jew was.

"Well, darling, the Sutreaus were brought up as Protestants and Anton was brought up a Catholic. And your Daddy and I were married by a Jewish rabbi and I promised I'd bring you up as a Jew."

"Anton doesn't believe in the Catholics."

"I know."

"And the Sutreaus don't believe in the Protestants. They hate those Protestants in Northern Ireland. You should hear what Catherine says about them."

"I know."

"Then why do you want me to believe in the Jews?"

"I don't want you to believe in anything you don't want to. I just want you to know about them and make up your own mind."

She thought that over for a few days and then she asked Anton, who, she was sure, knew all about everything, to tell her about the Jews. He started with Joseph and his brethren, and took her up through Judges and Kings to the Maccabees and the Diaspora. Vanessa was particularly fascinated by the flight from Egypt. She had just read *The Scarlet Pimpernel* and loved any stories of escape and pursuit. When Easter time came, she asked if we could celebrate the Passover.

Anton asked some Jewish friends, the Silvers, to invite us to their Seder. They lit the candles and the eldest Silver boy, David, read the passage from the Haggadah in Hebrew. On the way home, Vanessa made Anton tell her the whole story again and for the next few days she and her friends played crossing the Red Sea and the fall of Jericho.

"I'll be the Canaanites next time," I heard her promise one of the Sutreau children. "And you can blow the trumpet and be the Jews."

The Connemara Press continued to flourish. Irish writers began submitting manuscripts to Kevin Box. In the next year we published three of them. So long as they were Books on Ireland, we could count on a sale, through the airports and hotels and tourist shops, of fifteen hundred or even two thousand copies. Our production expenses were minimal, little more than the cost of the paper. The first year we showed a profit of 820 pounds.

I used part of the money to buy a sailboat and that summer before Timmy came over I made the mistake of trying to teach Vanessa to sail. She wanted to do everything herself at once and I knew how perilous a sailboat can be and I wouldn't let her. After that, whenever I suggested going out in the boat, she said she was too busy with her pony. It wasn't until four years later, when she was almost eleven, that she took to sailing.

That was in 1968. It was one of those years when history ran wild. Dubček and the Russian invasion of Czechoslovakia. The student protests in Paris that brought the whole city to a standstill in May. The assassinations of Martin Luther King and Robert Kennedy. Nixon in Miami and that other shameful travesty of a convention in Chicago. Riots on one campus after another and the lies and the lies and the lies from Vietnam.

When Timmy arrived at the beginning of June, he had come straight from Paris.

"It was such a wonderful month," he told me as we were eating in the kitchen his first evening. He had been with the students all the way, at the meetings at the Sorbonne, at the barricades in the streets. He had been clubbed and had seen his friends beaten unconscious and tossed into police vans.

"It was such a beautiful revolution. There was no doctrine, no dogma. They questioned everything. Why should we work making things we don't need so we can earn the money to buy them? That's a more revolutionary idea than anything Marx ever thought of. And we failed because we were right. Because we didn't have any leaders. We didn't believe in leaders."

"Write a book about it, Timmy, and I'll publish it for you."

He didn't want to write. He wanted to think. He had graduated from the London School of Economics the year before and he wasn't sure what he wanted to do next.

The phone was ringing. I answered it. A woman asked to speak to Kevin Box.

Kevin Box was becoming a nuisance, but I still needed him. There hadn't been a move from Max in six years and I hardly ever thought about him anymore, but if my name appeared in the Irish papers, there was always the chance of some American press service picking it up. I didn't want Max reading about Carol Stone and what she was doing in Ireland. The trouble was that as we published more Irish writers they kept coming to the house wanting to meet their editor, Kevin Box. I got tired of making up stories about him, that he was on vacation, on a business trip, sick in bed with laryngitis.

"You talk to her." I handed the phone to Timmy. "See what she wants."

"Hello," Timmy said. "Yes, this is Kevin Box speaking."

The woman was from the *Cork Examiner* and she wanted to do a story about the Connemara Press. She wanted to come over the next afternoon and interview Mr. Box.

That was how it began, as a charade.

Timmy was twenty-three and we thought Kevin Box ought to be a little older than that. He used glasses for reading so he wore them for the interview, slicked back his hair, and put on a suit and a tie. When he told the woman reporter he was twenty-eight, she wrote it down without questioning it for a second. He told her a lot of other lies, too. He said he had been born in Dublin and had graduated from Trinity College and had worked for a while on an underground newspaper in England before returning to Ireland and starting the Connemara Press.

The woman had brought a photographer with her, and a few days later there it all was in the *Cork Examiner* with a picture of Kevin Box working at his printing press.

Vanessa thought it was great fun, this game we had made up. She took to calling Timmy Mr. Box. After a while I didn't think it was so amusing. It was a bore. Now that Kevin Box had surfaced, more and more people wanted to meet him. They kept showing up at the house — writers, reviewers, literary hangers-on from Dublin. Timmy saw them all and told them the same lies. The Sylvia side of him thought it was a great lark.

"What am I going to do when you leave?" I asked him one evening. "What am I going to tell all these floods of people?"

"Why do I have to leave?"

We talked it over. Sylvia had come to stay for two weeks that summer and I knew she wouldn't mind. "I think it's wonderful, being a publisher," she had told him. "You might even become famous like the Olympia Press." There was Nigel, of course. He was Sir Nigel now. He was still trying to push Timmy into making what he called a decent career for himself. But Timmy had hardly spoken to his father for years, and I didn't think he was going to let Nigel push him into anything. At least he would have a steady job if he stayed. The distribution side of the business was becoming too demanding for me to handle alone.

"But I'm not going to have you starting any of that Paris business in County Waterford. I live here and I like it the way it is."

"I'm not interested in County Waterford. Not in that way, anyhow."

He *was* interested in Northern Ireland in that way. The civil rights movement was growing in the six counties. There were demonstrations and marches. The Paisley fanatics and the bloody B. Specials reacted the way Faubus and Bull Connor had in the deep South, with hatred and violence. I was incensed about it too, but Timmy was more active. As Kevin Box he had come to know a lot of people in Dublin and he was soon going up there to meetings every week. Through his Dublin friends he met Hume and Bernadette Devlin, and by the end of the summer he was going to Belfast and Derry as well and taking part in the marches.

Vanessa started school that fall. There was a Quaker school in Newtown just outside Waterford. One of the Silver children, Elsie, was going there. After that first Seder, we had seen more and more of the Silvers and Elsie had become Vanessa's best friend. The idea of being parted from Elsie all week was more than Vanessa could bear. She wanted to go to Newtown too, as a weekly boarder. She would be eleven in October and I thought it was time she went to school anyway. She had an immense store of general information, acquired mainly from Anton and the encyclopedia, but she had hardly touched algebra or geometry and, for all her reading, her spelling was abominable.

She came home every Friday evening for the weekend. She usually brought three or four friends with her. It had been so simple when they were small and could be given soup and rice pudding and tucked away four or five to a room. Now that they were older their needs were more complicated. They were very good about making their own beds and washing up, but some weekends, when Kevin Box had friends staying too, I was busy all day shopping and cooking and serving meals. I had a woman to help me during the week, but she wouldn't work Saturdays or Sundays and I didn't blame her.

I wasn't going to stop Vanessa from inviting her friends home — that was the whole point of having such a big house — but Kevin Box's guests were another matter. They drank a good deal and sat up all night talking and wanted breakfast and glasses of stout at odd hours. Sometimes when I went in to do the shopping on Monday morning, the whole back seat of the car would be filled with empty bottles to return to the pub. Besides, they insisted on talking politics at meals and Vanessa and her friends had to shut up and listen to them.

I didn't want Timmy to leave. I did want Kevin Box and his civil rights groups to have some place of their own where I wouldn't have to wait on them. There was the old carriage house across the meadow, which had once seemed to me a good place to seduce Anton. It seemed a good place to settle Timmy in now. It was pretty much a ruin, but the stone walls were still sound and it was quite a large building. A hundred years ago the people who built the house had kept two coaches in it, and upstairs there had been a dormitory for the grooms and gardeners. Best of all, there had been a separate drive to it from the road, and if I had it cleared and resurfaced, Kevin Box's political friends could come and go without my even having to see them.

The cost of building was going up every year; the sooner I got started on it the better. I went to see Mr. Coughlan, the builder who had done the house for me. He gave me an estimate and his men started work in November.

Timmy moved in on the tenth of April. The driveway had been cleared and he had his own gate with a small wooden sign that said "Connemara Press. Kevin Box, Editor and Publisher."

I remember the date because Anton scratched it on the wall of the barn to commemorate the day the Irish government announced the Finance Act of 1969. Anton was wildly excited about it. "No taxes," he kept saying as we listened to the news on the radio. "Just think of it. It's the most civilized act any government has ever passed. No income taxes for artists. For writers or painters or composers or sculptors. No taxes for poets."

"You've never paid any income tax in your life, Anton."

"That's not the point. It's the idea of it, Carol."

Over the next year I saw in the Irish *Times* that a number of English and American writers had bought houses around Dublin. I read this news with no more interest than the weather forecast.

It wasn't until two years later, in 1971, that it became any concern of mine. I was shopping in Waterford one afternoon in July. After finishing the shopping, I went to the Eldon Hotel for a drink. There were only three or four people in the saloon bar. I sat down at my usual corner table with a newspaper and a Guinness.

It wasn't until I was almost ready to leave that I noticed a man standing at the bar.

He was thin and white haired and well dressed in a way that didn't suit him. He must have been over fifty and his black polo-necked sweater and flared trousers were too young for him. He turned his head a little and I saw he was wearing dark glasses.

It was Chris Deniken.

Twenty-Three

Y ou should have married me."

"Oh, shut up."

"You should never have left me, Carol."

Chris and I were walking across the fields to his house. I hadn't wanted him to buy the house. I didn't want him living in the neighborhood. I had told him he would be much happier nearer Dublin. He had gone ahead and bought it anyway, a farm cottage with three acres of land.

When he had asked me to recommend a builder and to keep an eye on the work, I decided I might as well be helpful about it. If he was going to live a few miles away and go to the post office and the shops and pubs in the same small village, there was no point in getting into one of those bleak situations where we had to pretend not to notice each other.

The house was finished now; we were going out to look at it together before he moved in.

"You should have married me while you had the chance."

"Don't be a bloody fool, Chris."

I felt it was time to get the past straight between us. It all seemed so long ago, I could hardly remember what he had looked like in those Remo days; but I was tired of his waspish accusations.

"I didn't walk out on *you.* You went off to California with Iris and left me sitting in New York waiting to hear from you. Now I'm glad you did, because it would have been hopeless anyway."

"Why would it have been hopeless?"

"Because the first thing that went wrong, you'd have given up on me. The way you give up on everything."

"I've written eight books. Two of them were on the *Times* bestseller list. I've written three movies that got made, including one for your husband. Although he screwed me out of my solo screen credit."

"You gave up on that when Jason needed you for the final rewrites."

We had reached the edge of a field. I clambered onto the old wall of piled stones and jumped down the other side. Chris followed me. His foot slipped and knocked one of the stones off. He obviously wasn't going to do anything about it. I picked it up and set it back in its place. He watched me.

"You still have a hell of a nice ass, you know that?"

"We have a sort of agreement with the farmers. There are no trespassing laws in Ireland. You can go anywhere you like. But we close their gates behind us and if we knock a stone off their walls we put it back."

"Sure, you know. You wouldn't wear those tight pants if you didn't know you had such a nice ass."

I walked on. He caught up with me.

"Why don't you ever go to the States, Carol?"

"I don't want to live under Nixon."

We skirted a clump of gorse.

"Were you happy with that guy, Jason?"

"Yes. Very happy. That's why I'm glad you went off with Iris. If you hadn't, I might not have married Jason."

"He couldn't give you a child, could he?"

I kept walking. I was shocked and angry and uneasy and I didn't want him to see it.

"You may not have noticed, but Jason and I had a daughter. Her name's Vanessa and she'll be fifteen next birthday."

"She's not Jason's daughter."

"As a matter of fact, you talked to her in the pub yesterday, so you may have noticed her. She looks rather like Jason. She's got his hair and his forehead and she has a lot of his character. She sticks to things."

"Jason couldn't have kids. He was sterile."

"Who told you that shit?" I hardly ever used words like that anymore; it seemed natural, talking to Chris.

"A guy I met in California. Guy I met through Iris."

"How is Iris?"

"She's a big deal in that Genesis racket. She and the creep who runs it. That megalomaniac who calls himself Father Max. I saw them out on the coast and he kept storming on and on about Jason not being the father of your —"

"I hope you gave Iris my regards."

"I didn't know where you were then. It was before I ran into you at the hotel here."

"Have you seen them since?"

"Why?"

We had reached the edge of another field. I sat back against the wall and looked at him.

"Have you seen them since?"

"No."

I climbed over the wall. Chris followed me.

"He was madly interested in you. Kept asking me if I knew where you were."

"Did he?" I had to keep him talking about it. I had to know exactly what Max had said. "Why was he so interested in me? I haven't seen him for years."

"He said you'd kidnapped his child and disappeared with her."

"Oh, come on." I stopped and made myself look at him again. "What kind of shit is that? I suppose you believed it. You said yourself the man's a megalomaniac. He's a compulsive liar, too."

"Maybe."

"If you must know, he kept writing to me for years. Insane threatening letters about Vanessa. I had to get my lawyer to stop him. We went to the D.A.'s office in Los Angeles and got a restraining order against that fucking lunatic."

I was shouting. It didn't matter now; the angrier I sounded, the more convincing I would be. "I'm going to write to my lawyer about *this*. What you just told me. I'm not going to have that prick going around saying I kidnapped his child. I'm going to sue him. I'm going to —"

Careful. Don't go too far. You might have to follow through on it.

We were in sight of the cottage. "Oh, forget it. I don't want to talk about that maniac. Let's go and see your house."

The builders had done a good job.

"Well, I hope you like it," I told Chris after he had inspected it. "I hope you'll be comfortable here."

"Remember that time I laid you in a sailboat?"

I did my best to smile. I didn't think he would write to Iris or Max about me if we were going to be running into each other in the village all the time. But it was difficult to know what Chris would do. He had always been unpredictable. He had always been a shit, too.

"Are you going to spend most of your time in Ireland now?"

"You mean, am I going back to the coast?"

It was what I had meant. I didn't answer.

"You mean, am I going to tell that Father Max creep where you are?"

"You can tell him anything you fucking well like. I'm going to write to my lawyer about what you told me. And if you do go back to the coast I'd like you to give my lawyer a statement so I can take Max Ludlow to court."

I walked to the door. Chris came out to the drive with me.

Don't say any more now, I decided. Leave it at that. Chris wouldn't want to get mixed up with lawyers and court cases.

I walked away up the drive.

"You've still got a hell of a nice ass, Carol."

I told Anton all about it after dinner that evening.

"What do you think, darling?" I asked him. "What do you think Chris will do?"

"Why should he do anything?"

"Because he walked out on me all those years ago. And he blames me for it. And he wants to get back at me. Besides, I think he'd probably like to lay me."

"That I can understand."

Anton was sitting on the sofa and I was in my reading chair.

Over the years we had settled into that arrangement; it was part of Anton's complex delicacy. He would still sometimes jump me in the barn, but not in my living room. If I wanted him to make love to me there, I would go to him on the sofa.

"Do you think he believed you when you told him you didn't care if Max Ludlow does find you?"

"I don't know. I'm afraid not. You see, Chris knows so many of those movie people on the coast, people Jason and I used to see all the time. Some of them must have asked sometime, Whatever happened to Carol Stone? Not one of them's heard a word from me since Jason died. And then Chris runs into me in Ireland and he finds I've been living here for ten years. Ten years without sending anyone a Christmas card. He knows I've been hiding here, Anton, and now, after talking to Max, he knows why."

"Does she look like Max?"

"Not much." I had never been sure of the answer to that question. "Sometimes. A gesture. An expression in her eyes. The way she holds her head when she's listening. Probably nothing anyone else would notice."

"She is his daughter, isn't she?"

"Yes, of course she is. I've always known that."

Anton stood up and poured us both more wine.

"Does she remember Jason?"

"Not clearly. In flashes, I think. She was only four when he died. A couple of years ago I showed her some pictures of him. She looked puzzled, mostly."

"Very few people have any continuous memory of things that happened before they were four."

"I know. It's so strange. She was so close to Jason. He was her Daddy and she absolutely adored him. Now she can hardly remember him at all."

"What are you going to do about Chris Deniken?"

"There's nothing I can do."

"Try to keep him friendly?"

The quizzical way Anton asked that made me laugh.

"Don't worry. I'm not going to let him screw me."

Chris kept trying. It became a stupid, rather disagreeable game. Days, weeks would go by without my seeing him, then I would run into him in the post office or he would call and invite me over for a drink. I went to his house several times, but never alone; I took Timmy or David Silver or Anton with me. Chris would try to maneuver me into the garden or out to the studio he was building. If he did corner me alone for a minute, he would start in at once about my boobs or my ass or remind me of the time he had laid me on the floor at Charles Street or humped me over the coffee table or whatever.

"Do you remember?" he would say.

Most of the time I didn't. I remembered the sailboat because that had been a first. But the coffee table was a blank to me.

He went to New York for three months in the fall. It was a relief to have him out of sight, out of mind.

I was increasingly worried about Timmy at that time. He was still living in the carriage house, but he was away more and more, not just in Dublin or Belfast, but in Amsterdam and Paris and Berne. When he was home I would occasionally see people going to the carriage house to talk to Kevin Box. They were a different kind of people now. They didn't look like writers or literary hangers-on. They were young men in raincoats or older men in dark business suits. Some of their cars were Rovers or Mercedes.

The situation in Northern Ireland had changed completely after August 12, 1969.

Timmy had been there, in Derry, that whole week. When the fighting broke out he had used his car as an ambulance, taking the wounded out of the Bogside until the B. Specials overturned and set fire to it. After that, he was on the roof of a warehouse all night, helping to defend it against the screaming, jeering Protestants until they set fire to that, too.

"It wasn't like Paris," he told me when he came back. "It was insane, hysterical. Those Prods — not just the paramilitary thugs, but ordinary shopkeepers and shipyard workers — were out to kill every Catholic they could lay their hands on. If they had managed to break through into the Bogside, it would have been a massacre. We couldn't have held out another twenty-four hours if the British hadn't sent in troops to protect us."

"What's going to happen now?"

"The British soldiers are heroes now. The Catholics cheered them when they marched into the Bogside. But that won't last. After a while the army'll start siding with the others. They can't help it. The Protestants are their own people. They're pro-British. Then the poor bloody Catholics will have the troops to fight as well as the Prods. And there'll be no one to help them. Their only hope is something like the old IRA and they're bloody useless." During the fighting, the leaders in the Bogside had tried to get in touch with the IRA, Timmy told me. "There isn't any IRA. Half a dozen old men sitting around the Dublin pubs, reliving the great days of Michael Collins and squabbling about Marx. They haven't got anything, no organization, no money, nothing."

A few months later that changed, too. The Provos split off from the old IRA and within a year they did have money. And they had guns.

I didn't know how deeply Timmy was involved with them. He didn't want me to know.

"Don't worry," he assured me. "I'm not doing anything criminal. Old Kevin Box just acts as a post office for a few of the lads who need a safe address, or a place to meet and sort things out."

I soon realized that wasn't all he was doing.

Timmy had less and less time for the Connemara Press. I didn't mind that. David Silver had just graduated from Trinity and he didn't want to go into his father's jewelry business. He began to come over and set type and help with the binding until his father agreed to let me give him a regular job. He was a nice boy with long hair and a thin, delicate face, hard working and reliable and a natural editor. He didn't want to write, but he cared deeply about other people's writing.

After he had been working for me a few months, I decided it was time to drop Kevin Box altogether and make David chief editor and publisher. That September of '72, when Chris was in New York, I talked the idea over with Timmy.

"Well, I can't exactly drop Kevin Box," he said. "I know he's pretty useless to you these days. But I still need him. More and more."

"Don't you think it's time you told me what you're doing, Timmy?"

"No." The suggestion obviously dismayed him. "It's, well, it's safer for you if you don't know. But I can promise you one thing. I'm not doing anything that could make any trouble for the Connemara Press."

"Of course it could make trouble for the Connemara Press. That bloody Kevin Box *is* the Connemara Press."

"No, he isn't. Not anymore. My people think that's just a front. The trouble is it's *my* front. And it's the only one I've got, and I can't just drop it."

"What do you mean, front? Everybody in the village knows you're not Kevin Box. They know you're my nephew."

"Well that's all right, isn't it? I'm your nephew and you're Carol Stone, an American, and nobody knows much about you, really, do they?"

His voice trailed away into silence. I waited a minute.

"Go on, Timmy. Tell me what you're getting at. Go on."

"It didn't matter at the beginning, before sixty-nine. Hume and Devlin and Farrel and the others, they didn't care who I was. I was just another left-wing type who'd been beaten up in Paris during the protests there. Most of them were more or less Trotskyists, anyway, so Paris was fine with them, and they just accepted me. Good old Kevin, who was willing to get beaten up in their protest marches, too. It's different with these new men. They're up to their necks in —"

He made a quick dismissive gesture with his hand.

"Well, they're up to their necks in conspiracy of one kind or another and they don't trust anybody. They know my real name probably isn't Kevin Box. But they're used to assumed names. Their good friend who arranged credit for them in Prague, they don't think his real name is Mr. Freeman, either. But at least they don't know . . ." His voice trailed away again. He was sitting hunkered up on the sofa in the living room. Most of the time he had been talking, he had been staring at the floor, at his hands, at his knees. He looked up at me now. I was shocked by his eyes. They were the eyes of a prisoner, pleading and frightened.

"At least they don't know my father's Sir Bloody Nigel at the British Foreign Office."

It was no use Timmy's dismissing what the Provos were up to. Everybody knew what they were up to. It was in the papers and on the evening news. They were raising money in the United States and they were getting handguns and automatic rifles and explosives and even bazookas from all over Europe. There was a story that some of the arms were coming in from the Communist countries.

I asked Anton what he thought about that.

"The Soviets wouldn't care what those people believe in," he told me. "Whether they're left wing or right wing or what they think they're fighting for. They're a disruptive force. That's the way the KGB would look at it. And they'd be glad to help them. Give them a little lend-lease through the Czech arms industry."

I remembered what Timmy had said about the Provos' good friend Mr. Freeman, who had arranged credit for them in Prague. The more I thought about it, the more vulnerable Timmy's position seemed. As a revolutionary, he was such a romantic, and I no longer believed there was anything romantic about the IRA's activities in Northern Ireland. Whenever he was home, I kept nagging at him to drop it, to get out. He would listen and shrug. Sometimes I saw that look in his eyes again.

Chris returned in the new year. He called and asked me over for a drink. I knew I had to see him; he might have something to tell me about Max. I made a date with him at the beginning of February.

"And don't bring anyone with you," he said. "I want to talk to you alone."

I was going to ask him what about, but he hung up on me.

It was a cold, rainy day; I drove over around six.

He had lit a wood fire, and with the shaded lamps at either end of the mantlepiece the room looked like a cottage in a children's book. I sat on one of the built-in benches with my drink. I was wearing a tweed skirt, not in the least tight across my ass, and a cardigan that made my boobs look like a rolled blanket. I didn't want to give Chris any excuse for imagining I had come there to be seduced. I had come to find out if Chris had seen Iris.

He was sitting on the other side of the fireplace. He had a drink and a cigarette and he was just sitting there, waiting. It was an old trick of his to force the other person to speak first; he would make me question him about Max. I decided to wait him out. While I waited, I looked at him, the foppish clothes, those creepy shades hiding his eyes. What had I ever seen in him that I should have wept for him once?

"It's incredible how attractive you still are, Carol," he said at last. "Sexually attractive."

"Thanks."

"You don't even look forty."

"I'll be fifty-two in March."

There was another silence. This time I broke it. "You said you wanted to talk to me. What about?"

"Us."

"What about us?"

"I kept thinking about you all the time I was in New York. Remembering the way you used to be and the way you are now. It made me realize something. I was an idiot to let you go."

"We went over all that."

"I want you back."

"No, thanks," I didn't want to antagonize him too much. "I'm too old for casual affairs, thank you, Chris. And even if I wasn't —"

"I'm not talking about a casual affair. I'm talking about the way things used to be between us. If you think it would be awkward living together in a little village like this, okay, we'll get married."

Married? Marry *him?* He was out of his mind.

"No, thanks," I said again. And again I felt the need for caution. "I'm not going to marry anyone. I've got my own life. And I'm very happy with it. I've got a business to run and a big house and a child. And I've got Anton."

"Anton?" He stood up. "What the fuck good is he to you? That poor, bedraggled lame dog you picked up somewhere. It's time you got rid of that loser, Carol."

That made me very angry. I wanted to defend Anton, to explain him. But I knew it was useless to try. Chris could never understand Anton, his strength, that incorruptible honor that rested on self-respect. Chris had never had any self-respect, only a reckless vanity.

"I sure as hell don't need you as a husband, anyway," I said.

"Yes, you do. You do, Carol."

I heard the threat in his voice. I waited. He took my glass and his own and refilled them.

"I know it's sort of crazy. All the time I was in New York I kept thinking about it. Why have I got such an obsession about *you?* But I guess I know why. Because you're the only important thing in my life I ever missed out on. It was as much your fault as it was mine, the way we both were back then in the Village, but I screwed it up. Years later when I saw you in London, when I was working on that movie for your husband, seeing you two together, I couldn't get it out of my mind. I kept thinking *I* could have had you."

He stopped and took a drink.

"Then this last month in New York I realized something else. Okay, I missed out on you. But it wasn't too late. I could still have you. Maybe you think that's crazy. But I mean it. I'm going to have you. I'm not going to go on for the rest of my life feeling I screwed things up forever between us when I went off with Iris. Regretting it. Blaming the past for it."

If he hadn't been so obviously distressed by what he was saying, I would have laughed.

"I'm sorry, Chris," I said. "But it *is* too late now. It was all over years and years ago."

"No, it wasn't. It isn't too late. We can still make it together the way we used to."

I didn't want what was left of my drink. It had stopped raining. I picked up my raincoat and walked to the door.

Chris was standing in front of it. "I could force you to come back to me, Carol."

He smelled of American cigarettes and expensive cologne.

"Please let me by. We're both too old to wrestle in doorways."

"Okay, you don't have to decide at once." He didn't move, but his voice was reasonable, no longer distressed. "I'll give you three months, if you like —"

"I've already decided."

"You didn't let me finish. I'll give you until May. Then you're going to have to come back to me."

"Oh, come on." I was sick of this. "Will you please let me by."

"You're going to have to because you're such a good mother. You've taken such good care of your daughter all these years. Kept her hidden away here in Ireland. And I don't blame you. I wouldn't want any child to have Max Ludlow for a father." He stepped away from the door. "I wouldn't want him around, screwing up Vanessa's life."

"I don't understand a man like that," Anton said.

"He doesn't understand you either, darling."

I had driven straight to Anton's house after leaving Chris. I was suddenly terribly hungry. Anton had made me a huge bacon and cheese sandwich while I was telling him what had happened. I was sitting in his armchair, eating it.

"Do you think he means it? Do you think he would really be so cruel? He would hurt a child?"

"Chris isn't cruel. He's just careless. He hurts people the way he leaves the farmers' gates open — the hell with them."

"But do you really believe he will write to Max?"

"I don't know."

"You don't sound —"

"I don't care." I swallowed my mouthful of sandwich. "I was thinking about it while I was driving here. I kept wondering why I wasn't more worried. Now that I've had something to eat, I know I'm not worried at all. I'm relieved."

I put the last two crusts of bread in my mouth. Anton held up a bottle of wine, offering it to me. I nodded.

"For over eleven years, ever since Jason died, I've been hiding Vanessa from Max. I'm glad I did. I think it would have been terrible for her if he'd broken into her life while she was still a child, still had some memory of Jason. I think Max is dangerous and destructive and slightly insane and I'm glad I kept her away from him."

I drank some wine.

"I'm glad I brought Vanessa to Ireland. I think she's had a wonderful childhood here. Growing up in a village where everybody knows her and says Hullo, Vanessa. She's felt welcome everywhere ever since we came and I think it's been very important to her. It's given her a kind of confidence in herself that she'll never lose."

Anton nodded, agreeing with me.

"Anyway, she's fifteen now, and when Chris gave me that stupid ultimatum I thought, For God's sake, what am I doing? Am I going to try to hide Vanessa for the rest of my life? It's ridiculous, Anton, and not only ridiculous, it's impossible. Vanessa isn't going to want to live in Ireland forever. She's American and she's going to want to see her own country and travel around and go to Europe. And she should. She should go anywhere she likes."

Anton was holding his hand in front of his eyes, rubbing the bridge of his nose.

"You're going to tell her?"

"Of course I'm going to tell her."

He rubbed his forehead.

"Come on, Anton. What's the matter?"

"I wonder how she's going to feel about it. About you. Her mother. The things you're going to have to tell her about yourself."

"They're very good in that Quaker school, very frank and open."

"How many children in that school have divorced parents?"

"I don't know. I don't know of any."

"How many of their mothers are having affairs?"

"Well, I am, aren't I?"

"And you've done everything you could to hide it from her. I've never stayed over at your house." Anton poured some more wine. "I'm not saying you shouldn't tell Vanessa the truth about her father now. I think you're absolutely right to tell her. But I'm not sure how she's going to react to it."

Neither was I, now that I thought about it. Would she be shocked? She had more freedom with boys than I had had at her age, sailing, riding, going camping with them. But there was an extraordinary sexual innocence about those Irish boys. I had seen them help Vanessa ashore from their boats, handling her as unselfconsciously, as *indifferently,* as they handled a sail bag. And she appeared to feel the same way about them. She had formed close, rather romantic attachments to a series of best friends, but she had never shown the least interest in clothes or makeup.

And she was beautiful. That was the most astonishing part of it. She was absolutely lovely, with great dark blue eyes, small delicate features, and her skin was like Chinese porcelain. And she didn't seem to know it.

"Listen." I had a sudden, excited idea. "It's high time Vanessa saw something more of the world than Waterford. Have you got a passport?"

"I have my Irish citizenship papers."

"In June. As soon as she's out of school, we'll all go off together. We'll go to London and Paris and the south of France and Venice and maybe to New York. Vanessa can invite Elsie Silver to come with us."

"I don't know . . ."

"If you're worried about money, the Connemara Press can give you an advance."

"It's not the money. I've been a kept man for so long . . ." Anton smiled, a quick shameless smile that reminded me of Jason ordering champagne in Rome. "It's just the idea. I haven't been out of Ireland for over thirty years."

"All the more reason."

"I don't know."

It was an unexpected revelation to me, an unsuspected facet of Anton's character. It touched me. I went over and put my arms around him.

"It's not all that scary out there, darling. I'll look after you."

He leaned against me. I could smell the tweed of his jacket, the fresh soap scent of his skin. In the past few years, that combination had become a practically infallible aphrodisiac to me.

We went into Anton's small bedroom and for the next twenty minutes I was the happiest woman in County Waterford, in an oblivious way. When I finally, slowly regained my mind, I saw that he was laughing.

"What's so funny? You bastard, Anton. What are you laughing at?"

"Myself. For feeling so scared just now. What can they do to me?"

"Send you back to Prague and shoot you."

"Yes." He propped himself on his elbow. "That's exactly what I was frightened of. The irrational fears of a refugee. They'll send me back and the police . . . Oh, my God —" He grabbed my arm. "I forgot to tell you."

"What?"

"The police were here this afternoon."

Two plainclothesmen from Dublin. They had been very friendly and polite and Irish. They wanted to ask him a few questions about Kevin Box. Anton had offered them a drink, which they had accepted, and had started to talk about the Connemara Press, what a fine editor Kevin Box —.

That wasn't what they were interested in. What about Mr. Box's background, his family?

"I realized, of course, they were trying to find out the truth about Timmy."

"What did you say?"

"Nothing. I told them I didn't know anything. I showed them that old interview in the *Cork Examiner*. They said they had seen it and thank you. Then, just before they left, one of them said you could never trust newspapers, could you? Trinity College had never heard of Mr. Box."

I jumped out of bed and started to dress. Anton followed me into the living room.

"Would you like me to come with you?"

I shook my head; I thought it would be better if I talked to Timmy alone. Anton came out to the car with me. By that time I had had a chance to think it all over a little. Only one thing really frightened me.

"Are you *sure* they were from the police, Anton?"

They had shown him their identification. Sergeants Burke and Costello. Both in their forties. Costello had a mustache. Burke didn't.

"Burke? Costello?" Neither the names nor the descriptions meant anything to Timmy.

"They might have been from the police," he said. "Although I don't know why the police would be interested in my background."

I hadn't been in the carriage house for weeks. There were dirty glasses and dishes and cigarette ends all over the room. I didn't like the way Timmy looked, either. He reminded me of Max that winter in Rome. There was the same listlessness in him.

"If I called Dublin," I suggested, "would they tell me if they had two men called Burke and Costello?"

"Probably not. Not if they were from the special branch. Maybe I could find out. I could ask around."

I couldn't stand it, that flat fatalism. It had upset me in Max; it seemed much worse in Timmy. He was only twenty-eight and he was so bright, so kind. That day at the London airport, the way he had taken charge of Vanessa. It made me furious to see him like this. I had to do *something*. I started to pick up the dirty dishes and carry them into the kitchen. There was even more of a mess in there. I ran hot water into the sink and dumped everything into it.

I was almost finished when Timmy joined me. He leaned against the draining board, smoking a cigarette.

"For God's sake, Timmy." I couldn't help it; I was shouting at him. "What do you think you're doing? You know those thugs in the IRA don't stand for a damn thing anymore. They don't want a united Ireland any more than Paisley does. They're nothing but a bloody Mafia. They've got a hold on the Catholic districts and it's like a protection racket. They've got their own people terrorized and all they're out for is themselves. Their own organization. Their own power. They break every truce as soon as they sign it. They don't want the fighting and the killing to stop. Ever. They'd be in the shits if it ever ended."

"It didn't start like that." Timmy put out his cigarette; at least he did it in an ashtray. "Things deteriorate. Friendships, marriages, revolutions. Everything. People deteriorate."

I didn't believe that. Some people did. Max. Chris. Jason hadn't. Neither had Anton. "Not everybody," I told Timmy. "And I don't think you have. Not really. Not yet."

"What do you want me to do?"

"Get out. Go back to England. Anywhere. Get out of the whole filthy mess."

Timmy shook his head slowly, helplessly. "That's the worst thing I could do. Run. It would be absolutely fatal if I tried to make a run for it now."

He did seem a little less defeated over the next few days. He shaved; he exercised Vanessa's pony; he helped David with the press. Then, toward the end of the week, I noticed the carriage house was closed. There were no lights in it at night. Timmy had gone. I hoped he had gotten out, broken with those people. I was afraid it was more likely they had sent him on another of their bloody errands.

I had called Vanessa and asked her not to bring anyone home with her that weekend. I met her at the bus stop on Friday evening. We had supper in the kitchen.

"What is it?" she asked when she had cleared away our plates. "Has something happened to Timmy?"

"No."

"Then what is it? Oh, come on. You've got something to tell me."

I said Well, three or four times. And then I told her.

I tried to be as honest as I could, but I left things out. Mostly things about Max. If I was going to present her with a live father, all at once, after letting her think he was dead for eleven years, I wanted to present her with the best side of him first. I said I had been in love with Max for years. I had met him again in Rome. Jason and I couldn't have children and we had had a disagreement and Jason was in Madrid and, well, it had just sort of happened and I'd found I was pregnant. "And I was so happy and I wanted so much to have a child, darling, and it all turned out so wonderfully. I mean, it was you."

She had only interrupted me once or twice, funny detailed questions. How old was I then? Was Max living in a hotel?

When I had finished, she didn't say anything. She went over and started to wash the dishes.

I couldn't stand it for more than a minute.

"Vanessa."

"What?"

"For heaven's sake, say something."

"I'm thinking."

She stacked the dishes and came back to the table and sat down.

"I don't understand it," she said coldly.

"What? What, darling? What don't you understand?"

"I don't understand how you could behave like that."

Oh, God, she thinks I'm a slut. Anton was right. She'll never forgive me for being such a slut.

"Darling, I tried to explain —"

"I hate you."

She was looking at me, with accusing, dark eyes. Then, all at once, her delicate porcelain face was splintered with rage. Her mouth was half-open, the corners of her lips pulled down, and she seemed for an instant to be struggling to control herself and then with an angry shrug to discard all control.

"I hate you. I think you're *horrible.*"

I was on my feet, trying to move around the table to her, to take her in my arms, as though that were the only way I could defend myself.

She stepped away from me so fiercely it was like a slap.

"Why didn't you tell me?"

I stood there, stupidly shaking my head.

"Why didn't you tell me?" she repeated furiously.

"Darling, when —"

"How could you lie to me like that? All this *time.*"

"Darling, when you were small, you loved Jason —"

"I can hardly remember him."

She was telling me I knew that, and it was no use pretending I didn't.

"I know, but then later —"

How could I explain why I hadn't told her later without admitting the truth about her father?

"Then later, I wanted to wait until you were old enough to understand."

"You treat me like a baby."

We were still confronting each other across the table. If I could only touch her, hold her. I knew she wouldn't let me. I sat down. I must let her do what *she* wanted. I must let her accuse me.

"Go on," I said. "Tell me what I should have done."

"You treat me like a child. You and Anton. You don't even trust me enough to be honest about that. You have to pretend —" She brushed the back of her hand across her eyes. "I suppose you thought I'd be shocked if I knew you were going to bed with him."

Yes, I had thought that. I couldn't think of any way of explaining why now.

"As if it *mattered.*"

I was startled by the contempt with which she said that. In it was all the scorn reason feels for convention, candor for prudery.

"I suppose you thought if you told me Jason wasn't my father, I'd blame you for — for that too. I'd think you didn't have any self-control at all."

Self-control? She was centuries ahead of me, ethically.

"No, Vanessa, I didn't think —"

"It was a hateful thing to do." She brushed her hand across her eyes again. "All the time you knew my real father was alive and you wouldn't let me see him."

I was going to have to tell her at least part of the truth after all. "Max and I had quarreled, Vanessa. We had quarreled very badly. Very bitterly. He lives in California" — what the hell did that have to do with it? — "and I was afraid he'd make trouble. I was afraid he'd try to take you away from me."

"Why couldn't you let me make up my own mind? Why couldn't you ask me if I wanted to see him?" She was shouting, close to screaming. "Why couldn't you trust me? Why couldn't I see my father if I wanted to? Why did you have to interfere with my life?"

The force of her emotions suddenly seemed to exhaust her. She came to me, leaning against me, proffering her dismay, as years ago she had shown me a bruise, a skinned knee. I held her, pressing my cheek against hers, stroking her hair.

"All right now?" It was what I had always asked then.

"You should have told me," she said softly. "You know you should."

"Darling, I'm sorry."

Oh, Vanessa, waking in the night and crying, and the folds in your plump arms, reaching up to me, and your limbs straightening and tapering, and walking sturdily beside me, and running off to explore on your own, and you're grown-up now.

"Darling, let's go in the living room and sit down and talk it all out."

We talked and I was dying for a drink and I was afraid she would despise me if I had one. Until she went into the kitchen and came back with a bottle of wine and two glasses and poured us both a drink.

And we went on talking.

We went on talking and I brought out some pictures of Max, taken one weekend at Fire Island, and she said He looks rather nice, and I said Yes, he was, and I told her about the war and the POW camp, and thinking he might be dead, and how happy I was when I heard he was alive.

But I still couldn't explain why I had kept silent about him for so long.

"What did you quarrel about?"

At least I could be truthful about that. "You, in a way. I wanted to have children and he absolutely refused. He said I had no right to have a child." I remembered exactly what Max had said. Since Vanessa and I were talking as equals, I might as well be frank. "He said I was all fucked-up and I'd fuck you up, too."

That made her laugh. But a minute later she was serious and inquiring again.

"Does he know about me?"

"Yes."

"Did you tell him?"

"It was in the papers."

"In the papers? Why?"

I explained about that idiotic movie, the Epic, opening in New York, the indefatigable studio publicity. It was a relief to talk about Jason.

"He was what we used to call hot at that time. A celebrity. And the papers thought it was a nice story. A double event. You and the movie coming out at the same time."

"Did Jason think he was my father?"

"Yes." At least he had then.

"Why didn't you tell him the truth?"

"He loved you so much. He was so proud of you. He used to stand and just look at you for hours."

"All right. I can see why you wanted to pretend with him." She was holding her glass, symbol of our equality. She had hardly tasted it; she didn't like wine, any alcohol. "But he died years and years ago."

"I know, but then, after Jason died —" I had to risk giving her another glimpse of the truth. "Right after his death, I had some nasty letters from Max. Sort of blackmailing me. Threatening to make trouble. I felt it was better to keep you away from him."

"Why did he threaten you? How?"

"I felt he hated me." I didn't see how I could go any further than that without pouring it all out. The truth. I felt he didn't give a damn about you as his daughter. He only wanted to use you to get back at me. I was afraid he really would fuck you up if I let him. I felt your father, the man who gave you life, was a demented monster.

I couldn't say it to her.

For the rest of the weekend, at meals, popping in on me in the kitchen or my bedroom, she kept returning to her questions. What part of California did Max live in? What did he do there? How old was he? Did I ever write to him? Did I still feel he hated me? Had I ever sent him a picture of her? Did she look like him?

On Sunday evening when I was helping her pack her things to return to school, I saw she had put the Fire Island snapshots of Max into the pocket of her windbreaker.

I didn't say anything, but it made up my mind for me. Driving her to Newtown, I suggested it to her.

"If you like, we could go and see him. In June, when school breaks up. We could fly to New York and spend a few days with Jason's parents. Then we could go out to California and see him."

She was quiet and thoughtful about it. She asked if Jason's parents knew, and when I said they didn't, she was gently understanding. Although she hadn't seen them since she was four, their love had reached her in endless letters and presents. She saw how much it would hurt them to be told they weren't really her grandparents.

I drove her into the school grounds, to the door of her house, as the dormitories were called. She got out with her suitcase and then leaned back into the car.

"You sure?"

"Yes. I think it's time you met him. I want you to meet him."

Him? I still found it difficult to speak of Max as her father.

During the next few weeks, I arranged our plane tickets and made hotel reservations in New York and Los Angeles. Both our passports were okay. Although we hadn't been out of Ireland for so long, I had kept renewing them. In case Max showed up. In case I suddenly had to escape with Vanessa.

I was all excited. I didn't think about Max much. I thought of traveling, being in New York again, showing it to Vanessa. She and I would go to the States by ourselves and then fly to Paris from Los Angeles and meet Anton and Elsie Silver there.

"Aren't you excited?" I asked Anton.

"Yes, I'd like to see Paris again."

He had spent a year at the Sorbonne before joining the Czech diplomatic service. He had fallen in love with a French girl; he had wanted to marry her.

"Her parents wouldn't hear of it. Marry a Czech? Oh, that reminds me. I'm afraid your wedding has been called off, too."

"What wedding?"

He was teasing me. He had heard Chris had left and his house was for sale. I hadn't thought of Chris for weeks, hadn't noticed his absence. He had called several times in March, inviting me over for a drink. I had said I was busy; I had finally said I didn't see any point in our seeing each other. When he tried to pressure me through Vanessa — how would I like it if she found out about Max? — I told him to go to hell; she already knew all about him.

Now he had left. He had given up on me the way he gave up on everything at a certain point. And he would blame me, hate me for it.

Timmy came back from wherever he had been. He seemed a little less edgy. He told me he was trying to quit.

"Maybe I can ease myself out slowly. They might just drop me if they decide I'm getting stale, losing interest. It might be all right so long as I don't make any sudden moves."

The news from Northern Ireland was as full of senseless violence as ever. A woman caught in the crossfire in the Shankhill had to have both her legs amputated above the knee. Two men were killed by a bomb blast in a pub. Another shipment of guns was intercepted at the Amsterdam airport. A boy was blinded by metal fragments when a car exploded outside a store.

Vanessa came home for the Easter vacation. She was still full of questions, no longer upset, but intensely curious about Max. Did I think he had read *Catcher in the Rye?* She had just finished it. Was he a Republican? We had been listening to the news about Watergate. Did he like sailing? Horses? Was he the sort of person who thought girls ought not to wear jeans?

I answered her questions as well as I could. It was sixteen years since I had seen Max, over ten years since I had heard from him directly.

I didn't write and tell him we were coming. I had no idea how he would react to Vanessa, and if he met us at the plane the whole situation might get out of control. Since Jason's death I had associated all airports with confusion and disaster, and I didn't want to have to cope with Max at Los Angeles International. I would call him from our hotel and arrange Vanessa's first meeting with him, in our suite. On my own grounds. At the slightest sign of anger or hostility from Max, the least indication that he was making Vanessa unhappy, I would pull out with her, fly to Paris and forget him.

Timmy was away again for several days at the beginning of May. Another errand? I tried not to worry about it. By September, when we all came back from Europe, Timmy would have eased himself out altogether. He would be free of those thugs. I tried to believe that.

I was in the living room alone after supper, reading. The soft May twilight was so beautiful over the lawn and the trees that I hadn't drawn the curtains. I was playing Mahler on the phonograph.

There was a sound from outside like a stone striking against the wall. I looked up from my book. Timmy was standing to one side of the windows. He was beckoning to me. I went over and he gestured to me to draw the curtains. I pulled them closed. He waited a few seconds and then slipped into the room.

He was wearing a dark suit and tie. For a moment, absurdly, that reassured me. He looked so respectable. It wasn't until he tried to light a cigarette and couldn't manage to strike the match that I saw how frightened he was. He was like someone who has just come through a car crash, weak and clumsy with shock. I settled him into a chair and brought him a drink.

I didn't try to make him talk. Mahler came to an end. I switched off the phonograph. Timmy had finished his whiskey. I poured another inch into his glass and he managed to light a cigarette.

"They think I told them. They were waiting for me when I came home just now. They think I shopped them."

I didn't know what he was talking about. He still looked so scared I was afraid he would dry up if I questioned him. I waited.

"I kept trying to convince them I didn't even know they were being sent through Schiphol. But I couldn't make them believe me. They're still out there on the road. They're parked out there in their Rover, waiting. Waiting for me to run for it."

I was beginning to understand some of it, at least. Schiphol was the Amsterdam airport where the Dutch police had intercepted a shipment of arms to the IRA a few days ago.

"I didn't know," Timmy was saying. "I simply passed on their orders, the list of what they wanted. I didn't have the faintest idea how the stuff was going to be brought in. It could have been going through Brittany or Montreal, for all I knew."

"Why do they think anyone told the police?"

"Someone shopped them. That's what they kept saying. Someone shopped them. They were quiet about it, as though they were asking my opinion. Then I began to realize they thought it was me. They let me see that, when they were talking about the Dutch police inspector at Schiphol. 'Your man,' they called him. 'Your man knew all the arrangements, you see.' They think I tipped him off."

"Why? Why do they think it was you?"

Timmy shook his head helplessly. But I could already guess the answer to that. It made me angry with him. All that Kevin Box nonsense. How long could he hope to keep that up before they tied him to Sir Nigel? To the British Foreign Office? To all the bloody British secret service agencies Nigel must have to deal with?

He finally admitted I was right. Those two men who had questioned Anton hadn't been from the Dublin police. They had questioned other people in the neighborhood, too.

I wasted the next half-hour making useless suggestions, ways of getting Timmy out of the country, by plane from Shannon, by ferry from Cork. He knew he couldn't get beyond the end of the drive. Those men were out there in their Rover. They were parked on the main road, quite openly, watching him, as confident in their immunity as ambassadors. They knew the police wouldn't interfere with them so long as they kept it reasonably quiet. Timmy was sure the police wouldn't help him, either. To the Irish authorities it would seem like a private quarrel, best settled in the family.

"What would happen if you just sat tight? Stayed in the carriage house. Behaved perfectly normally."

"Depends. Depends what the Command decides." He didn't think they would do anything at once. They would go over his whole record, see if he might have been responsible any of the other times when things had gone wrong.

He was less shaken now. Talking, the whiskey, had helped him see his position more clearly.

"If I could only get in touch with Victor," he said presently. "He could tell them I didn't know about Schiphol."

I made him explain. Victor was the man to whom Timmy passed

along the orders, the lists of what was needed. He had once been the Tass representative in Dublin. Two years ago the Irish government had canceled his residence permit. Since then he had made his base in Paris. Timmy had had several dealings with him and they had become quite friendly. He thought Victor would help him, would talk to the Command. Victor could clear him at once by establishing his ignorance of the route used for any of the shipments.

"Then why don't you call him?"

"You think I've got his phone number?"

Timmy's smile when he said that infuriated me. "How do I know? I'm not a bloody secret agent. I'm just someone who thinks the whole thing's a rotten dirty mess. And you know how I feel about you being mixed up in it. Whatever happens to you serves you bloody well right."

It was all very well to say that, but I had known Timmy since he was eleven. I had picked him up at school in his gray flannel suit. I had taken him to tea and to the zoo.

"How *do* you get in touch with Victor then?"

It was complicated. Victor would be in certain cafés in Paris at certain times on certain days, never the same days from week to week. If he was in one café on Tuesday at noon, he would be there again the following Sunday at five and then the next Friday at ten in the evening. Timmy had met him in the Flore a few days ago, and from that he could work out the next time he would be there. He asked me if I understood. I did.

"Well enough to explain it to Anton?"

"Anton? What's he got to do with it?"

Timmy was wandering around the room, fingering things as though he had never seen them before. I realized he was embarrassed to look at me.

"I just thought — I thought perhaps Anton — he's going to Paris this summer, anyway — I thought perhaps he might be willing to go now."

He had picked up a framed photograph of Vanessa and was examining it with great interest.

"I don't know. No. No, I'm sorry, Timmy."

I knew Anton would go if I asked him, and I knew I wouldn't ask him. He had been born in Prague; from the Communist point of view, he was a defector. He had all the irrational fears of a refugee about that. I knew he would face those fears instantly without question if he thought he could help Timmy. That was exactly why I didn't want to ask him to go.

"All right." Timmy set the photograph back in its place. I could see his eyes now, the flat defeat in them. I couldn't stand it.

"Oh, come on," I said. "I'll go. Give me the times and the days and the places and tell me what the bloody man looks like and I'll take the plane from Cork tomorrow and go and talk to him for you."

I called Vanessa at school the next morning. There was the usual long wait before she came to the phone. I told her I was going to Paris for a few days, to do some shopping, buy clothes for New York.

"All right. Have a good time."

I thought I would be back by Friday, or Saturday at the latest, but in case I wasn't, perhaps it would be better if she arranged to spend the weekend with the Silvers.

"I'll call you Friday morning, anyway," I suggested.

"No, don't please."

She hated being called at school. She had to be fetched to the phone in the headmaster's office. From the hushed way she was talking, I could tell he was sitting there now, a few feet away from her.

"Elsie and I want to go camping this weekend, so it's fine. Have a good time in Paris and I'll see you when you come back. Bye."

She hung up before I could tell her I loved her. Oh, well, she knew that anyway, and I *would* do some shopping in Paris. I would buy her some really nice clothes for New York and California.

The Rover was still there when I started for Cork. They hadn't even bothered to pull it over to the side of the road. A man was sitting behind the wheel, reading a newspaper. Another man was standing by the gate to the carriage house; a pair of field glasses was hanging from a strap around his neck. He waved to me in a casual, friendly way as I drove past.

I took a taxi from Le Bourget and checked into a small hotel, the Crystal, in St.-Germain. Timmy had figured out that Victor should be in the Café Flore, just around the corner, that Thursday evening at five. I was there at four-thirty and found an outside table beside the entrance.

Across the boulevard was the Brasserie Lipp, where Jason and I had had dinner with Steve McQueen. I hadn't been outside Ireland, scarcely outside County Waterford, for over ten years. I felt strangely light and fragile being back in Paris. Then I understood why. I felt like a ghost, what the French call a *revenante,* a returner.

I also felt like a bloody fool. It is one thing to know from newspapers and magazine articles that men and women do move around our cities carrying torn halves of Jell-O box tops as identification. It is quite another matter to be involved in such shenanigans. The world of conspiracy and espionage had never held the slightest fascination for me. It had always seemed to me absurd, as outlandish as transvestism. Now here I was waiting to make contact with a man, a stranger, with no name except Victor, who was reputed to work for the KGB. Timmy had described him as around forty-five years old, well dressed, clean-shaven, with dark hair, brushed straight back, gray eyes, a gold upper-left molar, which showed when he smiled, slender, five feet nine or ten. He would be carrying a copy of *Le Monde* under his right arm.

As five o'clock approached and I looked at every man who entered the café or sat down outside it, I had to keep reminding myself that what I was doing was serious, not some childish game. Timmy's life, his *life,* might depend on my recognizing and talking to this man. I still could not altogether rid myself of the feeling that I was an impostor, an actor who had no right to be in this play.

A man paused in front of my table.

"*Madame. Cette place est libre?*"

He had a small brown mustache and wasn't carrying a newspaper. I shook my head rudely.

Only the French can shrug with their eyebrows; he did it.

"*Mais madame est seule.*"

Go away. Leave me alone. Can't you see I'm on a secret mission? Doesn't it stick out all over me?

I explained in French that I was waiting for a friend.

I waited until seven o'clock. I saw four men carrying copies of *Le Monde.* Each of them was either too old or too young, too short, too fat, too tall. One of them was bearded. I was accosted three more times. I had only myself to blame for that: as a secret agent I was a hopeless klutz; the way I stared at every man who passed would have been enough to get me arrested under the Street Offences Act in London.

At seven o'clock I pushed aside my fifth cup of coffee without tasting it and tried to think the situation through.

I did not believe I had missed recognizing Victor. Timmy had made a mistake in the hour or the day or the café. This Thursday Victor had gone somewhere else at five, to Deux Magots, or the Coupole, or one of his other regular places. He might have come to the Flore at noon, or he might be coming here at ten tonight.

There was no way I could get in touch with Timmy. We had thrashed that out before I left. All calls to our area in Waterford went through the switchboard in the village post office. It was just too damn easy, Timmy had warned me, to listen in on an open system like that, and he thought a call from the Continent, any call from the Continent, might be just enough to convince those men watching him that he was the one who had shopped them.

So I was on my own. It was up to me to figure out the best way to find Victor.

Once, a few years ago, I had taken Vanessa and Elsie to the zoo in Dublin. They had kept wandering off and I had kept searching for them until we came to an arrangement. "If we lose each other, go to the lion house. Don't try to find me. Go to the lion house and *stay* there. Wait until I come."

It seemed to me the same rule would be the most sensible one now. There were six cafés on Victor's schedule, three of them on the Right Bank. If I tried chasing around to them all three times a day, at noon and five and ten, I might just miss him in any one of them. If I stuck to the Flore at those hours, he would show up there sooner or later, within five days at most.

By ten o'clock on Tuesday night.

And so that became my way of life. I went shopping in the mornings. I bought several outfits for Vanessa, underwear, an Italian suede shoulder bag I thought would be perfect for her for traveling. I bought some things for myself. At noon every day, I was sitting at what became "my" table at the Flore. I waited there for an hour, sometimes an hour and a half. I had lunch. I lay on the bed in my room at the Crystal, reading paperbacks, or I went to the movies. I was back at the Flore at five and then again at ten.

"My" waiter came to know me and greet me. If any member of the Sûreté had happened to be staking out the Flore, he would have started a file on me at once. I had to cut down on the coffee; it made me too edgy. I varied it with Perrier, and in the evenings, wine.

A dozen times I was almost sure I saw Victor. Each time there was some detail of his appearance that didn't fit. Once a man in a hat, well dressed, gray eyes, slender, and so on, walked past my table and went inside the café. A moment later I followed him. He had taken off his hat. He was bald.

Twice I was so nearly sure I went over to a man's table.

"*Vous venez de Lyon?*" I asked. It was the recognition signal Timmy had taught me. Victor was supposed to say, "*Non, de Toulouse.*"

"*Non, madame, je regrette,*" one of the men replied. The other only shook his head. Both of them smiled at me. Neither had a gold molar.

I can't say this protracted routine bored me, exactly. I had only to think of Timmy in the carriage house, those men outside the gate watching him, waiting for him to make any move that would indicate to their practiced killers' minds that he was their man, and I was instantly overwhelmed with an anxiety, a near-panic of urgency, that made boredom impossible. What I felt most of the time was a sense of shame. It was much stronger than embarrassment. I felt like a doctor at a hanging: however innocent my own involvement, I was ashamed to be taking any part in this obscene ritual.

It was just after ten on Sunday night when I saw a man pause at the newsstand outside the Flore. He picked up a magazine and glanced at it before putting it back in the rack. I knew instantly that my waiting was over. Standing there, pretending to be interested in the magazine, he had observed the whole street, the café, every face in sight. I could sense his alertness like an aura as he walked past me and sat down a few tables away. I felt shy, breathless, relieved, but no flush of accomplishment. I watched the waiter bring him a *bock*. The man took the copy of *Le Monde* from under his right arm and opened it on the table in front of him.

I walked over and did my best to smile.

"Vous venez de Lyon, monsier?"

I expected him to be slightly startled, at least to glance up at me. He continued to read his newspaper.

"Non, madame," he said almost absently, turning the page, *"de Toulouse."*

"Vous permettez?"

"Avec plaisir."

I sat down. He still hadn't looked at me. It didn't occur to me until later that he didn't need to. He had *seen* me as he walked past on the way to his own table. He had seen and considered and evaluated me. He was no klutz at his profession.

"Alors?" he asked, closing *Le Monde* and sipping his beer. "Please speak English if you prefer."

"Kevin Box asked me to come and see you."

He nodded, go on.

I watched his face and especially his eyes as I talked. They were attentive, urbane. The things this man must have witnessed, I kept thinking. The things he must have done. The personal terrors he must have lived with, the fear of betrayal, arrest, torture. The fear of becoming suspect to his own people. I could see no indication of any of it in him. Except for that alertness that was like a latent vitality, he reminded me a little of Nigel. He had the same assured conceit.

"And you?" he asked when I had finished. "What is your concern in all this?"

"Kevin Box —" The name sounded more absurd every time I spoke it. "I've known him all his life, ever since he was a child. I care about him —" Did those words have any meaning in this man's world? "I care about him very much. I don't want him hurt."

He looked at me then. It struck me he was searching me with his eyes, like a customs inspector. Is that all you have to declare?

"You're putting me in a very difficult position," he said. "Because I think you're telling me the truth. You're not Irish. You certainly have no connection with the British authorities, either. On the other hand, you're not being quite frank with me, are you?"

I did not immediately understand what he was getting at.

"I haven't any reason to lie to you," I said.

"No?"

"No. None. I promise."

"Then what's all this nonsense about Kevin Box?"

I understood then.

"Timmy's my nephew."

"Sir Nigel is your brother?"

"Brother-in-law. He married my sister, Sylvia."

"Lady Sylvia?" Suddenly he was smiling; I saw his gold molar. "I met her once at a party at the French embassy in London. It was some years ago. I was the trade attaché at our embassy there. I found her charming, so fresh and natural."

All his alertness had left him. His eyes were hazed by the pleasure of his thoughts, his recollections.

"She sat next to me at dinner and we — as the English say, we got along like a house on fire. Unfortunately I had to leave London soon afterward and I never — we never . . ." He sighed and picked up his beer. "So Lady Sylvia is your sister."

"Yes."

I was completely lost. I hadn't understood this man before; now, I knew, I would never be able to reconcile all the aspects of his personality, his *existence,* into any understandable unity. Concentration camp guard; loving father. Not even that parallel could explain him to me.

He patted my knee. "Well, we'll see what we can do to get Timmy out of this spot of bother. I'll talk to those *merdes* in the IRA and tell them they're barking up the wrong tree. And now I'm afraid you'd better go. I have another appointment." His hand moved a little further up my thigh. He patted me again.

"Somebody may have been watching us, so we'll give them *un peu de comédie,* shall we? Lean over and kiss me."

I did. I kissed him on the cheek. His hand slid around my hip. He patted my behind.

"*C'est bien gentil.*" I glimpsed his gold molar again. "Now stand up and walk away and then turn and wave to me. And don't worry, I'll do everything I can."

I dropped a hundred franc note on my table for the waiter as I passed, and edged out between the chairs to the sidewalk. I turned to wave.

He wasn't looking at me. He had gone back to his newspaper.

It occurred to me that his bit of comedy had been staged less for anyone watching us than out of a nostalgic impulse to feel Lady Sylvia's sister's bottom. I waved anyway and hurried back to my hotel.

There was no direct flight to Cork until late the next afternoon. I caught the 1:00 A.M. plane to London. The noon London-Cork flight the next day would get me back to Waterford, to Timmy, several hours earlier.

I spent the night at the Heathrow airport hotel. After breakfast I called Sylvia. I had no idea how much she knew about Timmy's activities, but at least I could give her his love, and I couldn't bear to be in London without talking to her.

Her phone was busy. It was busy for twenty minutes. Oh, hell, I thought, she's having one of those lying-in-bed phone chats with her latest macker. When I finally got the ringing tone, she answered at once.

"Hello. Who is it?" She sounded both anxious and annoyed, as though she were waiting for an urgent call and had already guessed this couldn't be it.

"Hello, darling. It's Carol."

"Carol?"

"Yes, Carol. I'm in —"

"Carol. Where the hell have you been? I was trying to reach you all last night and there was no bloody answer. Where have you been? Where are you?"

"I'm in London."

"In London? What are you doing in *London?*" She sounded accusing now as well as annoyed. "Where have you been all this time?"

Why had she been trying to reach me?

Oh, no, please no.

"I had to go to Paris, Sylvia. I had to — Timmy asked me."

"Timmy's dead."

No.

"What's the matter? Can't you hear me? I said, Timmy's dead. He was killed in Belfast on Saturday."

She had to hang up now. She was expecting Nigel to call her. I found a taxi and went straight to her house in Kensington.

The maid showed me into the living room. Sylvia was talking

on the phone. She gave me a blank look and waved her hand, wait, sit down. She was immaculately made-up and was wearing a tailored suit and pearl earrings.

"I don't give a damn what you tell the newspapers," she was saying. "That's your business. But I want to know the truth. I want to know exactly what happened." She listened for a moment, her face cold with distaste. "Never mind your delicate bloody position, Nigel. Just tell me this minute. Was it or wasn't it? If you don't, I'll call every newspaper in London and tell them *you* shot him."

She listened again, said "Thank you," with icy detachment, and hung up.

"What the hell were *you* doing in *Paris?*"

She looked beautiful, her hair freshly washed, her delicate face as porcelain smooth, almost, as Vanessa's. But as she sat down facing me, I was shocked by the change in her. All the life, the fun, that wonderful spirit of daring I had envied in her all my life, had gone out of her eyes.

"I'll tell you about that in a minute, Sylvia. But first, please, unless you don't want to talk, or you can't, please, what happened to Timmy?"

"He was shot. Some stupid British soldier shot him."

"British *soldier?*"

"It was in all the papers yesterday. That useless British army in Belfast. They were patrolling in their bloody Saracens and one of them saw a man on a roof with a rifle. Nigel says there *had* been sniping a few minutes earlier. But then, you know Nigel, he has to pretend anything the bloody government does is like an act of God. Not for us poor mortals to reason why. Anyway, one of the soldiers fired and killed him."

"Was Timmy — did he really have a gun?"

"Yes. There doesn't seem to be any doubt about that. Nigel's over there now. He flew to Belfast as soon as we heard. He's been through it all with the army. The soldiers went up on the roof after the shooting. It was a warehouse or something. And Timmy had a rifle. He was slumped over the parapet sort of pointing it down into the street."

"But why? Timmy . . . He . . ."

"I know. It's all so stupid and useless, isn't it? But at least I suppose we ought to be thankful, at least the bloody soldier was a good shot. He got Timmy through the head. I mean, Timmy didn't, you know, it was all over in a second. There couldn't have been any pain. The only thing is —"

She had been leaning forward in her chair, head raised, as poised as if she were having her picture taken. Her voice didn't falter as she broke off, but her mouth twisted suddenly. She stood up and turned her back on me.

"The only thing is — Nigel just admitted it on the phone — the only thing is, Timmy's bloody rifle wasn't *loaded.*"

I started to cry. Not as I had cried at Jason's funeral, with wild release, but timidly, as though from cold.

"Oh, for God's sake, stop blubbing, Carol. You'll make me blub too. You always were such a *baby.*"

"I can't help it. I'm sorry. Timmy —"

I couldn't say any more. We were clinging to each other, wordless with memories and grief.

"What *were* you doing in Paris?" Sylvia asked me presently.

I told her. I had too much respect for her spirit and integrity to try to comfort her with lies. I told her the whole story, Timmy's gradual disillusionment with the IRA, their suspicion of him, his fear, my blundering efforts to find Victor in Paris, his promise to help.

She listened, intact and poised again, without interrupting.

"Oh, Carol. Oh, my God, isn't life horrible?"

"Sometimes."

"Poor Nigel."

"*Nigel?*" What was she talking about? "Nigel? Why?"

"He's such a fool. And he's so helpless, poor old sod. He's over there now, trying to hush everything up and he's caught right in the middle. The British army doesn't want to admit Timmy's rifle wasn't loaded. It'll look bad for them if they do. And Nigel has to side with them, naturally, because of his position in the bloody government. At least I made him tell *me* the truth, and you know what that poor sod said?"

I shook my head dumbly.

"He said, 'Of course you understand what that means. We'll

have to say Timmy was shooting from that roof and now those awful rotters' — that's what he calls the IRA — 'those awful rotters will insist on giving Timmy a hero's funeral.' " Sylvia's lips twisted again for an instant, and then she laughed. She laughed a little hysterically, but with unmistakable amusement.

"But they can't, Sylvia. You *can't* let them. Timmy hated those thugs. They —"

I had a startled understanding of the truth, of what must have happened in the carriage house while I was away.

"They forced him. They forced him to go to Belfast. They probably gave him the choice. Either *they* would kill him or he could go up there and *prove* his loyalty. Shoot a British soldier. That's the way they think."

"I know." Sylvia shook her head impatiently. "I understand that. What it really comes down to is that Timmy committed suicide. And Nigel will have to pretend he didn't. That's what I mean, poor Nigel. He cares so much what other people think and now he'll have to go on for the rest of his life, letting them think Timmy, his only son, Timmy, gave his life for those awful rotters. Poor old Nigel. Poor silly sod."

She straightened her skirt with a brusque, dismissive gesture.

"Would you like a drink?"

"No, thanks."

For some reason it was the last thing I wanted.

Sylvia decided she didn't want one either.

"I know," she suggested. "Let's go down to Brighton."

"Why? Do you want to tell Mother?"

"Oh. Oh, God, no. I forgot."

She had forgotten Mother lived in Brighton. She only wanted to go *somewhere*. She wanted to drive.

She backed her Porsche out of the garage and we took off West onto the M4. Once past Hammersmith, Sylvia let the car go. Seventy, eighty, ninety, she touched a hundred. She drove, as she did everything, with skill and flair. She swerved past the other cars, from lane to lane, with the grace of a falcon. Never faltering. Never hesitant. Never edging recklessness beyond control. Sitting beside her, I thought what I had thought so many times these past few years.

What a waste.

She had such quality, such style. She should have made such a shining trophy of her life. She should have married a man like Disraeli who would have adored and valued her. She should have been a resplendent hostess, a woman of influence in a time when influence still had principles. And she had wasted it all on a pompous snob. That poor sod, as she called him. She had helped him become Sir Nigel, a success by his own standards, but his eminence was that of a mediocre man in the mediocre government of a declining country. My darling, beautiful, daring sister, Sylvia. What a waste.

We drove to Bristol in two hours. There was nothing to do when we got there. The pubs were closed and we couldn't find a restaurant that didn't smell of stale dishwater. We bought some ham rolls in a café and drove, more slowly, back to London. We didn't talk much and hardly at all about Timmy.

It was seven by the time we got back to the house.

"Why don't you stay the night?" Sylvia suggested. Nigel wasn't due back until the next day and I knew she didn't want to be left alone. I called Vanessa's school. The phone rang and rang.

"What is it?" a man's voice finally answered. I had gotten the night watchman. I asked him if he could find Vanessa and bring her to the phone.

"Is it what you'd call urgent?" he wanted to know.

Vanessa's house was at least half a mile from the headmaster's office, and in his Irish way he was being sensible about it. He wasn't going all that way to fetch her unless there was a good reason for it.

I had to admit it wasn't all that urgent. The chances were Vanessa wouldn't be in her house, anyway. She would be down at the lake or in town. I asked him if he would be sure to see she got a message. Her mother had called. I was flying back to Cork the next morning and would pick her up at school at four. He said he would, all right. I could count on him.

Sylvia had found some cold pheasant and potato salad and a jar of caviar in the refrigerator. We took our plates into the living room.

"I know what we'll do," she said. "Nigel's got some prewar whiskey he's been saving for the day he gets his peerage. We'll drink the whole bloody bottle."

We did. We drank and we talked and we made less and less sense as we sat there in the long dying twilight and finally in the dark. We talked about Timmy and what a wonderful little boy he had been, and we talked about careers and causes and the way they destroyed people, and around midnight we agreed that nothing really mattered except getting on with it without complaining or feeling sorry for yourself.

My flight was delayed an hour at Heathrow the next day. I picked up my car from the parking lot at the Cork airport and, though I would never be able to drive like Sylvia, I reached the school at Newtown by five minutes past four. I pulled up outside Vanessa's house. I had hoped to find her waiting there. The car was packed with the things I had bought in Paris and I was going to take her home with me for the night so she could try them on.

There was no one I knew among the girls in the downstairs hall, but one of them asked if she could help me.

"I'm Vanessa's mother. I've come to pick her up. Could you tell her?"

"Vanessa? Vanessa Stone?" She seemed a little surprised.

"Yes."

"Oh. I don't know. I'll see."

I told her I'd wait for Vanessa outside. It was one of those schools where there was very little adult supervision in the houses and I always felt like an intruder in them.

I stood by the car. The grounds were full of boys and girls sitting under the trees reading and talking. I remember thinking how careless and young they all looked.

"Carol. What are you doing here?"

It was Elsie Silver.

"Hello, Elsie. I'm waiting for Vanessa. Has anyone told her?"

"Vanessa's not here."

"Well, where is she?"

"She went away for the weekend. I thought you knew."

The weekend?

"Elsie," I said stupidly, "it's Tuesday."

"I thought you knew."

"Knew what?"

It wasn't exactly fear; it was like a sudden sharpening of the senses, everything a little too clear, too stark.

"Someone called. They said she wasn't coming back for the rest of the term."

"Who? Who called?"

She shook her head, confused. "I thought you knew. He came and picked her up on Friday. We were going camping and of course she couldn't come. She was awfully excited because she wasn't expecting him."

"Who? Who came and picked her up, Elsie? Who?"

It *was* fear now. I couldn't keep it out of my voice.

"Him. I know it's supposed to be a secret. But Vanessa told *me*. She never thought he'd come here to see her. That's why she was so excited. You know who I mean. Vanessa's *father.*"

Twenty-Four

B ut you called me on Saturday morning, Mrs. Stone," the head-master said.

At least, he had naturally assumed it was me. A lady who sounded American and said she was Vanessa's mother. I had explained I wanted to take Vanessa out of school before the end of the term because we were going away. He hadn't seen any objection to that. "We'll be breaking up for the summer vacation in another week anyway, so, naturally, I agreed."

"Of course. You couldn't possibly know," I admitted.

"I don't understand, Mrs. Stone. You mean, it wasn't *you* I talked to?"

"I only saw her for a moment," David Silver said. She had come out to the barn for a sweater she had left there. She was happy and excited and she said she was going away. David thought she meant for the weekend and there was nothing unusual about that. Then she had gone to the house, to pack, he supposed, and a little later he had heard a car drive off.

That had been on Friday evening around six. I called the post office and the pub and several shops and no one in the village had seen Vanessa after that.

Happy and excited, she had gone off with Max.

Where?

The only certainty was that Max would not have stayed in Ireland with Vanessa. She would have kept wanting to call me, to bring him back to the house to see me after the weekend. On some pretext or another, he must have persuaded Vanessa to leave the country with him.

Where had he taken her? How could I find that out? How could I trace her?

I sat in the living room, staring at the phone. I didn't know where to begin. All the things that made living in Ireland so pleasant — the casualness, the trust, the lack of official formalities — were against me now. You could take the ferry from Cork or Rosslare without even giving your name. No one would ask you any questions. You just bought a ticket and walked on board.

I jumped up and looked in the drawer of my desk. Vanessa had taken her passport with her.

I sat down by the phone again.

I would go mad if I went on sitting there staring at it. I needed help. I called Anton. He started to say how sorry he was about Timmy.

Slightly hysterical, I said never mind that now. "Vanessa's been kidnapped. Come over at once, please, Anton, at once."

I was still staring at the phone when he arrived fifteen minutes later. I told him, disjointedly, what had happened.

"It's all my fault. I should have called her from Paris. I should have called her every day. I should never have gone to Paris and left her alone. I should never —"

"Rubbish. You've been living for ten years in a village where you don't even lock your doors when you go out. Where all the children go freely and safely wherever they want to."

"I should have realized when Chris left. I should have known he'd go straight to Max."

"You had no reason to think about it. You had already settled all that in your own mind. You were going to take Vanessa to see Max yourself in a few days. It was perfectly natural for you —"

"What am I going to do?" I was ranging about the room. "How am I going to find her? Where am I going to start?"

"You can start by sitting down and I'll get you something to eat and a drink and we'll try to be logical."

"I don't want anything to eat."

He brought me a sandwich and a whiskey anyway, and I finally sat down in my chair with them and I even tried to be logical.

"I could call all the airports. At least *they* have passenger lists, don't they?"

Anton considered that. "Dublin, Shannon, Cork. And we don't know what flight or even what day. And if you call the airports yourself, you'll get some girl at the information desk who won't be able to tell you anything." He was silent, rubbing the bridge of his nose. "If we are going to try to trace Vanessa that way, we must call the police for help or go to a private detective agency."

"What other way is there to trace her? Except find out where she went. I'm sorry, darling. I didn't mean to shout at you." I took a sip of the whiskey.

"Eat your sandwich. You shouldn't drink on an empty stomach." He was rubbing his forehead. "It seems to me the best way to find Vanessa is to look at the whole situation from Max Ludlow's point of view."

"How?" I took a bite at the damn sandwich.

"Max picks her up at the school. She is pleased and excited. She isn't expecting him, but he's her father. She'll believe anything he tells her. Perhaps he says he saw you in Paris. It was your idea he should come there and take her away with him for a few days."

"Elsie Silver," I remembered. "She kept saying, 'I thought you knew.' Vanessa must have given Elsie that idea. But she didn't tell Elsie where she was going."

"She probably didn't know yet. She had only seen Max for a few minutes before she ran upstairs to get her coat and things. Then she drives off in the car with him. She comes back here for her suitcase and her passport and then he tells her where they're going. To Paris to see you, or to London or New York or California to meet you there or —"

"Which? Where, Anton? Where did they *go?*"

"Carol —"

"I'm sorry."

"The point is, my darling, if Max told her it was your idea, how long can he keep that up? She will be expecting you to phone her. She will insist on phoning you."

"But she didn't even try." That was one of the things I had asked Mrs. Coughlan at the post office. There had been no phone calls from Vanessa. "She didn't try to phone me," I insisted impatiently. "That's why I'm so sure they left the country."

"But Carol, my dear. There are phones in London. There are phones in Paris, in New York, in California. Vanessa is a very intelligent, independent girl. She will not accept Max's evasions for long. She will go to a phone booth —"

"But she *hasn't*. She's been gone four days now."

"What I'm trying to explain to you" — Anton's patience was admirable — "what I am saying is, look at it from Max Ludlow's point of view. He has to take Vanessa somewhere where she *cannot* phone you."

"Where?"

Anton looked at me steadily. There was a terrible reluctance in his eyes.

"Somewhere he can stop her, restrain her. Keep her locked up if necessary without attracting attention."

I thought about that for several minutes in silence. I went over and sat beside Anton on the sofa. He put his arm around me.

"If I called . . ." I said.

"Yes. If you called person-to-person. Who could you say the call was from?"

"Chris?"

"Yes. Person-to-person from Chris Deniken. It's worth trying. If he accepts the call, at least you'll know he's there."

The post office had to put me through to Dublin to get the Genesis number in Santa Monica and make the call for me. The Dublin operator was friendly and helpful, but it took him a long time to get a transatlantic line. At last I heard it ringing.

A woman's voice answered at once. "What number are you calling?"

The Dublin operator told her.

"That number has been disconnected."

"Please." I was afraid she was going to hang up on me. "This is a long-distance call from Ireland. Could you please tell me if there's any other number listed for Genesis in the Los Angeles area. Or for Max Ludlow."

"I'll connect you with information."

I heard the ringing tone again. On and on. "I'm still here," the Dublin operator assured me cheerfully. Information answered on the twenty-third ring. I was counting. They said they'd check. There was only one number listed, the one I had been given.

I thanked the Dublin operator and hung up.

"Return to Go." Something in my despair had reminded me of Jason, his way of handling defeat. "Do not collect any money. Return directly to Go."

"Then you must call the police now," Anton told me.

"Dublin would be best, wouldn't it? I mean, the local Guarda —"

"No, no, the Santa Monica Police."

"What can they do? We don't even know —"

"Come sit down and finish your drink. That place, Genesis. It's a home for drug addicts. It's been going for years. If it has closed down for some reason, the police there will know about it."

I had always thought Anton was the most intelligent man I'd ever known.

"Santa Monica Police Department," the Dublin operator said as though it were the most routine request. This time he got a line almost at once.

"S.M.P.D." Again it was a woman who answered.

I explained what I wanted. She said she would put me through to Sergeant Gregory.

"Yeah?" Sergeant Gregory answered. "What can I do for you?"

I said I needed some information on Genesis.

"What kind of information?"

"The phone there has been disconnected and I —"

"What's it to you? You got that kind of trouble, call the state hospital. That's my advice."

"My daughter is missing."

There was a silence.

"Yeah," Sergeant Gregory said wearily. "You and how many others, lady? Okay. What's her name?"

I gave him Vanessa's name and age; I gave him a description of her.

"What makes you think she was hooked in with Genesis? She tell you she was going there?"

I realized it would be best if I went the whole way. "I have good reason to believe the man who runs Genesis, Max Ludlow, Father Max, as he calls himself, has kidnapped my daughter and is holding her against her will."

Another silence.

"Maybe you better come down and we can talk about it. Ask for me at the desk. Sergeant Gregory."

"I'm in Ireland."

"Yeah?" That seemed to shake his faith in my credibility a little. "You're calling from Ireland. You kidding?"

"Max Ludlow was in Ireland last Friday. I know that. He picked up my daughter at her school. And I think he flew her back to California with him."

"Yeah, well . . ." There was a certain caginess in Sergeant Gregory's voice, but I felt he was prepared to believe me again, believe at least that I wasn't a nut case. "I'll tell you this much, lady. This isn't the first complaint of that kind we've had against Genesis, and if you ever feel like making the trip over, I'll be glad to try and help you out. But there isn't much I can do for you in Ireland, is there? You'd do better to contact the police there."

"I'm going," I told Anton. "I'll get a plane from Shannon first thing in the morning."

"I'll go with you."

"No."

"I've got my passport."

"No, darling, listen." I sat beside him on the couch again. "I may be doing something absolutely crazy. We may be all wrong about this. It is just possible, after all, that Max took Vanessa to London or Dublin for a few days and he'll bring her back."

"She would have called."

"She may call. That's why I want you to stay. I want you to stay in this house in case she does, in case she comes back here. Oh, please stop rubbing your nose, Anton. It always means you're unhappy about something."

"I'm unhappy because I'm afraid you're right. He has taken her to California."

He agreed at once to stay in the house while I was gone. It

eased me to know how completely I could count on him. I could reach him at any hour of the day or night. He would never move out of hearing range of the phone. He helped me take the things I had bought in Paris out of the car. As a small act of faith, I put Vanessa's new suede shoulder bag into my own suitcase when I repacked it. I chose my best, most expensive things to wear in California. The more affluent I appeared to be out there, the more credible I would be to the police. I had eight thousand dollars in traveler's checks I had bought for the trip with Vanessa. I put them in my bag with my passport.

It was only a three hour drive to Shannon. I left at midnight in case I had a puncture or anything, and caught the 7:30 TWA flight to New York. I was lucky there and made a quick connection. I arrived at Los Angeles International shortly after noon. I rented a car and drove to the Santa Monica police station.

My only experience of police stations had been during those Remo days, going down to the squalid precinct house in the Village to bail out Roberta when she'd been busted for stripping on the subway. The Santa Monica station surprised me: it was all neat and freshly painted like a new suburban school. A very attractive policewoman took me up in the elevator to Sergeant Gregory's sunny cubicle of an office. He wasn't there. She asked me to sit down; he was probably in the cafeteria; she would tell him I was waiting for him.

I had, inevitably, formed a picture of Sergeant Gregory from his voice on the phone. About forty. Fat. Sloppily dressed. When a good-looking young man in a smart tan linen suit and a plain dark tie walked into the office, I thought he must be looking for the sergeant too.

"What took you so long to get here?" He closed the door behind him.

"Headwinds."

"Yeah. I checked with the switchboard. You *were* calling from Ireland. From Dublin."

"County Waterford."

My false picture of him had been understandable. His voice didn't match his appearance at all. I realized later that his tough, slightly slurred speech was a deliberate camouflage, but for a while it made it difficult to keep him in focus.

"Okay." He sat down behind his desk. "Go ahead. Let's have the whole story."

The whole story. I had thought about that very carefully on the plane. There was no demanding reason why I should tell the police Max was Vanessa's father. It made my position much stronger if I didn't. I could lodge a complaint against him for straightforward kidnapping. On the other hand, my experience with Victor had made me wary of withholding information from people whose profession it was to sense lies or evasions. It would also be extremely difficult to explain how Max had managed to pick Vanessa up at her school and drive away with her unless she knew him, had some close relationship with him. Any attempt to invent an alternative relationship would involve me in a whole web of lies.

I told Sergeant Gregory the truth. He didn't interrupt me.

"Jesus," he said when I'd finished. "So this guy Ludlow's the kid's father."

"Not legally."

"Yeah, well, it still makes it kind of awkward, doesn't it."

"No."

"How come?"

"Because I believe he's holding her against her will in that Genesis place, and that makes it kidnapping whether she's his natural daughter or not."

He frowned. There was a Thank You For Not Smoking sign on his desk. He turned it face down and offered me a cigarette. I said I didn't smoke.

"You're lucky." He lit one himself. There was a silence while he found an ashtray in a drawer.

"Yeah, well, I appreciate you've been honest with me, so I'll try and do the same for you. In the first place, Max Ludlow isn't holding your daughter in that Genesis building. The place is closed, empty, shut down tight."

He must have seen the dismay in my eyes. He looked at me quickly in a sensitive, almost shy way that seemed to add another facet to his already complicated personality.

"We closed it ourselves. I've got a good friend in the D.A.'s office and he gave us a lot of cooperation. It still took us almost a year to do it. Genesis is registered as a religious organization and that always makes it tough to build a case against an outfit like that. Then, too, Max Ludlow has a certain amount of clout. Or at least a hell of a lot of money. The reason we kept after him was that we'd had so many complaints. A whole stack of them. Assault. Forcible restraint. Kids being kept in straightjackets, force fed tranquilizers, starved. Most of the complaints came from parents like yourself. Some from citizens' groups. Anyway, my friend in the D.A.'s office and I kept after it and a few months ago we did it. We went in there with the fire commissioner. He found seventeen violations of the safety regulations, including a structural defect in the roof. The roof, that was my idea, and it clinched it. We could clear the whole place out and lock it if the roof was going to fall in. We turned the kids loose or sent them to Camarillo or returned them to their parents if they were minors. We held Max Ludlow and his lady friend for twenty-four hours but we couldn't make a case against them. The kids who'd been abused were either too scared to make statements or they were just too far out to hold up in court. So we had to let Father Max and his lady friend go."

He put out his cigarette.

"We tried to keep tabs on them. But they did a quick fade. We thought maybe they'd slipped off to Mexico, but I didn't figure they might be in Europe until you called."

He had come to a stop. I didn't say anything. There was too much to think about. Straightjackets. Force fed tranquilizers. Starved. I was trying not to lose control of myself, fall to pieces right there in the bright little office.

"You've been very kind, telling me," I said shakily, and then I couldn't keep it back any longer. "Please help me. Please help me find her."

Sergeant Gregory was frowning again. "You got any real reason to believe he is back here now?"

"No. Nothing. Nothing you'd call proof."

"Yeah, well, still it's a possibility. Some of those kids we turned loose from Genesis told me —" He seemed to check himself.

"What? What did they say?"

"I'll tell you what, Mrs. Stone." It was the first time he had used my name. "I'd like to get this guy. The way he treated some of those kids. I'd like to put him away. And you're right, of course.

Whether he's her natural father or not, if he's holding your daughter against her will, it's a kidnapping charge. The way you handle yourself, you'd be a good witness. We could make a nice tight case against him. If we can find him. I'll talk to my friend in the D.A.'s office about it this afternoon. Where are you staying?"

I wasn't staying anywhere yet. I had come there straight from the airport. He recommended the Hulton House.

"I'll pick you up there at seven, okay? There's quite a good Mexican restaurant on the roof and we could have dinner and talk some more."

I must have looked a little surprised at this friendly invitation. He smiled.

"Don't worry. I'm not trying to make a pass at you, Mrs. Stone."

He gave me that sensitive, slightly shy look again.

"There's no secret about it. I'm gay."

He said it so simply, so straightforwardly. From then on I trusted Sergeant Gregory forever.

The lobby of the Hulton House was full of airline pilots and hostesses. The sight of them reassured me. With guests of that kind, the hotel would be good about phone calls, taking messages. I was given a characterless, pleasant-enough room on the eighth floor overlooking the ocean.

I stood at the window, staring at it — gray-brown and sluggish, the long, tired rollers sweeping in over the breakwater. The Pacific. I hadn't seen it for over thirty years. Max and I used to take the streetcar out here from Hollywood and spend the afternoon on the beach or the pier.

It was almost four o'clock, midnight in Ireland. I called Anton. It was easier getting through, west to east.

He must have been sitting by the phone. He answered at once. I told him I missed him. I did. I gave him my news. He had some news for me, too.

"I had an idea. I thought it was worth trying. Max picked Vanessa up in a car, so he probably rented it in Ireland. I called the rental agencies at the airports and I was lucky. He hired a car from Avis at Shannon last Thursday and turned it in there on Saturday morning."

I told Anton he was wonderful.

As soon as we were settled over tacos in the roof restaurant that evening I explained the significance of Anton's news to Sergeant Gregory.

"You wouldn't fly anywhere from Shannon except to the United States."

"New York?"

"Or Boston."

"Yeah, well . . ." He had changed into a blazer and dark gray slacks and was wearing a silk scarf instead of a necktie. It didn't seem to make him any less many-faceted, but at least more informal, less of a policeman. "You can go to a lot of places from New York or Boston, can't you?"

"But Max was born here in California. He's lived here most of his life. All his connections are here."

"What kind of connections d'you mean?"

"If he's holding Vanessa somewhere, in some house, he couldn't just rent a place from strangers. He'd come back here with her. All the people he must have known over the years, the drug addicts who passed through Genesis. He'd take her to one of them. There was a girl called Iris —"

"Iris Gorman. That's his lady friend. The one we pulled in with him."

Gorman. It was the first time I had heard her last name. She had been simply Iris in the Village. Sometimes Iris with the pad on Christopher Street. Or Iris with the tits.

"Don't you think I'm right? He must be here."

"Yeah, maybe." Again I had the feeling he was holding something back. "I'll run a check on the airlines, anyway."

Don't crowd him, I could hear Jason saying. Listen to him. Get him to talk about himself.

I asked him how long he had been in the Police Department.

"Here? Here, only a couple of years. But before then . . ."

Jason had always known best about things like that. Sergeant Gregory *was* eager to tell me about himself. He had been with the Police Department in San Francisco and transferred to Santa Monica in '71.

"We felt we needed a man down here."

"We?"

"Gay Lib. We're trying to integrate the P.D.s all over the country.

L.A.'s still a closed shop, but we've got a couple of brothers in the Sheriff's Office in Orange County. And we'll crack them all in the end."

"Is it very difficult for you?"

"No worse than being black." He smiled. "Or a woman, I guess. How about you? You into that?"

I had to admit I wasn't. Not really. I was all for the ERA, but I had been lucky, I explained. Lucky in my marriage to Jason, and then living in Ireland, running a publishing company.

"What I hear, women in Ireland could do with a bit of liberating."

"I've never had much team spirit, I'm afraid." None. I had admitted that to Fitz thirty years ago.

Sergeant Gregory told me more about himself. His discovery at sixteen that he was homosexual. He hadn't tried to fight it. At eighteen, in the early sixties, he had decided not to try to hide it, either.

At least we had made some progress in America; we had come a long way since Fitz.

We finished our dinner. He had to get back to his office. I tried to pay the check; he wouldn't let me. I insisted on splitting it.

"You're a Women's Libber, all right. You just don't know it."

Then he was abruptly serious, a policeman again. "I had a talk with my friend in the D.A.'s office this afternoon. We worked out something we think you ought to do. When we pulled Max Ludlow in that time, he had his lawyer there. A guy named Tate. He had him there ten minutes after we got him to the station. The thing is I could talk to that lawyer, or the D.A.'s office could. We could try to lean on him to tell us where his client is. I don't think we'd get very far. He'd just claim privilege. But you might. You might get more out of him, just being nice. Just tell him you want to get in touch with Max Ludlow. I don't want to be personal, but can you afford to pay him something?"

"Yes, that's all right. You mean, bribe him?"

"He's a lawyer. He's in business. You give him a retainer and you're his client. I'm not saying it'll work. But I think it's worth trying."

He gave me the lawyer's full name and his phone number.

I called Harold Tate's office at ten o'clock the next morning. I said I was Mrs. Jason Stone. Mr. Tate had been recommended to me by my lawyer in New York. I wanted to make an appointment to talk to Mr. Tate about a personal matter. His secretary put me down for two o'clock that afternoon.

Harold Tate's office was on Wilshire Boulevard, not quite in Beverly Hills, just across the line in West L.A. The reception room didn't have that particular discreet gleam Jason had taught me to recognize as the patina of heavy money, but there was nothing seedy about it. I was wearing a Cardin suit I had bought in Paris and a string of pearls Jason had given me on our fifth wedding anniversary. They seemed to impress the receptionist, anyway. She said Mr. Tate would be right with me, Mrs. Stone.

Harold Tate was in his early fifties, gray haired, the sort of man who probably thought of himself as vigorous. He had a good tan and the sleeves of his jacket were cut tight to display his biceps. His office had two windows onto Wilshire Boulevard, prints of sailing ships on the walls, and a massive, highly polished desk with three phones on it.

He offered me tea or coffee. I thanked him, no. He asked how he could help me.

"I'd like you to represent me in a paternity dispute."

"Yes?" He looked disappointed in me. "You want to file for child support? Is that it?"

"No." What I was seeking was a reconciliation, an agreement with the father of my daughter, an arrangement for me to visit her.

"Yes?" The look of disappointment was gone. He took a legal pad out of a drawer and slipped the cap off an expensive ball-point pen. "I'll just jot down some of the details, shall we?"

It struck me as a good sign that he hadn't asked me the name of the lawyer in New York who had recommended him to me. I didn't think Harold Tate was in hock for that impressive desk, but he wasn't above accepting clients off the street.

"Mrs. Jason Stone. Is that right?"

I nodded.

He wrote it down on his pad. "Jason Stone," he repeated. He had recognized the name. Was my husband . . . ? and so on. He was. That seemed to relax him a little more.

My husband had been dead for over ten years, I explained. He had nothing to do with this matter. I had had an affair with another man. We had had a child. It was this other man I was seeking an agreement with.

"And his name?"

"Max Ludlow."

I was watching him carefully. He wasn't in Victor's class, but he knew how not to look surprised.

"Max Ludlow." He wrote it down.

"My daughter's fifteen now. Mr. Ludlow's taking care of her at the moment, and I'd like to, well, formalize the situation, make sure I have legal access to her."

"And where is Mr. Ludlow living at the present time?"

"That's what I'd like you to find out for me."

He slipped the cap back on his ball-point pen and put it down on his desk. He looked out the window over Wilshire Boulevard.

The time had come to offer him his retainer. I had never bribed anyone in my life. How did you begin?

"I'd like you to act for me as my attorney." It sounded phony, even to me. "I don't want to make any trouble for Mr. Ludlow. I'd like to see him, meet with him. I'd like to discuss the whole matter reasonably. If you could arrange that for me."

Should I mention an actual figure? How much?

"I realize, of course, that representing me would mean a lot of time and expense for you."

"I see."

He was still looking out over Wilshire Boulevard. The office was on the fifth floor and there was nothing to be seen from it except a rather ugly apartment house.

"Well, Mrs. Stone . . ." He turned back to me at last. "I normally charge a retainer of two thousand dollars before accepting a new client."

He let that hang there in the silence between us.

It seemed reasonable enough. There was the rent of this office and his dues to the golf and tennis clubs, a boat in a marina somewhere, probably. I took my checkbook out of my bag. He uncapped his pen again and handed it to me. I wrote him a check for two thousand dollars on my New York bank.

He thanked me and put it away in his desk.

"And if I can arrange this meeting, Mrs. Stone . . ."

He was looking at me, the Cardin suit, the pearl necklace. How much was I good for? Jason Stone must have left me pretty well fixed. But if he put the price too high, I might simply walk out and stop payment on my check.

"I'll require a further fee of eight thousand dollars."

"All right. Thank you."

I smiled briskly and stood up. He walked to the door with me.

"Thank *you*, Mrs. Stone. Please leave your phone number with my secretary and I'll call you tomorrow afternoon about this time."

I had eaten a sardine sandwich in a delicatessen while I was waiting for two o'clock, for my appointment with Harold Tate. I found the women's toilet on the fifth floor. I locked myself and vomitted up my lunch. My breakfast, too. Everything in my stomach. I had always been lucky in that way, like that night on the monkey island during the U-boat attack; I had a delayed reaction to stress.

When I had finished retching and had washed my face and hands, I felt steady enough to drive.

"Good. You did fine," Sergeant Gregory said when I called him from the hotel. There was a brief silence; I heard him sigh.

"Ten thousand dollars. That's a lot of money."

"Not if I find Vanessa."

"No."

"Do you think —" I was clutching at him. I wanted him to reassure me. "Do you think he *can* arrange for me to see Max Ludlow?"

"From what he said to you, it sounds like he's in touch with him. And then, well, if he wants that other eight thousand, he can lean on Max Ludlow a little."

"How?"

"Ludlow's in trouble. A kidnapping rap. Tate's his lawyer. He can offer to surrender his client to us. Plea bargain for a reduced charge. I'm not saying he'd do that, but if he suggests it to Ludlow, yeah, well, Ludlow's going to see what Tate's driving at. He's got him over a barrel. He's going to take his lawyer's advice about seeing you."

"He said he'd call me tomorrow afternoon about two."

"Fine. Don't lose touch with me."

"No." Not for a second. "No, of course not."

I stayed in my room the next morning trying to read. Trying not to think about what Sergeant Gregory had told me about Genesis. The enforced restraint. The starving. I called Anton twice just to talk to him. I closed the curtains so I wouldn't have to look at the ocean. I knew it was a long time until two o'clock. I didn't need the slow, measured roll of those breakers to remind me of it.

Harold Tate was mercifully punctual. He called at 2:15.

"I've talked to Mr. Ludlow, Mrs. Stone."

"Yes?" I tried unsuccessfully to sound casual. "When can I see him?"

"I have some instructions from him for you."

I hated him for pausing.

"I think it would be best if you came to my office and I can explain them to you."

I was there in twenty minutes, beating every orange light on Wilshire Boulevard. Harold Tate was wearing the same tight jacket and his tan hadn't faded since the day before. He probably had a sun lamp.

He offered me tea or coffee again. It was all I could do not to scream at him to get on with it.

"Mr. Ludlow was very pleased by your conciliatory attitude and he'd like to talk to you."

"When?"

"As I told you, he's given me some instructions for you, to arrange a meeting between you."

He explained them to me. I was to go to Guaymas, in Sonora, Mexico. I was to stay at a hotel. Tate recommended the Hotel Cortéz on the beach in an offhand way that made me feel this was part of the instructions. Every morning at ten o'clock I was to go down to the port. There was a jetty there with a statue at the end of it. The Fisherman's Monument, it was called. I was to wait under the Fisherman's Monument every day from ten o'clock until noon. A man — "a man named Lindsay," Tate added, as one might say, Let's call him that — would meet me there. He would be driving a white camper. He would take me to Max Ludlow.

"When? How soon?"

Tate couldn't tell me that. It depended on a number of things, how soon Lindsay would be able to keep our appointment. But he could assure me, from his conversation with Mr. Ludlow, that it wouldn't be more than a matter of days.

That was the end of the instructions. He asked me if they were quite clear. They were. Harold Tate looked at me.

I opened my bag and took out my checkbook. He handed me his ball-point pen. I wrote him a check for three thousand dollars.

"I haven't seen Max Ludlow yet. I'll pay you the rest of your fee after I've met with him."

He didn't like it, but he didn't insist on my giving him the other five thousand at once. I still had time to stop payment on that first New York check if he quarreled with me, and I think he was human enough to understand how desperately I needed to retain that hold over him. He was my only link to Max.

I didn't go to the women's toilet that day. I went straight to Sergeant Gregory's office.

"Yeah," he said when I had told him my instructions. "So he is down there."

"Where?"

He reached for the No Smoking sign on his desk and then decided to leave it as it was.

"I've got some news for you, too. Some good. Some bad."

"Give me the bad first."

"I'm not sure which is which. They're kinda mixed up with each other. First, Max Ludlow, Iris Gorman, and Vanessa Stone were passengers on United Flight 659 last Saturday from JFK to San Diego."

"San Diego?"

"That's where it begins to get bad. *The Emissary,* a forty-eight foot, diesel-powered cabin cruiser, registered to Iris Gorman, took out from the marina in San Diego Saturday evening and hasn't been back since."

"He's taken Vanessa to Mexico. I realized that."

"Yeah, well, I didn't want to tell you this before" — he gave me that sensitive, shy look again — "because there might not have been anything in it. But some of the kids we turned loose from

Genesis said Father Max had a place down there. Some kind of settlement he established two or three years ago. A commune. Whatever you want to call it."

"Where?"

"They weren't sure, exactly. Somewhere in Baja."

"But then couldn't we find it?"

"You know Baja?"

"No."

"I flew over it once in a small plane. It's one of the most isolated stretches of land left in the world. From San Felipe south, there's three hundred miles of deserted beaches, sand dunes, dried up arroyos, scrub, nothing."

I thanked him. I said I would be leaving for Guaymas at once.

He shook hands with me. "There isn't much I can do to help you in Mexico right now. If we asked the police down there to look for that Genesis commune, they'd sit on it for three months and then send us a bill for expenses. But if you find your daughter and she's in bad trouble, I'll try to get some action through the embassy down there. So keep in touch."

I said I would.

When I looked back at him from the door, he was lighting a cigarette. He hadn't bothered to turn the sign face down.

The only way to fly to Guaymas was by chartered plane from the Santa Monica airport. A company called Gunnel Aviation flew package tours down there for the fishing. I was lucky and got on a plane the next morning, an eight-passenger Cessna. I was hoping we would fly òver at least part of Baja, but we turned east to Mexicali and then over the delta.

I rented a VW at Guaymas airport and checked into the Hotel Cortéz on the beach.

The next morning, an hour before ten o'clock, I drove into town, and down the main street, and across the Plaza of the Three Presidents. I parked on the far side of the square and walked out to the end of the jetty.

I sat there under the Fisherman's Monument, waiting for a man in a white camper, a man named Lindsay, to take me to Max Ludlow.

Twenty-Five

It was noon.

The third day of waiting was over. There had been no sight of a white camper. No man had come walking out along the jetty to tell me his name was Lindsay, to take me to Vanessa.

I could not force myself to leave yet. Lindsay might have been held up in traffic, had a breakdown, a puncture. I decided to give him another hour.

The first two days, waiting on after noon, the second day until one-thirty, I had felt nothing but despair. Today my thoughts were more prescient. It was the prescience of rage, of hatred for Max. He could go on torturing me like this day after day. He could be sure he was doing it. From all our years together, he understood me so well. He would know how persistently I would keep the appointment. He would be able to figure, almost to the day, how long it would be before I gave up.

Gave up and did what? Returned to Los Angeles for further, different instructions from Harold Tate?

At 1:10 I left the jetty, retrieved my VW, and drove back to the hotel.

I could hear their voices all the way from the parking lot, rowdy and strained. They reminded me at once of those evenings in Rome, the men's voices then, their self-important rudeness.

The lobby was crowded with them. They were like members of some grotesquely extended family, on intimate, jeering terms with each other. They had a family likeness, most of them in their late fifties, big and male, with the same distended bellies, the same overfed faces.

"I fly by the seat of my pants," one of them was yelling as I edged my way to the desk for my key. "That's the way we flew them B-16's isn't it, Boy?"

I remembered then. The girl at the charter-plane company in Santa Monica had told me to expect a crowd after the weekend. "I warn you," she had said, though there was no warning in her voice; she might have been promising me a special treat. "There'll be a bunch of crazy pilots coming down to the Hotel Cortéz on Tuesday. The Fly-For-Funsters are having a get-together in Guaymas."

For pilots, their sensory equipment seemed surprisingly poor. They kept bumping into me as I stood by the desk. It took me five minutes to get my key. I went to my room and changed into my swimsuit and a short terry cloth robe. The Fly-For-Funsters and their wives were gathered at the pool. They had crowded the metal tables together and were spread around them drinking margaritas. I found an air mattress as far away from them as possible, claimed it with my robe, and dived into the water.

Fragments of their talk — it wasn't exactly conversation — carried to me as I swam.

"Paid forty thousand for it eight years ago . . ."

"One of the last custom-made models . . ."

"Remember how the P-47's at Guam . . ."

"In the present market . . ."

"The crankshaft on that model . . ."

I swam twenty lengths, back and forth. Swimming had always relaxed me; it eased my mind as well as my body. Nothing terrible could ever happen to me in the water. I was even intermittently free from anxiety about Vanessa.

My mind started to seethe again as soon as I returned to my air mattress. I put on my robe and lay down. Was it all just a trick of Max's to torture me? Did he ever intend to keep the appointment? Did the man named Lindsay even exist?

"Caught a sixty-pound marlin . . ."

"Redeveloped the whole area . . ."

"Off from San Diego with a full tank . . ."

If Max did intend to keep the appointment eventually, how long would he keep me hanging? What would be his estimate of my persistence? A week? Ten days?

"All the way down to La Paz . . ."

"Built an extension over the garage . . ."

"From Felipe to Rosalía, only saw two goddamn signs of human existence . . ."

I glanced up quickly to see who had said *that*. He was the largest and noisiest of the lot, the seat-of-his-pants man I had noticed in the lobby.

Felipe to Rosalía. I had spent hours over a map of Baja since I had been in Guaymas, trying to figure out where that Genesis commune might be. I did not even know whether it was on the east or west side of the peninsula. I had tried Anton's trick of putting myself in Max's place. Where would I establish a place of that kind? How would I supply it with the things needed for subsistence in a desert like that — food, water, some kind of shelter, even if only canvas tents? If Genesis was on the west coast, those necessities would have to come from the United States, from San Diego, probably. Brought down by sea from there. The transportation of any large quantities of supplies would involve questions, clearance papers from American authorities. It would be much easier, arouse less attention, to bring everything across the Gulf of California from Mexico, from Guaymas. If that was what Max was doing, then he would have established Genesis on the east side of Baja. Where? After trying to answer a number of other questions from Max's point of view, I had settled on the three-hundred-mile stretch of coastline between those two small towns, San Felipe and Santa Rosalía.

I was staring across the pool, watching the man who had flown over that whole coast and only spotted two signs of human existence along it. I was waiting, hoping he would say something more about them.

He was shouting at the waiter for another round of margaritas.

I stayed at the pool until four. He did not mention Baja again. I thought several times of strolling over, starting a conversation, questioning him. I decided to drop the idea for the present. The pool was too crowded, that group of men around the pushed-together tables too gregariously male. If I joined them, I would get nothing but boisterous kidding. I would try to approach him alone later in the bar or the restaurant.

I went back to my room and called Anton. We had no news to exchange. We talked for twenty minutes, clinging to the reassurance of each other's voices.

"No. No," Anton said when I told him my doubt that Max ever intended to keep the appointment. "That man will come, Carol. It's only been three days. He will be there tomorrow."

I knew that Anton was not simply trying to give me hope; he had never been able to believe in the infinite cruelty of others.

I showered and dressed, spending time over my hair and my makeup. The bar was off the lobby, a big cool room with red, plastic-covered chairs. There were only half a dozen people there when I walked in at six. The Fly-For-Funsters had left the pool. They were probably in their rooms, changing; they would all be in soon. I chose a table near the entrance with plenty of vacant chairs around it. If I gave him an interested smile when he walked in, I might be able to get the seat-of-his-pants man to sit with me.

The waiter came over at once, welcoming, more than usually attentive. The Mexicans were like Italians in that way, sensing any festiveness — a woman who had gone to the trouble to look her best — and reacting with impulsive approval. I ordered a tequila and tonic.

"Do you mind if I join you?"

A man was standing by the table. A white linen suit, long thin face, steel-rimmed glasses. He had not been among the group at the pool.

"I'm waiting for someone," I told him.

"I hope it's a long wait." He sat down in the chair across from me. "I saw you at the desk this afternoon."

"Did you? I didn't notice you."

"Those appalling people." He leaned forward and took a *frito* from the dish on the table. His fair hair was cropped so short I could see the bumps and ridges in his narrow skull.

"I thought, Thank God, there's one civilized person here."

That old trick of inclusion. You and I. Why was he taking the trouble with me? What did he want?

"Fly-For-Funsters. I should have known. I saw the announcement in the lobby. I was going to turn right around and sail straight home but I only got here today and I think we owe it to ourselves not to let other people force us into decisions, don't you?"

He was including me again. There was something repellently fascinating about him. The rather high-pitched voice, the thin lips that remained almost rigid when he talked, the peering eyes behind the steel-rimmed glasses.

"I guess that depends who the other people are."

"I know who you are. Your name's Stone. Carol Stone. I asked the desk clerk."

Three of the Fly-For-Funsters had entered the bar. The man I was waiting for wasn't among them.

I didn't say anything. Maybe if I didn't answer, he would go away. I didn't believe that. He probably felt he owed it to himself not to let other people's reaction to him affect him. He might even enjoy being unwanted. It occurred to me that was why he had had his skull cropped like that, like a convict out of Dickens. He knew it was ugly; it gave him some perverse satisfaction to intrude his ugliness on others.

"My name's Croy. Harvey Croy." He paused as though he expected me to recognize the name. "I own that chain of restaurants in Los Angeles, the Harvey Croy chain. You must have heard of them."

"No."

"Perhaps you don't live in Los Angeles."

"No."

"I used to be in electronics. I'm still a CB buff. Then I was going to a movie in Westwood one evening and when I came out of the movie I wanted something to eat. But I didn't want a hamburger. After all, you can't eat hamburgers all the time, can you?"

"No."

"That's where I got the idea. Soup and salad. I started with one restaurant, right in Westwood. I've got six of them now. One in Santa Monica. One in Venice . . ." He was going to tell me where every one of them was.

"Excuse me." I stood up. "There's the friend I was waiting for."

I started away from the table with my drink. He was on his feet, too.

"Why don't we have dinner together later?"

"No, thank you." I started past him.

"I'll look for you in the restaurant."

He would, too. He would come over to my table and sit down, without being asked, and tell me where the rest of his soup and salad places were. In the meantime, there I was, halfway across the bar, going over to join my friend, and I didn't have a friend to join. The room was full of Fly-For-Funsters now, but still no sight of the seat-of-the-pants man. A woman was sitting by herself at a small corner table. I headed for her.

She was about my age, dark, carefully made up, wearing tailored slacks, a silk shirt, and a whole storeful of jewelry — necklaces, bracelets, earrings, the lot. She was like a living showcase.

I stopped in front of her. "I'm sorry to bother you, but I wonder if I could sit with you for a minute. I'm being pestered."

"Lucky you." She waved a handful of rings at the chair beside her.

"Thank you." I sat down.

"Which one? Maybe I could go for him."

"Over there. With the shaved head."

"Ugh." She was drinking a margarita. She held the glass to her lips, licking the salt with the tip of her tongue, while she looked around the bar. "Come to think of it," she said, "there isn't a mother in this whole place I *would* want to be pestered by."

"I know what you mean."

"It's too bad, because I'm as available as a free lunch, in a manner of speaking. My husband passed out in the room half an hour ago. And I know him. He'll sleep till two o'clock in the morning. Two o'clock sharp. Then he'll wake up and want a beer."

I smiled, hoping she'd go on; she was a lot more fun than soup and salad.

"Used to be, ten years ago, he'd wake up and want *me*. But that boy can't hold his liquor anymore. He only had fourteen mar-

garitas at the pool. Fourteen the whole afternoon. And they hit
him like a Mickey Finn. They dropped him cold on the floor before
he could even get his pants off. I had to get two waiters to lug
him onto the bed. My husband's six foot five and weighs two hundred
and forty-eight pounds. All of it solid flab. But then most men
are, aren't they? Most of the ones I know, anyway. Squalid flab."

She looked at me suddenly, a frank, quirky look.

"You're not one of these three fucks, are you?"

"Three — ?"

"Fly-For-Funsters. Three effing F's."

"No. Are you?"

"Am I ever. That's how I got these." She held out an armful
of bracelets and wiggled her ringed fingers. "Every one of these
baubles was a bribe from my husband to get him to one of these
Three F get-togethers." She pointed to the bracelets one by one.
"Denver, Colorado, Vegas, Mazatlán. Oh, shit. I can't remember
them anymore. They're all the same anyway. The men sit around
telling lies about Guam and the good old P-47's, and the women
get tanned and screw a bellhop if they're lucky. But not me." She
clicked the bracelets together on her wrist. "I get one of these.
Every time. Because my husband knows fucking well he couldn't
get our plane there without me."

"You mean, you fly him to these places?"

She shook her head. "I'm his navigator. My husband couldn't
find his way to Manhattan on a clear night if he took off from
Welfare Island. On a clear *day*." She licked at the salt on her
margarita again. "My husband, as he likes to tell you, flies by the
seat of his pants. And you know what that means? He flies like
an asshole."

We had dinner together. Her name was Diane. She had three
grown children, none of them, as she put it, in jail yet, and a
house in La Jolla. She had navigated her husband to Three F meets
in La Paz and Loreto as well as Mazatlán, and when she found I
was interested she was glad to talk about the topography of Baja
in expert detail.

When I told her, after dinner, why I was interested, that I had
heard there was a hippie commune somewhere on the Baja coast
and I was afraid my daughter might have joined it, she came to
my room with me and we went over the map together.

She agreed with me that in desert land like that a commune would have to ship in all its necessities by sea — food, water, medicine — let alone all the things they would need to start it — tents, utensils, sleeping bags, clothing. She thought that if there were even as many as a dozen people there, they would need a fair-sized supply ship, either a barge or a trawler.

"Shit," she said suddenly. "I know exactly where it is. I wondered what that fucking jetty was doing there in the middle of nowhere."

She asked me if I knew anything about navigation. I told her not really, but I had done a lot of sailing. We drove out to the airport and she got some charts from their plane. We went back to my room and she laid out a course for me from Guaymas. By the time Diane left to take a six-pack of beer back to her own room for her husband when he woke up, I knew I could find that jetty.

I thought I could find Genesis.

I was at the Fisherman's Monument at the usual time the next morning. I waited only until 12:15. No white camper. No Lindsay. I had not really expected him. Max knew he could keep me hanging a lot longer than four days.

I didn't go back to the hotel when I left the Plaza of the Three Presidents. I drove on beyond it to a new development on the shore called Bahía San Carlos. It was a drab, littered-looking place of prefabs and mobile homes and an unfinished country club. Beyond the country club was a marina. I parked the car there and walked over to the office on the dock.

A young Mexican was reading a comic book in the office. I managed to explain to him that I wanted to rent a boat, a sailboat if possible.

No. He seemed sorry, in an apathetic way. There were no boats for rent, only private boats in the marina.

And in Guaymas? I asked. Would it be possible to rent a boat in Guaymas?

Perhaps. I had the feeling he was trying to let me down lightly. Perhaps it would be possible, but he didn't know of any. He didn't know of anyplace where I might go to find out.

Okay. Then I would buy a boat. Did he know of any boats that were for sale in the marina?

There had been one last month. He did not, as he put it, occupy himself with those things, but he remembered seeing a For Sale sign on a cabin cruiser.

I thanked him. I walked all the way around the marina, out along every jetty, and talked to several people. There were no boats for sale.

Okay. I would drive down to the port in Guaymas and ask around in the shipping offices and if I couldn't buy a boat there, I would steal one.

"Carol Stone."

He was coming up out of the cabin of a broad-beamed sloop with a can of Tab in one hand and a bag of *fritos* in the other. He looked different in his Mexican straw hat. Hiding his cropped skull, it deprived him of his only memorable feature.

"Hello there," I said.

"What are you doing down here?"

"I don't know. Just wandering around."

"Welcome aboard."

He put down the *fritos* and held out his hand. I took it and climbed onto the stern.

"I'm sorry I broke our date in the restaurant last night. I just couldn't stand those appalling people any longer."

"I forgive you," I said.

"Let me show you around."

He took me forward and into the cockpit and down into the double-bunked cabin and showed me everything — the electric winches, the automatic pilot, the two-way radio set. Taking my interest for granted, as he had about his soup and salad chain, he *explained* everything. Not simply how it worked, but where he had acquired it, how he had gotten the idea of having this and that installed, how useful it was when this and that happened.

I said oh and ah a great deal and called the galley the kitchen and the deck the floor. I tried not to overdo it, but my thoughts were jumping around like hot fat on a griddle and it was easier to quiet them if I immersed myself in my role.

"Did you really sail all the way down from Los Angeles? All alone?" I asked when we were back on the deck and he had brought out canvas chairs and another can of Tab.

"From Marina del Rey. I moor the *Aquarius* in Marina del Rey when I'm not using it."

He told me about that, why he had found Marina del Rey more convenient than San Pedro. Why he had called his boat the *Aquarius.* How he had put in at La Paz on his way up around the Baja peninsula.

"Are you planning to stay in Guaymas for a while now?" I asked him.

"Depends." He smiled at me with his curiously rigid lips. It reminded me of those junkies in Bickford's, their rictus smiles.

"Depends on what?"

"On you."

"On me? Really? Why?"

I was hopeless at looking coy, but I did my best.

"How would you like to go for a little sail with me?"

"Today? Right now?"

He was wearing one of those digital watches. He looked at it. "It's a little late right now. By the time we got out of the bay . . . How would you like to go for a little sail with me tomorrow?"

I said I'd love it. I had privately decided I was even prepared to have dinner with him, to put up with him all evening, if he asked me to. I was prepared to put up with anything to get aboard that boat the next day.

"What time?" I asked.

"We ought to get an early start."

He was looking at his watch again.

"I'll get her gassed up this afternoon and — " He didn't suggest dinner. "I'll meet you in the patio outside the hotel tomorrow morning. Is seven o'clock too early for you?"

"Seven o'clock sounds fine."

Fuck the Fisherman's Monument. Fuck the white camper. Fuck Lindsay. Fuck Max.

He stood up. Now that it was all settled, he seemed anxious to get rid of me.

"Bring a sweater," he told me. "And a change of clothes in case it rains. And — " He gave me his rictus smile again. "And you'd better bring a toothbrush."

"Okay." I didn't even try to look coy. I had not imagined he had invited me for a sail because he found me intellectually stimulating. He wanted to get me out there in the middle of the Gulf of

California overnight so he could do whatever it was he liked doing to women. I had an idea it might be something fairly perverse.

I thanked him and said I would be on the patio at seven o'clock the next morning, and I was looking forward to it so much, and it was going to be such fun.

When I glanced back from the dock, he was climbing down into the cabin. He had taken off his hat and his cropped skull looked pink and raw in the sunlight, like something in a butcher's shop.

I looked for Diane in the bar that evening. I wanted to thank her and tell her I had found a boat. She wasn't around. None of the Fly-For-Funsters were. They were probably having a carousal at some restaurant in town. I had a quick dinner, drove into Guaymas, and bought an overnight canvas bag.

I called Anton as soon as I got back to the hotel. I told him what I was going to do. He didn't sound happy about it; I could imagine him rubbing the bridge of his nose while we were talking. But he agreed I was probably right to try it. We arranged that if I didn't call him within five days, he would fly to Los Angeles and tell Sergeant Gregory what I had done and exactly where I had gone. I gave Anton the latitude and longitude of that jetty I was heading for.

I spent the rest of the evening going over Diane's charts again.

Harvey Croy was waiting on the patio when I got there at 6:55 the next morning.

"Okay. Let's go." No greeting. No rictus. He seemed curiously tense as we walked over to the parking lot. When I suggested driving to the marina in my own car and meeting him there, he cut me off at once.

"No. Leave it here. We'll both go in my car."

He relaxed a little once we were aboard the *Aquarius.* He set a canvas chair for me in the stern and told me to make myself comfortable. He started the auxiliary motor and cast off, easing away from the jetty between the boats moored on either side.

One of the things he had shown and explained to me the day before was his sextant. It was kept in a special waterproof, velvet-lined locker on the afterdeck. I took it out and pretended to be examining it. He glanced back at me irritably but he was busy steering around the bow of an incoming trawler and he didn't say anything.

I stood up, holding the sextant up to my eye in a clumsy way and pretending to be trying to take a sight on the country club.

"Please don't play with that. Put it away where you found it."

We were towing our dinghy; he had evidently been using it for getting around the marina. I figured he didn't intend to haul it on board until we were clear of the clutter of boats and jetties and out of the channel. It was on a short towrope, less than four feet from where I was standing.

I threw the sextant into it.

"Oh, God," I screamed. "Oh, I'm terribly sorry."

He was safely around the trawler. He idled the motor and turned and looked at me.

"I couldn't help it. I'm so sorry. I sort of tripped and it fell out of my hands."

We were in clear water now, a quarter-mile from the entrance to the channel. He left the engine in neutral and scrambled out of the cockpit.

"It's all right," I told him cheerfully. "It didn't go in the water. It fell in that little boat there. Look, you can see it."

You could see it clear as the moon, lying on the duckboards under the seat of the dinghy, his beautiful, treasured sextant.

"Oh, I do hope it isn't broken," I said.

I was betting my whole life on the chance that he wouldn't be able to wait to find out if his beautiful, treasured sextant was broken or not. That he would not risk hauling the dinghy aboard with the sextant in it. I thought I was fairly safe. He had spent a quarter of an hour lecturing me about the bloody thing yesterday afternoon.

I was right. He couldn't wait. He pulled the dinghy up under the stern and lowered himself into it.

I cast off the towrope, jumped down into the cockpit, and set the engine full ahead.

When I looked back at the entrance to the channel, he was standing upright in the dinghy holding the sextant in both hands. I couldn't see his eyes at that distance but his face looked like stone. Entirely blank.

"Don't worry," I shouted at him. "I'll bring your boat back. Don't worry."

The *Aquarius* was a lovely boat. She went out through the winding channel as though she could anticipate every move I wanted from her before I touched the wheel. Three miles out in the open sea, I hauled up the sails with the electric winch, killed the motor, set the automatic pilot on a course that would bring me within sight of San Pedro Nolasco Island within a couple of hours if the good southwest wind held, and went below to the galley to make myself some coffee. While I was waiting for the water to boil, I took off my sneakers and socks. I had always liked going barefoot when I was sailing.

I felt a little guilty about Harvey. But not very. He was lucky. His passionate obsession with himself and his possessions had saved him from something far more uncomfortable than being left stranded in that dinghy. If he hadn't gone after his sextant, I had planned to wait until he started setting the sails and then push him overboard.

As it was, of course, once he had recovered from his surprise, he would paddle back across the marina and try to rouse the Mexican authorities to go after me. I didn't think he would have much success. I didn't think the Mexican Coast Guard, or whatever, would waste much time chasing one gringo, female, to oblige another gringo, male. Apart from the apathy he would encounter, Harvey Croy would also find himself entangled in a lot of red tape. The chances were that his passport and tourist card and the ownership papers of the *Aquarius* were on board.

I took my cup of coffee and went to look for them.

The drawer of the small metal desk in the cabin was locked. Harvey Croy probably had the key in his pocket. It took me almost five minutes to force it open with a chisel. As I had expected, the papers were all there.

I looked through them. U.S. passport. That held a small surprise for me: Harvey Croy's profession was given as "Psychologist." Mexican tourist card. Permission to land in La Paz. U.S. registration for the *Aquarius.* Another small surprise: home port, San Diego. I turned to the next item, a sheet of white paper encased in cellophane.

I sat there staring at it. It was as though some abacus in my mind had come up with the expected answer. On the paper was a list of radio call signals. They were in alphabetical order. The third one down was Genesis.

I went back to the cockpit and settled behind the wheel with the fresh wind in my face and tried to think it all out.

I remembered the way Harvey Croy had kept glancing at his watch the afternoon before, how anxious he had seemed to get rid of me once I had agreed to go sailing with him. He had started into the cabin, with his hat off, the instant I went ashore. Had he been going down to put on his headphones, to switch on his two-way radio, to call Genesis, to tell Max it was all set, Carol Stone was on her way?

It seemed to me very likely.

"I can recommend the Hotel Cortéz," Max's lawyer had told me, as though it were part of the instructions. Max had known where to find me. A man named, not Lindsay, but Harvey Croy had approached me there and suggested a little sail.

It disturbed me to remember how readily I'd agreed to that. Considering the urgency of my daily rendezvous at the Fisherman's Monument, Harvey Croy might have been puzzled by my eagerness to skip it and go sailing with him. Maybe Max had never told him about that arrangement; in any case, Old Harvey had obviously never suspected I was anything but an unattached woman ripe for a little macking. If he had, he would never have clambered down into the dinghy.

Earlier, he had shown a certain caution; he had been very firm about my not taking my own car to the marina. It was okay if the rental company found it in the parking lot of the hotel; that was a dead end. If they found it abandoned in Bahía San Carlos, they might start asking people on the boats there about me. Someone might remember seeing me aboard the *Aquarius*.

What would Harvey do now? He had told me he was a CB buff. He might have access to another two-way radio in Guaymas. He might be trying to call Genesis right this minute. I went below and turned on the receiving set. For the rest of the day, sailing northwest across the gulf, I half listened to interminable conversations in Spanish on the citizens band, alert for any American voice or the Genesis call signal.

I sighted San Pedro Nolasco Island just before 10:00 A.M. and altered my course to pass west of it. An hour before sunset, I was skirting the eastern shore of the island of San Loreno. It was a deserted strip of rock and scrub about twelve miles long, pointing northwest, ten miles off the coast of Baja. I found the cove I had marked on Diane's charts as a good place to lay over for a few hours. I took down the sails and eased into the cove, using the auxiliary engine, until I judged I was close enough to the beach to have the full shelter of the lee shore and still be certain of two fathoms of water at low tide. I dropped the anchor.

I made myself a sandwich of corned beef and rye bread and opened a can of Tab. There was no beer or liquor on board; Old Harvey evidently didn't drink. I decided not to show any lights; I had seen nothing but a few Mexican fishing boats all day and I thought there was little or no risk of any other craft putting into the cove and ramming me in the dark.

I pulled the mattress off one of the bunks and lay down on the afterdeck. The stars were like the lights of a distant friendly city; the moon was in its first quarter.

I thought some more about Harvey Croy. Psychologist. It seemed to fit. Croy was probably an old associate of Max's; he might have worked with him at the Genesis drug-abuse center in Santa Monica. I remembered what my friend Sergeant Gregory had said: "Max Ludlow had a certain amount of clout, or at least a hell of a lot of money." He had either paid or pressured Harvey into sailing to Guaymas to get me, to trick me on board his boat and take me to Baja.

Why? Why trick me instead of keeping the appointment at the Fisherman's Monument? Thinking it through now, I could see I'd been stupid ever to expect that Max would stick to that arrangement. It would have given me too much time, too much opportunity to find people who would help me. The American consul, a well-connected Mexican lawyer; I might even have managed to interest the Mexican police in helping me rescue my kidnapped daughter from Baja. Max's contact, "Lindsay," meeting me by appointment, could have found himself having to answer a lot of official questions before he got me on board a boat.

At ten o'clock, when there was still no sound of anyone calling

Genesis or the *Aquarius,* I turned off the radio, set Harvey's electric alarm clock for 4:00 A.M., and went to sleep on deck.

The location of the jetty Diane had spotted from the air was on the north side of Las Animas Point, just under forty miles from my anchorage. I had been afraid I might miss it in the dark. If the wind held, I should reach it now soon after dawn.

I sighted Las Animas at six-thirty in the morning, a two-mile spit of hilly land, running east and west and ending in sharp rocky cliffs. Rounding the point, three miles offshore, I could see the jetty. I turned the boat into the wind and got Harvey Croy's Zeiss binoculars from the cabin.

The jetty was about twenty yards long, wooden struts, wooden pilings, sturdy mooring posts. It all looked fairly new. There was no boat tied up to it, no sight of Iris's cabin cruiser, *The Emissary,* anywhere in the bay. I focused the binoculars on the rim of land beyond the jetty.

I'm not sure exactly what I'd been expecting. Prefabs? Tents? Thatched huts? Antlike communal activity?

I could see nothing on that crescent of land. A strip of sandy beach, dry gullies, a streak of open ground littered with flinty stones sloping up to the top of a low hill. No huts. No one.

I sat down on the deck, suspended between fear and anger, fear for Vanessa and anger at myself. I had jumped at the obvious, the jetty Diane had seen from her plane, and it had turned out to be a false lead.

I tried to think out what to do next. I could sail south as far as Rosalía, hugging the coast and searching for Genesis myself. If I didn't find it, I could turn back north and sail up as far as San Felipe. I still believed that somewhere along this three-hundred-mile stretch of deserted shore between those two towns Max had established his commune and was holding Vanessa there.

I started back to the wheel and then stopped. I picked up the binoculars and went over every square yard of the hill. That streak of open, flinty ground was certainly no road, but it might have been deliberately cleared. I focused the glasses on the jetty again. Those new-looking beams and pilings bothered me. Someone had built that jetty quite recently.

I lowered the sails and, turning on the auxiliary engine, moved closer to the shore, pausing now and then for another look through the binoculars.

I could still see no evidence of human life. Even when I was only a hundred yards offshore, I could find no sign of tracks or tire marks on that streak of clear ground. I remembered what Diane had said: Max would have to bring in everything by sea — food, water, everything. If he had established his commune inland, the water, at least, would have to be trucked there. I eased the boat into the jetty and cut the engine. I hadn't much hope, but since I had come this far, the least I could do was go over the ground on foot and see if there *were* any tire marks.

I tied up to those sturdy mooring posts, furled the sails in case a sudden wind came up, and went down into the cabin for my socks and sneakers. While I was there I realized how hungry I was. I gulped down some cold coffee and started to fix myself a sandwich to take ashore with me.

I was putting the second slice of bread on top of the corned beef when I heard it. A sudden, full-throated bellow of laughter. It scared the breath out of me. It was so loud, so deep and hollow, that it sounded unearthly and yet accusingly personal.

I put the sandwich back on the table and did absolutely nothing until the laughter stopped. I went on doing nothing for several seconds after that, waiting for it to start again. It did. Closer this time, just above my head.

Then, Don't be a damn fool, I told myself. It's a burro. I hurried up on deck.

It *was* a burro. It was standing on the jetty a few feet from me, its head lowered in a waiting, patient way.

Vanessa was riding it.

"Hello," she said. "Why did it take you so long? I've been expecting you for ages."

She slithered down off the burro's back and I was on the jetty, reaching for her, holding her against me. I didn't say anything. I couldn't speak.

She hugged me for a moment, then stepped back, looking at me, a little startled.

"What's wrong?" she asked. "Are you all right?"

I nodded, searching her face with incredulous relief. There was no need to ask if *she* was all right. She was clear-eyed and tanned and smiling. In her favorite jeans and dark red shirt, she looked as composed and secure and as much at home as though she had just ridden in from the fields in Waterford.

"I've been climbing the hill every day to watch for you," she said. "Several times a day, and then this morning there you were, tying up. It was wonderful. I've been longing to see you. So I rode Beano down to meet you."

I was searching her face. She did look pleased; in her own quiet way, excited. But there was no relieved anxiety in her eyes or her voice. She might have been longing to see me, but she had evidently never for a moment been afraid I wasn't coming.

"This is Beano," she said, patting the burro. "I've been riding him a lot and Max has goats and chickens, too."

There were so many questions I wanted to ask her, so many things I wanted so urgently to know. But I was afraid to cross-examine her; she was so obviously, cheerfully "safe."

Once when she was eleven years old she had gone sailing with one of the Sutreau boys. They had been very late getting back and I had become frightened. When they did finally show up, it turned out there had been nothing to worry about, they had been sitting on the beach. But I was faintly hysterical by that time, and I frightened and disturbed Vanessa with my own fear. It had ended with Vanessa in indignant tears. "But we were all right," she kept saying. "We were perfectly safe." Later that night I understood that I had behaved like an idiot, a selfish one, too, relieving my emotions by heaping them, like accusations, on Vanessa.

I was determined not to do that now. I needed to sit down with her, let her talk, let her tell me her own version of what had happened since Max had picked her up at her school in Waterford two weeks ago.

"I was just going to have a sandwich," I said. "Are you hungry?"

Yes, she was rather. She hadn't had breakfast yet. We went down into the cabin together.

"Oh, how lovely," she said when she saw the corned beef. "We don't have any meat, except chicken sometimes. We don't have any coffee, either. We only have herb tea, though I must say I quite like it."

She was looking around at the galley, the cabin beyond. "Are you alone?" she asked. "Didn't Max's friend bring you across from Guaymas?"

"No, I came on my own. Was someone supposed to bring me?"

"That's how Max thought you'd probably be coming. With his friend. Of course, we don't have a telephone, only a two-way radio, and it's a bit difficult to get through on it sometimes, it keeps conking out, but he told me you were flying on to Guaymas from Los Angeles and he was trying to arrange with this friend of his to bring you across."

He had certainly done his best to arrange that.

She was silent for a moment, eating her sandwich. "Max is longing to see you, too," she said. "He's been looking forward to your coming almost as much as I have. He was terribly disappointed you weren't home that weekend in Ireland."

Was he? Hadn't he called Mrs. Coughlan at the post office and found out I was away before he went to Vanessa's school?

"Did you tell him I was in Paris?"

"Yes, of course. It was so exciting when he suddenly showed up at Newtown. But then you know all about that from the letter I left you before we went off to Shannon."

There had been no letter from Vanessa when I returned to Ireland that Tuesday evening. Max must have slipped back into the house on some pretext or other and destroyed it before they drove off.

I was so angry that I did almost blurt it all out then — my frantic anxiety when I had found her gone, chasing Max to Santa Monica, the instructions from his lawyer, Harold Tate. I was trying to find a way of telling it as calmly as I could, without accusation. But Vanessa spoke first.

"He's awfully nice," she said. "He's so kind. He's, I don't know, sort of wonderful. The people here seem to love him so much." She hesitated and the sudden coolness in her eyes reminded me of that evening when I had first told her about Max.

"I'm not blaming you," she went on. But she was. "I know you'd had a row and you thought he hated you for some reason. But it seems awful now that I spent all those years without even knowing he existed. Without knowing I had a wonderful father like that."

I walked over to the stove and made myself very busy pouring

the warmed-up coffee into two cups. My head was full of voices.
"I hate you. I think you're horrible. Why didn't you tell me?"
Vanessa was screaming at me in the kitchen in Ireland. "Yeah,
well," Sergeant Gregory was telling me. "The reason we kept after
him was that we'd had so many complaints. Assault. Kids being
kept in straightjackets, force fed tranquilizers." Vanessa, no longer
screaming now, but with a wondering affection in her voice, was
saying, "He's awfully nice. He's so kind."

I put the coffee cups on the table and sat down. "Tell me all
about your trip here," I suggested. "From the time you left that
letter for me at the house."

"It was great fun. I liked him at once. He asked me so many
questions about school, my friends there. Not prying, but the way
you'd expect a father would. He was so interested in me . . ."

They had spent the night at a hotel in Shannon. Iris had been
waiting there for them. Sometime that evening she must have called
Vanessa's headmaster, pretending to be Mrs. Stone, saying Vanessa
wouldn't be returning to school that semester.

"I'm afraid I don't like Iris much. She's all right, but there's
something pushy about her. I'm glad she doesn't live here at Genesis.
Max says she hardly ever comes here anymore . . ."

Early the next morning they had all three taken the plane to
New York.

"I would have called you from there, but I didn't know where
to reach you."

I had still been in Paris.

"I did try to call Jason's parents in New York. Don't worry, I
wasn't going to tell them Jason wasn't really my father. But then
we had to catch the plane to California and Max said we didn't
have much time . . ."

In San Diego they had taken a taxi straight to the marina and
gone aboard Iris's cabin cruiser, *The Emissary*. They had sailed
that afternoon.

"It's a terrific boat, like being on board a yacht, and it can cruise
at twenty knots. Iris has a couple of young men who crew it for
her. I think they're her boyfriends. At least, she spent a lot of
time in her cabin with them . . ."

They had put in at La Paz to refuel, then sailed straight on up the east coast of Baja. They had reached Genesis on Tuesday after-noon, about the time I was landing at the Cork airport, hurrying back to Waterford to pick up Vanessa at her school. My eager haste then reminded me of something.

"Oh, I brought you a present from Paris, darling." I found the suede shoulder bag I had packed as a small act of faith. Vanessa undid the tissue paper.

"Oh. Oh, that's lovely." She stood up and put the strap over her shoulder. "It's exactly what I wanted. And Max'll be pleased, too. We go out collecting herbs sometimes and I don't have anything to carry them in."

She came over and kissed my cheek.

"It's lovely," she repeated. "And it's so wonderful you're here at last."

There was one question I could ask.

"How could Max be so sure I was coming?"

"But that was all arranged weeks ago. Before you even went to Paris."

"Did Max tell you that?"

"Of course. I know it was supposed to be a surprise for me, coming here with him instead of meeting him in Los Angeles. That's why he was so disappointed you were away when he came to Ireland. He had been hoping we could all travel here together."

Had he?

"Wasn't he worried when he didn't hear from me?" I asked.

"But he did hear from you. Last Thursday. At least, I think it was Thursday. The days here never seem to matter much. He man-aged to get through on the radio to a friend in Los Angeles. Harold someone."

"Harold Tate. He's Max's lawyer."

"I guess so. Anyway, he said he'd seen you and you were on your way to Guaymas."

Yes, I was. On my way to that daily rendezvous at the Fisherman's Monument. Obeying Max's instructions.

"And then the day before yesterday, the radio was working again and a friend of Max's in Guaymas said you were there and he was bringing you across on his boat."

Harvey Croy.

Vanessa put our empty coffee cups in the sink. She looked around the beautifully appointed galley and cabin again. "Where did you get this marvelous boat?" she asked.

"I sort of borrowed it."

"From Max's friend?"

"In a way."

She turned the water on and washed the cups and dried them. "Don't you have to take it back to him?"

"Sooner or later."

"Iris will probably be stopping by sometime. She's supposed to bring some tools over for us. Maybe one of her boyfriends can sail the boat back for you."

Over my dead body.

I was as confused as I had ever been in my life. Sergeant Gregory's warnings had prepared me for horror, and here was Vanessa, not only safe and happy, without a shadow of fear or suspicion in her mind, but entranced by her whole experience these past two weeks. There had been no kidnapping, as far as she was concerned. It had all been an unexpected and exciting adventure. Her wonderful new father had brought her here on a terrific boat and arranged for me to join her.

I was relieved, almost to the point of shock, that she had experienced her abduction in such a carefree way. But *I* hadn't. I had seen it all from a different, frightening angle. I did not believe Max was either nice or kind. And Old Harvey's *Aquarius* was my lifeboat, the only way of getting out of here, of getting Vanessa out of here. With luck, Iris might not be stopping by for several days yet, but when she did I had no intention of letting one of her boyfriends sail off with my only means of escape.

"I do hope we can all make a go of it here together now," Vanessa was saying as she replaced the cups in the rack. "It's really a wonderful place. I can't describe it. It's so natural and peaceful. Wait till you see it."

"I'm dying to." I stood up.

"Come on then."

She skipped out of the galley and climbed onto the jetty. I followed her.

"Don't you want to bring your suitcase?" She was looking at

my empty hands. "It's all arranged for you to share my tent with me. Or you can have one of the cabins, if you like. But the tents are cooler."

I didn't have a suitcase. I had an overnight bag with my passport and traveler's checks, a change of clothes, the toothbrush Harvey Croy had recommended to me. I fetched it from the cabin. Vanessa took it from me.

"Would you like to ride Beano?" She hung my bag from the wooden saddle.

"No, thank you. You ride him, darling." I was afraid I would look ridiculous astride the burro. I felt I had enough problems to deal with without looking ridiculous to my daughter.

"All right. Then I'll walk, too. It isn't very far."

She started down the jetty, leading Beano. I was pleased that she had not hung her new suede bag from the saddle. She kept it hanging from her shoulder, clasping it with one hand as though she treasured it. My small act of faith.

We climbed that streak of clear ground I had seen through the binoculars. There were certainly no recent tire marks on it. It struck me like a start of fear that if Vanessa had not come down to the boat, if I had climbed that hill alone and found no tracks on it, I might have gone back to the *Aquarius* and sailed away.

We reached the top of the hill. Vanessa stopped, prompting me to pause beside her. She was telling me to look.

I looked. Three or four miles away was another line of hills and beyond them a high range of mountains. Directly below us in the hollow were palm trees, fields of corn, meadows and vegetable gardens, windmills, several white painted cabins, one of them as long as my barn in Ireland, tents, and grazing animals. It was an oasis, a green, welcoming valley in the desert land.

"Isn't it heaven," Vanessa said. It wasn't a question.

I nodded. Beano started forward again, eager to return to those nourishing pastures. Vanessa restrained him.

"How did Max ever find this place?" I asked.

"He didn't find it. He created it."

Like the God of Genesis.

"There was a Spanish mission near here once, over three hundred years ago," Vanessa explained. "So he knew there had to be water

around somewhere and he kept drilling until he found an underground stream. That's what the windmills are for. They pump up
the water and irrigate everything. Then he brought the people in,
and the tents and wood for the cabins and all the other things
they needed. He had to ship food in for the first year or so, too.
But he doesn't anymore. We can grow just about everything we
need now."

She paused, stroking Beano's nose. "Don't you think it's wonderful?"

I nodded silently again. I could see the people now, working in
the fields and the vegetable patches. They were not the kind of
people I had expected to find in Max's commune. The ones who
were close enough for me to see their faces were mostly in their
thirties and forties, tanned and relaxed looking in their white shirts
and cotton pants and Mexican straw hats.

"How many people are there?" I asked.

"About forty, I think, including the children."

"There are children here?"

"Oh, yes, lots. All ages. There are even two little ones who were
born here. One of the first people to come was a doctor and his
family, and there's a woman who's a schoolteacher, although Max
teaches most of the older ones himself." She pointed to the long
wooden cabin. "In that big building there. That's where we have
meals, too." She glanced at her watch. "They'll be coming out of
school in a few minutes now, and then we can go and see Max.
He'll be so glad you're here. Come on."

"All right." I started down the hill. There was no immediately
visible path, but there was a way, twisting between rocks and boul-
ders. It was obviously as familiar to Vanessa as the back roads of
County Waterford. She went ahead of me, leading Beano, guiding
me until we reached the first fields.

In spite of the grilling sun overhead, I felt the instant coolness
of being among green, growing things. There was only occasional
shade from a date palm, scattered chaparral, or what looked like
Joshua trees, but the verdure itself was such a contrast to the arid
glare of the land behind us that it seemed almost temperate in
the valley. My feet stopped hurting at once.

"It's so peaceful," Vanessa had said. I could feel what she meant.

On the far side of the field, two men and a woman were hoeing between rows of beans. They glanced up as we passed; they did not speak, but they did not look unwelcoming. They seemed absorbed in themselves, incurious about us.

We reached a wooden lean-to. Vanessa unsaddled Beano and stowed his harness and saddle carefully away at one end of it. Spades, pitchforks, hoes, axes, were hanging from pegs on the walls. Each tool was shining clean, each in its ordered place. I took my overnight bag from her, and we walked on to a meadow surrounded by a low wall of loose stones that reminded me of Ireland. Several other burros were grazing there. Beano broke into a deep braying laugh at the sight of them. Vanessa unlatched the gate and he trotted in to join his kind.

Tools, burros, saddles — everything obviously had its place at Genesis. The peace Vanessa had remarked on was a noticeably ordered, disciplined peace.

"It's all so neat," I said. "Like a rather strict school."

"I know what you mean. But it isn't *really* like that." Vanessa was frowning uncertainly. "Of course, they do have to have rules in a place like this, but everybody seems to sort of enjoy obeying them."

"What kind of rules?"

"Well . . ." She was thoughtful. "They all work on the land for four hours every morning. And they all eat together, with everyone taking turns to cook the food and wash up. And then Max *is* rather strict about sex. If two people want to live together, they have to wait six months, and then they have a ceremony and Max marries them."

"How?" I did my best to sound amused, rather than prying. "He was never ordained and he isn't a justice of the peace, is he?"

"I don't know, exactly. I've only been here about ten days and there haven't been any weddings yet."

"What are the other rules, darling?"

"It's really a kind of self-discipline. Everyone trying to fit in and get along with everybody else."

"Suppose they don't. Suppose they have a quarrel?"

"Then Max talks to them. He helps them focalize, as he calls it. Oh, good." Vanessa took my hand. "They're coming out of school. We can go and see Max now."

A dozen children were filing out of the largest of the buildings. A man stood in the white sunlight, watching them as they dispersed silently, without haste, to their tents.

It had been sixteen years since I had seen him. Outside the airport in Rome after that terrible taxi ride from his hotel. He had looked pale and thin and sick and tormented then. I'm not sure I would have recognized him now if I had passed him in a crowd. His face and arms were a deep brown and the cotton T-shirt he was wearing revealed the muscled strength of his chest. His graying hair had looked so dead in Rome. Although it had turned white, it was bristling with life now. His features, his nose and cheekbones and chin, so sharp then, had assumed a firm, impressive emphasis. There was an overwhelming authority in the whole cast of his face.

He reminded me of someone; it took me an instant to remember who. Then I realized it was not any actual person my mind had recalled, it was my own adolescent fantasy of a leader, a scout of the Western plains. It was the image I had created of Max himself that long-ago summer in Hollywood. He was no longer the young American I had idealized then, although he did not look even middle-aged, but he had that same aura of quiet, dependable confidence I had fallen in love with at eighteen.

"Hello, Carol." He was walking toward me, that rangy stride I had once found so attractive.

"Hello, Max." We shook hands. He smiled and touched Vanessa's shoulder. She was looking at him with the unguarded admiration he had inspired in me all those years ago.

"Why don't you take your mother to your tent and help her settle in." He was smiling at me now. "I can't tell you how wonderful it is to have you here, Carol. I wish I didn't have to run off like this when you've only just arrived, but there are things I have to do."

"Max has to inspect all the farm work that's been done every morning. You're sort of the overseer, aren't you?"

I'll bet he was.

Max laughed good-naturedly. "Well, I'm not exactly the gang boss, Vanessa. I just have to check things." He turned back to me. "I'll see you at lunch in half an hour."

I said I'd look forward to it. Vanessa showed me to her tent. It was quite large, with vertical sides and a pitched roof. There were two wooden cots. I put my bag on the one she told me was for me.

"Isn't he wonderful looking?" Vanessa was saying.

I had to agree that he was.

"And it's amazing what he's done here," she went on. "There are showers and toilets and even electricity. The electricity comes from solar energy. Everything runs on the sun or the wind here. That's what I meant, it's all so natural."

Natural and very carefully and thoroughly planned. No wonder there had been no tire tracks leading away from that jetty. For over a year now, Genesis must have been almost entirely self-sufficient. A whole independent, separate world in itself, enclosed by the ocean on one side and the mountains on the other.

Vanessa took me in to lunch at noon. A plain wooden table ran the length of the room. Max stood at the head of it, placing me and Vanessa on either side of him. The children were at a smaller table by themselves. We all helped ourselves from a buffet along the wall. Squash, beans, corn, a salad of papaya and sliced mango. When we had filled our plates and returned to our seats, there was a sudden silence. Max bowed his head. The woman next to me reached out and took my hand. I didn't understand why for a second; then I saw everyone was linking hands around the table. Max was reaching his toward mine as he took Vanessa's. Submissively, I clasped his hard, dry palm. The chain was complete.

"The land flourishes and produces in abundance." Max had raised his head and was speaking in a stern, carrying voice. "But man has despoiled the earth and wasted its abundance. He has wasted and destroyed the awareness of his oneness with the earth. But the sentient being still lives in our hearts. In the realization of this sentient being is the absolute awareness of the true way of life. Realization of the sentient being knows and knows that it knows. The sentient being is uplifted into the truth of our way of living . . ."

He went on like that for several minutes. The words meant very little to me, but in the people around me I could feel the response to the conviction in his voice. I had heard that persuasive timbre of conviction before. Once it had championed the workers' ownership of the means of production; then the mystical reality of subjective experience; then psychoanalysis and Freud; then the church of Rome. Now it was the sentient being.

I glanced at Vanessa. She wasn't fidgeting; there was no hint of protest or boredom in her eyes. She had accepted that ring of clasped hands, Max's hollow rhetoric, as unquestioningly as she had once accepted the lighted candles, young David Silver's reading in Hebrew of the story of the Passover, the whole ritual of those Seders in Waterford. Why not? An unquestioning private tolerance had always been a part of her naturally private character.

Max had come to the end of his endorsement of the sentient being. We ate. There was little conversation during the meal. Max did not say anything. The woman beside me did not ask me any questions about myself. When she spoke to me at all it was only about the food, the wild herbs in the squash, the flavor of the homegrown sesame seeds that had been sprinkled on the beans. From what I could hear of the rest of the conversation around me, it was largely concerned with those same topics.

When we had finished eating, we all joined hands again. Max did not favor us with another sermon. He bowed his head for a minute in silence. We all bowed our heads.

It was a relief to escape from that devoted hush into the sunshine outside. Max and Vanessa joined me there. I watched the others file away. They did not chatter among themselves, not even the children. As I looked at their faces, I was struck by a similarity in their expressions. They all seemed to be cherishing the same emotion. It took me a minute to define it to myself. The closest I could come to it was a self-righteous serenity. They were like a few of the nuns I had seen in Ireland: they weren't going to make a thing about it, but they were self-evidently superior to other people; they were following the True Way.

"Vanessa's been very helpful," Max was saying. "She looks after the small children for an hour every afternoon."

He was dismissing her. We were to have a private talk together. Good. I had a lot to say to him. Vanessa went off to one of the cabins. Max and I strolled across a field to the shade of a date palm and sat down on the grass.

Max sat cross-legged; it wasn't quite the lotus position, but his straight back and tucked-in ankles conveyed some of that Eastern guru effect.

"I can't tell you how long I've been wanting to bring you here, Carol."

He reached out to take my hand. I pulled it away from him.

"If you'd really wanted me here, you wouldn't have destroyed that note Vanessa left for me at the house in Ireland. You could even have left a letter for me yourself, telling me where you were taking her and how to get here."

"Would you have come?"

"Of course."

"Alone? Would you have come alone?"

No, I wouldn't. He was right about that. I would have brought Anton with me, and perhaps a lawyer, too, depending on the tone of the letter. And of course Max had wanted me here alone, without interfering friends or associates. I had already realized that was what all that man-named-Lindsay crap was for, to get me to Guaymas, where Harvey Croy could lure me, alone, on board his boat.

"It was mere chance I got here at all," I pointed out. "You couldn't possibly count on my finding your lawyer in Los Angeles. And he had no way of reaching me. It was only with the help of the police that I ever got in touch with him."

I was watching him carefully when I mentioned the police. I thought I did see a flicker of annoyance in his eyes.

"Of course I knew you would find Harold Tate, Carol," he told me. "Because I wanted you to." He clasped his hands together in front of him; it heightened the guru effect. "You see, I believe if you want something in the right way, want it with your whole sentient being" — I made a gesture of impatience; he didn't seem to notice it — "the way I wanted you here at Genesis," he continued evenly, "then whatever you want will manifest itself."

"I didn't manifest myself here. I went through ten days of absolute hell trying to find my daughter."

"Our daughter." He half closed his eyes, but not before I had seen the abrupt anger in them. "The daughter you kept from me all these years."

"You got well paid for that."

"What do you mean?" His eyes were completely closed now.

"Jason paid you around twelve thousand dollars to stay away from Vanessa. And please don't say what do you mean again. I found the canceled checks and that note I wrote you at the Inglaterra in Rome among his papers after he died. You were blackmailing Jason for three years."

He opened his eyes; the anger was gone.

"I was going through a confused time," he said quietly. "It wasn't until much later I even understood my own behavior, my own motives."

"I could have explained them to you. You made them quite clear the last time I saw you, in Rome. You hated me for trying to destroy your soul, as you put it. And you were going to make me pay for it if it took you the rest of your life. You couldn't quite figure out how to get at me at that point, so you made Jason pay instead."

"I felt it was my mission to help others. Those pitiful young drug addicts. I needed money to fulfill my mission."

"I know all about that, too. Those young addicts were pitiful, all right. Especially after you got your hands on them. The police had so many complaints against you, for assault, abuse, cruelty of one kind or another, that they went to a lot of trouble to close you down."

"Is that what they told you?"

"With all the details, including the straightjackets." I stood up. "You've managed to fool Vanessa for a few days here, Max. But she's a sensible girl. She's going to see this wonderful commune of yours in quite a different light when I tell her about your other Genesis in Santa Monica."

I had expected to see that anger in his eyes again. He was smiling.

"I think you should tell her, Carol."

"I will."

I walked back to our tent.

Vanessa was still looking after the smaller children in one of the cabins. I lay down on my cot. What exactly was I going to say to her? I would tell her about that other Genesis, certainly. I was also going to make it clear to her that it had been far from a charitable, nonprofit organization. Max had gotten very rich from it. What else? I had seen enough of those self-righteous people at lunch, their worshipful attitude toward Max, to suspect the true nature of their commitment to this place. Their serenity was the serenity of the self-deluded. Or the Max-deluded. I could understand their habitual silence now. They didn't talk because they had nothing to talk about. They had abandoned the human custom of thinking. Isolated in their fertile valley, they were preoccupied with nothing but their immediate needs, the small pleasure of sesame seeds on their beans, and their devotion to Max. Vanessa had said they seemed to love him. If they did, it was a love that had been deliberately cultivated in them, an implanted religion. It probably had an element of fear in it. Most religions did.

I recalled the anger in Max's eyes when we had been talking just now, all the other times in the past I had been the victim of his sudden fury. "What happens if the people here quarrel?" I had asked Vanessa. She had explained that Max talked to them, "focalized" them. I could imagine those talks, the threat of his rage, its effect on these passive and dependent members of his commune.

He had managed to hide that side of himself from Vanessa. It must have taken great self-control. He had shown her only how nice and kind he could be. It appalled me a little to remember how much — and for how long — I had once loved and admired him for those same qualities.

The tent flap was lifted aside. Vanessa entered. She sat on the other cot.

"Did you make it up?" she asked.

"What?"

"Your old quarrel with Max. Is everything all right between you again now?"

I sat up and put my feet on the floor. I realized the danger of antagonizing her, but I had to risk it. "I do hope we can all make a go of it here together now," she had told me. What had she meant? Make a go of it for how long? I had no intention of staying even one night if I could help it.

To persuade Vanessa to leave with me — and I certainly wasn't going without her — I *had* to try to make her see what Max was doing here through my eyes. As I saw it. An exercise in power and self-glorification. Max had realized that dream he had once explained to me in a pension in Pescara in Italy. A group of abject

followers who would look up to him and obey him. I had hated
that dream in Pescara. I hated it even more now when it was a
reality.

I started to tell Vanessa about that other Genesis in Santa Monica,
what the police had told me.

"Oh, I know all about that," she interrupted me. "Max told
me the whole story. There was a group of psychiatrists who were
jealous of him. He was much more successful than they were and
they were furious because he wasn't even a doctor. So they made
up a lot of lies about him and the police believed them."

It was Max's word against mine and he had gotten to her first.
I tried a different attack.

"That two-way radio," I said. "Is anyone allowed near it except
Max?"

"I don't know."

"When he told you I was in Guaymas, he knew where I was
staying, he had a friend there he was in contact with. But he wouldn't
let you try to get in touch with me, would he?"

She shook her head; a little doubtfully, I hoped.

"I did ask him," she admitted, "but he said the sender had conked
out."

"It conks out whenever it suits Max to pretend it has." I leaned
forward and took her hand. "Can't you see, darling, Max is the
only person here who can reach the outside world. All the rest of
the people are completely cut off. They couldn't leave even if they
wanted to. Max rules this place like his own little kingdom. The
others are virtual prisoners here —"

"Prisoners of hope, Carol. Certainly they are."

Max was standing in the entrance to the tent. He must have
been listening to us for some time. He stepped in and sat down
on the end of Vanessa's cot.

"Prisoners of their own hopes," he continued. "And at the same
time, they represent hope. Hope for the future." He turned so that
he was addressing us both. "The rest of the world is slowly, suicidally
destroying itself. Vietnam. Pollution. Watergate. A loss of faith in
its own leaders. A loss of faith in everything except violence, which
in its ultimate form means the hydrogen bomb . . ."

He went on about that. He had always been good at marshaling his arguments and he had a lot of them now. I couldn't even disagree with most of them. The world was in a bloody mess, all right, that summer of 1973. There were times when it didn't seem it could survive its own self-destructive insanity much longer. Except that I was still illogically sure that it would.

"But we'll survive here," Max assured us. "We'll survive because we don't need the rest of the world and because we have faith. We're like one of those monasteries in Ireland in the eighth century that kept the flame of hope and belief alive when the rest of Europe was dying in its own savage darkness."

He stood up and moved over to my cot, and sat beside me with his arm around my shoulders.

"I knew you'd come here, Carol," he said with that persuasive conviction I remembered so well. "That's why I established this refuge for us here. A small, perfect world where we could be with each other."

I tried to pull away from him; his arm tightened around me.

"Haven't you ever realized that was what was wrong all along?" he asked. "Even at the beginning, in Hollywood. And then later in New York after the war. There was never anything wrong between *us*. It was the world we were living in. A distorted, uncontrollable, destructive world. It almost destroyed us, Carol. The kind of love we had was too perfect to survive in it. It needed an environment that was a reflection of itself. We needed to be loved as we loved each other. We needed to be worshipped as we worshipped each other . . ."

I realized he was no longer really speaking to me. These were words he had repeated a thousand times to himself, the words of a long, bitter, private obsession.

I glanced at Vanessa; she was frowning, puzzled.

"You knew, didn't you?" Max was saying. "Right from the beginning. Almost thirty-five years ago in that hotel off Times Square where we first met. You knew we'd been waiting for that meeting all our lives. You knew we could never escape each other again. You knew it in Rome when you let me make you pregnant, so you could bear our child. You knew that sooner or later we'd be together forever."

I turned my head and faced him. He was looking beyond me, as though at some image he saw there.

"And now we *can* be together, Carol. For the rest of our lives. And we'll have our child with us. We'll teach her to think as we do. As sentient beings. And we'll have the life we were always meant to have, Carol. We'll be together, the three of us, in a world of our own choice. A world I made for you."

I managed to break away from him at last. I stood up, looking at Vanessa. She was staring at me, waiting for my answer. What did *she* want me to say?

I didn't know.

Fifteen years ago in a hospital in New York she had come struggling out of me, red and shriveled and helpless. My child. We had scarcely ever been parted for more than a few days since then. And yet in some ways I knew so little about her. She was Max's child, too. How much of his nature had she inherited? Did she share his hunger for absolute answers, his yearning need for commitment, not to other individuals, but to some shifting dream that he called belief?

She was fifteen now, a woman. I had been wrong earlier. I could no longer try to make her see things through my eyes. I could only hope there was more of my questioning, foolishly hopeful independence in her than there was of Max's zealotry.

"What do you think, darling?" I asked her. "Do you think Max is right? Do you think this is a perfect world he's created here? Do you think we should both stay and share it with him?"

"For how long?" She was frowning again.

"Forever, Vanessa. The way Max told us."

"But I've got my school-leaving exams next year. I've been studying for them for ages. And you said we were going to meet Anton and Elsie in Paris next month."

Max was standing too now. "You think that's more important?" he demanded. It was the question he had once asked me, sitting on a bench at a streetcar stop in Hollywood in 1939.

"More important than what?" Vanessa asked, as I had.

"Than what I've done here. What I'm planning to do. Create the microcosm of a new, ideal world."

"I think it's wonderful what you've done here, in some ways, Max." Vanessa shook her head slightly as though trying to clear it. "Making things grow in the desert and using solar energy for everything. But you can't expect me to spend the rest of my life in a place like this. There are too many other things I want to do."

"What? What things?" Max stepped a little closer to her; he still sounded gently persuasive. "Live in a city where the air itself is a poison? Have your mind corrupted by the lies on television and in the newspapers? Have to pay *money* for everything — food, clothes, anything you need to stay alive? Be surrounded and jostled by people who either envy or despise you, and who are only interested in what they can get out of you? You're my daughter, Vanessa. You're too good for that. If you stay here, you'll be treated with the respect and dignity you deserve. And this is only the beginning. What I've created here for you will grow and grow. There'll be a hundred people here soon, and one day several hundred, thousands. And in time you'll be the one who makes the decisions for them all, who makes sure they live in health and in truth. You'll be the one who leads them. Isn't that something to give every hour of your life meaning?"

Vanessa shook her head again, more positively this time. "I'm sorry, but I think that sounds terrible," she said. "I wouldn't want anyone making all my decisions for me. So why should I make them for other people?"

"You only say that because you don't understand what human beings are really like. How fallible and unself-disciplined they are."

I could see the stillness in Max's body. It reminded me of that night in the Trotskyist apartment in New York. I wanted to get up, to protect Vanessa against the rage I could sense in him. I didn't move. It wasn't only that I felt I had no right to interfere; I was restrained by the bright confidence in Vanessa's eyes.

"People need to be told," Max went on. "They need to be saved from themselves. You'll understand that when you've learned as much about the world as I have. When you've seen —"

"I'm not going to learn much about the world in this place, am I?" Vanessa interrupted him calmly. "It's full of people who all think alike. They've sort of given up. I don't want to be like *them*. I've got my whole life ahead of me and I'm going to make the most of it. You can count on that."

"What life? That stupid Irish school where they don't teach you anything worth knowing. Your little friends there. All the things you kept prattling about on the trip down here. Your pony and your sailing races and the silly books you've been reading. Do you think any of that matters? I was hoping, once you'd seen this place, you'd begin to grow up. You'd understand what was *important.*"

I was proud of her then. She didn't respond to his anger. Her beautiful, porcelain face expressed nothing but disdain. It reminded me of Sylvia.

"I'll make up my own mind what's important to me, thank you," she said quietly.

"You haven't any mind. You're nothing but a child who's been spoiled with vanity and materialism. You —" He turned abruptly on me. "You've done this to her. You've infected her with your own shallow, frivolous selfishness. You never could see beyond your own trivial little life." He was shouting. "And you've brought up my child to be just as undirected and irresponsible as you are. You —"

"Shut up, Max," I told him sharply. "I've heard it all before. Too many times. When I didn't believe in your Trotskyism. When I refused to be psychoanalyzed. When I wouldn't leave Jason and stay with you in Rome." I felt I had been waiting for years to say this. "I'll tell you what's always been wrong between us. It had nothing to do with an imperfect world. We're two entirely different kinds of people and we always have been. You don't give a shit about human beings. You never did. They're just figures in some idiotic theory to you. Some *cause* that gave you an excuse to feel superior to them. And you've reached the bottom this time, with your bloody Genesis. It's nothing but a racket you dreamed up to make emotional slaves of a few poor, credulous losers, to feed your own vanity —"

He hit me. He hit me with his fist across the side of the head, knocking me down onto the cot beside Vanessa. She reached for me at once, protectively. I saw the shock and indignation in her eyes.

"I'm all right, darling," I told her. I got to my feet. "You'd better pack your things. We're going back to the boat and getting out of here."

"You're not going anywhere." Max was standing in the doorway of the tent. "You're staying here. Both of you. And don't think you can run away, either. The people here will do anything I tell them. They'll make sure you never get aboard that boat."

He smiled suddenly; there was a sickening edge of cruelty in his smile.

"You're not the first people who've tried to leave here, and no one's ever made it. It's impossible without a boat. They all came crawling back after a couple of days in the desert and the mountains. They came crawling back begging me to forgive them, promising anything if I'd let them stay."

"Don't be ridiculous, Max." I turned away from him as I pushed the few things I had unpacked back into my bag and helped Vanessa gather her clothes together. "If the police in Santa Monica don't hear from me in five days, they're going to call the embassy in Mexico City. And they know exactly where I am, latitude and longitude. I made sure of that before I left Guaymas. This place'll be swarming with helicopters before you know it. You don't want that, do you?"

I was exaggerating a little; but I was counting on Max's past experience, too. He had had at least one unpleasant encounter with the Santa Monica police. They had held him in jail overnight and only reluctantly released him. He must know they would be eager to press further charges against him.

I bent over the cot, helping Vanessa pack. When I looked back toward the doorway, Max was still standing there. I couldn't see his face — the light was behind him — but there was no suggestion of defeat in his stance.

Then with a quick, decisive movement, he turned away and was gone.

I zipped up Vanessa's canvas tote and snatched up my own bag. We left the tent together.

"Is there any way Max can get to that boat before we do?" We were hurrying, half running between the rows of beans.

"He does have a jeep."

I'll bet no one except Max was allowed near that either.

We reached the meadow where the donkeys grazed. Vanessa opened the gate. "It'll be faster if we take the burros," she said. She darted into the lean-to where the harnesses were kept and came back with two halters. "We don't need saddles," she explained running past me to the grazing donkeys. She had always been good with animals. She had Beano and one of the others bridled in less than a minute.

I was no longer afraid of looking ridiculous in front of my daughter. Vanessa had already put her tote across Beano's back and mounted him. I heaved myself astride the second burro, holding my bag in front of me with one hand. She kicked her heels into Beano's sides and he trotted amiably through the open gate. My donkey obediently followed him.

Vanessa only spoke once as we wound our way up between the rocks to the top of the hill.

"I'm not surprised you quarreled with him," she said. "He can be absolutely crazy, can't he? And then *hitting* you."

It was easier once we were over the crest; that streak of cleared land was a straight descent. But I could hear the sound of the jeep's engine behind us now. Some superstitious fear kept me from looking back over my shoulder. Using the loose end of my rope bridle as a whip, I struck my burro back and forth across his neck. Protestingly, he trotted a little faster. I patted his head.

I did look back when we reached the jetty. The jeep was jolting and bouncing down the hill toward us. Max was alone in it.

"Come on." I scrambled off my donkey and started to run to the boat. Vanessa could run faster than I could. By the time I got to the *Aquarius,* she already had one of the mooring ropes loose. I cast off the other one and we both jumped on board. The jeep was on the jetty now.

Thank God for Harvey Croy's passion for nautical efficiency. The auxiliary engine started at once. As Max jumped down from the jeep, I swung the wheel to starboard and reversed the boat away from him.

There was a second when the prow was only a yard from where he was standing. He might have been able to leap on board during that one second. He appeared to be considering it. He had always felt uneasy about boats and had never learned to swim. The next second it was too late. He stood there, watching me as the gap between us widened, and I was safely out of his reach.

"Don't go, Carol." It was more of an entreaty than a command.

I idled the engine, letting the boat continue to swing around of its own momentum until the bow was pointing out to sea. The tide was already carrying us away from the land.

Max followed us to the end of the jetty. He put his hands on his hips. The afternoon sun emphasized the strong planes of his face. For an instant then, I saw him again as the idealized figure of my adolescent fantasies. The illusion was as fleeting as a déjà vu.

I straightened the wheel. Vanessa had gone forward and was unfurling the sails. All her attention was occupied with that. She wasn't looking at Max; I don't think she had glanced at him once since she had seen we were safe from him.

"I pity you, Carol."

I set the engine full ahead, starting out across the bay.

"I pity you because you've wasted your life. You've wasted it on yourself. There's a terrible emptiness in that, Carol. Never caring about anything bigger than your own day-to-day concerns."

He was twenty yards away now. I switched on the electric winch so that Vanessa could haul up the sails.

"But you're better than that, Carol. And it's still not too late for you. You can still do something important with your life."

Vanessa had the jib set. The offshore wind caught it. We gathered speed. I turned off the engine as she began to set the mainsail.

"You'll see, Carol. You'll see in the end I'm right."

He was shouting. His voice carried quite clearly across the widening stretch of sea between us.

"You'll come back. You'll find you need me. You need this world I created for you. You need me. You need me. Do you hear me, Carol?"

He was almost out of sight now, fading into the afternoon haze over the gulf, but I could still hear the conviction in his voice.

"You'll come back, Carol. You'll come back. Back to me. To my world."

It was little more than a faint echo at last, but as the coastline and the hills vanished into the haze, I could still hear the sound of my own name, repeated insistently, like an accusation.

"Carol."

"Carol."

"Carol."
